D1150874

TimeFlyer

by

Jeff Cargill

Copyright © 2005
by
Jeff Cargill

All rights reserved. No part of this book may be reproduced in any form, except for the inclusion of brief quotations in a review, without permission in writing from the author or publisher.

ISBN: 0-977374-00-9

LCCN: 2005909354

Printed in the United States by
Morris Publishing
3212 East Highway 30
Kearney, NE 68847
1-800-650-7888

Background

The fall of 2004 was a special time of spiritual reflection for this author. I was able to spend quite a bit of time studying the Bible. What God revealed to me during this time was that He wanted me to honor my parents, and in particular, my father.

Please understand – it wasn't that I didn't love him. However, we had never been particularly close. He was a well-respected and admired physician in our community. I was a hyperactive gearhead who eventually made my way into the computer field. We had different interests. He was a busy man.

Our extended family Christmas celebration was in early January of 2005. In order to follow God's direction, I determined to stand up and explain to the family some of the things I had come to recognize about my father's life, and name some of the spiritual and character gifts he had passed on to me that I had not previously appreciated. And so, before we started opening Christmas presents, I stood up, asked by father to stand beside me, and verbally went through the dedication on the following page. It wasn't nearly as eloquent as what you will read – I was nervous, and hadn't memorized the speech, so I stumbled through the things I wanted to say. But I did it. And I felt good when I had finished, because the things I said were spoken from the heart.

I could tell my father appreciated what I had said. We are closer now than we have ever been in the past. My mother and siblings told me they appreciated what I had said. I think it caused all of the adults in the family pause a little bit to consider his life and his values.

As the Christmas celebration came to a close, it was time for me to load up my family and drive the three hour trip back home. It was late on a Sunday night. My wife and children were sleeping, exhausted after spending a long, fun weekend with the extended family. I was driving down Interstate 39, a relatively quiet road that passes through Illinois farm country. And as I drove, I suddenly imagined a flying wing airplane traveling back through time, and a military research group trying to come to grips with an evolutionary versus creationist timeline for Earth's natural history. I instantly realized that it would make a compelling tale.

I believe that this imagery was a gift given directly from God, an example of the blessings promised to those who honor their parents. So inspired, I determined that, sometime before the end of 2005, I would write and publish the story that was given to me on that lonely stretch of Interstate. The result is this book.

There were people involved in the process too, of course. I would like to thank Jessica Leman, as well as the 'Growing Kids' group, for their support and encouragement. Thanks to Donald Broquard, Michael Brown, Greg Burger, Dr. Sue Lenski, Charlie Liebert, and Mark Streitmatter for reviewing various copies of the manuscript and providing feedback. Jason Saunders did a wonderful job on the cover art, and you can see more of his work at www.jsaund.com. Finally, a large thank you for my gifted, intelligent, long-suffering wife for putting up with yet another of her husband's pet projects.

And so, dear reader, the Almighty Jehovah, Creator and God of the Universe, and I, his mere scribe, invite you to sit back, relax, and enjoy *TimeFlyer*.

Dedication

Dear Dad,

Several weeks ago, I met one of your cousins, who told me a story of an incident that happened to you when you were growing up. He related how you had come out to their farm, and they had taken a trip into town. They had provided an old Model A truck for you to use while helping with some of the chores. What they hadn't told you is that the brakes on the truck didn't work. When they returned from town, they found you trying to figure out how to repair the section of fence that had served to stop the dysfunctional vehicle.

What occurred to me when I heard the story was how it was a reflection of so many experiences in your life. So many times, it seems, you found yourself in situations where there was damage, hurt feelings, and disappointment. Situations in which you would never have willingly involved yourself. You were the one who was left to deal with the damage, to pick up the pieces, or deal with the broken remains.

It started as a child, when your father left your mother, married another woman, and left that part of the country. He left behind five children, of which you were the oldest. Such an action was absolutely scandalous in small town America in the 1950's, and you were left with the burden of finding your own way in the world.

But I must admit I never was able to reflect on your life until I had experienced some hardships of my own.

When I was accused of stealing information from my employer

and using it to benefit myself, I remembered your business partner who tried to manipulate the office structure to get as much of the income as he could. And I remembered how you accommodated him, willing to allow a greater share of the profits to go his way in order to keep peace between the two of you. You were a living example of turning the other cheek. The memory helped me endure a four hour grilling and follow-up investigation in which, in the end, I was exonerated.

But the hardship didn't stop there. Before long, I found out a member of my management team was having an affair with an executive, the same executive that was in charge of the investigation. It became obvious that the ploy was to discredit me, and give my manager credit for my work, in order to get her promoted. Further, no one in the company was willing to give my plea any consideration because of political power of the executive. And I remembered how our local church congregation was also divided when your business partner divorced his wife and left his family, many being very supportive of him and willing to justify his actions. And I remembered how you were willing to let people voice their support for him, never saying anything negative about the man. The man was politically powerful in the congregation, to the point where most of the church leadership was on his side. And you were willing to turn the situation over to God and let him deal with it, even though there was all kinds of things you could have told people to help them understand the man's real character. And that memory helped me to turn my situation over to God, waiting for Him to do His work in my situation as well.

When I decided to move to another section of the business to get out from under the authority of that executive, I found myself in a position where the job duties were unclear, and I didn't have enough work to keep me busy. Weeks stretched to months while I waited for the high volume of work promised by my managers to come my way. It never did. Meanwhile, I searched the Internet for four or five hours per day, attributing my time to 'basic research' on my timecard. And I remembered that you were also once hired by a hospital, and endured two years of almost no work while the hospital tried, and failed, to start a new healthcare program. In the end, you were fired, and had to start over again.

Then came the day when I walked up to the doors of my workplace, knowing that I faced another day of almost nothing to do, bitter about the past mistreatment, and I didn't want to go in. I stood there, wanting desperately to turn around, go home, and call in to tell them I had quit. And I remembered how you had submitted to your employer, willing to endure boredom and frustration in order to try to make their program work. I remember saying to myself, "If your father could endure it, so can you," and resuming my walk toward the door.

And it was at that moment when my thoughts ran over the events of the previous years, that I finally understood just how much your example, character, and values had shaped my life. I finally appreciated the imprint your life had made on mine. And I realized just what a Godly example you had been to me.

And so, Dad, I want to say thank you for your influence on my life. Thank you for showing me what it means to turn the other cheek, to walk two miles with your adversary when he asks you to walk with him but one. Thank you for being willing to trust God with so many of these aspects of your life, to wait patiently for Him to work instead of taking matters into your own hands. Your life has been a blessing to the lives of many, not the least of which has been mine.

Your Son,

Jeff

Prologue

Choi Daesang tried not to wince as the vehicle he was guiding – driving was hardly the right word for what he was doing – jolted over yet another lump in the uneven terrain. He was acutely aware of the group of men who were watching him from a distance of 10 meters. Despite the beautiful, cool springtime weather, he was perspiring. Months of work had gone into this moment. Indeed, his entire future depended on what happened in the next few minutes. *If I haven't already missed it,* he thought.

The vehicle had once been a tractor. Someone with a knowledge of farm machinery might still recognize it as such. Tractor wheels remained on the back, and the engine and transmission were still the power source. However, anything attributed to aesthetics had been stripped off long ago. The engine was now exposed to the elements. The original pneumatic front tires, wheels and steering mechanism were gone, replaced by a single solid wheel. Angle iron bracing had been crudely welded to hold the front wheel in place. The steering wheel was long gone as well, replaced by a tiller, which Choi was using to guide the contraption. He was seated on a wooden bench, which had been bolted to more angle iron bracing welded to the frame directly in front on the engine. The crude combination had the disagreeable side effect of transmitting the slightest unevenness in the ground directly to the occupant's anatomy. Choi was resolutely ignoring the protests emanating from his rear end and lower back.

It helped that he had to focus so intently on a panel located underneath the tiller. The panel looked remarkably like one might have on a boat to find fish in the Western world. In fact, that was its original function before being converted to display something else entirely. It was wired to a large, flat metal plate suspended between the single front and double rear wheels, hanging horizontally about 25 centimeters off the ground.

A group of men dispassionately watched the progress of the machine. Their uniforms made them look somewhat intimidating, but it was their eyes from which the intimidation came. The oldest of them was barely 50 years old. All were thin, not unusual in the Democratic Peoples Republic of Korea, where more than 10% of the population had died of starvation in the previous decade. All had lips that might smile, but eyes that had been forced to ignore far too much suffering to allow that sentiment to be exhibited. The focus of their collective attention moved slowly; so slowly, in fact, that any one of them could keep up by walking. But none tried.

After moving about 15 additional meters, the driver stopped the machine. Then he turned to the group and waved. They walked toward the machine, led unhurriedly by the Colonel, who was the highest ranking member of the group.

When they neared him Choi pointed to the former fish finder panel, "I believe I have found the tunnel, Comrade Colonel." He raised his voice to be heard over the clatter of the engine directly behind him. "Do you see that pattern, Sir? On the bottom of the screen, that row of dots indicates a hollow spot under the ground. If the tunnel is not too deep, my invention should be able to follow it back to where it surfaces."

The Colonel did not speak, but paused instead to consider this information. After a moment of awkward silence, Kim Yuntae, Choi's commanding officer, spoke up. "Comrade Colonel, if you will follow me, I will show you the path of the tunnel." The group turned, and followed Kim, who turned and led the way toward the north, up a slight rise. At the top of the hill, he turned and looked back behind him toward the south. About 150 meters away was the first set of barbed wire that separated North and South Korea. At his feet was a rag that had been tied to a stake.

"Comrades, the tunnel lies directly under this marker." He indicated the rag with his foot. "If you look toward no-man's land, you should be able to see a telephone pole." The group's line of sight traveled over the rows of barbed wire on each side of a seemingly empty strip of land. The telephone pole could be seen on the far side. "The tunnel passes very near that pole before it makes its exit. Note where the tunnel detector has stopped." The modified tractor was directly between them and the telephone pole.

"How deep a tunnel can the machine detect?" asked the Colonel.

"We shall have to ask our comrade inventor." He nodded toward Choi, who had stayed behind long enough to park the machine. When he joined them a few moments later, the Colonel repeated his question.

"Comrade Colonel, the machine is able to reliably detect tunnels to a depth of three meters. Below three meters, detection depends on the makeup of the soil, the amount of moisture in the soil, and other factors. In the best circumstances, tunnels can be detected to a depth of five meters."

The Colonel turned to Kim. "Is three meters enough to detect tunnels?"

The guide nodded quickly. "Most of them. There may be some that are lower. But, please remember this is the first demonstration of this technology. I am confident that Comrade Choi can and will improve it. With your permission, of course," he added lamely.

"And my money," noted the Colonel.

"Yes."

"Are you absolutely sure that Choi did not know the location of the tunnel before this demonstration?"

"I am positive. He did his testing on one of our tunnels 30 km to the west. As you recall, we found another tunnel that was being used illegally by our own people. That activity has been stopped and we arrested the traitors who were found using it." He didn't have to add that they had been shot. The punishment for such a crime was well understood in North Korea.

"Very well. Let us return to the compound and discuss exactly what you will need to continue with this program."

Choi turned and headed back to the tractor. He was not to be a part of the coming discussion. That was to be done by his commanding officer. Choi and Kim had already spent hours discussing what Choi needed in order to continue with the development of his ground-penetrating radar. Returning to the rear of the tractor (the wires for ignition and electric start hadn't been moved to the front by the driver), he started the machine and then climbed up into the bench

8

seat. Disengaging the brake, he used the tiller to guide the machine in a large circle back toward the military garage where it was stored.

It was May, and there had been enough rain this spring to make the countryside lush and green. The hills had changed from their brown winter color several weeks earlier and the sky was blue, with light fluffy clouds. *Almost pretty enough to want to make a person sit still and admire the scenery.* He knew that wouldn't do at all. He hadn't earned the privilege of driving this escape tunnel detector by admiring pretty scenery.

He hoped the discussions between the Colonel and Kim were fruitful. He was intent on finding as many tunnels that led to the relative paradise of South Korea as he could. Not, however, because he was a patriot. He didn't mind that a few of his countrymen were able to escape to freedom.

In fact, he hoped to do so himself.

* * * *

As Dan Labinsky rode the escalator from the subway up to street level, he looked outside for signs of rain. As much as he enjoyed the spring rains that transformed the natural environment from its drab winter colors, he was glad there was none this morning. He had dressed carefully. He and his boss, Nola Smith Nielsen, had an appointment at the White House at 10:00, and he was well aware that rain always made his carefully ironed shirt and suit pants look less crisp. Not to mention the occasional spot of mud that always seemed to find its way onto his shoes in wet weather.

The familiar walk from the subway station to his office in Washington, D.C.'s interior building took the usual eight minutes. He arrived at 8:14 AM and greeted his secretary, Linda, who was already at her desk. The coffeepot was on and he could smell its rich aroma as he walked in the door. After hanging up his overcoat, Dan assembled his usual concoction of coffee and milk, no sugar, and headed into his office. He reminded himself that he had to be careful with the coffee. It would not be good to be too hyped up on caffeine around the President.

An hour later, after catching up on the mail (electronic and otherwise), he retrieved his overcoat and walked across the hall to the office of the Director of the Interior.

"Good morning, Dan," came Nola's usual cheery greeting. "It's such a nice day. Would you mind if we walked over to the White House?"

"Sounds great to me. Still no idea what's on the President's mind?" He asked hopefully.

"No, and even the rumor mill has failed me this time." Washington was a town where it seemed impossible to keep a secret, and Nola was as well connected as anyone in government could hope to be. The only ones more in tune with the grapevine of 'The Hill' were members of the press.

They took the elevator down to street level and walked the five blocks to the White House. It was always interesting to observe the people on the street. There was the usual mix of university students and tourists mixed in with the senators, house members and their staffs. It was easy to spot the government people – they were the best dressed.

Dan and Nola arrived at the White House five minutes early. Security was the usual tight affair, after which they were shown into the waiting area. They were summoned into the oval office at 10:02 AM.

"Hello, Nola, Dan. Always good to see you." The President extended his carefully manicured hand and flashed his million-dollar smile, which his critics called his only redeeming quality. "I don't know if you have met General Greg Collins? No? Well, high time we got the three of you together."

They shook hands, and the President urged them to sit on the sofa. General Collins took one wing chair, the President the other. The General was a bit shorter than average, Dan thought, probably 5'4" or so. But he obviously never let a lack of height stop his rise in the military. Dan noticed the tinges of gray which his crew cut helped to hide and guessed he was a little over fifty. He was obviously physically fit. Dan was already wondering why a military general was part of this meeting.

A steward brought in a coffee tray and set it on the coffee table in the middle of the precisely arranged furniture. Nola reached forward and helped herself to a cup of coffee. "Thank you, Mr. President. It was such a nice day that Dan and I walked. Turned out to be a bit chillier than I expected and that will make the coffee especially enjoyable." Dan and the General both politely refused a cup.

"Well," the President began, "the reason I asked the two of you to come here is because we have a military project that I think will be of great interest to you. General Collins has been overseeing its theoretical aspects , so I'll let him give the overview. The details are so far over my head its like trying to explain a jet engine to a rabbit." He flashed his smile again, "Please, go ahead, General."

"Thank you, Mr. President." The General's voice was surprisingly deep. "I would ask that you please keep the contents of our conversation in the strictest of confidence. As you will see, the implications of what we are about to discuss are substantial, and the fewer who know about it, the better.

I would like to explain a project that we think will revolutionize our knowledge of ourselves and all living things. As you may know, the last several years have brought about an explosion in biological science information. We have powerful computers that allow us to examine the DNA of ourselves and other living things. We have better mathematical models, which help us to learn how various parts of our bodies operate at the molecular level. There are many medical applications, of course, but for various reasons this science is also of interest to the military." A chill ran through Dan at the thought of the military keeping a copy of his DNA on file. "If nothing else," the General continued, "based on scientific advances, we like to know about possible chemical or biological threats to our nation."

"Of course," Nola smiled and nodded.

"About a year ago, the President received a letter from a Ph.D. candidate in Geology from one of our nation's Universities. This gentleman claimed that he had made a breakthrough in obtaining biological information from fossils, as long as the fossils met some specific criteria. The President had some people check it out, and it seemed legitimate, so they invited this individual to do a briefing. I was asked to attend. It turns out that his idea was all theoretical, and just from a practical level, would take considerable effort to implement. Some advances needed to be made in applying non-invasive examination techniques to rocks. As you can imagine, this is not viewed as a terribly high priority in the scientific community. Examining how pieces of rock interact on the atomic level is not like finding a cure for cancer.

However, I could see that there were perhaps some military applications for this technology as well. For example, what if scientists

11

could replicate a bacteria that hasn't been alive on earth for over a million years? Who knows what kinds of things they could do. This could be beneficial."

"General, are you saying that you think you can re-create bacteria that have been extinct for a million years?" asked Dan.

"Yes, the research looks promising," responded the General.

Dan turned to Nola. "This could be revolutionary."

"Why?" asked Nola.

"Well, we know from the earth's fossil records that over 95% of all species of living things have become extinct. What we see today is the last 5% of all living things that have ever existed. If we could get information about the other 95%, it would expand our biological knowledge immensely."

"Exactly., nodded the General emphatically.

"I see." Nola sat quietly thinking for a moment. Then she turned to the President. "However, I still don't see a link between this project and the Department of the Interior."

"Nola, what if I told you that it seems possible to not only replicate bacteria, but anything that has previously been alive, including animals?" asked the President.

"You mean, like dinosaurs?" asked Nola coolly. The President nodded with a subdued smile playing around his lips. "Are you really serious?" When the two men nodded, in an uncommon show of emotion, she sat suddenly upright in her chair. "So this means we might have marauding dinosaurs running through our towns and eating people like in the movies?"

The General chuckled. "No, not at all. I don't know how useful it would be to have a resurrected Tyrannosaurus Rex. However, there are some species in which you would probably have an interest, like some of the extinct species of bears. How about boosting the population of endangered species like the peregrine falcon? Wouldn't it be marvelous to bring back the saber-toothed tiger? There are all kinds of possibilities."

"So you are saying that we could resurrect almost any extinct creature?" clarified Nola.

"Within reason. The remains of the animal would have to meet some criteria. But yes, we believe such things would be possible. The implications for the environment are substantial." The General finished with a rather obvious understatement.

12

"Well, of course we would be interested. But it sounds like there is still work to be done. Is there some way that we can be of assistance?" she asked.

It was the President who responded. "It is going to take a substantial amount of money to do the research required to develop this technology. We would like you to volunteer some of the budget from the Department of the Interior to help fund the project."

"How much?" asked Nola.

"Two percent of your annual budget for the next five years," responded the President.

One of the traits that had helped Nola risen to her current position was her ability to hide her thoughts. She looked at Dan, but Dan couldn't tell what she was thinking. She turned her attention back to the President.

"This is very unusual. Would all of the funding from this project be supplied from my area?"

General Collins answered. "No, this would be a joint venture. I have already committed three percent of my budget for the next five years. I really can't afford to commit any more than that."

"When you say your budget, what do you mean?" Nola wasn't sure which budget item was being discussed.

"I mean the total amount of money budgeted to the Department of Defense."

Dan tried to remember the size of the defense department budget and failed. "Three percent of your budget dwarfs two percent of our budget. Your budget is, what, 20 times larger than ours?"

"Actually, almost 40 times. So yes, we are making a sizable contribution. But every little bit helps. And, with this arrangement, you would get a commitment to use the results of this research in ways that benefit the Department of the Interior as soon as they become available. We would have to keep methods secret, of course, but you would be able to display these formerly extinct animals, perhaps re-introduce them back into their native habitats. It would be fantastic PR for you."

The politics of the moment became immediately obvious to Dan. It was no secret that his boss, Nola Smith Nielsen, was hated by environmentalists. Among other things, she had advocated logging, and oil exploration and drilling, on federal lands. No matter that she was supporting the President's agenda, and that there were valid scientific and economic reasons for her positions. The environmental lobby wielded considerable influence in Washington, and the President was eager to turn his choice for Director of the Interior into a political asset instead of a liability. If she could demonstrate that she was involved in an effort to resurrect extinct species, her own political fortunes, as well as that of the President, would immediately soar.

"Are we the only department involved?" queried Nola.

The President responded. "No. There are several others. I don't want to share which ones, because they are still making their decisions. But I want this to be a joint effort. There are so many potential benefits to this research. Medical, pharmacological, biological, geological, and a whole lot of other ...ogicals."

"How soon do you expect to be able to start bringing extinct animals back to life?" asked Dan.

"Three years. Of course, that figure could vary widely. A lot of this depends on technology that still has to be invented and refined," said the President.

"Predicting such things is difficult at best," added the General. "But, we would expect to have solid evidence of our success in three years, with obvious developments along the way to indicate progress."

"When do we have to get an answer back to you?" asked Nola.

"Can I ask for a decision by the end of next week?" asked the President courteously.

Nola feigned exasperation. "Of course you can, you're the President." The men all chuckled.

"Very well. General, why don't you share your contact information with them? If you have questions, please direct them his way. He will be the man in charge of the operation, and is the most knowledgeable about the project. He might not be able to share some of the technological details, but he will share with you any other information that you think might help you make a decision."

The President stood. "Thank you for coming today. I appreciate your taking the time to come and discuss this. I think it will be a very good thing for your department, but I want your buy-in. I am not going to force it on you." *Of course not*, thought Dan. *Nola is either going to support the project and keep her job, or hesitate and be pushed aside in favor of a more politically acceptable cabinet member.*

"That is very thoughtful, Mr. President," Nola responded graciously. She turned to General Collins, "And thank you, General.

14

Technology is an amazing thing, is it not?"

"Indeed." he replied. They shook hands all around. After a few more pleasantries, Dan and Nola turned and headed for the door. Dan noted that the General remained behind. Probably to discuss their reaction and try to predict their answer.

Back on the street, Dan and Nola walked the first block in silence. Then Nola turned to Dan. "What do you think?"

"Something's wrong with this picture," observed Dan. As Deputy Director of the Interior, he had as much experience as anyone with Washington, D.C. politics. He was thinking out loud. "Sure, such a development would benefit the Department of the Interior. But our money is such a small amount compared to theirs. And we are not involved with national security. Face it, we're an ornament. We are one of the least important departments in the President's cabinet. There has to be another reason why they want us included in this." He didn't point out the obvious political angle. He knew Nola had already discussed her political vulnerability with several members of the President's staff, including his chief political strategist.

"My thoughts exactly. Although the truth of your statement is rather painful to admit," sighed Nola.

"Well, how about we sleep on this for a day or so and get back together to discuss it. How about on Thursday?"

"Thursday it is. Have Linda set up an hour for us. Maybe we'll think of the real reason we are being pulled into this."

* * * *

The night was cold, but Choi had anticipated that. He wore a dark jacket and pants and crawled as far into a bush as he could to conceal himself. The moon was covered in clouds, although some light still shone through – enough to see, barely.

It was creepy waiting for something to happen at night at the edge of a cemetery. Choi was not a religious man and he didn't believe in spirits or ghosts. Dead people were dead, he tried to reassure himself. End of story. Done. Finished. His logical arguments, however, didn't ease his anxiety. The goose bumps on his arms and legs were from the cold, he told himself – and it was probably even partially true.

He was taking a terrible risk. By now, he would be missed at his dormitory. He hoped the dorm mentor, who was a known agent of the secret police, would just assume he was working on his tunnel detector again. He had purposely stayed late and worked far into the night four times during the last several weeks, just to generate the impression that he might occasionally be gone late into the night without arousing suspicion. The first night, when he returned, he had faced a thorough chewing out. He had given the mentor Kim Yuntae's name. The mentor did not wait until daylight to call – he called him at 1:30 in the morning. Kim assured the mentor that Choi was working on a legitimate project. Choi had to explain that he had come up with an idea to improve the machine, and wanted to get the improvement in place so that it could be used immediately. The mentor had finally dismissed Choi with a few more threats and warnings.

Kim had really come through for him. He had called the Colonel, and the Colonel himself put in a call to the mentor. Once the mentor found out that Choi's project really was being sponsored at a senior military level, he had begun to treat Choi with considerably more respect. Not only that, he had chatted amiably the next three times Choi returned to the dormitory late.

The tunnel-detecting machine worked quite well. During the previous month, Choi had detected four tunnels with it, and traced them toward the North as far as he could. One of them had run into a military compound. It was no secret that North Korean spies regularly infiltrated South Korea to gather information and evaluate the threat level. Tunnels were one way the North Korean spies went back and forth between the two countries without detection. Choi knew that he had to report any tunnel he found being used by the military apparatus of his country. Failure to report one of these tunnels would arouse considerable suspicion.

It was not, however, those tunnels in which the Colonel was interested. It was the ones that were made by North Koreans trying to escape from their own country. Incredible as it seemed, people had actually dug tunnels over two kilometers in length using just their hands and primitive tools. It was not known how many people had escaped this way, but there was no doubt it happened more frequently than his country was willing to admit. North Korea had tried to keep the matter a secret, and to investigate it as an internal affair. That ended up being impossible when two men, tunneling underneath no-man's land, hit a mine. It killed them instantly, but the resulting explosion had also alerted South Korea to the tunneling attempt and

16

caused international embarrassment for the North Koreans. Such things were not to be tolerated. Choi's proposal to build equipment that could detect these underground tunnels had been the right thing at the right time, and so his project was funded. It was suspected that the South Korean military had also found some of the tunnels and sent their own spies into the North.

Choi had reported the military tunnel he found, as well as another one that he suspected. However, there were two others he had not reported. One seemed to lead into a house. Choi ruled that one out for his own use. But, another led directly into an old cemetery. He had not driven his machine into the cemetery, so he didn't know where the entrance to the tunnel was located. In fact, the tunnel might have gone right through the cemetery and continued on the other side. Choi, however, doubted that. A cemetery would be an excellent place to put the entrance to a tunnel. And who would suspect dirt being moved around in a cemetery?

This cemetery was old. Several of the headstones where raised above ground level, something that no North Korean except those high up in government could afford – and those people lived far from this place. Therefore, it had to have existed before, or perhaps during, the Korean uprising over 40 years before.

There were also other markers. Some were stones placed at ground level. Some were polished and engraved. Others were simply rough stones with writing that had been painstakingly cut by hand into the rock. More than a few graves had a single stone for a marker, with no writing or memorial at all. Such was the fate of the common North Korean.

Choi's plan was simple. Now that he had potentially located an escape tunnel, he would hide and watch to see if he could find someone using it. He would wait until those using it had gone a sufficient distance ahead, and then follow. He carried with him the stump of a candle and a cigarette lighter. Once started, he didn't expect his escape effort to take over an hour.

What he hadn't fully anticipated was keeping himself calm for an extended period of time waiting at the edge of a cemetery. He was simultaneously terrified and bored: terrified of the remote prospect of being caught, terrified that he might not find someone actually using the tunnel, terrified that the person he found using the tunnel would detect him following, and even more terrified that person was loyal to the North. But probably the most terrifying aspect of all, was that no one would come and show him the path to the South and freedom, and that all of his planning and work would be for naught.

He thought back to memories of his family. He had left home at 17 to go to the University. During his last couple years at home, he and his father had several interesting conversations. Not conversations in the usual sense, however. These talks were written on the edges of the pages of North Korean propaganda pamphlets. One of the few things readily available in a country where starving to death was an all to likely prospect; the pages were thrown into the little wood-burning stove as soon as they had been read. Even inside the walls of their home, it was too risky to talk out loud about the things his father taught him in those painstakingly handwritten notes. The discovery of such a thing would have meant an immediate prison sentence for his father, and probably for Choi as well.

And so they wrote their notes back and forth. Mostly, it was notes from his father to himself, giving him advice and encouragement. He had two older brothers and one younger sister. Only one of his older brothers had similar conversations with his father. The second son displayed too much loyalty to their North Korean masters for his father to risk giving his true feelings away. But he was comfortable with Choi. The thought of his father's trust sent a momentary course of warmth streaming through his cold body.

His father had started by telling him about life before the communist uprising, when food was more plentiful and the country was generally peaceful. After he determined that he could trust Choi with those simple secrets, he had shared his true feelings about the government of North Korea. Choi had been surprised at the depth of feelings expressed by his father, who was normally so stoic and quiet. He had never realized the pain and frustration that lay in his father's heart.

Choi's father had encouraged him to go into the military and to get as much education as possible. He had told his son to wholly support the government and teachings of North Korea. He warned him of the risks of revealing any trace of disaffection with the government. He had explained that government spies would try to gain his confidence and get him to admit that he was not totally committed to their country. No one was to be trusted. Choi had been thankful for that lesson more than once. He knew first hand of three classmates at the

University who simply disappeared, with no explanation given. It was suspected they had revealed some trace of doubt about their loyalty to the government to an informer. Thanks to his father, he never made that mistake.

But his father had also been explicit about another matter. "If ever you have a chance to escape, do so," he had written. "Do not hesitate, and do not waver. You will find freedom to be worth any pains taken to obtain it. Always be careful. Trust no one. And if you get the opportunity to escape, take it. Never look back, and never question yourself. Better to spend one year of your life as a free man than 20 years in North Korea."

Which was why he was sitting here, in the dark, on the edge of a cemetery, chilled to the bone. His father's exhortation had aroused a passion that surprised him. He had worked for years to learn enough science and mathematics to figure out a way to make escape realistic. He had considered building a hot air balloon, or a boat. He had even considered building a submersible craft with batteries and an electric motor driving a propeller, to cross from North to South by way of the sea. All of these ideas were possible, but keeping such projects hidden was almost impossible. There was absolutely no privacy in North Korea, especially at a University. He had considered escape possibilities for four years, with no realistic alternatives, until he read an article in a scientific journal about ground penetrating radar.

As he read the article, an incredible inspiration struck him. What if he could adapt this technology to detect tunnels? There were always rumors about escape tunnels dug from North to South. Not that anyone he knew could provide any solid evidence to support such ideas. It was more the stuff of legend, like tales of the Old West in the United States, where a few isolated incidents between outlaws and law-abiding citizens had been enhanced and expanded so they hardly resembled the original occurrences at all.

And yet, Choi had reasoned with himself, many legends are based in fact. Was it possible that there was some truth to the existence of secret tunnels between his country and his free comrades to the south? Were there actually smugglers who would take you to freedom for a price? The more Choi thought about it, the more he came to realize that such a thing was indeed possible. And so, he had spent a considerable amount of his free time learning about radar and other forms of electro-magnetic radiation.

Then the two tunneling North Koreans hit the mine. Two days after the story swept through his dorm, and was officially denied by the authorities, Choi presented his idea for a tunnel detector. He had made his presentation both to his University professor and his commanding officer.

He shivered and tried to draw himself further into the thin cloth of his coat. He figured he could risk waiting out here, during the night, three times before the risk of someone checking up on him became too great. He wondered what time it was. Probably about 1:30 AM, he guessed. A great yawn forced its way through to his mouth, despite his efforts to suppress it. *Do suppressed yawns yearn for freedom as much as he did? Do they yearn for escape through a great open mouth, out into the open air to show openly to the world the mental state of the body from which they struggled toward freedom?*

Choi, he thought, *that was one of the dumbest ideas you have ever had.* But it was so hard trying to stay still and quiet, hour after hour, in the dark and cold. He realized that he would have to return to his dorm soon. He was getting too tired, and when he started imagining his yawns yearning for freedom, he knew his body was demanding sleep and that alone would restore lucid thinking. Just a few more minutes, he thought to himself. He was acutely aware that the sleepiness might be the onset of hypothermia.

It was then he saw a black shape stealthily emerge from some trees about fifty meters in front of him and slightly to his right.

He focused all of his attention on the spot, and after another minute was rewarded with more movement. He continued to stare until he could make out four larger shapes, with a slightly smaller shape next to last. They were moving his way. He shivered and willed himself to stay absolutely motionless. As they came closer, he could make out the form of people crouched low and walking as quickly as their stooped forms could carry them. They were heading directly toward him.

He suddenly wondered what would happen if they discovered him. It was something he had not seriously considered before. He had been far more worried about being discovered by an informer. *But if these people were trying to escape, surely they would let me go along, right? It would be better for them to allow me to escape to the south with them. They could kill me, but then what would they do with my body?* He decided he didn't want to pursue this course of thought any more.

20

The people kept coming. Closer and closer they came. Now he could make out which were male and female. Soon he could make see that they all wore dark clothing. About the time he realized that two of them were barefoot, they stopped. Choi breathed a sigh of relief. The one in the lead made a motion, and they all dropped to the ground.

The lead man seemed to be on his knees, working on something on the ground. Choi heard what sounded like two hard objects colliding, but muffled somehow. Then the lead man turned toward the group and made another motion. Choi watched as the four others moved toward the lead man and, one by one, they disappeared. Finally, the lead man disappeared too. Choi heard that muffled impact twice more, and then all was silent.

Exhilaration flooded through his body. He was right! There was a tunnel, and he had discovered someone using it. He was almost too giddy for rational thought. Now, to wait for a few minutes and follow...

Which turned out to be much harder than he expected. Despite the cold, he found himself sweating with anticipation. He wanted to jump, he wanted to run, and he wanted to scream that *HE HAD FOUND IT*. Forcing himself to remain perfectly still took more willpower than he knew he possessed.

Finally, he felt like it was safe to follow. He had detected no other movement. He uncurled his body, ignoring the pain from muscles and joints that had been in one position for far too long. But he found that he couldn't walk. His legs had become stiff, and wouldn't support his weight. They started to tingle, and then burn. Undaunted, he crawled toward the place where the people had disappeared into the ground. His legs moved in clumsy lurches. He was looking carefully for a place that would indicate the location to the entrance to a tunnel.

But he couldn't find it. He crawled in a circle in the area where they had vanished, then in a larger circle. Nothing seemed out of place. All the gravestones in the area were level with the ground. They were pre-communist era, he saw, because they were polished and engraved. He started to panic. He had never thought that he might not be able to find the entrance to the tunnel. He circled again. He thought about flicking his lighter for more light, but he immediately squelched that thought. Might as well step into the light of the searchlights that were continuously scanning the ground immediately around no-man's land, he thought to himself.

He felt panic rising, and stopped himself. *Stop it,* he told himself. He had just seen five people disappear into the ground. There had to be a way. He forced himself to stop moving and just look. Scrutinize everything in the area closely. He examined the grass and gravestones carefully.

And then he saw it. An area of flattened grass just to one side of a grave stone, as if something heavy had been placed there. As he watched, he could see individual blades of grass springing back upright. By morning, there would be no indication of anything amiss. He crawled to the spot; it was immediately adjacent to a gravestone. In fact, the flattened area seemed to be the same size as the closest gravestone.

Choi turned his attention to the gravestone. He could see nothing on it to suggest it was anything unusual. He ran his finger around the edge. He found that, on two sides, there was a hollow space between the ground and the stone. The spaces were just large enough for him to slip his hand down. He pushed one hand in, and about ten centimeters down, found the bottom edge of the stone. He positioned himself in a crouch above the stone, and placed one hand in each hollow. His legs were feeling much better now and the burning was almost gone. Gripping the underside of the stone, he pulled. Nothing. Pulled again. Again, nothing. Finally, he gave it a mighty heave. It resisted for a moment, and then he was able to lift it high enough that he could slide it out of its resting place. He looked down.

He was looking into a dark opening.

He put his legs into the opening and lowered himself. It was deeper than he expected. Taking a deep breath, he forced himself to drop down into the hole. His feet hit a solid surface. He found that he could stand full height, and the top of his head was just about level with the ground's surface. He reached up and grabbed the edge of the gravestone. With considerable effort, he dragged the stone back into place. It dropped into place with a solid clunk. He recognized the sound as the one he had puzzled over when he watched the people disappear just a few minutes before.

When the gravestone dropped back in place, it was pitch black. He had never experienced such total darkness before. He reached into his pocket and tried to retrieve his lighter. The surrounding walls were so close that he had difficulty getting his arm into the right position. Finally, he reached across with the opposite hand and awkwardly pulled the lighter out of his pocket. He flicked it, and as the flame formed, he took a quick look at his surroundings.

The opening wasn't even large enough for him to turn in a circle. The walls were hard, harder than just plain earth. *They must have had some cement mixed in to make them so hard*, Choi supposed. He looked down and was shocked to discover that he was standing on the top of a coffin. After regaining his composure, he looked more carefully around the bottom of the walls. Sure enough, to one side, was another dark opening. He carefully placed one leg into the hole, but found the space too tight to drop his other leg into the hole without the aid of his hands to help support his weight. Grimacing, he put the bottom of the lighter in his mouth. Then he placed his hands against the walls. Pushing hard, he got the weight off his feet, and slipped them into the hole. Then, as carefully as he could he lowered himself into a sitting position on the coffin. He dropped the last half-meter with a thud, and somehow managed not to drop the lighter. Removing it from his mouth, he flicked it again, leaned back, and peered into the opening where his legs protruded.

He was surprised to find himself looking into a relatively roomy space. His feet were dangling more than one meter above the floor. He allowed the lighter's flame to go out and slid down into the little room. He dropped to the floor, then sat down and pulled out his candle. He lit it and looked around.

The room looked just about big enough to hold six people comfortably. There was even a rug on the floor. It was considerably warmer underground that it was above. *Almost pleasant if you didn't mind one of your walls being the side of a coffin.* He turned to look at it. It was a plain metal box. No rust. *Must be made out of stainless steel or aluminum.* Choi surprised himself by speaking to it.

"My apologies for using your bed as a stepping stone, Uncle." he said. Despite the teachings of communism, it was difficult for any Korean to ignore the sensibilities of the ancestors.

Then he turned and crawled to the tunnel entrance on the other side of the room. The tunnel was large enough to crawl through, but not large enough to stand in. Holding his candle in one hand, he began to crawl forward.

It took 35 minutes to crawl to freedom.

* * * *

23

The following Thursday, Nola and Dan spent an hour discussing the President's proposal. It was obvious to both of them that he was using their department to shield himself from accusations that such a highly funded project was being directed to exclusively military purposes.

"We still need to decide if we are going to support the project," said Dan. " I guess we have to decide whether we think it reasonable that we can resurrect extinct animals from fossilized remains."

"It sounds too fantastic to be true," said Nola. She was obviously not very happy about being used as a pawn in a political game, even if she was extremely loyal to the President. Of course, a woman in her position could hardly expect otherwise.

"Perhaps," Dan said, "but I don't think the President would offer such a thing if he didn't think it was theoretically possible. Obviously, he is getting something out of this project. No doubt, the military is planning to get a lot of new information. The question is, do we really think that we might be able to benefit?"

"Pulling animals from extinction? That sounds quite compelling, if it can be done," replied Nola. "I would be willing to be used as a pawn if we could get a saber tooth tiger or a woolly mammoth out of the deal. Still, I find such a thing difficult to believe. How can you get biological information out of fossils? It is just rock, after all."

Dan shrugged. "I agree. However, there is a long history in our country of people standing up and saying something can't be done, and then getting embarrassed by someone who goes and does it. Think about, uh, radio, for instance. The inventors would have had to explain how they could transmit voices and signals through the air, in a way that couldn't be detected unless you had some special electronic equipment. It would be invisible. It would be silent. It probably sounded quite unbelievable at the time."

Nola sat thoughtfully, looking out the nearest window. It was raining, which was not unusual for springtime in Washington, D.C. The dull gray sky seemed to reflect the possibility of success with such a mad venture. Still, she had to admit Dan had a point. Scientists and inventors did seem to have a way of making the unimaginable turn into reality.

Dan sat quietly for a moment, waiting for her. When she didn't respond, he decided to play his hand. "I think we should cooperate. I know it's a risk. But you have to remember that reward is commensurate with risk. If this turns into a fiasco, we won't be the only ones under the microscope. But if it actually works, it would be an astounding triumph of science, and we would be at the front of the line to receive the benefits."

Nola stared out the window for another few moments. Then she turned to Dan. "I agree, I don't think we can allow this opportunity to slip past us. I'll call General Collins this afternoon and tell him that we agree to the proposal, in principal. The next question is how to divert two percent of our budget toward this effort."

"I think he probably has all those details thought out already," Dan responded. In this assessment, he was more correct than he would have ever guessed.

Chapter 1

Before he married, Steve Harrison had never considered his willingness to kill people. Killing people was part of war. It came along with armed conflict, just like mowing grass came with a yard. And for a poor Kansas boy with a dream of being a pilot, the military seemed like the best way to achieve his goal.

For as long as he could remember, Steve had dreamed of being at the controls of an airplane, roaring into the heavens, flaunting his defiance of gravity. He wanted to soar among and above the clouds, to be pressed back into his seat on his takeoff roll. He wanted to feel the nose of the aircraft come up, and the rear wheels leave the ground. He wanted to fly in precision formation with other skilled pilots. He wanted to test his skill against the enemy in a combat aircraft. When other boys were talking about the newest muscle cars and figuring out ways to bolt on superchargers and nitrous oxide, Steve was dreaming of afterburners, flaps and super-cruising.

His best friend in high school, Drew, had begged Steve to come along on the maiden voyage of his newly souped up rice burner. Drew took him out and demonstrated cornering forces in excess of 1G. Externally, Steve had shown appropriate respect for the accomplishment. He never had let Drew know, however, that he was thinking of modern fighters that could turn so sharply that anyone but a well-trained, physically fit occupant would immediately black out. When other boys were talking about their girls, who was hot and who was not, Steve was dreaming of being catapulted from the nose of an aircraft carrier, where the launch forces are so great that a pilot cannot place his hands on the controls of the aircraft until the catapult had hurled the airplane off the front of the ship.

During his junior year of high school, he applied to the only place he wanted to attend – the Air Force Academy. He was accepted, and he worked extremely hard, with a major in electrical engineering. The competition was intense, both physically and academically, but his determination and poise had earned the respect of his classmates and officers alike. He graduated high enough in his class to choose which aircraft he wanted to fly.

His classmates were astounded at his choice. He had not chosen the F-15 Eagle, the king of modern fighters, which would have led him eventually to fly its replacement, the F-22 Raptor with its stealth and super-cruise capabilities. Nor had he chosen the F-16 Fighting Falcon, the single engine fighter revered around the world for its maneuverability, multi-role capability and integrated technology. Instead of any number of other airplanes – The B52, B1, or B2 bombers, the F-111 fighter-bomber, even the Vietnam-era F4 Phantom wild weasel – he had chosen to pilot the A-10 Thunderbolt II.

Considered one of the absolute ugliest of the modern fighting aircraft, the Thunderbolt II didn't even have afterburners on its twin engines. It was so awkward looking, it was known as the Warthog. It was designed and built around a cannon, a 30mm machine gun with seven rotating barrels. Its gun was actually considered a primary weapon, instead of the secondary weapon as in the other fighter aircraft.

The Thunderbolt II is designed to get into close contact with the enemy on the ground, and its weapons are designed to destroy the enemy's assets – people, trucks, tanks, and personnel carriers. It turned out to be quite effective against buildings as well, especially multi-story buildings constructed of steel-reinforced concrete. During the Gulf Wars, there were more than a few stories of Army or Marine personnel being pinned down by the enemy firing from within abandoned concrete buildings. Normal machine guns, rockets, and other firepower seemed to have little effect. However, when a Warthog rolled in, its bullets would penetrate into the core of the building, blasting chunks of steel and concrete loose and scattering debris in a wild melee. The building wouldn't necessarily collapse, but no one inside could live through the depleted uranium bullets, steel and concrete that blasted through the interior at the speed of sound.

When his academy classmates asked why he had chosen to fly the Warthog, he had tried to explain the thrill of getting close to the battle, to use his own eyes and judgment to pick his targets, to be in constant danger of surface-to-air missiles. He didn't want to feel like he was at the controls of an elaborate video game, which is what he felt like with the F-15 and their ilk. He wanted to be in the thick of things, flying close to his targets, using a fighting aircraft to make a difference to the soldiers on the ground. What was the fun, he asked them, of shooting missiles from 25 miles off and watching your radar to determine if you had hit or missed your target? Modern fighter pilots trained for dogfights, but in real life, such encounters were so exceedingly rare that most fighter pilots never experienced one in their entire career.

Flying the A-10 was different. Wars are won and lost on the ground, Steve explained, not in the air. There would always be the need for soldiers to come in direct combat with the enemy. In an A-10, he explained, he would be going to meet the enemy, to support the ground troops who actually won the battles, and thus the war. The need for his type of support aircraft would never go away. Technology would never replace the judgment of a pilot engaged in direct contact with enemy forces.

His colleagues, most who had chosen (or wanted to choose) flying the more exotic supersonic fighters, argued with him until he got to the technology argument. He found that, at that point, they changed the subject. They knew as well as he did that the next generation fighter aircraft would not have a pilot in the aircraft. The pilot would be sitting on the ground or in a support aircraft, flying the fighters remotely when they needed a human hand at all, which was not often. Steve didn't rub it in.

If you wanted to win a war, you had to defeat the enemy, and the easiest way to defeat the enemy was to kill his soldiers. It was his bride Jill who had brought up the issue. Which is exactly how he found himself sitting in the waiting area of Pastor Howard Olofson with her.

They didn't have to wait long. Barely a minute after they had been seated in the waiting area, Pastor Howie's familiar bulky frame and crew cut filled the door to his office.

"Steve. Jill. How are my two newest lovebirds this afternoon?" Pastor Howie looked on Steve and Jill with unconcealed affection. He had joined a lot of couples in holy matrimony, and he couldn't

28

remember a couple who at first glance had seemed so unsuited to each other, and who ultimately ended up so well matched. Steve was the perfect picture of an Air Force professional pilot – a little shorter than the average, round shoulders, small hips, blond hair cropped short, back as straight as a post, leg muscles that strained against the fabric of his pants. A happy-go-lucky grin and a firm handshake. Blue eyes that took in everything at a glance, and a keen intellect that didn't forget the details of what his eyes reported. Steve jumped up and gave the pastor his firm handshake, while Jill stood by more sedately to give him a big hug and a quick kiss on the cheek.

"Ah, my dear girl, thank you. Pity the man who can't appreciate such a genuine token of affection. Come in, come in," he encouraged as he held the door for the young couple.

Jill led the way. She had taken care of herself that day, Howie noticed. Her hair was done, she had applied the tiniest bit of makeup, and was nicely dressed in a blouse and skirt. Her black hair fell in full, curly waves around her shoulders. She was quite attractive – yes, he would say even genuinely beautiful – when she took the time to make herself so. Which hadn't been often until Steve came into the picture. The pastor had known Jill for years, as her family had attended church there since Jill was a little girl. And a most extraordinary girl she was.

* * * *

Jill's family had struggled with her until she was diagnosed with Asperger's syndrome, a mild form of autism. Once diagnosed, and with guidance and support from both psychologists and self-help groups, she had matured much more quickly. The syndrome manifested itself in the ability to concentrate intensely, so much so that she often forgot to eat meals. Her parents had schooled her at home until the age of 13. By that time, her father had taught her all the math he knew, which included calculus.

Jill and her parents had gone to a local community college to inquire about more math classes. The enrollment counselor had listened to her parents, and instead of trying to give advice, had sent them to visit with Dr. Herb Zeller, one of the math professors. Dr. Zeller had quietly listened to Jill's father, and then, saying nothing, had written four equations on the board. He had then turned to Jill and asked her to solve them. It actually took a little longer than her father expected. She filled up one white board and had to erase two of the problems and put them on another board on the other side of the room. But they were solved in less than five minutes.

Gail, Jill's mother, could see that Dr. Zeller enjoyed watching her daughter's abilities. When she was done, he turned to her parents.

"You have a most impressive young lady here," he told them. "In my opinion, this college has very little to offer her. She is ready to learn differential equations, but those courses are not usually offered at the community college level, and certainly not here. She belongs at a university." Turning to Jill, he had inquired about her interests.

Jill hadn't known how to answer him, and had stood silently. That's when Jill's father explained about the Asperger's syndrome. Dr. Zeller listened, and stood thinking quietly for a moment. Then he asked Jill to step into the hallway for a couple of minutes while he visited with her parents. Jill had been glad to do so.

It seemed that she waited in the hall for a long time. Not that she minded, of course. There were quite a few interesting things to look at and think about. There were posters of different four-year colleges and Universities, along with descriptions of their programs. There were announcements about student activities. Jill was intrigued to find out there was such a thing as a robotics club and that it was organized by students. *That sounds like fun,* she thought to herself, and spent the remaining minutes thinking about the kind of robot she would like to build. She eventually decided a robot that would clean her room would be perfect.

When her parents finally came out, they drove straight home. They hadn't said much to Jill about the visit and she was relieved. That seemed to end the matter.

The next morning, however, there was a phone call from another professor, this time from Dr. Zeller's alma mater, American University in Washington, D.C. Within a week, Jill found herself, accompanied by her father, talking to Dr. Irene Wemhaus, Professor of Physics. The two fell quickly into a conversation about mathematics applied to modern physics that Jill's father didn't even try to understand. A month after that, after preliminary testing, Jill had a full scholarship and began taking courses at the University. She rode the train into downtown Washington, D.C. with her father. He went off to his job as a Deputy Director of the Interior, while she went on to the University. She earned her B.S. in Applied Physics at the age of 16, and promptly continued into graduate school. By the age of 21, she had completed her Ph.D., and since her graduation had been working for a technology consulting company near her home.

Jill and Steve had met in Georgia, volunteering separately through their churches for hurricane cleanup work. He had been stationed at Moody Air Force Base in Valdosta, Georgia, while she had traveled from the Washington, D.C. suburbs of Virginia. They ended up working together at an emergency shelter, getting people in touch with support resources in the community. Somehow, they had fell into a conversation about aircraft, and Steve was amazed to learn that she could understand how the thickness of an aircraft's wing could affect its performance envelope. When it came time to finish their work, Steve said, "Listen, how about we continue this conversation over some dinner?" It seemed to him that she was reluctant to accept, but he managed to talk her into sitting down together over a dinner at the shelter that was provided by the Red Cross and some of the other volunteers.

When Steve asked her if he could see her again, he had been as surprised at her answer as his Academy classmates had been at his choice of aircraft. "Are you willing to get permission to date me from my father?"

"Are you serious?" He asked. He had heard of getting permission to marry a girl from her father, but not just for a date.

"Yes, I am."

"Well, sure, I'll ask him. Do I have to come up to Virginia to meet him personally, or can I just ask him over the phone?"

"I'm going back home tomorrow. Are you interested in coming all the way up to Virginia for a date?" Jill, surprising herself at her audacity. She wasn't usually comfortable enough with a member of the opposite sex to speak so freely, unless it had something to do with physics.

"I'll come to Virginia," he responded immediately, surprising himself almost as much as Jill. He had met a lot of girls over the last few years, there had been no lack of attention from them, and some of it was so obvious it embarrassed him. But none of them had intrigued him intellectually – in fact, he considered most girls to be anywhere from slightly above average to downright dumb. That's what comes from attending the Air Force Academy, he reflected to himself. While there were some girls in the academy, attendance was overwhelmingly male. Majoring in Electrical Engineering had further limited his exposure to girls. At the time, he had made a conscious commitment to focus on Academy work, and purposefully had not dated. He knew that a woman could be a distraction, and he hadn't allowed himself that distraction during his Academy tenure. The girls he had met, whether out on the street, at church, or at social engagements, seemed shallow to him. Jill was the one of the few girls he had met who seemed capable of thorough thinking.

"Well, you can meet my father when you come to Virginia," she replied sensibly. They exchanged e-mail addresses and phone numbers, and two weekends later Steve made the trip.

Jill's father, Dan Labinsky, was a couple inches over six feet, in his early 60's, and thin for his age, Steve observed. He obviously has a lot of energy. He and his wife Gail made Steve feel quite welcome as they ushered him into the house. Steve had decided to dress in his formal uniform, in an effort to create a positive first impression. It certainly seemed to work on Gail, but he wasn't so sure about Dan. After a few moments of light talk about his drive up, Dan, Steve and Jill settled in the living room while Gail returned to the kitchen to continue working on supper (which was already smelling quite inviting to Steve).

"Mr. Labinsky," began Steve, "I enjoyed meeting Jill a couple of weeks ago while I was working in Georgia. I asked her for a date, and she asked me to get your permission. So I came up here to ask you if I could date her."

"Steve, I appreciate you taking the time to come and visit me in person," replied Dan. "And I appreciate that Jill asked you to visit with me. You see, when she became a Christian, we attended a seminar as a family that focused on living a Christian life. One of the recommendations was that, instead of using dating as a means for young people to find out about one another, we use courtship. Jill agreed to using the courtship model instead of dating."

"What's the difference between dating and courting?" Steve interrupted.

Dan grinned at him. "Well, for one thing, I'm involved in the process." Steve chuckled appreciatively. "For another thing, it means that you and I get to know each other. It is a way for me to safeguard her. I am sure you know that there are young men out there who wouldn't hesitate to take advantage of Jill. If I am involved in the relationship, I can safeguard her and help her make good choices. It is also a way for me to communicate to you my desire for a healthy, appropriate relationship between the two of you. I trust you understand the implications."

"Yes, Sir, I understand," Steve answered. The implication was clear – hands off.

"Good. The other part about courting is that I ask you to respect not only her body, but her heart as well. In other words, if at any time you decide you are not serious about getting to know Jill, please let either she or I know and break off the relationship. She has already agreed to do the same with respect to you." Jill nodded at her father soberly. "I want nothing more than for her to have a healthy relationship with a young man who might, at some point, potentially be her husband." He must have seen some twitch on Steve's face, because he smiled and held up his hand. "I am not expecting you to pop the question or make some kind of commitment to her now. I am just asking that you respect her as a woman and treat her in the same way you would want your mother or sister treated in the same situation. Don't play with her emotions. She is not a toy. She is my daughter, whom I love very much, and I only want the best for her."

"That's understandable, Sir."

"Please call me Dan. I know you're a military man, and saying sir comes naturally. But you are quite welcome to be less formal in our home."

"OK, Dan. Thank you, Sir." replied Steve.

Gail poked her head in the living room door. "Supper is ready. I hope you're all hungry. Come and sit down."

"Yes, Ma'am. I am hungry, and it smells delicious." Gail beamed at the compliment. They all stood and made their way to the table. After being seated, Dan asked a blessing on the food and Gail began to serve the pot roast.

"So Steve, tell us about yourself. Where did you grow up? Why did you decide to enter the military? Are you a Christian?"

Over the course of the dinner, Steve related his childhood in Kansas. He shared how his father had divorced his mother and left the family when he was eight. Steve had a younger brother and two younger sisters back home. "Mom didn't have a college education, and Dad wasn't very good about paying child support. So, Mom ended up working as a seamstress at a men's clothing store in Topeka. She did other odd jobs too. I helped as much as I could. I started a lawn care business, which helped put food on the table and allowed us to have a few extras and take a short vacation a few times."

Dan, Gail and Jill were listening intently. Dan was impressed by the willing contribution that Steve obviously had made to the family. Jill was impressed by his ability to speak so frankly about his past. Gail was impressed at the amount of pot roast, potatoes and carrots that were being consumed between sentences.

"The man that ran the clothing store where Mom worked was a Christian. He invited us to church. At first, I didn't think Mom wanted to go. But we went a few times, and my brother and sisters and I made friends and enjoyed Sunday School so much we kept going. After about a year, Mom became a Christian. I became a Christian when I was 14." Steve looked earnestly at Dan. "Mom's boss was a great man who treated her very well. He explained to her how God was able to fill in the hole left when Dad took off. I think he taught her a lot. He was my Sunday School teacher one year, and I remember how he took extra time to share with me how God wanted to be my Heavenly Father. I mean, I could talk to Him like He was my real father, and He would help me through life just like my real father would have. I didn't believe it when he first told me, but he read me all the stories in the Bible about people who didn't grow up with their fathers, and how God always seemed to pay special attention to them. I liked that. It was easy to become a Christian when you believed that God was so interested in you."

The meal continued for well over an hour. Steve ended up answering a lot of questions about life in the Air Force. None of the Labinsky family had ever been in the military. Gail managed to talk Steve into accepting a second helping of peach cobbler with ice cream.

At the end of the meal, Dan said, "Well, you didn't drive all this way to answer questions about Air Force life. Why don't you and Jill go and spend some time visiting in the living room? I've enjoyed visiting with you, but I can see that she wants to spend some time with you as well." Jill blushed, but didn't deny her father's observation.

"Well, thank you for supper. It was delicious. I don't think I have ever eaten this well, even at home." Gail's smile at this compliment lit up the room. "I'll have to run some extra miles next week to work all this off."

Jill led Steve into the living room, and they sat facing each other on the sofa. "Thanks for driving up all this way. I'm glad you came. I

34

think Mom and Dad like you."

"I like them too. They are really nice. Do you eat meals like that all the time?"

Jill laughed. "Well, Mom is a good cook. When I was living here, we tried to eat supper together every evening. But no, we don't always eat that nice of a meal."

"So you don't live here? I thought you did," said Steve.

"No, I have an apartment now, about four miles from here. I live with a couple of other girls that I know from church."

"So what do you do, exactly? I don't expect that you spend all your time studying airplane wings."

"I'm a physicist. I work for a company that does consulting work, mainly for the government or government contractors. Usually it is work for military applications, but sometimes we get some other things. Right now, I am working on a way to focus gamma rays for a medical application. The contracting company makes machines that give radiation treatments to cancer patients. They are trying to get more radiation into tumors and less into the surrounding tissue, to try to improve the patient's quality of life."

After some prompting from Steve, Jill told him about her college career and her graduate degrees. Steve listened in amazement.

"So that means you're a Doctor?" asked an amazed Steve.

"Well, yes, I have a Ph.D. But I'm not a medical doctor."

"Wow. You must be brilliant. And here I am, thinking I am going to teach someone with a Ph.D. in physics about the thickness of airplane wings." he said.

Jill reached over and touched his hand. "Don't feel bad. Actually, it was nice for me to have someone treat me like a normal woman. People think I am really smart and I guess I am," she allowed. "Having brains doesn't do much for a social life, though. It was hard going to college with people that were almost twice my age. We could relate on an intellectual level, but not socially. I always felt a little out of place."

They continued to talk until Dan walked into the room.

"It's 10:00 folks. Time to turn in. Steve, some good friends of ours, Paul and Karen Schneider, have volunteered to host you overnight at their place. They attend church with us, so you can just go with them to church and meet us there. Then you two can spend some more time together tomorrow after church, until you have to drive back to Georgia."

"Sorry, Sir. I guess I lost track of time," said Steve.

Dan chuckled. "No problem at all, but it wouldn't do for us to be winking and nodding at the minister in church tomorrow because we've been up all night, would it?"

"No, Sir. Well," this to Jill, "I guess I had better get going. I'll see you tomorrow."

"OK. Thanks for coming up this weekend." she replied.

Steve arrived at the Schneider residence twenty minutes later. He met Paul and Karen, and they all chatted for a few minutes. The children were already in bed. Steve was tired from his drive, and they all quickly turned in.

The next morning, Steve woke at 7:00 AM and went for his usual three mile run. When he returned, he was met by Paul and Karen Schneider's daughter, who was 13, and their two boys, who were six and five. They were amazed when they found out he had been out running before breakfast. The two boys obviously had a lot of energy, and didn't stay in one place for any length of time. It made Steve wish he were back at his own home in Kansas with his younger brother and sisters. After a breakfast of scrambled eggs and sausage, Steve went to get showered and dressed for church. After inspecting his formal dress uniform, he donned it and walked back out to where the Schneider's were waiting. When the boys saw him in his uniform, they stared in amazement and had a sudden attack of extreme shyness. Then they started whispering together. Finally, the five year old gathered up enough courage to ask, "Are you a good guy or a bad guy?" Their mother, Karen, nearly died of embarrassment, but Steve and Paul got a good chuckle out of it.

They arrived at church just a couple of minutes before the Labinsky family. The Schneiders shooed their children off to Sunday School. After everyone had arrived, they all entered the sanctuary. Dan and Gail led the way, then Jill and Steve, followed by Paul and Karen.

Steve enjoyed the service, especially the sermon delivered by the pastor, Howard Olofson. Afterwards, they all went out to a neighborhood restaurant for lunch. Steve wanted to spend some more time with Jill, but everyone lingered over lunch until the Schneiders excused themselves. After they left, Dan turned to him and he noticed that Gail seemed suddenly rather nervous.

"Steve, you seem to be a fine young man." began Dan.

Uh-oh, Steve thought. *Sounds like the beginning of 'I don't want you to date my daughter.'* He was surprised at what came next.

"Gail and I talked this morning, and we would be glad to have you court Jill. But there is a thing or two that you should know about her. Jill isn't very comfortable talking about this, but I thought that you should know a little more about her. I want to make sure you understand that she has some considerable gifts, but those gifts have both positives and negatives." Dan went on to talk about Jill's amazing power of concentration, and her diagnosis of Asperger's syndrome and autism. Steve listened carefully. He was surprised to see Jill trying to keep back tears.

After Dan finished, everyone was quite for a moment. Then Steve said, "Thanks for telling me. I am glad you let me know. I can see this gift of Jill's has been a challenge for all of you." Dan and Gail nodded together. Jill was avoiding his gaze. "You know," Steve continued, "it seems to me that everyone has their challenges in life. I would have preferred not have my dad leave our family. That has been hard on the rest of us. You would prefer that Jill not have this hamburger syndrome, or whatever it's called. But there are some things in life that we just can't control. All we can do is try to deal with them the best we can. That was part of my attraction to Jesus when I was 14. I could see that he would help me through life. I could see that having God as my Heavenly Father would help me to be a better person than I would be otherwise. That is one of the lessons that the Bible teaches us over and over – being a Christian doesn't mean avoiding challenges, it means dealing with challenges in the right way."

"That was well said." Dan responded after another moment's silence.

"Well, it 3:00 o'clock, and I really need to be heading back toward Georgia. Can I spend the last few minutes with Jill?"

"Of course," Dan said. They all stood up and he reached out and shook Steve's hand. "Thanks for coming up and spending the weekend with us. Consider yourself having an open invitation."

"Thank you, Sir. Er, Dan."

Steve reached out to shake Gail's hand. She ignored it and gave him a big hug instead. "God bless you, Steve. Thanks for driving all the way up to meet us." Then Dan and Gail turned and headed toward the exit, holding hands.

Steve sat back down. Jill remained standing, still hesitating to look at him. "Jill," said Steve. She looked at him hollowly, "Please sit down.

37

I can spend a few more minutes here with you, and I do enough standing in the military. I try to avoid it when I am off duty." He smiled at her. She braved a smile back at him and sat down. *Whew, I guess we touched a real sensitive spot here,* Steve thought. "Jill, it's OK. I meant what I said. Everyone has their challenges in life."

"You don't think I'm weird?" she asked.

"I think you are an extremely bright girl who has a unique gift. Actually, I envy you. Your parents are really fantastic people. I think I would rather have hamburger syndrome and have my parents still married. They obviously love you a great deal."

Though her eyes were still moist, Jill smiled at him. "It's Asperger, not hamburger. And, yes, Dad and Mom are nice people. I guess I should be more thankful for them."

"I'll say. Have you ever thought what life would be like if you didn't have one or both of them?" He went on to describe times at home when they didn't know where their next meal would come from. "Winter was especially tough. You can live without air conditioning, even in a Kansas summer. But you can't live without heat in a Kansas winter. There were times when we thought the electricity was going to be shut off. But God always got us through."

"You have a lot of faith," she observed.

"I have some experience with God providing for me in amazing ways. Like, I didn't think I had a chance of entering the Air Force Academy and it was the only place I really wanted to go to school. I injured my knee during football practice before my senior year of high school, and only ended up playing two games at the end of the year. You have to have a record of participating in athletics to attend the Academy. But there was an Air Force recruiter at the last game who watched me play. He had some good contacts, and somehow they got me in."

"But you can still relate to people," Jill said, "I can't. All I can relate to is sub-atomic particles and magnetic fields."

Steve chuckled. "I'm envious. They don't talk back, or order you to give them 50 pushups."

Jill laughed. Her eyes were dry now. "I never thought of that. I'm glad my gamma rays don't order me to do pushups." Steve nodded encouragingly. "You help me see things different."

"Good. I get the feeling that you need to realize that your Asperger syndrome really is a gift, and not a burden. See, my God made you, and my God doesn't make mistakes. You are the way you are for a reason. You just need to figure out the reason."

"Thanks," said Jill. "That's the nicest thing any boy has ever said to me."

"Well, I really do need to be heading back. Monday morning happens way too early in the military."

"OK. Thanks again for coming," she said. They stood up and walked outside. Steve's car was closest. As they walked toward it, he took her hand.

"Can I come to see you again?" he asked.

"Oh, please do. I would like that."

Steve pulled her hand up to his mouth and kissed it. "I will. Your family is great. I enjoyed spending time with them. And with you." He released her hand and climbed into his car. "I'll call you," he said through the open window.

"OK. Bye." she said.

Steve did a lot of thinking on his way back to his airbase in Georgia. He thought about what he wanted in a wife. As a Christian man, he understood that the Bible commanded that he marry a Christian woman. At the same time, a major portion of his life had been defined by the abandonment of his father. He was determined that he would never do the same thing to the woman he married. The one absolute requirement he had for a wife was a woman who was committed to making a marriage work. Quitter was not a word in his vocabulary, and he didn't intend for it to apply to any aspect of his marriage.

He saw in Jill and her parents a dedication to each other that attracted him. Dan was obviously the man in charge of the family. Steve didn't have enough experience to know how he treated Gail, but he sure seemed to be taking care of Jill and meeting her unique needs. He was obviously very supportive of her and quite protective. Steve had a deep appreciation for people who helped other people. Growing up, his family had been aided a number of times by friends and neighbors who helped them make ends meet. Seeing Dan's care of Jill gave Steve a great deal of respect for the family, their faith, and their commitment to each other.

And what about Jill? *What would it be like*, he wondered, *to have a wife smarter than me?* No sense trying to deny it – someone who earned a Ph.D. in Physics at the age of 21 was no slouch. She would probably have more income earning potential than he ever would. Was he comfortable with a working wife? Well, his mother had worked most of the time she was raising him – but not out of want, out of necessity. It was not an idea that was foreign to him; he didn't feel threatened by it. But what if they had kids? *I would probably have to stay home with them,* he concluded. That sounded OK with him. He loved kids, and had done a lot of supervision with his own younger siblings while his mom worked.

The other thing about Jill was that sensitivity to her Asperger's syndrome. Understandable if she never was able to go to school with people her own age. She seemed to be a very sensitive girl. She had obviously learned to trust in her father, and that trust would automatically migrate to her husband, he thought, unless that husband really blew it somehow. He thought about having a smart, sensitive, attractive woman trusting in him. And that is when he knew she was going to be the one. And, as with most other things that Steve set his mind to, it had come to be.

* * * *

"What can I do for my newest young couple today?" the pastor asked after they had all been seated in his office. He had married them barely three weeks before, and was hoping and praying this wasn't the beginning of some trouble in their ability to relate to each other.

"Well, Pastor," began Steve, "Jill and I have been doing a lot of talking over the last few weeks. I didn't realize how important human life was for her. She is really bothered about my work, since I might one day have to kill people. I guess I never really thought about it before. She says that the Bible says we shouldn't kill. I always thought it was OK for a soldier to fight for his country. I mean, I wouldn't go out and kill someone on the street. But she says a person who is willing to kill is not able to please God, even in a time of war. Is she right?"

"Hmmm," the pastor responded. "That is not an easy question. Of course, I shouldn't expect easy questions from you two. Actually, I had to think through this issue myself some years ago when I first became pastor of this church. We serve a fair number of people who are in the military, due to our proximity to our nation's capital. So, I'll share my thoughts. Now, that is just a beginning. You also need to do some

40

research of your own to see what you think the Bible says about this topic. Different denominations have different views on warfare. Some say it is OK for a Christian to serve in the military, whereas others strictly believe that killing is never justified in the eyes of God. So, when you come to ask my advice, you're going to hear my interpretation of what the Bible says.

"First, we have to recognize the difference in attitude between the Old and New Testaments.

"The most obvious Old Testament revelation on this topic is the life of King David. He was a man of war, even more than King Saul before him. As a military leader, he killed many of Israel's enemies. In fact, the women of Israel used to sing a song, 'Saul has killed his thousands, and David his tens of thousands.' So, David was obviously very capable of killing his enemies in armed conflict and he was a man that God loved very much."

The minister continued, "However, there is a very interesting passage when David asked God for permission to build Him a temple. Nathan the prophet told David to proceed. But that night, God appeared to Nathan and told him to forbid David to build the temple. The reason? Because David was a man of war, and had shed the blood of his enemies, God didn't want him to build his temple. This is a fascinating passage of scripture. It shows us among other things that God is a god of degrees. In other words, in God's sight, things aren't always black and white. God approved of David's conduct, and loved David, but didn't want his house to be built by a man that had shed so much blood. He wanted his house to be built by a man of peace. That man ended up being David's son, Solomon, who didn't have to fight so many battles against the enemies of Israel.

"Now, Israel lived under the Old Law, which specifically forbade murder. However, Israel engaged in warfare throughout its history. Therefore I conclude that God views killing in war as different from murder."

He could see from his expression that Steve was following his every word and he went on, "Next, we move to the New Testament. Just before Jesus' ministry began, John the Baptist was preaching in the wilderness. He was approached by some Roman soldiers who asked what they should do to obtain salvation. John told them, 'Do violence to no man, neither accuse any falsely, and be content with your wages.' Interestingly, he didn't tell them to leave the military.

41

Next comes Jesus. There was a Roman Centurion who sent a message to Jesus asking him to heal a servant. The message encouraged Jesus to just give the command and the servant would be healed – Jesus didn't have to travel all the way to the Centurion's house to do the healing. The Bible says that Jesus was amazed at this man's faith, and told his followers that he had not found such faith in all of Israel. The centurion's servant did indeed recover. So here was a man who was not a Jew, and who was in charge of a garrison of soldiers, who obtained the favor of Jesus because of his faith.

"There's also another example that illustrates the same point. One of the first Gentile converts to Christianity was another Roman Centurion, a leader of something called the Italian Band. We don't know for sure what that was, but I suppose it might have been some kind of Special Forces unit. The Bible records this Centurion as a man who was fervently seeking God. In a vision, God specifically sends Peter to explain the gospel. In fact, he used this Centurion to show Peter that both Jews and Gentiles can be saved. Again, this Centurion is not commanded to leave his military position. We read about him in the book of Acts.

"Jesus taught that we should turn the other cheek. When someone asks you to travel with him one mile, you travel with him two. When he asks you for your coat, you give him your shirt also."

The pastor turned and looked directly at Steve. "How do you think that meshes with killing in war? Based on these words of Jesus, do you think he would approve?"

"I wouldn't say approve, but he seems to accommodate it," Steve reflected.

"I think we need people of faith in the military, just like we do in most other parts of life," Pastor Howie explained thoughtfully. "God needs witnesses there just like he needs witnesses in schools and workplaces. And here is where I think we need to draw a line between God's perfect will and his permissive will.

"I think it is clear that God's perfect will is that no one ever kill another person under any circumstance. And that includes military action. However, I believe he also knows that wars will happen, and that killing people in war is not the same as murdering your neighbor in cold blood. So, I do believe that people in the military can be Christians. But I also believe that he prefers to have people who would refuse to bear arms."

"So, you are saying it is a matter of degrees?" clarified Steve.

"Yes, that is what I am saying. Let me give you an example. I ask my children to put their bicycles in the garage at nighttime. If they bring their bicycles in but drop them over on the floor without using the kickstand, that is unacceptable. They have done what I asked, but not with the care that I intended. If they bring in their bicycles and stand them up correctly, that is acceptable. If they bring in their bicycles and spend a couple of extra minutes arranging the contents of the garage so that there is enough room for their bikes and my car, that is pleasing to me. I appreciate that they took the time to think of my needs. They are showing their love for me in their actions."

"So the absolutes are not absolute?" asked Steve.

"Perhaps it would help if I showed you a very clear example where there are differences in holiness to God. The apostle Paul understood this principle. People in various churches asked him about marriage. He told them that to marry is good, but to stay single and devoted to God is better. However, he also made it clear that there were some that could follow the command to stay single, and some that couldn't and who should marry. Paul wrote that there should be no command to forbid marriage in an effort to get a whole group of people more devoted to God. The decision to remain single is a very personal matter between an individual and God.

"Steve, I believe that God will accept you if you are a member of the military. But if you want to be more than just accepted of God, if you really want to please him, I think he would be more pleased if you decided not to conduct warfare."

Jill could tell that Steve was getting a little tense. She laid a hand on his arm. "Steve, ask him the same questions you asked me." She turned to their minister. "Steve can't figure out how a nation could defend itself if everyone decided not to bear arms. The country would be taken over in a few weeks."

"Actually, that is probably the easiest question to answer," Pastor Howie replied. "In order to see why, we have to go back to the Old Testament, to the time of King Hezekiah. Do you know anything about his reign?" He asked the couple.

Steve shook his head, but Jill brightened. "Yes, isn't he the one who got some extra time added to his life?"

"That's the one. He acquired a terminal illness, but God healed him and added 15 years to his life. But an even more remarkable thing happened to him before that. Here's the story. The Assyrians came up against Jerusalem, intending to take it over and wipe it out. They were very good at doing that – they were the dominant power in the known world at the time. They could break down the walls of a city, annihilate the people, and carry off everything of value in a week or less. They were an incredible fighting force. When they approached a city, they would command the city's leadership to give themselves up without a fight. If that happened, those captured were still carried off to Assyria, but they were treated quite a bit better than those who chose to fight. If a city chose to fight it out, they were invariably all killed, or tortured and then turned into slaves.

"Anyway, the Assyrians came up to the walls of Jerusalem and commanded the people to give themselves up. They insulted the God of the Jews, Jehovah, and asked if he was more powerful than any of the gods of the other cities that had been captured and destroyed. They wrote out a letter and sent it in to Hezekiah, insulting Jehovah and demanding that Hezekiah give himself up.

"Hezekiah knew the situation was helpless. There was no way to win against the Assyrians. So, he took that letter and brought it to the temple, and prayed to God asking him what to do. He pointed out the insult and asked God to somehow spare the city. God listened to that prayer, and sent a prophet to Hezekiah telling him that no Assyrian would set foot inside the walls of the city. Hezekiah sent a message back to the Assyrians saying that he refused to give up the city.

"Within a week, the main contingent of the Assyrian army was camped around Jerusalem, preparing for siege warfare. The night before the siege started, however, a disease struck the Assyrian army. The Bible says the disease killed 185,000 soldiers. The remaining Assyrians had to give up and return home. As they left, they sent another letter to Hezekiah warning him that they would be back. However, the Assyrian king was killed by two of his sons when he returned home, and as a result of the political chaos, the Assyrians never again tried to take over Jerusalem. So, to make a long story short, if our entire nation prayed and asked God to protect them, God himself would fight for the nation."

"So, what you are telling me is that all the wars that have been fought have been unnecessary?" challenged Steve.

"God will protect his people if they ask for protection. Of course, there have always been more than enough people who are willing to conduct warfare. So, no, I don't believe that all wars have been unnecessary. There has always been war. In a perfect world, there would be no warfare, but we don't live in a perfect world, now, do we?"

Steve sat back against the couch. He had always viewed God as purely black and white. He had never considered that God might have an unacceptable, an acceptable, and a perfect will. "You know, this would be easier if God just told us exactly what he expected," he said.

The pastor laughed. "I'm not so sure that wasn't what God implemented in the Law given to Moses. Turns out that humans can't measure up to God's law. So, in the New Testament He has taken a different approach. He gives us his principles. Jesus said 'Love God with all your heart, soul, and strength. And love your neighbor as yourself.' In other words, he wants us to memorize those principles and apply them as we go through life. I personally think that is even more difficult than the Old Law. On the other hand, it does give us a much clearer picture of the nature of our Heavenly Father."

"Tell Steve some of the other times that God fought for his people." prompted Jill.

"There are many stories. Let's see, there is the Israelites escape from Egypt. The Israelites were trapped between the Egyptian army and the Red Sea. God made a path through the Red Sea, and the Israelites escaped. When the Egyptian army followed, the Red Sea returned to its normal area and the entire Egyptian army drowned.

"Then there is the story of Gideon. God instructed him how to conduct psychological warfare. He took on an army of 20,000 soldiers with 300 men. God caused such a panic in the opposing army that they ended up killing each other. Oh, I could go on and on. But you need to read some of these stories yourself. I can assure you that God is pleased when people ask him for deliverance from their enemies."

"That sounds pretty incredible." Steve said.

The pastor's eyes twinkled as he replied, "That is because these events were pretty incredible. And God is still capable of protecting his people. The problem is that people generally try to solve their problems by themselves, and don't ask God to solve them. God won't fight our battles for us unless we have enough faith to trust him completely. If we don't have that faith, we have to solve our problems ourselves."

"So, you are saying that God would be more pleased with me if I asked for protection and decided not to take another person's life?" concluded Steve.

"Yes, that is what I am saying. Your conduct would move from acceptable to pleasing in the sight of God." replied the pastor.

"Well, I don't know how I can get out of the military. I still have a four-year obligation to fulfill. I don't think they would agree if I walked in on Monday and told them I was now a non-combatant."

"Steve, you're not applying the lesson," replied the pastor gently. "The specific point was that God would fight for people if they asked him. But if God is willing to fight for people, don't you think he would be willing to help solve other problems, too?"

"So you think I should ask God to solve this problem?" he asked.

"Of course." The pastor's bushy eyebrows shot up, "Jill will be glad to help, too, I'm sure."

"Yes, of course." she replied eagerly.

"How can you help? This is my problem." Steve retorted to Jill, with a hint of frustration in his voice.

"Whoa, Steve. I seem to recall a certain ceremony that you participated in three weeks ago." He interjected, "As I recall, you are no longer Steve, you are now half of something known as 'Steve and Jill.' Am I right?" he challenged.

"Yes, yes. But how can she help? She doesn't have any experience with the Air Force."

"But she does have a lot of experience with prayer. If you want God's help with a problem, don't you think you have to ask? And can't Jill share this burden with you? Of course she can, that is what marriage is all about. What happens to one affects the other, and you help each other along in life. Jill is perfectly capable of praying for you and asking God to help solve your problem. I should think you would be glad of her help."

"I guess I am not used to asking other people's help in solving my problems," acknowledged Steve.

"Well, as a Christian, that is exactly what you need to do. Ask God for help. Stop relying only on yourself. You used to ask God for help when you were growing up in Kansas, didn't you?" Steve nodded affirmatively. "And you have told me before that you believed God answered those prayers and provided for your family then. Well, don't stop just because you're an adult. God is just as willing to help you now as he was then."

46

Steve turned to Jill. "I'm sorry, I didn't mean to insult you. I guess my thinking was just too earth-bound."

Jill laid her head on Steve's shoulder. "It's OK, Honey. I would like to pray for you if you will let me."

"Of course." He responded. The pastor's heart warmed as he listened to their exchange. One of the benefits of being a pastor was to see God work in the lives of men and women who truly trusted in Him. It happened all too rarely to suit him – it seemed that one of the characteristics of being human was the inability to totally trust God with life's problems. But when it did happen, it was always worth watching. And he had the feeling that God was going to do something special in the lives of these two rather unusual young people.

Chapter 2

The next morning, Steve and Jill sat in church near Dan and Gail, as they always did when they were visiting Jill's parents. But Steve found that focusing on Pastor Howie's sermon was difficult. He knew the minister's advice from the previous day had been sound. From the first time Jill brought up the issue of sanctity of life, and her opposition to his willingness to take the lives of other people, even in battle, it seemed as if a weight had settled on his shoulders.

Steve could see the truth in Howie's argument that killing was not on Jesus' agenda, even for one's enemies. He realized that Howie was right about asking God to protect and fight for himself, his spouse, and even his whole nation. He sincerely wanted to please God. But he felt that, if he continued with his present career plans, his choice would not be entirely pleasing to God – or rather, that God had something different, and probably better in mind. But Steve sure couldn't see it from his viewpoint. He had never experienced this level of uncertainty before, and it was not a good feeling.

He had received significant financial help from the Air Force to get through the Academy. For every year of education, he had to serve one and a half years. And there was no easy way to back out. Once you made your commitment to the military, they intended to keep you. Steve didn't hold any grudges about his situation. He knew what he was getting into when he signed up, and he had readily agreed to the military's terms.

But what about now? Would the Air Force listen if he went to them and explained that he was having pangs of conscience about killing people? He knew if any one of his superior officers knew about his questions, he would be grounded immediately. Would they accommodate a change in religious viewpoints midway through a person's term of service? Getting those questions answered involved hiring a lawyer versed in military law, which sounded very expensive. Jill would probably be willing to pay for it, but he hated to spend her money that way. He had spent half the previous night tossing and turning in bed, trying to find a solution to the dilemma, but a solution hadn't presented itself to him.

He realized with a start that the service was almost over. One more hymn, then a closing prayer, and the congregation started filing out. He guiltily realized he couldn't even remember the topic of the sermon. *What a Christian you are,* he scolded himself, *worrying about your future and ignoring the sermon.* The people in the bench ahead stood and started filing out. He held out his hand for Jill and together they walked into the visiting area outside of the sanctuary.

"Wasn't that a nice message today, Honey?" She asked, "Pastor Howie does such a nice job. I don't think I had ever thought of the relationship between Jacob and Esau like that before."

"I agree," he replied. *And I still haven't.*

Steve and Jill found themselves in a clump of other chatting people. He recognized nearly all of them, and figured he could probably put names on about one out of three. Steve was pretty good with names, but this was only about the fifth or sixth time he had attended church here, and he had been so focused on Jill and her parents that he hadn't really tried to learn the names of more people. He had felt sorry at the wedding reception that he couldn't name more of them, since most of the people at the reception had been from this church group.

Pastor Howie broke into the circle of chatting and smiling people. He was greeted enthusiastically, and took time to shake hands and give hugs all around. The last ones he greeted in the group were Steve and Jill. He gave Jill a quick hug and shook Steve's hand with a smile. Then he managed to pull Steve closer to him and a little to the side.

"I had a thought after our conversation yesterday," he said to Steve. "Have you ever thought of applying to Test Pilot School?"

Steve's thoughts jumped back to the worst six seconds of his life.

He had been going through weapons training with his A-10 squadron. The training area was in Arizona. He had been pleased with his mastery of the aircraft – not that it required a tremendous amount of skill to fly. It was a relatively simple airplane, after all, compared to more sophisticated fighters like the F-15 or F-16. But he wanted to be confident about the basics before he started working on learning to use the weapons.

The A-10 has a rather checkered history in the Air Force. The basic problem was that it performs so well that the Air Force cannot get rid of it. Designed during the late 1960's and early 1970's, during the Vietnam "conflict" when America's younger generation was getting "liberated," it was the era of the Cold War. And although the military planners in government might have been uncomfortable with Vietnam, their daily focus was the Soviet Union and its latent threat to Western Europe. The new weapons systems of the era were designed to deal with a ground war in which the Soviet Union or her "allies" came across the Iron Curtain for an entirely different kind of liberation than that being practiced by the youth of the United States. The Vietnam conflict, which had never been officially declared a war, was considered nothing more than a nuisance to the top military planners of the United States, compared to the threat of exposing hordes of troops to a nuclear-equipped enemy force intent on the conquest of the part of Europe they hadn't gotten during the last great war.

With that perspective had come the identification for the need of a new ground-attack airplane, capable of taking on masses of mobile armor that the Soviet Union could deploy in short order. Two competing designs had been submitted for evaluation, and the model submitted by Fairchild Republic had gotten the bid. First flight had been in May of `72, and the Air Force had begun to take deliveries in `75.

The aircraft designated A-10 is named in honor of another famous ground attack airplane, the P-47 Thunderbolt. The P-47 had made a name for itself as the best airborne friend a WWII soldier could have. The A-10 is therefore named the Thunderbolt II.

There is another name synonymous with the aircraft, however. While officially the Thunderbolt II, it is perhaps even more widely known as the Warthog. While the origins of the name are unknown, it probably came from the row of pylons that extended from each wing and fuselage. While the top of the plane looked somewhat aerodynamic, the bottom looked lumpy and warty, especially when no ordinance has been hung on any of the pylons.

There are four pylons under each wing and three under the fuselage. To these can be attached a total of 16,000 pounds of ordinance. The A-10 can deliver 500 or 1000-pound gravity bombs, or the fearsome Maverick missile. The original Maverick had a TV camera in the nose, which the A-10 pilot uses to aim the weapon. The Maverick is a "fire-and-forget" weapon, which meant that after launch the missile steers itself to its target without any more intervention from the pilot. Upon contact, it blasts a stream of molten metal into its target. There is no known armored vehicle that can stand up to the blast of a Maverick missile. It is so successful, in fact, that an infrared version of the original missile was designed and built as well, for use during darkness and low-visibility situations.

The A-10's pylons can also hold pods that can deploy magnesium flares to distract heat-seeking missiles, and chaff pods that can scatter clouds of small metal fragments to distract radar-seeking missiles. The pylons can hold external fuel tanks, which could be dropped after being emptied, although this is rarely done. The aircraft can be refueled during flight from an airborne tanker, and in war situations there has been enough tanker coverage that mission planners opted to use the pylons for extra weapons instead of fuel.

Remarkably enough, all of those weapons are considered secondary. The main weapon is the seven-barrel Avenger cannon. It is the most fearsome firing weapon that has ever been deployed on any light aircraft from any country in the world. It can fire more than 30 bullets per second. The bullets are made up of a unique alloy of uranium (for density) and titanium (for strength). In fact, the aircraft is literally designed around the gun, and not the other way around. The nosewheel is offset from the centerline, which is reserved for the barrels of the cannon. The engines are mounted in separate pods above the fuselage, instead of being integrated into the fuselage like almost every other fighter ever built. This is necessary because, when the cannon fires, the shells contain large amounts of powder. When fired, the powder turns into extremely high-pressure gas in a fraction of a second – gas that contains no oxygen. The canon fires so fast, and as a result spits out so much spent gas, that it can actually extinguish the flame inside a jet engine. Having an engine flame-out in the middle of a gun battle turns out to be somewhat unpopular with pilots, and so the engines have been mounted up high, above the fuselage, to keep them out of the path of the gases generated by the firing canon. It makes for an awkward looking – but a highly effective - airplane.

The rest of the airplane is built to survive ambushes and tough firefights from close encounters with the enemy. There was no doubt at all in the designers' minds that the airplane was going to get hit by anti-aircraft guns and missiles. This airplane was designed to take this punishment and still get the pilot home safely.

All of the flight controls are attached, with mechanical linkages, directly to the flight surfaces. There are no computer controls on this airplane. Each flight control is hydraulically assisted, not much different from the power steering in an automobile – the difference being that there are multiple independent hydraulic systems, so that if one fails, another can take its place. All the hydraulics are routed through the airframe on different paths, so that if a part of the airplane were shot up, and a hydraulic system was lost, the redundant system would still be able to operate. In the unfortunate event that all the hydraulics are lost, the plane could still be flown with its mechanical connections to the flight control surfaces. It wouldn't be pleasant – similar to driving a power steering equipped car without the power steering working – but it could theoretically be done.

The twin tails of the airplane were another nod to survivability. The thought was that, if one of the vertical stabilizers was shot off, the airplane could still fly with the remaining stabilizer in place. The two tails are identical, to facilitate easy maintenance in the field.

Finally, but most importantly, is the survivability of the pilot himself. The entire cockpit, and most of the critical flight systems, are surrounded from the canopy down with a titanium shield. Titanium is horrendously expensive. But it is also light and incredibly strong. The shield is designed to protect the pilot from the impact of up to 23 caliber bullets. In actual tests, it did even better, deflecting bullets of up to 50 caliber. The engines also have titanium shields around their critical center sections.

Other sections of the airplane are designed from the standpoint of survivability. The fuel tanks have self-sealing capabilities. When punctured by bullets or shrapnel, they exude foam that hardens and plugs the leaks. Surprisingly enough, although the nose gear retracts and folds up inside the nose, the main gear does not. The wheels of the main gear stick partially outside of their housings when fully retracted. What seems like an incredible oversight on the part of the designers, by exposing the tires to bullets and shrapnel, is actually quite ingenious. An A-10 that gets shot up to the point of being unable to lower its landing gear could still theoretically crash land on its nose and main gear wheels without ruining the entire airplane. When fully retracted, the main wheels are still low enough that they can support the airplane without the center section of the airplane touching the runway. During the first Gulf War, at least one A-10 delivered a pilot safely home in this manner.

The U.S. Air Force has tried to decommission the A-10 several times. There was no malice or disrespect in this decision, but there was an extreme sensitivity to maintaining unneeded or ill-suited weapons platforms. This was another legacy of the Vietnam era. When the conflicts in Asia started, the Air Force had a mix of airplanes that were designed for a relatively focused purpose – delivering weapons against the Soviet Union or her allies. These airplanes were designed to penetrate Soviet air defenses at high speeds, to go up against the newest generation of MiG aircraft that were being fielded by the Soviet Air Force. Tactics required allied fighters to take off and climb very quickly to engage enemy forces on short notice. Those with ground strike capabilities were designed to penetrate Soviet-controlled air space at a high speed in order to deliver their deadly nuclear payload. An example of this type of airplane was the F-104 Starfighter. Such airplanes were ill-suited to precision air-to-ground attacks. Fighting against mobile targets on the ground requires precise maneuverability at relatively low flying speeds, while the Air Force planes of that era were designed for stability when flying at a high speed and in a straight line.

The result of the focus on the Soviet threat was an Air Force found itself quite ill-equipped to fight in Vietnam. For example, a tour of duty for F-104 pilots was considered to be 100 missions over enemy territory. There was a bet among those pilots that surviving 100 missions over Vietnam was not possible, because so many pilots and aircraft were lost in combat long before the 100 mission mark was ever reached. There were eventually a few F-104 pilots who flew 100 missions, but the rate of loss for these types of airplanes remained high for the duration of the conflict.

As if high loss rate wasn't bad enough, there was another factor that made the situation unacceptable to Air Force brass – the Navy. Their colleagues at sea were quite effective in their air-to-ground campaigns and the competition between the two military divisions resulted in an abysmally poor showing for the Air Force. The reason was obvious – if you were going to land an airplane on an aircraft carrier, it had better be able to maneuver at relatively low speeds. That ability turned into a tremendous asset when the Navy's aircraft were forced to fight against the Viet Cong. Airplanes like the A-6, considered underpowered and ungainly, became the airborne stars of the East Asian conflict.

Not content with above-average performance, during the same era, the Navy started the Top Gun School with the idea of pairing promising pilots with experienced veterans to pass on the tricks and tips that would lead to survival in the skies above the jungle. Military planners have long understood that most pilots are lost during their first 10 missions. Top Gun was the Navy's way of providing their new pilots with the critical skills they needed to get through those first 10 missions. The Navy's already good showing increased when Top Gun pilots began deploying to the aircraft carriers.

To anyone with any knowledge of aircraft, it was easy to see that the Air Force had planned for the wrong mission. There had been such a focus on a possible war in Europe that there had been no consideration for fighting the type of war exemplified by Vietnam. Ever since that time, the Air Force has been very sensitive to the types of weapons platforms that they keep ready for deployment. No one in the Air Force wants to experience a situation in which the bulk of their weapons are wholly unsuited to the mission assigned. This experience seared into the Air Force brass the desire to constantly re-evaluate their weapons platforms and get rid of any weapons that seemed inappropriate.

The problem with getting rid of the A-10 was that there was not an acceptable replacement in the Air Force inventory. A special version of the F-16 fighter/bomber had been proposed. The F-16 is a marvelous showcase of technology. It is designed to do both air-to-ground and air-to-air fighting. But there were several problems with this proposed solution. The F-16 is designed to operate against ground targets from medium-to-high altitudes, 5000 feet or higher. It is not designed to get into the equivalent of a knife fight with the enemy. Its low-and-slow capabilities leave quite a lot to be desired. In addition, all of its technology makes it a much more fragile airplane than the A-10. It cannot take nearly the amount of punishment that an A-10 can take and survive.

Various solutions were proposed to overcome these limitations, including different wings and additional armor to protect vital systems. But there was one factor that couldn't be overcome. The F-16 is a single-engine fighter. The engine is tremendous, to be sure – with it, a lightly loaded F-16 can accelerate while going straight up. But there is only one. In fact, the pilots of America's most fearsome fighter – the mighty F-15 Eagle – tease their F-16 compatriots about this shortcoming. In the twin-engined F-15, the loss of a single engine mandates the transition to emergency mode and getting on the ground as soon as possible. An F-15 pilot will say the F-16 is in emergency mode as soon as it leaves the ground. The -15 jocks refer to the -16 as a lawn dart. And with a single engine, there is not enough redundancy in the -16 to justify using the base platform for any kind of situation at which the A-10 excels.

With the fall of the Soviet Union and the end of the Cold War, the need for a low-level attack aircraft of the A-10's capabilities was seen to be rather foolish. After all, was the reasoning, what other nation had huge amounts of armored vehicles, combined with the poor judgment, to take on the U.S. military? Such a scenario was considered unlikely at best – until 1991 when a fool named Saddam Hussein ordered the Iraqi army to invade Kuwait, fielding an army with as many as 100,000 tanks. The A-10s were called in with some reluctance, and played a huge role in reducing that mighty army's mobile armor to heaps of worthless junk. A-10s fired 90% of all Maverick missiles used in that war, and the combination of anti-tank missiles and canons, along with the ability to absorb anti-aircraft and even ground-to-air missile hits, proved that this airplane was going to continue a long and successful career.

Steve knew all of these things, of course. He had known about them long before he entered the Air Force. The thrill of going one-on-one with an armed enemy at close range, while in constant danger, was the thrill for which he lived. Flying an A-10 compared to other aircraft is not just flying – it is bungee jumping compared to jump rope, parachuting compared to jumping on a trampoline, and NASCAR racing compared to trips to the grocery store in the family automobile. Flying a heavily armed airplane at low altitude, fighting from 1000 to 20 feet from the ground, in a one-seat aircraft where the pilot has to fly and fight at the same time, with the threat of anti-aircraft guns and missiles pointed your way, was the challenge and thrill that he had dedicated his whole life to pursuing.

On this particularly fateful day, Steve and the rest of his squadron were going through live fire exercises with the canon for the first time. They had already gone through drills and simulations. Ammunition had been loaded, and the pilots briefed. They were to fly to the gunnery range and practice on some old trucks that had been hauled from a junkyard.

What Steve didn't know was that there was a problem with his flight suit. It had a small hole in one pocket. For some reason – probably just force of habit, he thought later – he had tossed his car keys in that fateful pocket. There was no reason to do this. Most of his other personal items were in a locker back at the base.

It was a wonderful day for flying, typical for southern Arizona in the winter months. Cold in the morning until the sun came up, the heat typically rose to 60-70°F. The flight group, seven planes today, had taken off at about 8:30 A.M. Steve was number four, the second plane on the left hand side of their V formation. Takeoff had been quick due to a light load. He had formed up with the rest of the group, waiting for the remaining aircraft to fall into formation, and then they turned together toward the practice range.

As they approached the range, Steve could see the collection of junk that was the excuse for a target. The plan was for the group to form a circle around the target, and one by one, in order, dive and make passes, firing the canon in two-second bursts. As soon as firing became impractical, they were to turn more than 90 degrees to the left and climb back into the circling pattern until it was their turn again.

When Steve's turn came, he broke out of the circling pattern and prepared to dive. This involved deploying the airbrakes on the A-10. The flaps on the wings are split into upper and lower sections, and the sections can be spread so that the upper section is in the slipstream above the wing and the lower section is in the slipstream below the wing. The increased drag allows the airplane to move more slowly through the air while still keeping engine power up.

Steve lined up and dove at the target. He focused his gunsight on the center of the pile of trucks and let go with a one second burst. The sound of the firing canon rippled through him. It was not a chatter of most machine guns, but rather a continual high-pitched roar of sound. It was like God himself had reached down and was ripping the sky apart at the seams. He could not only hear the sound, he could feel it resonating through the aircraft. The firing mechanism is directly behind and below the pilot, and the sound carries through the entire structure of the airplane. Simultaneously, he felt himself being pushed against the seat harness as the gun's recoil slowed the aircraft's speed. A little closer to the target now, he nudged the stick and sighted on a vehicle on the edge of the mass of junk, again firing off a short burst. It was a near miss. He corrected slightly and shot again. This time he was rewarded with a burst of glass, plastic and metal fragments. Now it was time to pull out of his dive. He pulled back on the stick and felt himself pressed down into the seat. He retracted the airbrakes, banked the 'hog to the left, and started contracting his leg and torso muscles to keep blood from being pulled from his head and losing consciousness, as he had been taught. "Urgh" he grunted, partly from the strain of clenching his muscles and partly from the push of the G forces on his body. As the airplane began to turn up at the bottom of the dive, he felt the G-suit fill with compressed air. At high G forces, the suit squeezes a pilot's legs and abdomen, to assist his muscles in keeping blood in his head and upper body. Without it, a pilot can lose consciousness. It felt like several giant blood pressure cuffs, one around each lower leg, one around each upper leg, and a looser one around his abdomen. As he completed his turn and the plane turned into a climbing trajectory, the forces fell. His compression suit deflated, he relaxed his muscles, and began looking around to see where to insert himself into the rest of the flight group circling above. Looking to his left, he could see plane number five of his group beginning his dive.

"Nice run, Four" came the call from his flight leader over the radio. "Several short bursts. Just the way we like it." Steve felt the glow of accomplishment spreading through him. He found it rather difficult to believe he was being paid to do this.

The rest of group completed their first round. The only one that had a problem was Six. He had let the canon roll for about three seconds, and it had misfired at the end. There was a bullet stuck in one of the barrels, and it would be an unhappy mechanic's job that night to pry the bullet out of the barrel without detonating the powder charge.

That also meant that Six wouldn't be able to complete the next two passes. *Tough luck*, thought Steve to himself. But this was as important a part of their training as the firing practice. *Equipment malfunctions happen in real battles*, he reminded himself, and that's the reason they still had people in the pilot's seat instead of computers – people could think through and compensate for unexpected situations in ways the computers could not.

After a few additional remarks from flight lead, they prepared to go again. Lead went through his firing run without problems, as did Two and Three. Then it was Steve's turn again. He rolled his aircraft left, deployed his airbrakes, then pitched forward and down to begin his dive.

His airplane wasn't the only thing that began diving at that moment. The keys in his pocket had found their way through the hole in the flight suit pocket and slipped forward, inside the leg of the suit. They stopped momentarily when they hit the backside of his knee. Then, as the reverberations of the firing cannon began pulsing through the aircraft, the keys shook loose from their precarious perch and dropped down to rest against the backside of his calf. Steve, focused on his mission, didn't pay any attention to the slight feeling of the keys moving down his leg.

He fired his three short bursts, very much enjoying the shower of debris kicked up by the devastating impact of his bullets on the junk below. Then he pulled back on the stick, simultaneously retracting the airbrakes and tightening his muscles in preparation for the high G turn. "Urgh" he grunted as the forces quickly built, he began to bank his aircraft sharply to the left. Then the pressure suit inflated. It pushed the keys into the back of his calf. Unfortunately, the keys had fallen so that the sharp points were digging directly through the skin and into the muscle.

The pain was totally unexpected. "Aaaah," he cried. This was not the sound of a pilot trying to keep blood in his head. This was the cry of a man who was getting hunks of sharp metal dug into his leg. He leveled his aircraft and the G forces dropped away. As his pressure suit deflated, the pain lessened a little. He tried to reach down to push the keys further down the leg of his suit, away from the sore spot, but his safety harness wouldn't let him bend over that far. So he reached up to his chest and undid the chest strap .

"Four, what's going on?" came the call over the radio. But Steve was bent over, intent on digging the metal out of his leg. When he leaned forward, however, he had also pushed the stick forward, and the aircraft began to pitch down toward the rocks, sand, and scattered sage and cacti of the desert floor. He managed to get the tips of his fingers on the keys and, with a push, they moved to a less painful position. Then he sat upright in his seat, glancing out front as he did so.

What he saw was death – the desert floor rocketing toward him at over 100 miles per hour. Steve yanked back on the stick as "Four!" came over the radio speaker from flight lead. He saw the horizon beginning to move down his canopy toward its normal position. Everything seemed to be happening in slow motion now. One hand was on the throttle, moving to max power, but with the knowledge that turbine engines take a second or two to react to throttle inputs.

Just as the horizon seemed to reach a reasonable position, he felt a jolt, and his airplane shuddered. Then the nose started to move up. His eyes leapt to the airspeed indicator as the stall warning began hooting at him. With the desert floor mere inches underneath him, he kept the airplane's nose pointed just above the horizon and willed the engines to push him back toward a reasonable flying speed. He was hanging in space, too slow to fly but too fast to come down. It seemed like an eternity that he hung there wondering if he was going to go up or finish his unseemly descent. He could hear the engines winding up from their previous setting, and then his airspeed indicator began to move slowly to the right. Another second, and the stall indicator stopped hooting at him. He kept his aircraft's altitude the same for another three or four seconds, and then he pulled the stick back to begin his climb toward the welcoming blue sky.

"Four, you OK?" came the call over the radio.

"I think so," Steve replied. That's when he felt himself began to shake. Perspiration was pouring down his fact, and he felt like he had been underwater for a long time and had just broken the surface. He was sucking in air like he had just finished a 250-yard sprint.

"You got way to close to the desert floor back there, Harrison. What happened?" called flight lead.

He thumbed the switch on the mike. "Car keys fell down my flight suit leg, and the compression suit dug them into it. I felt a bump; I think I might have hit the desert floor. Where are you?"

"We're behind you. Get back up to altitude and head due north. I want to do a visual on you." Steve thumbed the switch on the mike on an off in response, then banked his aircraft north.

By the time he climbed back to 5500 feet, he had gotten his breathing under control. He was still shaking, but he could feel the adrenaline beginning to drain from his bloodstream. He settled his aircraft into level flight, and looked left and right. He saw his flight leader off to his left and behind him. He reduced the power on his engines to allow his leader to catch up to him, and then sat quietly, feeling the last of the adrenaline leaving his body.

About one minute later, the radio crackled again. "You did hit. There is a tear in the bottom of your fuselage. OK, any emergency lights on?"

"No, everything shows normal."

"Let's try deploying your landing gear and make sure that works."

Steve complied. He heard the whine of the hydraulic motor, and within a few seconds, the roar of air over the landing gear, as well as the three indicators on the panel that went green, indicated wheels down and locked. "Looks OK from here," he reported.

"Concur. OK, here's what we're going to do. The entire group is going to fly directly back to base. I want us to form up in extended formation with Steve in the lead. I'll take number two position. Two, you take three, and three, you take four. When we get back to base, we will land in reverse flight order, like usual. Steve, you wait until you get word from the tower that it is OK to land. I'm going to make sure emergency vehicles are on both ends of the runway before you come down. I think you're going to be able to land OK, but we're not going to take any chances. Pull your gear up. The rest of the group, form up."

The rest of the group acknowledged their new orders and, in less than a minute, had formed up on both sides of Steve, separated by 200 feet. It took less than 15 minutes before the runways of the base appeared below them. Steve lead the group in a circle around the perimeter of the airfield while the other six aircraft dropped out of formation and landed.

As soon as the last of the other six aircraft had cleared the runway, the tower radioed him that he was cleared to land. He banked more sharply to line up with the runway, then deployed his landing gear and settled into the glide path. As he got nearer, he saw the red and white emergency lights flashing on the taxiway near the end of the runway. He passed slightly overhead. He felt his descent slow as the airplane entered ground effect, and then the rear wheels bumped. It felt normal – tires were apparently intact, thank the Good Lord – and then the front wheel settled and he turned on the thrust reversers and deployed his airbrakes. The landing turned out to be entirely routine. At the end of the runway, he waved off the waiting emergency vehicles and taxi'd back to his hanger.

When he got out of the cockpit, he found out he couldn't put much weight on his left leg. The keys caused a deep bruise, and it took almost three weeks before the leg felt like normal. Fortunately, the bruising was confined to muscle and not bone.

He was grounded while an inquiry into the accident was conducted. The conclusion of the inquiry was that the keys falling through the flight suit was an accident, attributed to faulty equipment. But Steve was faulted for undoing his chest harness and leaning forward to try to push the keys away from his leg. The inquiry board found that, because he had released his chest harness, he had pushed the stick forward, and that almost resulted in the loss of both the aircraft and the pilot. A letter with this conclusion had been placed in his personal file, forever after exposed to the Air Force command structure.

* * * *

Steve's attention snapped back to the present. "I don't think I would be accepted into Test Flight School," he responded to the pastor. "I had an accident while I was in basic flight school, and there is a letter in my file stating I was partially at fault."

Pastor Howie looked at Steve with a curious expression on his face. "Steve, my God is the God of impossible. Is yours?"

Steve was taken aback. Then he realized that the pastor was issuing his own challenge. Steve had to give the pastor credit – Howie had obviously analyzed his personality and realized that Steve was not the kind of person who would back down from a challenge. "Well, Test Flight School would be great, but it would take a miracle to get me in at this point." He responded.

The bulky pastor nodded. "God bless you, Steve. And please keep me informed of how things work out. I get the feeling He has something special ready for you and Jill."

Chapter 3

Dr. Choi Daesang walked into the conference room. It was rather sparsely finished, like the rest of the complex. Thank goodness, it was air conditioned, he thought. Nothing like Nevada desert heat in the summer to make a person appreciate air conditioning.

The others hadn't arrived yet. He checked his watch: several minutes early. Walking over to the single window at the narrow end of the room, he looked out. Heat waves shimmered off the metal roofs of the nearby buildings, the pavement of the parking lot, and the nearby runway. No activity right now, he saw, which was normal. Everyone who had to work outside tried to do it before the sun was too far overhead, or after it had made steady progress toward the western mountains. Even if the humidity was far lower than his native North Korea, 105 degrees was 105 degrees. You worked up a sweat just as fast. It just took longer for your shirt to dry in North Korea.

The door behind him opened, and two men walked in. They were about as close to polar opposites as any two men could be with the same color skin. General Collins, who was short but had the straight back and shoulders of a lifetime soldier, looked small compared to his companion, Dr. Andrew Stark. Stark had pieces of hair that always managed to find funny angles to project themselves from his head. He didn't wear a tie, and his dress shirt was opened to the second button, exposing his bushy chest hair. Sweat stains stood out under his arms and across his chest. His stomach protruded over his belt. His mustache looked as unkempt as ever, but at least he had shaved the rest of his face that morning. His pants were nondescript, and his shoes would make the shoeshine men in any airport of the world groan in despair. Dr. Choi knew that none of that mattered when the man's head carried the next breakthrough in physics.

"Hello, Dr. Choi. How are you this fine day?" asked the General with his baritone voice.

"Hot," replied Choi as he reached out to shake his hand. "Hello, Andy."

Dr. Stark grunted something nondescript and shook Choi's hand loosely. Stark's hand was sweaty and cold. They each pulled a chair away from the conference room table and sat down. The General sat at the head, Dr. Stark on his left, and Dr. Choi on his right.

General Collins jumped right in. "The reason we wanted to talk to you today is to ask you to become the Director of Implementation for the project. Are you interested in the job?"

"Really?" Choi was startled. "Why me? There are several others here that are my senior."

The General's face didn't change. "There are indeed several good men here. But in our judgment, you are the best at taking theory and producing a working product. A lot of these folks write impressive research papers. Very few have the ability to read a paper and figure out how to build something useful. When Dr. Stark and I looked at all the resumes and experience, we were struck with how many different ways you had managed to implement theoretical concepts. Your design of a pebble bed nuclear reactor is quite impressive. You have worked extensively on implementing things related to the electro-magnetic spectrum. Your ideas for ways to detect our stealth aircraft are... well, may I just say, I am glad you are working for us and not for North Korea."

"Thank you," breathed Choi. He had not been expecting this at all, and was more than a little surprised.

"We saw a pattern all the way back to your escape from North Korea," put in Dr. Stark. "In fact, it was that escape that convinced me that you were the right man for the job."

"But that story cannot be confirmed," Choi countered. His growing surprise had become evident to the other two men.

"On the contrary," said General Collins with a smile. "We asked South Korea to try to confirm the story, and they did so. Confidentially, of course. There are people who escaped North Korea

63

after you that were able to confirm enough elements of your story that it convinced us it was true." He didn't mention that confirming the escape was necessary to make sure Choi was not spying for a foreign country. The Russian penetration of the Manhattan Project, over 50 years before, was a security breach that the General was not about to let happen on this project.

"If you accept the job, you will be reporting directly to me. You will be the implementation side. Dr. Stark, of course, is the Director of Theory, and he will be reporting directly to me as well. Your job will be to take his theory and build a workable machine."

"I don't know very much about aircraft." Choi replied.

"Don't have to," retorted Dr. Stark in his characteristic abrupt manner. "We got most of the good retired people from our defense industry to do that stuff. Details. The airframe isn't a problem. The problem will be stuffing a nuclear reactor into it, plus the space-warp drive. It's going to be tricky. Got to keep the thing from melting the airplane when we turn it on. You can get those problems solved for us."

"How much of the airframe is designed already?" asked Choi.

It was the General who responded. "It's 90% designed. The final design and build can wait until you give us the specs for the amount of interior volume and surface area you need. We generated rough estimates about how much a nuclear reactor would weigh that could generate the power we need. That wasn't too hard; we've been doing that for ships and submarines for over 30 years now. We had to fudge a bit for the space-warp drive. But there should be enough room. The biggest challenge will be keeping everything and everyone cool. Weight and packaging will be secondary challenges. And I've already spoken to the airframe guys. They have some ways they can change the shape of the wing to accommodate about a 20% increase or decrease in weight. We're not building a high performance fighter. All the thing has to do is fly straight for about 60 seconds, and then land and take off on either side of the space-warp event."

Choi was only half listening. He already knew what the challenges were. He had spent the first three months here getting his head around the theory, and the next three months working on ways to actually get the theory to work. He hadn't been able to poke a hole in the theory, and he had some ideas about how to actually build the machine. But, being offered a director position! And he wasn't even 40 yet! There were people here who were in their 50's, with over 15 years more experience than him in all aspects of modern physics!

Could this be a setup, he wondered? *Are they offering this to me because they expect the first implementation to fail, and they already have someone else picked to do the real implementation? It doesn't seem reasonable to put me in this position. On the other hand,* he reminded himself, *I have done some pretty good work over the last 10 years.* He certainly had the respect of his colleagues. They were treating him well enough, and he was making enough money that he wouldn't have to work another day in his life when this project was over, assuming it lasted for another four years, as they projected.

It was the money that allowed him to convince himself that they had to be serious, that they really did want him to be in charge. Where else could he work for $250,000 per year, with all his food and housing paid? AND, because of a special arrangement within government circles for people working on the most secret of secret projects, his salary was being exempted from income tax. There were over 20 people that he would consider more senior than himself here. *They must be getting paid about the same,* he reasoned. He was beginning to get excited about the possibility of setting the direction for building the space-warp mechanism.

The General saw Choi's eyes focus back in on him. "I am very honored to be asked to fill this position, and I accept," he said humbly.

"Excellent!" said Dr. Stark with uncharacteristic enthusiasm. "Couldn't have picked a better man for the job." He stared at Choi. "You were the only one among us who I 100% trust can build this thing. We have a lot of brainiacs walking around here, but actually designing something that will work is more art than science. You've got it, Choi. I am looking forward to seeing how you're going to actually get this thing built. It will be a treat to watch it take shape."

"Indeed it will," said the General more quietly. He looked at Choi. "Start a list of the things you need. You know money is not much of an object. Probably need to focus on materials first. If we need to develop some new kind of metal or plastic or something, probably need to start with that. Just let me know what you want. Oh, probably want to think about who you want on the implementation side with you. Got to think about forming teams, assigning responsibilities, all that management stuff. We'll try to keep most of the actual management burden off you. We want your head down with your team leads, doing actual design. If you have people problems, I'll most likely be here every other week, and I can handle them. I'll fly out from D.C. in a moment if you call." He smiled at Choi. "For the most part, the theory is done. Lots of people want this to work. You're the boss now. You say jump, I ask how high on the way up. That goes for everyone else here too, and I am going to make sure everyone on this base knows that."

"We'll announce this at our staff meeting tomorrow morning, unless you want us to wait. You probably want to think about who you want as team leads," the General finished.

"I know most of the men, but it would help if I knew more about their formal education and experience. I have some ideas about team leaders, but I would like some additional information," Choi requested.

"I'll make sure you can get into the files. We have everyone's resume, credentials, and all the papers they have either written or contributed to. Will that be enough?"

"That should be quite sufficient."

"Well, then, on to the next challenge," grunted Stark as he stood. The others rose too.

General Collins thrust out his hand. "Thank you, Dr. Choi. We were hoping we wouldn't have to twist your arm too hard to get you to accept. You are by far our first choice."

Choi shook their hands. He opened his mouth to say something, but couldn't seem to come up with the right thing. Stark grinned, "Don't get too excited. You'll be swearing at us in six months for asking you to do this, and swearing at yourself for accepting. But it'll get done. Nothing worthwhile gets done without a little effort, eh?" And he and the General turned and walked out of the room.

Choi felt a little dizzy. He wondered if he had done the right thing.

* * * *

The Wednesday morning staff meeting started as usual at five minutes after nine. Brian Masulis called it to order. He was a post-grad working on a Ph.D. in library science when he had been recommended to Dr. Stark as someone who could get things organized. Calling Brian detail oriented was like calling the Nile a long river. He chafed at having to wait until five minutes after the hour when the meeting was supposed to start at 9:00 AM. But, Stark had explained to him, the people in this meeting were more important than starting on the dot. There were some people who would arrive at 9:10 if the meeting was stated to begin at 9:05. If you moved the meeting to 11:00 AM, they would make it in at 11:05. Just the way things were. In projects like this, you accommodated the talent and their idiosyncrasies.

"First item today – the project has been assigned a new name. From now on, we are project Opera. If anyone from outside asks, we are working on a nuclear-powered aircraft. A security class is just about finished..." he was interrupted by a chorus of groans, "...which, yes, we will all be happy to attend. It will be a four-hour course. You and all your staff will need to complete it before the end of next month. No exceptions. Any questions?"

There was the usual scattering of questions like, "what happens when new people come on the project?" Stark, sitting on one side of the table, was often amazed that such bright people could come up with such dumb questions. Problem was, when he was running the meetings, he often told his staffers what he thought. It was one of the reasons why Collins had 'encouraged' him to find someone else to run the meetings. It hadn't taken too much to convince Stark to delegate that task to Brian. Brian had difficulty with the difference between a neutron and a proton, but he didn't call smart people dumb to their face, and certainly not in front of their peers.

"Next item," continued Brian. "Dr. Stark?"

"I – uh, we..." he nodded toward Collins, sitting in the background in a corner of the room, "have an announcement to make. Up till now, the project has been mostly the development of my theory. As you know, we now have enough theoretical knowledge that we can start thinking of building a device to take advantage of it. That means a bit of a shift in focus for the project. I am a theorist. We needed someone to head up the implementation. We have asked Dr. Choi to become Director of Implementation, starting immediately, and he has accepted."

The heads of the men and women automatically swiveled toward Choi, sitting closer to the end of the table. Almost all were friendly. After a second, applause spontaneously broke out. Stark was well respected, but Choi was simultaneously respected and well liked. This obviously was going to be a popular decision. They all knew they were fortunate to be able to work on a project like the one that Opera was becoming. That didn't mean they enjoyed working for, or with, Stark. The man had a notoriously short temper, and didn't like spending time with people who were less intelligent than he, which was almost everyone. He had trampled on a lot of feelings during his career.

After the applause died, Stark took a deep breath and continued. "Now that Dr. Choi has been appointed, I want to make sure everyone understands our change of focus. The focus of this project is getting something useful out the door. We have changed from theoretical science to applied science. That means Dr. Choi is going to be setting direction. I, and the people who remain on my team, will be moving into the background. I think our fine General has some things to add."

"Indeed I do." General Collins stood and addressed the group. "As Dr. Stark has said, we are now starting implementation. Our entire project organization chart is going to change over the next couple months. Most of you will be asked to move from the theoretical side to the implementation side of the project. As you probably expect, Dr. Choi will start by appointing key people to positions that report directly to him. There will be interviews for some positions. Positions will be posted on our internal website. You can apply for an interview on the website as well. However, Dr. Choi has the right to choose someone from outside to fill certain positions, even without having interviewed them. They have to pass the security screening, of course. The message is that the final decision rests with Dr. Choi."

The General went on to make a few more points, including how Stark and Choi were peers and would both be reporting to him. Then he turned more serious.

"With the change in focus for our project, there will be some other big changes coming. Building a flying machine that can take advantage of a space-time warp is a huge challenge. We are going to have a lot more people coming in to help build this thing. Of course, we will send as much of this outside our base as we can. However, we anticipate that we will be adding another 2000 people to this base as the aircraft is built. That means it will be virtually impossible to keep this a secret. Everyone in this room knows the real reason for this project. That secret must be very well contained. You and your staffs will continue to be tested." By that, he meant that counter-espionage agents would continue to try to win their confidence and get them to reveal what they were really doing. Anyone who revealed anything, intentional or otherwise, would find themselves in the General's office, with two possible exits – removal from the project for inadvertent slips of the tongue, or jail for those with criminal intent. "This project is more important, in regard to our national security, than anything that has ever been done before. We can take no chances. If any of you has any doubt about what can or cannot be revealed, than take the on-line security class called 'State Secrets' again. Memorize the script if you have to. We've had two incidents up till this point, which is two too many. That's all. Back to you Brian."

One of those in the meeting was Desmond Wallace. He was one of only two black men in the room, although there were other minorities in attendance. His colleagues loved him because he could always think of something funny to say to lighten up a tense situation. Talkative and outgoing, he also was a lifelong Democrat with memories of the Civil Rights Movement. He had supported the movement whenever it didn't interfere with his college education. He had marched behind Dr. Martin Luther King, and been jailed once by some of Alabama's finest. His anger at their unfair treatment had nearly convinced him to drop out of college and join the Civil Rights Movement full time. He was fortunate to have been counseled by some of the leaders in the movement, who had seen his potential and encouraged him to finish his education. He had done so, but the memory of his arrest during a peaceful demonstration march had ingrained in his usually easygoing nature an intolerance for injustice.

It was Desmond who had marched into Dr. Stark's office after the second of their colleagues had not returned from a weekend home and demanded an explanation. The two men had almost come to blows and in a fit of exasperation, Stark had called General Collins, who was in Washington, D.C. at the time. Collins had flown in that evening and met with Desmond for nearly four hours the next morning.

After that meeting, a few of his colleagues had tried to get some information out of him. He had only told them two things. First, that those who had mysteriously not returned to work would be released after the project was over. Released from where? He wouldn't say. Second, never, ever tell anyone anything about the project.

Collins initially regretted revealing to Desmond as much information as he had in that four-hour meeting. Over time, however, he had decided it was one of the best things he had ever done. Having the usually happy-go-lucky Desmond exhorting the project members to take their security seriously was much more effective than the continuously recurring 30 minute lectures about the need for secrecy. The counter-espionage team had reported that project members had become more reluctant to engage in any kind of conversation than they had been previously. That suited the General just fine. Keeping this kind of secret contained at this base was the only part of the job he – hated? No, that was too strong a word. But it was probably the most challenging, he admitted to himself as the meeting continued. It was also the part that had the potential to sink his career faster than any other. He loved his job, and being a part of this project was a privilege that he wouldn't trade for anything. The work being done here would change the world and it was his job to make sure that the primary beneficiary was America. If a few people with loose tongues had to be restricted for a few years while the work progressed, he had no problem with that. Great leaps were never made without some sacrifice. It was his job to make sure the great leap happened.

General Collins was a man accustomed to success, whatever the cost. And he had already determined that this project was going to be successful. There wasn't a man, woman, or congressional subcommittee in existence that was going to interfere with that. He had the President's backing to make it happen. A lifelong member of the military, freedom was not a word he would usually associate with any of the jobs he had been assigned over the last 35 years. But he couldn't think of a better word to describe the lack of restrictions placed on his ability to accomplish his current mission.

And that suited him just fine, too.

* * * *

"Good morning, Mr. Patchinsky." Melanie Graber was standing at the door to his office, but he was hunched over his computer and had his back to her.

Randall Patchinsky looked up and around from his work. "Ah. Good morning, Melanie. Come on in." He stood up and motioned her over to a chair next to the small table in the front corner of the crowded office. "That budget stuff is keeping you on pins and needles, I'll bet."

Melanie sat in one of the three chairs around the small table, and Randy took a seat across from her. "Actually, Mr. Patchinsky, it's the other way around. I need to sit on pins and needles while I am working my way through the budget. That stuff is a sure cure for insomnia."

Randy laughed. He enjoyed working with Melanie more than most of the other college interns who were hired on at the newspaper offices for the summer. She was frank in a way that was refreshing, but with a sense of humor that allowed the two of them to trade barbs in a comfortable way, despite the 20 year age difference between them. This was to be the first meeting between them to review some work he had assigned her, and he was eager to see the results.

Randy liked to start his interns with something rather boring and mundane. During his last seven years at the paper, he had found that it was a great way to weed out the ones who didn't have the drive, the zeal, or the sense of purpose, to be a good reporter. Some news stories were just luck, being at the right place at the right time, but most were just plain grunt work – chasing down leads, examining budgets and contracts, trying to find things that just didn't add up. It wasn't what was in the documents that tipped you off to a story, he was fond of telling those who hoped to emulate his award winning journalistic career. Most often, it was the missing information. Following a paper trail was like putting together a jigsaw puzzle in order to discover the one or two pieces that had been left out.

Randy had assigned Melanie the job of working through the proposed Federal Budget for the coming fiscal year. The budget was hundreds of pages long, filled with mostly mundane items and, of course, numbers. Each federal department had their own section, so wading through it was manageable if it was broken down into pieces. Still, almost everyone Randy knew considered it tedious work and tried their best to avoid it. When Melanie received the assignment, the other interns had teased her about it, but she had graciously accepted it and appeared to dig in like a woman on a mission.

"So, did you find anything that kept you awake?"

"Actually, I did. I started out with the Department of the Interior budget, like you recommended. I did find that all the numbers added up. But I found one line item that was strange, $2.3 million for something that was just labeled Bohemia." Randy's rather bushy eyebrows arched in surprise. "Do you know what that is?" she asked.

He shook his head thoughtfully. "No." He looked down at the papers without actually seeing them, thinking through this piece of information. "Hmm. Rather unusual, especially for this department.

71

Actually, this is a good introduction to some of the things I need to teach you before you start digging into the budget for the Department of Defense. How soon do you expect the final version of these documents?"

"I was told to expect them July 23."

"About three weeks from now. OK, what we'll do is make a note of this line item and check to see if it shows up in the final revision."

"What will that tell us?" pressed Melanie. Good, thought Randy, she doesn't want to drop this little trinket of information. Persistence is one of the most basic qualities necessary for a reporter.

"Depends. What I am about to tell you probably doesn't apply to this situation, because I don't ever recall the Department of the Interior playing games with their budget. But there's always a first time. Have you ever heard of a black project?"

"No."

"A black project is a project that is so secret that the government will never openly acknowledge it. Above top secret, very hush hush, if I told you I'd have to kill you, that type of project." Melanie nodded, encouraging him to continue. "Well, those projects need money – usually lots of money. So, what the government does is make several copies of the budget. There is the public version, which is what we have here, and that most members of Congress see. Then there is the secret version, which contains all the line items for the hush hush projects. Only a very few members of Congress get to see that version. It would probably include the leaders from both political parties, and the chair of the Armed Services committee, people like that."

"So most of the Senate is voting on a budget where they can't see all the details?" asked Melanie in surprise.

"Exactly."

"How much money are we talking about?"

"A lot. For example, up to 25% of the total budget for the Air Force goes to black projects."

"Wow." Melanie considered that piece of information. "Wait a minute. If the line items are missing, how do you know how much money goes to these projects?"

"Because the numbers don't add up. All you have to do is add all the line item amounts for the things you see and compare it to the total. The difference, the amount that's missing, goes to black projects."

"Oh. Well, duh. I should have figured that one out." Melanie's looked disgusted with herself.

Randy continued with his lesson. "This Bohemia thing looks like something that happened back in, oh, I think it was '92. The proposed budget for the Department of Defense had a line item labeled Aurora. It was for tens of millions of dollars, and of course, the amount would be a lot higher today because of inflation. Anyway, reporters asked about it, and the military people started acting real funny. After a couple of days, they got their act together and said that it was a mistake. Then when the final budget came out, the item was gone. But the amount of money missing for that section of the budget came close to the original amount listed for Aurora in the previous version."

"Did anyone ever track it down?"

"Nope, and if you ask anyone in the military about it, you will be told 'If there were such a program, I could not discuss it.' It's their standard response to things they have been ordered not to discuss publicly. But the general thinking is that Aurora was the code name for the development of a new spy plane which has never been made public."

"Do you think this Bohemia could be something like Aurora?"

"A black project for the Department of the Interior?" Randy snorted derisively. "That department has all it can do to pay the salaries of their forest rangers. I don't think they would throw money at a secret project. Besides, what would they be developing? A top-secret method of processing manure?"

Melanie looked soberly at Randy. "You never know. Just think how much good it would do to be able to process manure more efficiently. We could turn it into pavement for streets, bricks for building," her voice was rising in mock enthusiasm, "why, the possibilities are almost endless."

Randy chuckled. "Maybe you should take up environmental engineering instead of journalism," he suggested wryly.

Melanie wrinkled her nose, "I would rather wade through budget documents than work on a top secret manure project."

"I suspected as much. You don't seem like the manure type."

"Well, thank you, kind Sir. That's the nicest thing anyone has said to me today."

"Really? You must be having a bad day," he teased.

"Let's just say the day hasn't achieved its potential yet. Anyway, what do I do about this?" she indicated the line item.

"Let's wait till the final budget revision, and see if this item is still there. Things change all the time between this revision and the final version. If Bohemia still shows up, or if the money disappears, we can start checking into it. Good job spotting that line item, by the way. What else have you found?" And they turned their attention back to the documents on the table.

Chapter 4

There was something about being a professional pilot that made it difficult to turn right when boarding a jetliner, Steve thought to himself. It wasn't easy to give the responsibility of the airplane in which he was riding to someone else. Logically, he knew there was no way he could move into the cockpit and do anything beyond the most rudimentary tasks. About the only thing this airliner and his A-10 had in common was that they both had two jet engines. This airliner was flown using a side-stick controller, compared to the center stick in his A-10. This airplane was probably 100 times larger than an A-10 in both weight and volume. He had no doubt that, if someone got the engines started, he could get it into the air, but getting it back down intact was another matter entirely. This airplane had a glass cockpit – all the data was presented in a series of computer screens, instead of the mechanical dials that populated the instrument panel of his Warthog. In fact, Steve thought to himself, he probably wouldn't even be able to figure out how to turn on the intercom to tell everyone to buckle their seatbelts – not that anyone but the flight attendants would actually notice, he thought as he settled into seat 31B. It always amazed him that so many people didn't bother to learn about the most basic safety procedures. Of course, they were boring, and most of these people probably flew at least once a month. After all, how many times could you look at a safety card and learn something new? Still, one of the things he always did was make sure he knew the location of every door in the airplane, not just the ones nearest to him. Only a fool would strap himself into a machine that had to get up to 135 miles per hour to begin operating properly, restraining himself only a few feet away from thousands of gallons of combustible jet fuel, and not check the location of the exits.

He was flying across the country from Ronald Reagan Airport to LAX on his way to Edward's Air Force Base. Flying commercial was the easiest and most convenient way to travel such a distance. He had a series of interviews scheduled with several officers who were part of the admittance process for Test Flight School. He was amazed that he had gotten this far. After Pastor Howie's challenge about God doing the impossible, he had started checking into the entrance requirements for Test Flight School. He had found the entrance requirements even more rigorous than he had first imagined, and he harbored no illusions about gaining entry at this point in his career. It was going to take nothing short of a full-blown miracle for someone with his relative inexperience, and the accident on his record, to be admitted. And he really didn't expect God to send Michael, the archangel, down to command the Air Force brass to allow him entrance into the school.

Despite his doubts, he was going ahead with the interview. Whatever else he might be, he wasn't a quitter. He was determined to see this thing through. Then he would go back to Pastor Howie and solicit more suggestions. *Maybe he'll tell me to apply to NASA next. Becoming an astronaut is not much more far-fetched than getting into Test Flight School,* he thought. *As long as I'm aiming high, why not go for the moon and stars as well?*

Steve had spent the last few weeks going back through the Bible's books of Matthew, Mark, Luke and John, examining the words and actions of Jesus and comparing them to the advice given him by the pastor. Everything he read verified the pastor's advice. It didn't help much. He still wasn't sleeping as well as he should at night, and was still wondering what to do about it. *Jill has been such a good sport about the whole thing,* he reflected as the plane lifted its nose and rose majestically into the air. They had prayed together every night before going to bed, and he knew that she was praying for him often during the day when he wasn't at their apartment. Still, it was difficult to believe that their prayers, imploring God's wisdom and direction, made it much higher than their bedroom ceiling.

The trip to California was uneventful – Steve only wished he had brought more reading material. He had brought along some classroom-oriented material about how the Air Force was supposed to work in conjunction with the Army, Navy, and Marines during wartime. It was educational, but after two and a half hours, he had put it aside and started casting about for something else to occupy his time. The in-flight magazine had lasted for 20 minutes when a gentleman across the aisle recognized the symptoms of boredom and offered him the remains of a newspaper. With that, he managed to pass the time until they touched down at LAX.

They left the east coast at 8:00 AM, and touched down in California a little after 10:00 AM local time – still enough time to get his rental car and see something of the Golden State, Steve thought. He hadn't checked any bags, so he went directly to the rental car booth and found himself departing the airport by 10:45. He headed southeast out of LA and found himself drawn towards Edwards Air Force Base. The base had so much history, and he had never been there before. Just over the mountains from LA, in the desert, it was one of the Air Force's premier air bases. The weather was just about always perfect, at least for flying purposes – it tended to get a little too hot for comfort for people in July and August, but the aircraft didn't mind the hot air as long as they weren't too heavily loaded.

Arriving at Edwards, he had gone straight to the base's flight museum. Among other things, Edwards was the alternative landing location for the Space Shuttle, if the Florida site wasn't available for some reason. Edwards had a runway 10 miles long to accommodate its landing – 10 miles long! *In the length of that runway I could log five takeoffs and landings in my Warthog without ever having to change direction.*

Edwards had also been home to the other airplane that Steve held in awe – the incomparable SR-71 Blackbird. Designed by the legendary Clarence "Kelly" Johnson, it had been designed with slide rules in the 1950's and still held records for speed, altitude, and endurance. It was the replacement for the U-2 spy plane that had been shot down by the Russians, and had helped keep the peace for nearly 40 years. Shortly before its retirement, it crossed the state of Montana in 15 minutes, and gone coast-to-coast in under 62 minutes. It was so fast that the pilot had to wear an astronaut suit to protect himself from the heat generated by the friction of the airplane flying through the air – after all, the airplane could cruise faster than a bullet fired from a high-powered rifle. In fact, the friction from the air through which it traveled made it so hot, the expanding metal actually lengthened the aircraft by six inches during flight.

As he wandered through the exhibit, Steve had to wonder – *What am I doing here?* He stopped at a series of exhibits that discussed the feats of Chuck Yeager, the first person to fly an airplane faster than the speed of sound in the X-1 research aircraft. What Yeager hadn't revealed at the time was that he had accomplished the feat with a broken rib. *How in the world did I let Howie challenge me into applying to Test Flight School?* It seemed only natural to follow up on the challenge back in the comfort of the church in the Washington, D.C. suburbs. Now that he was actually here, what had seemed like a rather far-fetched idea turned into an absurdly foolish one. Steve thought about the pastor's challenge - "My God is the God of the impossible. Is yours?" Steve was beginning to realize just how much of a miracle it was going to take to get him accepted. *Yeah, they'll be calling me Chuck Yeager II in a few years. Maybe I can test fly the SR-78 Purplebird with a sprained ankle and a concussion.*

He heard a terrific roar and wandered over to a window. Several F-15 Eagles were taking off. They were magnificent machines, afterburners sending out waves of pure power that could be felt as well as heard, even through the wall of the building. As the Eagle reached flying speed, the pilot would keep the airplane level and simply retract the wheels. The airplane would continue to cruise down the runway for another several hundred feet, its belly only a few feet from the ground, until the pilot would bank into a vertical climb and thunder away into the light blue sky. Steve stood watching until the basso profundo reverberations from the last airplane had faded, and it was merely a speck in the distance.

He thought it far more likely that he would be assigned to clean the 10-mile long runway. *Maybe I can get one of those fancy scoops and brushes the attendants used at amusement parks. Might even be able to talk my superiors into a nice uniform with a baseball-type cap to keep the sun out of my eyes.* That position seemed a lot more likely than the other.

* * * *

When he reported for his interview the next day, Steve was met by five officers who introduced themselves and tried to make him feel at ease. They started by asking about flight theory and aerodynamics. Steve thought he probably answered those questions adequately. After an hour, they took a 10-minute break, then started going over his record.

This turned out to be the most uncomfortable part. They asked a lot of questions about his accident. The only thing Steve felt he could do was answer as honestly as he could. He related the pain of the keys digging into his leg, the gut-wrenching fear when he saw the desert floor filling his windscreen, and the feeling of hanging in the air in stall condition before regaining flying speed and recovering his aircraft. He also related how he now tended to double-check everything. If he had been prudent before the accident, he would describe himself much closer to detail-obsessed, bordering on paranoia if there was any doubt in his mind about any aspect of flight preparations now. He saw the officers glancing at each other, and wondered whether they would regard this as a positive or negative.

Next topic was his motivation for applying to test flight school. Steve explained that it was a childhood dream to fly. Having accomplished that, he wanted to help advance the technology, to keep America in front of her enemies. He explained that he believed in deterrence through strength, that is, the way to avoid getting involved in a war was to demonstrate such a degree of superiority that no lucid enemy would dare risk America's involvement.

"I do believe one of the ways to keep the peace is to have weapons and equipment so obviously superior to your adversaries that it can prevent wars from starting in the first place." He had explained. "For example, our country has nuclear weapons, but it would be terrible if we ever had to use them. Thankfully, ever since the end of WWII, we have never had to do so, and these weapons probably prevented our going to war with Russia during the '60's and '70's."

He didn't mention the spiritual and ethical dilemma he was facing. He knew if he voiced his consideration of becoming a non-combatant, he would be yanked from even flying the A-10. It wasn't that the Air Force discriminated against those with such convictions. If military action suddenly became necessary, however, and Steve's squadron was called to battle, the Air Force didn't want anyone who wasn't 100% willing to do the job in the pilot's seat. It would be unacceptable for a man to decide not to fight once the battle started. According to Air Force protocol, not only might such a man hesitate to fight, but his attitude might affect some of his squadron mates, causing them to hesitate as well. Besides weapons and tactics, modern warfare depended on psychology. Every good commander knew the attitude of his own troops, as well that of the enemy, had a huge impact on the success of any battle.

The interview wrapped up shortly before lunchtime. The officers cordially shook his hand and thanked him for his time. As the interview ended and the stress started to ebb, Steve found that he was tired. He decided to leave the base and head back toward LAX, electing to stop at a restaurant along the highway for lunch. At least, that was his plan until he left the building and headed out toward his rental car.

"Steve. Steve Harrison," he heard someone call. He turned and looked to see someone waving at him. He looked closer and recognized the young man jogging toward him across the parking lot. It was the contrast of white teeth against the black skin of a very characteristic grin, as well as the sound of the voice, that allowed Steve to identify the jogger.

"Scoot, is that you?" Scott Johnson, better known to his colleagues as Scoot, had been in the same squadron in the Air Force Academy as Steve. Students in the Air Force Academy are divided into squadrons. Squadrons made for easier scheduling of all the groups training on a limited amount of equipment. It also fostered a spirit of competition among the cadets. Scoot and Steve had both been in Squadron 15, the War Eagles. Their friendship had been the best kind between two young men – they challenged and pushed each other to succeed, competing fiercely in academics, athletic ability, and anything else that came their way, but also helping each other to compete against all the others in their class. Steve had grown up in Kansas, Scoot on the south side of Chicago, so in many ways they were quite different. But both had been abandoned by their fathers, and both had benefited from people in their lives who stepped in to help fill the gap. Both had set their sights high, and both had never accepted anything other than complete success. At graduation, Steve was several places higher in class rank, but he had to admit that Scoot could adapt to aircraft faster then he. Steve strapped himself into an aircraft, which he then controlled. Scoot strapped the aircraft onto him and without any apparent effort became one with it.

"How are you doing, Buddy?" Scoot threw an arm around him, and then stepped back for the more socially acceptable handshake. "What brings you out to the beautiful barren wilderness of Edwards? I thought you were out East flying the Warthog."

"I am. Actually, I just had a first interview in an application for Test Flight School. Just finished up 10 minutes or so ago. I was going to head back to the airport."

"Can you spare a few minutes? If you haven't eaten lunch, my treat. I've got to hear more about this. Test Pilot School? Doggone, I never heard of anyone getting in without five years of experience. You do have some time, right?"

Steve turned willingly back toward the buildings with Scoot. Scoot was a loyal enough friend that he felt comfortable sharing his spiritual struggle, even though Scoot didn't profess any kind of faith. By the time he was done, they were sitting at a table in the cafeteria. The remains of soup and sandwich were on Scoot's plate. Steve's chef's salad was still relatively untouched.

Scoot was shaking his head. "That is one of the weirdest stories I have ever heard. No offense, Man." Steve smiled and shook his head. "I knew you were cut pretty straight, but I never would have believed you would become a non-combatant. What are you going to do if you don't get accepted?"

"I don't know." Steve replied truthfully. "One thing at a time. Anyway, enough about me. What are you up to nowadays?"

"Funny you should ask. You know I've been flying the Eagle for the last couple of years. Awesome bird. Man, I can't believe you went for the Warthog. You haven't lived until you're doing a 9-G inverse loop and you've got someone on your tail ready to send you to meet your maker." He grinned enthusiastically. "The instructors out here are awesome. They are some kind of talent, man. I never met a guy I didn't think I could match in the pilot's seat with some experience, but when I started out here, some of the teachers could take my Eagle apart one feather at a time, if you catch my drift. I finally caught up with most of them, but I'm still working on a couple."

"Actually, funny you and I should meet just now." Scoot continued with a less infectious tone. "I just started doing some work on the side for a special project out at Nellis. Can't say too much about it, but the project is looking for a couple more pilots. I am trying to get transferred there full time. I could put in a word for you if you're interested."

"What can you tell me about it?"

"Not much, except to say it will probably last four years. The first two years will be boring as all get-out, but the next two years will make up for it. More like flying an airliner than a fighter, but it's the payload that will make it exciting."

"Exciting for the pilot, or just the people in the back?"

"Exciting for the pilot. Sorry, I can't tell you any more, except the last two years will be hazardous duty pay. There are considerable risks. No weapons involved, if you are worried about that. Civil as well as military applications for what they're doing. Wish I could tell you more. Interested?"

"Yeah, I'm interested."

"I'll put in a good word for you. You better start eating your food before it starts growing bacillus."

"I've done most of the talking here," Steve said. "Tell me what you're doing when you're not up in an airplane. Girlfriend? Engaged? What are you driving these days?"

Scoot laughed. "Steve, I got me a fine lady. She lives in Denver. Her daddy's a banker, and she's a sharp cookie. Good looker, too." He winked at Steve. "I am working up the nerve to pop the question. I didn't think I could fall so hard for one of them critters. Oh, it will be a sad day for the rest of the women in this country when my engagement is announced."

Steve almost choked on a piece of hard-boiled egg. "You mean, every father in the nation will celebrate because the streets became a little safer for their little girls."

"Hey, now, I can't help it if I'm a chick magnet?" retorted Scoot. "I didn't need to go looking, they came to me." Which, Steve had to admit, was true. Scoot was dedicated to his scholastics, but he always reserved Saturday night for R&R, as he put it. Always seemed to have a date and somewhere to go.

"How long have you known her?"

"Almost a year. Her name's Carla. Every week without her seems like a lifetime, and every weekend that we can't be together is like torture. Wait until you meet her. Here… " he pulled out his billfold, "I have a picture of her. Isn't she pretty?" He waved a photo at Steve.

Steve took it an examined it. "Wow, she's a beauty, all right." He responded. "Here, let me show you a picture of my wife." He dug out a photo of Jill and passed it back. "We've been married for almost four months now."

Scoot sucked in his breath. "Steve, my man. How did you manage to catch this lovely thing? I thought you were, like, allergic to women."

Steve laughed. "Someday I'll tell you the story. It's a little unusual. But I need to head back to the airport. If I get caught in rush hour, I'll never make it back in time."

"Alright, Man. Doggone, it's good to see you. Hey, give me your contact information. Phone, e-mail, all that stuff. I'll try to get word to you about the project as soon as I can."

They exchanged information and reminisced about life in the Academy while Steve finished his meal. After a few more goodbyes, Steve found himself back out in the parking lot. It was still a disappointing trip, but seeing Scoot brightened things up considerably. He found himself singing along with the radio on his drive back into LAX.

* * * *

It was two weeks later when Jill walked in to their apartment to find Steve sitting forlornly on the couch. "Hi, Love. Is something wrong?" She went and sat down beside him.

"I got called in by my commanding officer this afternoon, after lunch. He told me I had not been accepted into Test Pilot School."

"Oh, Steve. I'm sorry." She encircled his broad shoulders in her arms and placed her head on one shoulder.

"I'm really not surprised."

"But I can see you're disappointed."

"Well, sure I am. Now what am I supposed to do? I'm back to square one."

"I don't know. But God does. Just you wait and see."

"Sometimes it's hard to believe," he said doubtfully.

"What did your CO tell you, exactly?"

"Actually, he gave a pretty good report. I was rejected based on my lack of experience, nothing else. They didn't even hold the accident against me. In fact, they said it seemed like I had made a nice recovery when I hit the desert floor, and handled an unexpected situation pretty well. And they said they liked the fact that it had made me more careful about checking everything thoroughly. They also said they get a lot of guys apply who think they are God's gift to airplanes, but someone like me is a lot easier to work with. They said I should re-apply in three to four years."

"Well, that sounds pretty good to me."

"Yeah, overall it was pretty positive. Still, it hurts to get turned down."

"I know. But they did ask you to reapply in the future. It's not a failure, Steve. In fact, I would classify it as a success, compared to the way you were talking before you went out there."

They sat on the coach quietly for a few moments. Steve was glad he had Jill to share this with. He turned to her, "I'm glad we're married."

"Me too. Hey, how about going out to eat? I don't really want to make supper tonight. I know you like that little Italian place on Rosedale Avenue. Let's call it a 'Re-apply In Four Years' celebration."

"Jill, I love you. You know how to make me feel good even about a disappointing situation." He gave her an appreciative kiss.

She beamed back at him. "Let's go."

* * * *

Later that night, Steve was laying on the bed, waiting for Jill to get done in the bathroom so he could brush his teeth. She poked her head out of the bathroom door. "Honey, I want to pray about your job tonight." She moved to the doorway, brushing out her hair. She had her pajamas on. It was nearly 10:00.

"OK. But I'm getting sleepy," he warned.

"I'm coming." She disappeared, and reappeared a moment later to kneel down by the side of the bed. She reached for his hand. He rolled over and knelt beside her.

"Heavenly Father, we come before you tonight to ask what we're supposed to do." Steve began. "You know I didn't get accepted into Test Flight School, and now I am not sure if I should look for another position." The phone in the kitchen started to ring. Steve stopped praying.

"Ignore it." Jill whispered. "The answering machine will get it."

"Um, yes. Ah, well Lord, we are just trying to figure out your will, and we want to please you." After four rings, the answering machine started to speak the recorded greeting in the background. "Please show us what you want us to do. And thank you, Father, for everything you have given us. We don't mean to be ungrateful. We are thankful for your love, and the love you have given us for each other."

84

A familiar voice came over the answering machine's speaker. "Hey, Steve, this is Scoot. Got some info for you about that project."

Steve jumped up. "I've got to take this call," he said to Jill as he dashed away into the kitchen. He picked up the phone. "Hey, Scoot, this is Steve. I'm here, don't hang up." Jill, who was waiting by the bed, wondered what kind of man would call himself Scoot. *That's what comes from marrying an Air Force flyboy,* she reflected. Most of them had some kind of nickname they had adopted during flight training. She listened to Steve's side of the conversation, which didn't amount to much. "Yeah, I remember... Yeah, I'm still interested... No just found out today that I wasn't accepted, but they want me to apply again in a few years... OK, his name is what?... How do you spell that?... Yeah, I'll call him first thing tomorrow. If I come out, will you be around? ...Great... Congratulations. Have you set a date? ...Awesome. Hope I can meet her soon... OK, thanks for calling. Great to talk to you... Yeah. Bye."

"Who was that?" asked Jill, walking into the kitchen.

"Scoot Johnson, an old friend from the Air Force Academy. We were squadron mates in the Academy. Did I tell you I met him when I went out to Edwards?" Jill shook her head. "No? Well, anyway, I had lunch with him after my interview. He was working on some kind of project out in Nevada, as a pilot. He stopped flying the F-15 Eagle to take on this project, so it must be some kind of special. He said they were looking for a few more good pilots, and asked if I would be interested. I told him I was. Anyway, he just said the brass out there wants me to come out and talk to them. He gave me this guy's name and number, wants me to call him in the morning."

Jill's eyes were sparkling. "See, Steve, we had just started praying about a direction, and you get this phone call."

"Yeah, well, this project is in Nevada. You know, heat and desert and salt flats and no fast food joint for over a hundred miles in any direction. And anyway, I don't even know what's involved."

Jill looked at him seriously. "Steve, if this is God's will, I will go with you, even to Nevada. In fact, I would go further than Nevada." Her eyes grew rounder. "I would even go with you to someplace as foreign as California. Well, probably."

Steve laughed. "You goof. I hope you would." Jill started laughing too and he kissed her. "Alright, Babe. If you think this might be an answer to our prayer, I'm willing to check it out."

There were times when Paul Schneider was glad his dad had insisted he get a college degree. And then there were days that he was especially glad his dad had insisted he get a college degree. Today was the latter.

'Big Joe' Schneider, Paul's father, was a minor legend in the Washington, D.C. Fire Department. He had joined the department straight out of high school, and worked his way up to chief, a job he kept for 15 years until his retirement. Paul had always wanted to become a firefighter himself, and often pointed out to his dad that a firefighter didn't need a college degree. Big Joe disagreed. Over the course of his career, he had seen more technology, technical education, and management enter the department every year. There was no question that a fireman with any aspirations to move up in the organization would need a college degree. So, Paul had complied, earning a Bachelor's Degree in criminal justice. He had then promptly applied, and been accepted, to the department.

Paul enjoyed the physical challenges of being a firefighter, but he also had a fairly inquisitive mind. He found himself fascinated by forensics, so when an arson investigation job became available, he applied and was accepted. He had pushed hard to bring the department's investigative ability to the cutting edge. He had managed to persuade city management to fund two arson investigation dogs. He also ended up going back to school at night to learn more about chemistry, so he could learn the science behind his day-to-day detective work. His drive had allowed him to help the police bust an arson-for-profit ring with ties to organized crime.

As his success grew, so did the reputation of the department. Paul had noticed the drop in arson activity for a full year before terrorists attacked the nation with hijacked jetliners in 2001. When the Department of Homeland Security was formed, Paul had decided it might be a good place to apply his investigative skills. He had been quickly accepted, and as a result of being at the right place at the right time found himself closer to the top of the department than the bottom.

He was thinking about the events of the day as he drove home in his pickup truck. He had been called into his supervisor's office and asked if he would be willing to head up the internal security team for an above-top-secret project related to the military. Paul asked why his department was being asked to be involved in internal security for a military project, and was told that the President himself had stipulated there be civilian involvement in the security aspects of this particular project. Apparently, there was some pretty significant knowledge being developed, and the sitting President didn't want to have a legacy involving the loss of secrets to the enemies of his country, as had happened on the Manhattan Project.

Paul had asked for an evening to check with his wife before he committed. It would involve more time away from home, because the project was being conducted at a top secret Air Force Base in Nevada. He was assured, however, that most of the work could be done from his Washington D.C. office.

He didn't think his wife, Karen, would mind. The increased pay for being away from home several days a month would be helpful – to pay for his pickup if nothing else. He had bought it the day after Karen had gotten upset with him about something and complained about his previous pickup – she had called it an impractical, gas-guzzling monster – which it was, he had to admit. After all, with three children, they couldn't fit the entire family in his truck anymore. So the next day he had gone to a dealership and purchased a brand new, loaded, extended cab pickup, which held his wife and their three kids comfortably, without telling her beforehand. Paul had opted for a diesel engine, which made the truck almost as economical to drive as a large car, but it also added $5,000 to the base price. As a result, it featured a 72-month payment plan, which Karen didn't find quite as comfortable as the leather seats.

The resulting 'disagreement' between them caused Karen to complain about her marriage to a friend, who had told her to go visit a pastor Howard Olofson. Out of pure frustration she did, although neither of them attended church regularly, and had never attended the one that Pastor Howie shepherded. The good pastor had convinced Karen to become a Christian. She had, and Pastor Howie had mentored her in the art of being a Christian wife and mother. The resulting change of heart in Karen had intrigued Paul enough that he began to attend church, and six months later, he had given his heart to the Lord as well.

Their marriage had gotten a lot better, even though the truck payments were still a burden. They were 51 payments into the truck. It would be nice to get it paid off. From the time he became a Christian, Paul never made a major decision again without involving Karen, and also praying about it with her. The first few years of marriage had been rough – he was a city cowboy who thought he had the right to live just the way he wanted, and she had found that an independent, self-confident boyfriend could turn into a non-communicating, self-focused husband and father. Jesus had changed both of their hearts. Paul used to think that Christians were a bunch of self-righteous fools who tried not to have a good time. He had been surprised to find that becoming a servant to his wife and family led to more contentment than he would have ever believed possible.

Chapter 5

It had taken three weeks for the preliminary security check to clear before Steve and Jill were allowed to transfer to Nellis Air Force Base in Nevada. They found a suitable apartment on base in the married housing section. They were to be stationed there until a more thorough check of them both could be completed, at which time they would be moved to another, undisclosed, location.

Steve learned that, just as Scoot had reported, the first two years were going to be dull. *Dull probably wasn't the right word to describe it. It will have to climb up several notches on the excitement meter to rate dull.* He was being trained to fly a 55-passenger commuter airplane with a jet engine driving a large propeller on each wing, commonly called a turboprop. Once certified, he would be mainly shuttling people and parts back and forth between different areas of the huge air base. Every other Friday and Sunday afternoon, he would be flying jaunts between the base and the Las Vegas International Airport for project members who wanted to leave the base for the weekend.

The only other thing he was told was that he would eventually be training to pilot a large flying wing aircraft with a top-secret cargo. The missions would be dangerous, but not because of weapons. The danger came from environmental factors. That was all he was told.

Not that he really minded. He and Jill were able to spend a lot of time together, as well as meet some of the others who were working toward getting their in-depth security clearance for the project. Jill had quit her job to be with Steve in Nevada, and wasn't too interested in pursuing another until they learned where they would be settling more permanently. One weekend they flew to Denver to attend Scoot's wedding. They had met Carla, Scoot's fiancé, when she had come to visit Scoot at Nellis, and she turned out to be as refined and dignified as Scoot was outgoing and unpretentious, a classic example of opposites attracting.

There were quite a few others in their section of the base who also were waiting for advanced security clearances. Steve and Jill were surprised to find that many of these people had advanced engineering and physics degrees. Jill was a bit skeptical about their claims of some of their accomplishments until she researched some of the papers they had written.

"It's amazing the kind of knowledge some of these people have," she reported to Steve one evening. "I met three people in the last week who have done design work on pebble bed nuclear reactors. I didn't think there were three people in the country who had ever even done any work on them."

"You're going to have to translate. I understand the nuclear reactor part. What's the pebble bed part?"

"It's a new kind of design for a nuclear reactor. You know in most nuclear reactors, the fuel is in long rods, right? In a pebble bed design, the nuclear fuel is built in little balls, about the size of billiard balls. That's what they call pebbles. When the reactor operates, the balls heat up because of nuclear fission. The balls expand from the heat, and the small amount of expansion separates the pebbles by a fraction of an inch, but enough to slow down the nuclear reaction. If you do it right, it is supposed to be almost melt-down proof, much safer than current designs."

"Sounds promising. Are there any in operation?"

"No, not in our country anyway. China is probably going to build some, and they have been discussed in Europe. Not here though. After Three Mile Island and Chernobyl, nuclear plants aren't even a possibility anymore in the U.S. It drives Dad crazy. He thinks nuclear is the only way to solve our dependence on foreign oil, and he says burning coal sends more radioactivity into the atmosphere than any nuclear reactor ever will."

"He's might be right. I wonder why nuclear reactor designers are being hired for a military project to build a flying wing airplane?"

"Could you power an airplane with a nuclear reactor?" asked Jill.

Steve thought about that. "I suppose it could be done, in theory. After all, there are nuclear reactors in ships and submarines. The Navy's in love with the things. But they're not very practical for airplanes. If you need to go long distances with a military aircraft, you do air-to-air refueling. The Air Force has been doing that since WWII. Plus, if a nuclear-powered airplane went down, it would make a huge radioactive mess." He grinned at her. "Can you imagine if the Sierra Club knew there were nuclear-powered airplanes on the drawing board? They'd put up a stink that you could smell all the way to Jamaica."

"What about a payload?" pressed Jill. "Would you need a nuclear reactor to power something in the airplane?"

"That doesn't make a lot of sense either. If you need that much power, just hook a generator to a jet engine. On that commuter plane I'm learning to fly, the jet engine drives a propeller. Well, you can hook a jet engine up to a generator and make gobs of electricity. A jet engine drinks fuel like crazy, but again, if you need more fuel, you just do air-to-air refueling. The risks of putting a nuclear reactor on an airplane just isn't worth it."

"You're right," admitted Jill. "It doesn't make much sense." She was silent for a moment, then concluded, "I guess we'll just have to wait to find out."

The wait ended up being two months. By the time it was over, Steve was fully qualified to fly the turboprop and had started flying people and packages around the base. He was surprised to find that it was such a huge complex. Located Northwest of Las Vegas, the base covers an area of Nevada desert the size of the state of Connecticut. Steve found there were additional sub-bases within that huge area of land. There were strict procedures about getting clearance to fly into some of these inner bases. The rules were enforced by a F-16 at Nellis that was always ready to roll, and it was armed with Sparrow and Sidewinder air-to-air missiles. Steve also found out that the security staff had less of a sense of humor than his drill instructor back in basic training.

Finally, the day came when they learned that all the security access had been granted. They were to pack their belongings, leave them in boxes near the door of their apartment, with their names clearly labeled on each box, and come to a briefing which began at 8:00 AM on a Friday morning.

The briefing ended up lasting three hours, and two of those were additional security briefings. Along with the rules and warnings, and lists of things they could and couldn't say, they found out that there was an entire team of counter-espionage agents who would try to get them to reveal something about the project. They might be approached on base, back in their hometown, or just about anywhere. If they did reveal anything secret, or if they even suggested that what they were involved in was anything related to secret military technology, they would be restrained in a 'military holding facility' until the end of the project. They were amazed to learn that there was already more than one person who was being detained until the end of the project.

After the 'briefing,' they were fed lunch, and then they boarded a bus and were driven out to climb on one of the commuter planes which Steve had qualified to fly. They were flown to a section of the base called Minion Lake. Most of this section of Nevada, Steve explained to Jill, was made up of dried up lakebeds – apparently, most of Nevada had been underwater at some point in the distant past. There was no standing water now, and the dry lakebeds made for large, flat expanses of ground that were quite useful for testing military 'stuff.' Another benefit of the location was a ring of mountains, which surrounded the various dry lakebeds, to keep prying eyes away. About the only thing able to peer into these super-secret sections of the base were spy satellites.

After they landed, they were escorted to an auditorium for an introduction to the project. Steve and Jill examined their new home on the way. The Minion Lake complex was a collection of buildings, many of which seemed to have been recently constructed. They shared the common trait of having been singularly ignored by any architect with a creative streak.

The auditorium had seats for about 700 people, Steve guessed. It looked functional, if perhaps a bit spartan. The only thing he found odd was a contingent of mobile whiteboards at the back of the stage – there must have been at least 20 or more. Many of the whiteboards had mathematical equations written all over them. It looked like something from a mad scientists' convention – except, Steve realized, they were probably generated by a bunch of scientists who were most assuredly not mad, if the people they had been meeting back at the main part of the base was any indication.

Steve turned to Jill. "Look at all of those equations on those whiteboards up there. Do they tell you anything?"

"Not much. They definitely seem to be related to nuclear fission, though."

A young man stepped up to the podium and introduced himself as Brian Masulis. "Welcome to Minion Lake. We are delighted to have you here. What I will be doing is giving you a brief orientation of our facilities. That should take about 45 minutes. After that, we will have a 15-minute break. There are a few of you who are not directly involved in the project. We will dismiss you at that time, and you will get a chance to wander around the base, pick out your living quarters, etc. The rest of us get to stay and find out what this project is all about."

Steve looked at Jill. It was obvious to him that she was disappointed at being left out, but was trying not to show it. She kept staring at the equations on the whiteboards. "Bummer, huh?" he asked.

"No."

"Christians aren't supposed to lie."

"Oh, you. Just let me be your wife for awhile."

"If you're sure that's what you want."

The 45-minute briefing took almost an hour. The buildings themselves may have been spartan, but the military had not been thrifty when it came to outfitting them to keep the occupants engaged. Besides the usual amenities like a cafeteria and laundry facilities, there was a whole spectrum of recreational facilities – everything from a physical fitness center with state of the art equipment, to a bowling alley, to a building built solely to contain convertible tennis/volleyball courts, to a mall with quite a few independent stores run by retired military personnel. There were a total of 10 swimming pools scattered around the complex. Every apartment had a full contingent of cable channels provided free of charge. And the list went on.

After it was over, the group broke up. Of the 40 people who made up the original group, 27 were dismissed, including Jill. The remaining 13 assembled back in the auditorium 10 minutes later.

Brian returned to the podium. "Before we begin, I am going to need all of you to produce photo identification, please." There were mutterings from a few of the people in the group, but everyone complied. A couple Air Force officers circulated through the ranks, carefully comparing the photo on the card to the card's owner, and asking for confirmation of some information like a birth date or social security number. As they did, they checked off names on a clipboard. After they had completed their rounds, the two officers met to compare notes, then gave Brian the thumbs up. He nodded, and then turned toward the group.

"Thank you, Ladies and Gentlemen. I know the security may get a little tiresome, but after our briefing, I think you may understand why security is so tight here. Anybody think we're being a little paranoid?" A couple of hands went up, "Well, we have a saying. Just because we're paranoid doesn't mean there's not somebody after us." There was a collective chuckle, and the tension in the room subsided a bit. "How many people here have learned about the counter-espionage tests?" Everyone raised a hand. "I know you have probably already heard it several times, but from here on out, any information about this project is above Top Secret, on a need to know level only. If you reveal anything about what I am about to tell you to any person, even your spouse if they are not working on the project, and we find out, you will be in very serious trouble indeed. Please spare yourself, and us, the trouble by keeping what you are about to learn in the strictest confidence.

"Before we begin, I need to tell you that I am not a scientist. I am going to give you a high level overview, but you will have to wait for technical details from the teams to which you will be assigned. We have a range of people here, from mechanics to theoretical physicists. This is merely an introduction. From experience, we have found that it takes people a day or so to even begin to believe that what I am about to describe is possible. Tomorrow, you may begin to dive as deep as you wish into the theory and reality of making it happen.

"The name of this project is Opera. It is a randomly assigned code word, it means nothing. Project Opera was started at the order of the President of the United States. He ordered the project into existence based on the research of Dr. Andrew Stark, who is now here at Minion Lake. There are two phases to the project. The first phase was to hire some of the best physicists and mathematicians in the country to try to find a problem with Dr. Stark's theory. That work has been done, and no significant holes have been found. That phase of the project took 18 months. I, personally, have been here for the last 12 months. The project is now gearing up for the second phase, which is to build a machine that will take advantage of his theory.

"Let's do a quick science history lesson before moving on. Albert

Einstein proposed the theory of relativity, which states that there is a relationship between gravity and time. In very simple terms, the more gravity at a particular point in time, the slower time goes at that point. This is a proven principle. For example, the Global Positioning System has software that compensates for the time shift. The satellites, you see, are further away from the earth than we are, and their clocks are therefore running a bit faster than clocks on the earth's surface. If the system didn't account for that, eventually the GPS system would become unusable.

"Ever since the development of the Theory of Relativity, physicists have tried to either extend the theory, or come up with a new theory, to enhance their understanding of the functionality of the universe at a sub-atomic level. The Theory of Relativity explains more observable behavior than Newton's theories did, but there are still observations being made on the sub-atomic level that we cannot explain. You may have heard the term 'Grand Unified Theory.' There have been various theories proposed, but they never have completely and satisfactorily explained the behavior of matter in the universe.

"Teams of physicists are probing atoms at the sub-atomic level, trying to understand quarks, muons, and who knows what other particles that make up the most basic unit of matter. Dr. Stark, however, decided on a different approach. He decided to try to further describe the relationship between space and time on a purely mathematical level. What he discovered was a mathematical relationship between space, time, and gravity. Einstein's Theory of Relativity explained that gravity could bend space. Dr. Stark discovered that, with sufficient gravity, you could not only bend space, you could manipulate it into different shapes instead of just plain sheets, which is how we usually think of gravity. At least, those of us who have ever spent time thinking about gravity, which, I must admit, I never did before coming here." There were a couple of subdued chuckles and agreeable nods from the group.

"Anyway, when he discovered that space could theoretically be manipulated into shapes, he went back to the relationship between space and time. What he discovered was that, with enough distortion of space, he could also theoretically distort time."

Brian stopped talking. The room was absolutely quiet as the group sat and tried to fathom the implications.

"So, what you're saying..." the voice trailed off for a moment, as if

95

the speaker was trying to decide whether to finish verbalizing the thought. The speaker was a thin, nervous looking man sitting in the front row. Brian nodded at him to continue his thought. "..what you're saying is that phase two of this project is to build a time machine."

Brian nodded, "You are absolutely correct. We are going to build a machine, which will allow us to bend space into certain distinct shapes. This will also bend time. With the proper shape, this machine should be able to travel through that bent space, and therefore, through time."

He stopped talking, and let that thought settle for a few moments.

"Now, if you would set aside your incredulity for a moment, I will describe the machine we will build to make this time travel attempt.

"As I tried to describe earlier, there is a relationship between space, time, and gravity. Well, obviously we are all subject to gravity. In order to properly manipulate space, this machine will need to take into account the effects of gravity. The Earth itself is the largest source of gravity, although we are also subject, to a much lower extent, to the effects of gravity from the moon and the sun. The gravity of other objects in our solar system can affect us as well, but we believe their effects to be negligible to the point of being able to ignore them. Now, let's just say it is possible to build a machine which can travel through time. Let's get some audience participation here. Do you think we should build a land-based machine?"

The same thin man who had guessed the purpose of phase two spoke up. "Absolutely not. It would be suicide."

"That is the conclusion that we also reached. Can you briefly give us your reasoning?"

"Because, there is no guarantee you would travel back to the exact same spot where you began. And even if you did, the ground might not be in the same place as when you left. A difference of more than an inch or two would mean disaster."

"Excellent. You're exactly right. In other words, Ladies and Gentlemen, over time the level of the ground changes. Earthquakes raise or lower the ground level. Water covers parts of the planet, or drains away from other parts. We are here at Minion Lake, which is dry. Can you imagine what would happen if we traveled back in time to a point when the lake wasn't dry? So, a terrestrial machine is definitely out. What's left? How about a submarine? Anyone want to help us think that through?"

There was silence, and then a heavy-set woman spoke up. "That is better, but you still would have problems."

"Such as?"

"Water pressure varies quite a bit at different depths. You would have to have a machine that could accommodate rapidly changing water pressure if you came out of your time travel at a different depth than where you entered."

"That's right. In addition, there is another problem. Water is not compressible."

After a moment of silence, the man immediately to Steve's right spoke up. "So?"

"When you completed your time travel, you would be trying to occupy the same space as a bunch of water. If you entered the different time too fast, it would be like hitting a brick wall. Something would have to give. Water won't give, it can only move out of the way. But because water has a significant amount of mass, it might not do that quickly enough. Something else would have to relieve that strain. That means that the machine would have to give. Quite problematic."

By now, Steve had begun to see where this logic was leading. "So that means an airplane," he said.

Brian nodded to him approvingly. "That's right. Air is quite forgiving. It is compressible. If we come out of our time travel at a different altitude than we entered, there might be a pressure difference, but we think we can build an airplane that can handle that. So, our time machine needs to be able to fly. There are other advantages to a flying time machine as well. It can travel long distances much more quickly than either a land or water-based craft. That means more options for our researchers.

"Now, going back in time any more than 50 years presents significant problems for an aircraft. It means there will be no infrastructure built to handle it. No runways, no navigation, and no fuel. So, the aircraft needs to be self-contained and self-sustainable. It also needs to be able to land and take off. After all, what's the use of doing time travel if all we can do is peek out of an airplane window? Oh, it would probably still be useful, but it would be more useful to get out and explore. Run tests. Do real science. Things we can't do just by looking out a window. So, we will be using a nuclear power plant to produce the power needed to operate our aircraft. A nuclear power plant has the advantage that it will not need to be refueled for a period of years, so that eliminates the need for fuel during our time travel.

"The next thing is to accommodate the space and weight of a nuclear reactor in an aircraft. The project had decided to build a flying wing, or blended wing body aircraft. The advantage of a flying wing over a traditional fuselage and wing airplane, to which you are accustomed, is that most of the interior volume of the wing is able to hold equipment. In other words, a flying wing makes the most internal volume available compared to any other aircraft design of similar size and weight.

"Finally, it wouldn't be practical to expect to find suitable landing and takeoff sites more than 50 years ago. Therefore, we will do the same thing that the early airlines did as they ferried passengers between the American West Coast and Asia. Does anyone know how they managed?"

Steve raised his hand. "They had flying boats. Airplanes that could land and take off from the water."

Brian nodded. "Right again. So, we shall build a flying wing that can both land and take off on water.

"Now, you may think we are out of our minds, but I assure you that we are all quite serious. And while you are pondering the things that I have explained to you this afternoon, you might want to ponder some practical applications for this technology, including military applications. And then you might think about the value of this technology, and the way it might be abused by a hostile foreign power. After that, I would encourage you to go back and think about our security measures. As I explained at the beginning of the lecture, there is a reason why we take security seriously here. We believe that the technology we are working on here is the most significant technology ever to be developed in the history of mankind.

"I will take a few questions, but again, I am not a scientist."

The first question came from a husky young man with a ponytail. "Are you planning to go both forward and back in time? Also, how many years are you planning to travel in either direction?"

"Excellent questions. At this point, we are only planning on going back in time, and then returning to the present. We'll see how that goes. Going forward in time presents quite a few additional challenges. We have a pretty good idea what happened to our planet in the past, so we think it is much safer going back than going forward. What if we went forward and found ourselves in the middle of World

War III? It might be a bit uncomfortable.

Second, theoretically, we can travel back millions of years. We are planning a series of missions, going back in numbers of years that are solutions of 2^n power. In other words, a trip of n=2 would mean going back four years, a trip of n=8 would mean traveling back 256 years, etc. We haven't settled on a formal schedule yet, we're just kicking around ideas.

"The amount of power needed to travel back one million years is not much different than for traveling back five years. The reason is that it takes a tremendous amount of power to twist space into the shape required for time travel. Once space is in that shape, adjusting the shape is simply a matter of fine tuning, and that takes relatively little power."

"Could you travel all the way back to the age of the dinosaurs?" Someone asked.

"Theoretically, yes. In fact, Dr. Stark has told me off the record that he would like to travel all the way back to the end of the Mesozoic Era, to find out what really caused the dinosaurs to become extinct. The Mesozoic Era is the last era in which dinosaurs flourished. They became extinct about 65 million years ago."

A petite blond spoke up. "May I ask in what field your degree is in?"

Brian looked embarrassed. "Uh, yes. I have a Masters degree in Library Science."

"What is someone with a degree in Library Science doing on a project like this?" The blond may have been smart and fairly attractive, thought Steve, but I wouldn't give her any points for dealing with people.

"My primary responsibility is finding ways to organize the information that is being generated in a way that can be easily found and accessed by all the researchers. When you are generating new information in theoretical physics, previous methods of information access might not prove adequate. I am planning on writing a doctoral thesis on various ways that I have come up with to organize this information."

There were no more questions, so the meeting broke up. Steve was glad. He had been thinking so hard he had a headache. He exited the auditorium to find Jill waiting in the hallway.

"Well, what do you think?" she queried.

Steve shook his head. "Let's just say it sounds too fantastic to be true. I think you would be intrigued, though. I think you should apply for a job here. The stuff that these folks are doing is right up your alley, my little physics doll."

"I'm sure it is. But you can't talk about it, can you? Come and look at the apartment I picked out. It's the only one I found that has a view of the mountains."

* * * *

"Are you ready?" Randy asked Melanie. He had managed to get a high quality speakerphone for the coming call. It didn't look at all like a traditional telephone. It had a numeric keypad like a regular phone, but it was low and flat with three protruding arms resting on the table. The speaker, from which the caller could be heard, was in the middle. Each protruding arm contained a highly sensitive microphone.

"Yes, Sir," responded Melanie enthusiastically. Randy had decided to let her conduct the phone call. He had tossed the decision around for a while, wondering whether it was the right thing to do. If this were something regarding the Department of Defense, he would have handled the call himself. However, it was only the Department of the Interior, so it couldn't be all that important, could it? And it seemed like a good opportunity for Melanie to personally follow up on something she had found. She was coming along nicely, Randy decided. She seemed to have a reporter's instinct for a good story. He had decided to reward her attitude and effort by allowing her to make the call.

The official budget documents had arrived earlier in the week, and Melanie had promptly checked the Department of the Interior budget for Bohemia. It wasn't included in this version of the document. More telling, the numbers didn't add up, and the missing amount was $2.3 million, exactly what was listed on the line item for the earlier copy. It definitely deserved a followed up.

"Right-o. Let's start at the top. The higher up the chain we get, the more authoritative any information becomes." He coached, "Let's start with Nola Nielson, the Director."

Melanie pulled out the list of names and phone numbers she had compiled, found the number for Nola's office, and dialed the number. It was picked up after two rings. "Department of the Interior,

Director's Office. How can I help you?" asked a secretary with a perfunctory voice.

"This is Melanie Graber calling from the *Times-Herald*. I would like to talk to Director Nola Nielson, if she is available."

"Ms. Nielson is out of the office at the moment. May I take your number?" asked the secretary.

"Yes, please." Melanie gave the information, and the call ended. "Who's next?" she asked Randy.

"The Deputy Directory, Dan Labinsky." Melanie dutifully dialed the number and reached Dan's office. After identifying herself to Dan's secretary, the secretary put her call through to Dan.

"Good morning, this is Dan Labinsky." came a male voice over the speakerphone.

"Mr. Labinsky, my name is Melanie Graber. I am a reporter for the *Times-Herald*. I was reviewing some of the budget documents over the last several weeks, and had a question about a line item. What can you tell me about Bohemia?"

"Nothing," came the firm, and equally unsatisfactory, response.

"Sir, there was a line item labeled Bohemia listed in the preliminary budget. It was for 2.3 million dollars. That's a lot of money. Can you tell me anything about it?" Melanie was being polite but firm.

"That item was a mistake. It is not in the final budget, is it?" responded Dan.

"No, but there is 2.3 million dollars that is not accounted for in the final budget."

"I'm afraid that I'm not at liberty to discuss that."

"But Sir, that is the taxpayers' money. They have a right to know how their money is being used."

"I am not at liberty to discuss that," repeated Dan.

"So are you refusing to account for that much money?" pressed Melanie.

"I am simply unable to discuss that," came Dan's reply.

"With all due respect, Mr. Labinsky, that answer is unacceptable. It's not right for the government to simply not account for 2.3 million dollars."

"I'm afraid I can't discuss that. Is there anything else that I can help you with today?" he asked.

"Can you tell me the name of someone who can discuss this item?"

"No, I'm afraid not."

"Mr. Labinsky, your office reports to the President. Does the President know about this?" Melanie wasn't put off by Dan's evasion attempts.

"I'm afraid that I can't discuss it."

"So the President does know about it?"

"I'm sorry, Melanie, but I cannot discuss the item in question." His voice was firm.

"So it is a valid line item, then?" asked Stephanie.

"It is not in the final budget. Other than that, I cannot discuss it."

"Well then, perhaps you can answer this question. Does the Department of the Interior fund any secret projects?" asked Melanie.

"I can't discuss that."

"It sounds like you can't discuss much of anything," she said, pressing hard now.

"On the contrary, we are making excellent progress with our reforestation efforts in several of our national forests. Do you know how many trees we planted last year?"

"Does the number of trees have anything to do with Bohemia?"

"I'm afraid I can't discuss that."

"You just told me you could."

"I can discuss with you the number of trees, yes."

"Does the number of trees have anything to do with Bohemia?" she repeated.

"I cannot discuss that," Dan repeated in turn.

"Very well. Mr. Labinsky, will you be able to tell me anything about this at some future date?" Melanie was grasping for any piece of information that might be valuable now, giving up hope that she was going to get anywhere with this conversation.

"I am not at liberty to discuss that."

"Very well, Sir. May I leave my name and number in case there comes a time in which you can discuss it?"

"You can contact us at any time. I'll be glad to have my secretary take your contact information. Just a moment please." The call was transferred to another extension. It was picked up after two rings by Dan's secretary. Melanie left her name and number, and then ended the call.

Randy nodded at her, very pleased with her performance. "Very good. You didn't let up, and you kept asking the question in different ways. You did very well."

"Thank you."

"You're welcome. Who's next on your hit list?"

* * * *

After transferring the reporter's call to his secretary, he thumbed through his contact list until he found General Greg Collins' number. He called, and reached the General directly.

"General Collins, this is Dan Labinsky. Just wanted to let you know I received a call a minute ago from a reporter asking about Bohemia."

"Very good." The General was quite pleased with that bit of news. "What did you tell them?"

"Nothing, I just told them I was not at liberty to discuss it."

"How did they respond?"

"It was a woman, and she pushed pretty hard. She told me there was money missing from the budget, the people have a right to know, asked if we were hiding the money or funding a secret project. I didn't answer any of her questions." Dan and Nola had been coached by the General about how to answer any inquiries about the item in question.

"Excellent. Has Nola also had a call?"

"Nola is out of the office all day today. She is meeting with some suppliers."

"Please warn her that she will probably also be contacted. You two are the only people we have briefed about this but the reporter will probably contact others in your department. No one else has brought up the issue of the missing $2.3 million yet, have they?"

"No. When they find out, there are going to be some unhappy people in this department. Our budget's pretty tight, and a lot of my department heads could have used that money."

"Then it's a good thing you know the questions are coming. Please set up a morning meeting with Nola, you and me as soon as possible. I'll let you know where we go from here."

"Yes, Sir. I'll have my secretary do that."

"Thank you, Dan."

Dan hung up the phone and thought about the last couple of conversations. General Collins hadn't given him much information, just told him to respond to any queries about the missing money by saying he was not able to discuss it. He had instructed Dan and Nola to call him when and if anyone queried them about Bohemia, a word the General had supplied, or an unaccounted for $2.3 million dollars, but had refused to provide further instructions.

The General had come up with the idea of including the line item on the preliminary budget and then removing it in the final draft. He, too, was familiar with the legacy of Aurora, and had decided to use the same technique to his advantage.

After discussing the ploy at length, Nola and Dan came to the conclusion that their department was being used as bait. Well, they had definitely got a nibble. And it was a big one, too, the *Times-Herald*. Dan wondered if the next step was to set the hook. He also wondered who was holding the rod and reel.

* * * *

Life had started to settle into a routine. Jill stayed in the apartment during the day while Steve flew or worked with the team programming the flight simulator, providing input on its development. In the evening, they usually stayed home for dinner. Two evenings a week, Steve played volleyball in a league formed from members of the base, as Jill enthusiastically cheered him on while visiting with the few other married women at the base.

Steve encouraged Jill to apply for a job on the project, but she was hesitant. "I just want to stay at home and be a good wife for you," she would tell him. After giving it some thought, Steve realized that her mother had always been a homemaker, and Jill's conservative Christian upbringing had taught her that being a wife was far more important than going and getting a job. Steve, on the other hand, had a mother who had always worked, out of necessity, and he found Jill's interest in staying at home something he hadn't anticipated when he considered marriage with her. Not that he didn't enjoy the attention she lavished on him, of course.

Three weeks after they had moved onto the base, Steve and Jill arranged to have lunch together. They had done this a few times, so he was surprised when she wasn't at the cafeteria at noon as they had arranged. She was characteristically quite prompt. After 10 minutes of waiting, he decided to start walking toward the apartment, expecting to meet her on the way. But he didn't. When he reached the apartment, he opened the front door with his key and looked in.

Jill was sitting at the kitchen table, still in her pajamas. She had some kind of empty bottle set upside-down on the table, and was peering into it intently. Off to one side sat a few pencils and some sheets of paper, on which appeared to be random scribbles.

"Hey, Babe. Weren't you going to meet me for lunch?"

"Yes." she responded absently. She continued to peer intently into the bottle for a moment. Then suddenly she seemed to come out of her reverie. She sat up straight and looked directly at Steve. "Uh, what time is it?" Her black hair flew away from her head as she whipped around to get a look at the clock. "Oh, no. Oh, Honey, I'm so sorry. I can't believe I did it again." She jumped up from the chair. "I'll be ready in just a minute. Oh, Steve, I'm sorry." She ran back toward the bedroom.

He walked over to the table and examined the bottle. It was a glass applesauce bottle, which had been washed clean. He looked inside, and saw a little black housefly, which apparently had been trapped there.

"Hey, Love. What were you doing out here?" He called back toward the bedroom.

"I trapped a fly, and I was looking at it," came Jill's muffled voice from the bedroom.

"What are these drawings?"

"I was trying to figure out how a fly's muscles for its legs and wings are arranged inside its exoskeleton."

Steve shook his head. Then he looked at the fly. "I'm jealous."

"What did you say, Honey?" Jill called from the bedroom.

"I was just telling your fly that I'm jealous," Steve called back.

"Oh, Steve. I'm so sorry," came her answering wail.

* * * *

They made it to the cafeteria by 12:40, grabbed some food and found seats at a booth. As they began eating, Steve asked her, "You said something about it happening again back there in the apartment. What did you mean? What happened again?"

Tears sprung to Jill's eyes. "It's a symptom of Asperger's syndrome. You get so intensely focused on something that the rest of the world just goes away. I try not to let it happen." She set her fork

105

down. The tears were beginning to run down her cheeks. "I just hate it. I was so happy. I hoped that it would never happen again." Steve stared at her in amazement, which quickly turned into concern as she appeared to be getting more upset with every passing moment. Her eyes were fixed sightlessly on her salad. She grabbed for her napkin, and used it to cover her face. "Oh, Steve, I'm so sorry. I'll try not to let it happen again." Now he saw her shoulders start to move up and down as the tears turned into outright crying.

Steve had seen enough. He stood up from his seat, moved around, and sat down beside her on her side of the booth. He put both arms around her and pulled her tight. "Whoa, Babe. Take it easy. Calm down. Goodness sakes, take a deep breath, Girl. There's no need to get so upset." He continued talking calmly to her, saying nothing in particular, and after a couple of minutes felt her shoulders stop shaking. He was clutching her tightly with one arm, and using his other arm to run his hand up and down her arm. After another minute or so, she lowered the napkin to reveal a tear-streaked face.

"I'm sorry."

"Are you OK?"

"Yeah. I'm just so embarrassed. I hate myself."

"That's enough of that kind of talk. I don't want to hear you say that again." Steve said in a voice that was so commanding it even surprised him.

"OK," whispered Jill. Then, "can we go back to the apartment?"

"Yeah." Steve let her go, then gathered her salad and his sandwich. Fortunately, they had both been served in containers that could be folded over and closed. He grabbed the food with one arm, stood up, and with the other reached out to Jill. She took his hand and stood up, and they walked toward the door. Steve tried to ignore the stares from the other patrons. Once outside, it took just a few minutes to walk back to their apartment.

Once inside, Steve guided Jill to the couch. He turned back, placed the food on the kitchen table, and then went and sat down by her. He knew he was going to have to be very careful about what he said next, and how he said it.

"I, um, I'm a little confused," he said.

Jill said nothing for a few moments. Then, she said, "I just want to be normal."

"I am not sure what you think normal is, but I didn't marry

106

normal. I married Jill."

She turned to him. "You know what I mean. I don't want to be weird any more."

Steve shook his head. "You're not weird. You are an extremely smart, talented lady." She dropped her eyes and said nothing. "Has this happened before? I mean, focusing like that?"

"It happens about once a week. I was able to hide it before. I hoped you wouldn't see me like that." She paused for a moment. "Do you still love me?" she whispered.

"Oh, Jill! Of course I do. What a silly question. Why would I stop loving you? Goodness sakes, you are blowing this way out of proportion. And besides, it's an incredible gift."

"It is not."

"It most certainly is. Look, Babe, you're way smarter than me. And that's great, I have always been attracted to smart women. But you have this huge hang-up about this thing that you have, this ability to concentrate. Jill, God gave you that talent."

"But I don't want it!" was her anguished reply.

"Tough. You've got it anyway. Look, Jill, remember when Pastor Howie told me that God was the God of impossible? Well, I believe that. I also believe that he doesn't make mistakes." He reached over, put his finger under her chin, and lifted her head so that she was looking into his eyes. "Jill, you are not a mistake. I love you just the way you are."

"Oh, Steve." Again her eyes grew moist, but not in the same way as before. She put her arms around him and rested her head on his shoulder. "I'm sorry. You're so good to me. Maybe I am blowing this out of proportion."

"Well, you are obviously very sensitive about it. I hope that I can help you to accept that part of yourself." Steve sat thinking for a minute. "Look, you did really well when you were single, working at that consulting company. Weren't you happy then?"

"It was OK. But I was afraid I would never get married. All my friends were getting married, and they all seemed so happy. Ever since I can remember, I wanted to be a wife. And I was afraid that my brain would never let that happen."

"Your brain is one of the reasons I was attracted to you, remember?"

Jill nodded. "I know. I guess I thought maybe that wasn't really

107

accurate. I have had trouble relating to so many people in my life. I was afraid that, if you found out how I really am, you wouldn't love me anymore."

"Sorry. It is going to take a lot more than your brain to keep me from loving you."

"I do get bored, sometimes." Jill admitted.

"That's what I thought. OK, if you are feeling better, I think you and I had better take a walk over to the Muriel building." The Muriel building was where the project coordinators and top researchers had their offices.

"Why?"

"Because you need a job."

The walk over was quiet. When they arrived, Steve led Jill toward the office of Brian Masulis. Before reaching his office, however, they met him in the hallway. He was walking toward his office with a couple of other men Steve hadn't met yet.

"Hey, Steve. How are you doing?" Brian called. He turned to the other two. "Have you met Steve? He is one of our pilots, joined us about a month ago. Steve this is Dr. Choi and Dr. Stark. And who is the lovely lady?"

"My wife, Dr. Jill Harrison. She is looking for a job. I thought maybe you could point her in the right direction."

"Ah. Medical doctor?"

"No, actually she has a PhD in applied physics."

Both Dr. Choi and Dr. Stark peered more closely at Jill. "From where?" asked Dr. Stark.

"American University in Washington, D.C." she replied.

"Which she earned when she was 21." added Steve. Jill looked frowningly at him, but Dr. Stark didn't seem to notice.

"Is this true?" he asked.

Jill nodded. Dr. Stark turned to the others. "I am going to try her out," he said.

Steve noticed how the others deferred to him. He realized with a start that they were talking to THE Dr. Stark, the one who had come up with the time travel theory. He had been so focused on talking to Brian about a possible position for Jill he not paid enough attention to Brian's companions.

Brian held up his hand. "Hold it." He turned to Jill. "Have you been cleared by security?"

"Same clearance as me, I think," interjected Steve.

"Let me do a quick check and confirm that." He turned and stepped into his office. That left the rest of the group suddenly standing in an awkward silence.

"Ahem." Dr. Choi cleared his throat. "Ah, well, I must be going. Nice to meet you, Steve and Jill." He turned back to Dr. Stark. "I'll check on those heat-radiant coatings and let you know how it works out." He nodded politely to them, then turned and walked off.

Without a word, Dr. Stark turned and walked into Brian's office. Steve and Jill followed. Brian had a drawer to a filing cabinet open, thumbing through the files. He pulled one out, opened it, and started skimming it. Then he looked at Dr. Stark. "She's clear," he announced.

"Fine. Come with me." Dr. Stark motioned to Jill, then he turned and walked back out the office door.

Jill hesitated, looking toward Steve. "Go on," he said gently. She turned and walked after him. Steve and Brian stood staring after them. Then Brian turned to Steve.

"All this security, and somehow she doesn't come to our attention. I guess everybody was so focused on security risks they didn't think to tell us about latent talent." He shook his head. "How long have you been here? A month? Does she already have a job? What has she been doing?"

Steve chuckled. "Entomology. Thanks, Brian."

"No need to thank me, I didn't do anything. She studies bugs, too?"

"Only when she's bored. I don't think that is going to be a problem anymore."

Chapter 6

Steve and Scoot had been eager to see the flying wing aircraft that the project was building. They had studied the plans, and had a pretty good idea of what was being built. Imagining the end result from a set of plans, however, was nothing like seeing the real thing, even if the real thing was still under construction. It was November when they were able to fly down to a remote aircraft construction facility in northern New Mexico to see the progress being made on the aircraft.

The New Mexico site was formally owned by the Federal Government, but leased to one of the primary defense subcontractors. A lot of secret construction and testing of airframes, electronics, and other aircraft systems was conducted at the site. During the last six months of the first stage of Project Opera, when it became apparent that there was indeed going to be a second stage of the project, an enormous hanger had been built at the New Mexico site to house the construction efforts for the project's flying wing aircraft. It was now five months into the second stage of Project Opera, and the aircraft was starting to look like something that might actually take to the air.

The group flying down from the Nevada site consisted of Steve, Scoot, Dr. Choi, Dr. Stark, General Collins, and Brian Masulis. Dr. Choi and General Collins where the only two who had been to the site before, each of them had made several previous trips. This trip would allow the first glimpse of the unique aircraft for the other members of the group. They had been warned not to say anything about the primary purpose of the aircraft. The space-warp drive and its functionality had not been revealed to any of the aircraft assemblers.

After the turboprop landed, they were greeted by Gene Miller, the project manager who was overseeing the construction of the flying wing aircraft. After introductions, they were led into the ground's administrative offices, picking up security badges on their way to the hanger where the actual construction was taking place.

"Are you still behind schedule?" Dr. Choi asked Gene as the group walked.

"I estimate that we are now two weeks behind," Gene answered. He went on to explain that they had been three weeks behind, but had gained back a week in the last month by rearranging some of the construction tasks. "The delays have mostly been due to parts acquisition problems. We've had to rearrange some tasks in the schedule to compensate for the delay, but we're pretty close to being on track."

"What are you working on now?" asked Scoot.

"Routing all the hydraulic and electrical lines inside the aircraft. We're already starting to test some of the electrical subsystems. The fuselage and wing are built, except we have some skin on the top of the aircraft that we won't put on until the nuclear plant is installed. Here we are." Gene announced as they reached a door on the side of an enormous building. He scanned his badge, the door buzzed, and Gene held it open so the group could file in.

Steve was the last one through the door before Gene. As he walked in, he looked ahead to get his first glimpse of the airplane. Then he stopped in amazement. "Oh, wow!" he said.

The aircraft was huge. It wasn't as long as a conventional jetliner, but it more than made up for that with its enormous width. At the edge of the wing, an enormous vertical stabilizer rose majestically into the air, ending close to the roof of the building. The propellers had not yet been mounted. The skin was gleaming polished aluminum. There were only a few windows on the aircraft, around the cockpit area, but the glass hadn't been installed yet. Instead, thousands of strands of wire had been run in through the windows. Scaffolds surrounded the aircraft on multiple sides, and wires, air hoses, and other unidentified lines were running in, around, and over the aircraft. Steve thought all the lines made the aircraft look like it had been caught in some kind of a giant, prehistoric spider's web, except the number of people moving around in and out of the aircraft made it look more like an ant colony.

"If you want, you can climb up the stairs on our left," Gene offered. "That leads to a walkway that provides a good look at the topside of the aircraft." Steve and Scoot immediately turned and headed up the stairs, followed a moment later by General Collins and Brian.

It took several minutes of climbing to get to the walkway that went around the interior of the building, close to roof level. It was noticeably warmer in comparison to floor level and they were all puffing as they reached the walkway, which was more than 80 feet above the floor.

From this angle, the group looked down on the upper surface of the aircraft. They could see four of the six vertical stabilizers that had been installed, and the enormous gaping hole near the trailing edge of the center section where the nuclear plant would be lowered into the aircraft. The gleaming machine stretched from close in front of them toward the far side of the hanger.

"Ain't she pretty?" Steve heard Scoot mutter.

"Prettier than an F-15?" Steve teased.

"No. Just a different kind of pretty. The Eagle's a warbird, this is a workhorse. Big difference. What do you think?" He turned to ask Steve.

"She's a beauty, all right. I didn't expect her to look so big."

"The wingspan isn't any larger than some of the big jets. It's just that the whole wing is so thick, it makes everything look larger, I think."

"Looking forward to flying her, boys?" asked Collins.

"Yes, Sir." Steve answered for both of them. "I can't wait to ease her off the ground for the first time."

After a few more minutes, they descended the stairs and joined the rest of the group again. They were able to tour the interior. "Take time to enjoy the engine room now, Gentlemen," said Collins. "After the nuclear plant is installed and running, nobody will be able to go in except the technical staff, and then only between flights."

Scoot expressed surprise at how small the crew accommodations were. "From the size of the aircraft, I expected more room inside."

Gene answered. "We made sure to allow plenty of space for the nuclear plant and whatever else you're carrying. You've got the cockpit, the engineering control room directly behind the cockpit, and then a couple of other small rooms. There is a small cargo hold that you can reach through a hatch in one of the rooms."

For the next several hours, Brian Masulis met with Dr. Choi, Dr. Stark, General Collins, and Gene, taking notes about their conversations. Meanwhile, Steve and Scoot explored every inch of the aircraft, climbing in, around, and through every place they could fit, to the annoyance of the aircraft mechanics who often had to make way for them. After they had explored every inch of the aircraft, they rejoined the others working in a conference room built against one wall of the hanger.

Their work ended about 1:00 PM. The group grabbed some sandwiches and soft drinks from a series of vending machines and ate a quick lunch before heading back to Nevada. After they thanked Gene, they walked back to the turboprop. On the way, Scoot asked a question. "General, does the airplane have a name?"

"No. We have a model number."

"Well, isn't it the lead pilot's job to name the aircraft?"

"Depends on the name. What do you have in mind?"

"I'm going to call her *TimeFlyer*."

* * * *

"We've had a good month. In fact, the best month since we started the project," began Paul Schneider. General Collins and Brian Masulis were sitting across the table in the same plain functional conference room where Dr. Choi had been asked to become the Director of Implementation. Beside Paul sat Captain John Brier, who was chief of facility security at Project Opera. "My folks have made 17 attempts this month to try to get various project staff members to tell us something. We've had eight flat refusals to talk, and nine gave us the approved cover story. Of the 17 attempts, six were off-site, five were while workers were in transit between home and the base, and the rest were attempts on the base itself."

"Excellent," breathed the General. It was no secret that he didn't approve of civilian oversight of Project Opera's security measures. He was professional enough, however, to set aside his personal distaste in deference to a direct order from the President. Paul had found him easy enough to work with – suggestions for improvement were usually implemented immediately. But, Paul had to admit, he had learned more than a few things about security from his military counterpart across the table. It was turning out to be a learning

113

experience for both of them, the best kind of symbiosis as each learned from the other.

While Brian reported directly to Dr. Stark, and his official capacity was project librarian, General Collins also found him a useful go-between to aid in communications between Washington, D.C. and Nevada. His detail-obsessive nature translated into excellent notes, and his library training meant that, anytime in the future, the notes could always be found if there was ever a question about any previous happening.

"Of the people we probed, 11 were technicians, four were administrative support, and two were scientists. In fact, one of the scientists was Dr. Choi." General Collins' eyebrows rose questioningly. "He did well," responded Paul to the obvious question. "We were totally rebuffed by him."

"No checks of our on-site security staff?" asked Captain Brier.

"No. We expect to have a few of those this month. In addition, we are going to try to target a few of the retired military folks who run some of the shops in the Mall. But our primary focus, of course, remains project staff. In addition, we are continuing to bring more of our own people on-line. At the beginning of the month, we had only eight people working in internal security. We now have 13, and by the end of next month, we expect to have 24. So, you can expect the probes to continue to increase in frequency. Offset, of course, by the continued increase in the number of project staff members."

"Can I pass the results along in the newsletter?" queried Brian.

"Absolutely. Let your folks know they did well, and that we will be continuing to try to subvert them. As usual, you can pass along numbers, but no names."

"Alright. Anything else on that topic?" asked the General. After a brief silence, he continued. "Next topic – electronic security."

"I would like a paper describing any and all security measures implemented for data and voice communications in and out of the base." Paul stated. "High level at this time. We will probably follow up in a month or two asking for more detailed reports for various subsystems if we decide we want to know more."

"I'll handle that," volunteered Captain Brier. "I can give you the basics now, if you would like."

"We have another 10 minutes allotted for this topic on the agenda. Might as well use it," said the General.

"First of all, we start with workstation protection. We only allow regular PCs and Unix workstations running Starburst Unix."

"What's Starburst Unix?"

"It's an adaptation of a commercial Unix system that has been hardened by the folks in the Army's electronics warfare unit. They tell me, in addition to all the regular patches they get from the vendor, they have found 22 security flaws in the operating system so far, that they have fixed and the vendor hasn't even discovered yet. We feed those back to the vendor – slowly. Having a known security hole in a popular Unix distribution sometimes comes in handy. We keep several to ourselves in case we need to 'examine' the contents of a suspicious machine somewhere. It is a capability that has been quite useful."

"OK. What else?"

"Of course, all the PCs have a security package installed consisting of a firewall and an anti-virus package. The firewalls send an alert on all suspicious activity to the network administrator for immediate follow-up. Ditto on the anti-virus protection. These packages were written by the Army's electronics warfare unit and are constantly monitored for intrusions, bugs and any potential security updates that might in any way be warranted."

"We do have a connection to the Internet, which has been identified as a risk. However, we take extensive precautions to make sure we don't get hacked. For example, the Internet runs a data protocol called IP Version 4. There is an update called IP Version 6, which is not in widespread use. Every packet of data, whether in or out, gets translated from IP Version 4 to IP Version 6 and back again on its way in and out of the network. That in itself prevents a lot of problems. We scan every piece of e-mail that goes in and out. We block a number of services in the interest of security – there is no chat capability allowed to the outside, for example, although we do have a couple of internal chat servers."

"One thing we are doing on this project for the first time is routing all of our telephone traffic through our data network. It's using a technology called Voice Over IP, or VoIP. You can't tell that the telephone is any different. But every conversation in and out is recorded, and we have software that scans the recorded conversations listening for certain sound patterns that might indicate someone is talking about things relevant to the project. Also, conversations are picked at random and monitored by some of my staff in real-time.

That tends to be a rather popular assignment. It's amazing the things people say on the phone."

"I can imagine," responded Paul dryly.

"I could go on, but I think you are getting the picture. We try to keep a close watch on information in and out. We have two full-time people from the Electronic Warfare unit working full time on security for the project. Happens to be one man and one woman right now. They are sharp cookies, let me tell you. I used to think I was fairly good at running a PC, but I can't understand anything when those two are talking to each other. Oh, we also regularly scan for signals in the entire electromagnetic spectrum looking for unusual activity, like an unauthorized transmitter. The month before you started on the project, we detected something unusual and checked it out. Turned out a new technician was a short-wave radio operator, and had brought in a transmitter. We detected him while he was still setting up his system. Claimed it was just a hobby, but you never know. He isn't on the project anymore, by the way."

"Sounds like you have thought things through." replied Paul. He saw the General's mouth tighten. Paul understood. He would probably resent it if the President appointed a military officer to oversee a project he was running for the Department of Homeland Security. Well, can't be too careful in this business, he thought. In fact, Paul himself didn't know the real purpose of the project. He knew it involved nuclear power and aircraft, but beyond that, he had no information. His job was to try to learn more in any way he could. If he could present more information to General Collins or his bosses, there was a security leak. The proof was the knowledge that Paul or his team could dredge up and present. It was a challenge that Paul relished. He had been disappointed he hadn't learned anything substantial in the four months that he had headed up his security team. But this project was going to last for at least another two years. Time was on his side, he knew. One seemingly fundamental characteristic of people is that they liked to impress others with their knowledge. Paul and his team just had to find the person who felt the need to impress one of his team members with their knowledge, stroke their ego a little, and they would sing like a canary, he was sure. In so many ways, it was a game, and he was a master player up against a bunch of amateurs.

It was just a matter of time.

* * * *

Dr. Choi decided to spend the weekend in Las Vegas. He had made his first trip to the American city of sin several months prior, and had played a slot machine for the first time. He was more intrigued than he would have believed when, after a few attempts, a shower of coins spewed out of the front of the machine. Too smart to be completely taken in, he nevertheless enjoyed trying to beat the odds and come out ahead. After all, he had the money, and there wasn't much else to do with it in Nevada. His incredible salary, combined with a lack of income tax, meant he had more money that he would have ever believed a person could have when he was a poor graduate student in North Korea. And if he lost, well, he figured there was more than one way to pay an income tax.

This was his third trip, and he was determined to play blackjack. He had spent an evening on his previous trip observing the action around one of the tables, and then bought a book and taken it back to base with him when he returned. It had taken him only a few evenings reading through it, and he was ready to apply his knowledge. Something to take his mind off the challenges of getting all of the heat of the nuclear reactor out of their flying time machine. He needed the diversion. It was turning out to be a bigger challenge than he had anticipated.

It was Saturday afternoon, and he was about $6,000 ahead. He was enjoying himself immensely, even as he watched the $6,000 diminish to $2,500, and then drop further into a loss of close to $3,000. He had fought his way back to a loss of $2,500 when the table closed. *Ah, well. Next time things will be better,* he thought to himself. He knew full well that they probably wouldn't, but people did beat the odds. Maybe his luck would turn.

He decided to go get something to eat. That was something else about Las Vegas, everything was so cheap. The gambling subsidized the food and room expenses, and the gambling establishments spared no expense on either. They even had decent vegetables, something that was particularly difficult to find in a typical American restaurant. Vegetables and rice had accounted for the bulk of his diet before he escaped North Korea. His tastes had become more westernized, but he still appreciated a good meal of rice mixed with onions and bok choi.

He wandered from the gambling rooms to the restaurant nearby and got a booth on the side of the dining room. He chose a vegetarian meal, starting with a salad and then moving on to a vegetable pasta. This one featured artichoke hearts and whole cloves of garlic. It sounded like something his family would eat at home, if they had access to the wide choice of foods offered in the West.

He had finished his pasta and was trying to decide if he wanted a dessert when he unexpectedly found two men standing next to his booth. They both looked Korean.

"Dr. Choi. May we join you?"

Choi knew what this was. Another counter-espionage attempt that he had been warned about so often back on base. "I would rather that you find your own table," he responded as politely as he could. This was the second approach in a month. Choi made a note to himself to talk to Brian Masulis about it. He was beginning to wonder if he was being singled out for some reason.

"Thank you, Dr." said the first man, as if Choi had invited them to join him. He seated himself across from Choi, while the other man took a seat next to him, forcing Choi to move closer to the wall.

"This is a little, uh, forward, don't you think?" asked an unpleasantly surprised Choi.

"We have some information that we think you will find quite interesting," said the first man. It took Choi a moment to understand the message. When he realized why, he felt a cold shiver run down his spine. The man had spoken to him in Korean, with a North Korean accent. The stranger who had spoken nodded to the second, who leaned down to open a briefcase he had been carrying, and lifted out a folder. He handed this to Choi.

Choi opened it. It was a series of pictures – of himself, he was startled to discover. The first few were taken while he was living in Canada, working on completing his Masters degree. There was two of him in his apartment sitting at his kitchen table. In the first, he was eating, and in the second, he was studying. The next picture was of him climbing out of the shower. The next two pictures showed him working in the lab at the University in Canada.

"What is the meaning of this?" he demanded in English.

"You have been very treacherous to the homeland, Dr. Choi," replied the speaker, continuing to speak in Korean. "But we have left you alone because we suspected that you would learn information that might become very useful to us. And it appears that you have. You are

118

now working on a secret American military base. We would like you to return to North Korea to share what you know."

Choi's mind was racing. If these were counter-espionage agents, they were being quite thorough. This didn't seem to fit the American style, though. It surely would fit the North Korean style – win at any cost. It was very possible that they had tracked him all these years, in case he became 'useful' to them. "Are you serious?" he asked, stalling more than anything.

"Quite."

"You are out of your mind. I will never go back."

"There are reasons why you might consider our request," continued the man in Korean, as if he hadn't heard. He nodded again at the silent man seated next to Choi. The man reached in and pulled out another folder, which he handed to Choi.

Choi took it and opened it rather reluctantly. The first picture showed an old Korean man, sitting on a stone floor. One hand was chained to a stone wall, against which he was leaning. The man looked thin and ill. He looked closer, and felt his abdomen tighten reflexively.

It was his father.

"Look at the next one," prompted his antagonist, again in Korean.

This picture showed an old woman in much the same situation. Through his sudden blur of tears, Choi recognized his mother. Her exposed arms and legs were pinched and thin, as were her cheeks.

Choi lifted his eyes to the man seated opposite him. He felt anger growing inside him, a terrible anger that screamed to him to take the man by the throat and choke the life out of him. Never before in his life had he felt such hate.

"I will never give myself over to you."

Another nod. Another folder. This contained pictures of his brothers and sister, apparently in labor camps. The last picture showed a boy, probably about the age of six, staring innocently up at the camera. "That is your nephew. When any children are born into your family, we allow them to stay with their mothers until the age of four. They are then taken in as wards of the state, because the parents are not fit to care for them. There are two more children who are going to be taken into our custody in the next two years, another boy and a girl."

Above his anger, Choi was also beginning to feel ill. "What would happen if I agreed to come back?"

"Ah, that is more like it. We like agreeable people, Dr. Choi. It means that all your family is released from their confinement. You will be given a choice of where to live in our country, as long as you are contributing scientific information to us. We will treat you with the utmost care and respect. You will get free food and housing. We will provide you with whatever you desire. Whatever women you want. As many as you want. You will be treated with the utmost respect as an esteemed North Korean with a Western scientific education returning to bring that knowledge back to the homeland. You may lecture and teach our students, or you may conduct your own research, if you like."

"You are liars. I cannot trust a word you say."

The man frowned. "So you say. But think of your family. They will all die, eventually, if you do not do as we say. Their deaths will be on your conscience. You will have no one but yourself to blame for their tragic deaths."

Choi's mind was racing. How could he tell if these people really were from North Korea? Was this just an elaborate ruse?

"Listen to me," he said suddenly. "Your story does not make sense. If my brothers are in prison, how could they be having children that you claim to be taking away from them? You claim that I have a six year old nephew, and another nephew and niece about three and four years old. If my brothers were in prison, these children could not be theirs."

"Very good, Dr. Choi. I was told you are very sharp. This is what we do. Every two years, we allow your brothers to return home. We tell them they no longer have to pay for your crime. Then we simply watch their family. It is evident when the wife becomes pregnant. Then we come and arrest him again, and return him to prison."

Choi sagged in his seat. Only North Koreans would be this devious, and this cruel. He had absolutely no doubt that they were telling him the truth. He felt absolutely defeated. He had lived in the West for eight years now, thinking that he had escaped his former life, never suspecting that he was being carefully tracked by agents from his homeland. He had hoped against hope that his family would not suffer for his defection. He knew the families of other defectors were treated badly. But he had never suspected that the North Korean government would go to such extremes.

He lifted his head and looked firmly across the table.

120

"Nevertheless, I will not go back."

"Give him the card," said the first man to the second. The second man reached into the briefcase, and handed Choi a business card. On it was printed the name of a dry cleaning shop with a Chicago address. "If you ever decide to become more reasonable, you may contact anyone at this address. Call, write, or e-mail. Say you want to see the sun and moon. I am 'Sun', and this is 'Moon'. Give a time and place. We will find you."

"One more thing. It would be quite unfortunate for your family if we found out you had contacted any law enforcement agencies about us." Then they stood up and left.

Choi stared at their departing backs without really seeing them. It was as if life itself had stopped for him. The double shock of finding out he had been tracked so carefully all these years, along with his family's mistreatment, was something he could hardly comprehend. He felt like he was emotionally drowning, as if he was swimming in all the hate, malice and guilt that existed in the world, and he couldn't get to the top to take in a single breath of peace, happiness or reassurance. Maybe it is all just a bad dream and I will wake up, he thought to himself. Surely, it is a bad dream. It has to be. This could not be real. He looked down at his hands. One was holding the business card they had handed him.

It was real. All too horribly real. His parents were alive and suffering because of his escape. And the children of his brothers were being torn from their mothers' arms. All because of him. He knew the government of North Korea was evil, but would have never believed that he personally would become the focus of that evil.

As soon as the men left, he pulled the wallet out of his back pocket and threw two $20 bills on the table. Then he stood up and walked out of the restaurant to the hotel lobby, on his way to the elevator. In the hallway, there was a men's bathroom. He walked in, entered a stall, and latched the door behind him. Then he turned around and was violently ill.

Chapter 7

With the arrival of *TimeFlyer* in Nevada scheduled in four months, Scoot and Steve were instructed to start conducting interviews to select their first officers. The job openings had been made available to Air Force personnel, of course, but also to pilots in the Navy, Marines, and Army. Few people realized that, if helicopter pilots were included, the Army had nearly as many pilots as the Air Force.

Scoot had chosen a 34-year-old man named Jacob Plattner, known to everyone as Jake. Jake competed in hang glider stunt flying for fun, and was the first person to have performed triple somersaults with a hang glider in competition – no, the first person to have *survived* the maneuver, Steve reminded himself. There had been two others who had tried before Jake. The first one had died when the frame of his hang glider, which had been subjected to large forces over a period of several years of aerobatic flying, collapsed under the stress of the maneuver. The second had failed to maintain enough speed into his third loop and stalled as he approached the top of the loop, without enough room to recover. After the second failed attempt, the hang glider association had banned any more attempts at triple somersaults. Jake had done it anyway.

Steve didn't find a candidate he liked right away. He was looking for someone he could count on in a crisis situation, an individual that he could count on to maintain their judgment and nerve no matter what happened. He didn't know exactly how that quality might manifest itself. The best option, he decided, was someone who had flown in combat. However, there weren't too many combat-experienced pilots in the service anymore, and none appeared eager to fly an overgrown cargo plane. That was obvious because not a single one of the applicants for the job had combat experience.

He was scheduled to conduct an interview today with a man named Gale Derrman. Steve had flown to the main base at Nellis to conduct the interview. Gale was a S-3 Viking pilot in the Navy, flying the anti-submarine/refueling aircraft off of aircraft carriers. Steve wondered what a man with the first name of Gale would be like.

He turned out to be nothing like he expected. When he walked into the waiting room to get Gale, there were two men there. One was of medium height, dressed formally in a suit and tie. The other was short and wearing a cowboy hat and boots. "Gale Derrman?" called out Steve, and was surprised when the cowboy responded.

"Just call me Tex. I hate the name Gale," said the cowboy as he walked up to Steve and they shook hands. Steve was surprised again when the face looking up at him from underneath the hat was Asian, not Caucasian as he expected.

They made their way to a conference room and sat down. As Steve started through the interview, he found that Tex was originally adopted from South Korea by a couple from Britain. When he was three years old, the family had moved to the Houston, Texas area, where his father worked as a consultant for the oil drilling companies.

"My parents thought they were going to get a little Asian boy who learned to play the violin, ace every test in school, and generally made them proud." explained Tex. "But I never really enjoyed school. Oh, I could do OK if I tried, but I spent most of my time hanging out with some friends who owned horses. Eventually, I became a rodeo junkie. Every weekend I would be at a rodeo. When I was 16, I entered my first bucking bronco contest. My parents hated rodeos. They were real formal people, you know, tea and crumpets and raised pinkies. When I graduated from high school, they were determined to send me to college. I joined the Navy instead."

They discussed Tex's flight experience. He had good marks from his instructors. "What was the worst part of flying the S-3?" asked Steve.

"Hunting for subs. Boring as all get-out. You just circle and look for a big magnetic disturbance. It got a little better when we could drop sonobouys. But it was still pretty boring."

123

"So you don't like being bored?"

Tex shrugged. "Who does?"

"Why did you do it, then?"

Tex grinned. "Carrier landings are a blast. Especially at night. You really have to know your stuff. And air-to-air refueling is pretty intense, too. One little mistake and two airplanes turn into flying torches."

Steve was beginning to think that Tex just might be the one who fit his criteria. "So you like a challenge?"

"The tougher the better." he answered.

By the end of the interview, Steve had decided that Tex was his man. "Were you told anything about this job?"

"I was told it was flying a large aircraft, more like a transport aircraft, and that there was an element of danger involved."

"I'm afraid there will be a lot of boring flying time. The danger is from environmental factors, not anything related to combat."

"So really more like flying a cargo plane, right?"

"Yeah. We'll usually be carrying a crew of from eight to 20 people, but the cargo is the most important thing for these flights."

"It really doesn't sound any more challenging than what I am already doing."

"I don't think it will be. In fact, I think it will be less challenging."

"Well, I don't think I am interested in the job, then."

Steve was disappointed. He decided to try a different approach. "Do you miss rodeo? There can't be too many opportunities to ride horses on an aircraft carrier."

Tex chuckled. "No, horses and aircraft carriers don't mesh too well. Those ships are big, but not that big. But, to answer your question, yes, I miss rodeo a lot."

"Did I tell you that Las Vegas has some kind of rodeo almost every weekend? And I think they hold the championships here, too, at least some years."

"Yeah, that's right. I didn't think of that," said Tex, and he suddenly stuck out a hand to Steve. "Alright. When can I start?"

Steve grinned and shook the offered hand. "As soon as the paperwork is done."

* * * *

Because of the expected size of the crowd, the briefing was being held in the main gymnasium. Steve and Jill arrived 15 minutes early, but still had to sit near the back. The bleachers could hold about 1500 people. Steve estimated that 1200 were already there, which was amazing since the total number of people on the project was probably less than 3000, and this was only the first of three briefings. Apparently, everyone was excited to hear about the plans for the first flights of *TimeFlyer*.

Steve had been so impatient to arrive early at the briefing that he hadn't thought to bring something to keep his mind occupied. Jill had been smart enough to grab a book that she had been reading. It was a biography of Niels Bohr, the Danish physicist who had discovered and explained the structure of the atom in the early 20th century.

As Jill read, Steve watched his colleagues around him and reflected on the amazing progress that this team had made. The team had built and tested a stand-alone time-warp device. In order to test it, the device had been loaded onto a cargo plane and shipped down to Houston, Texas. There, it had been placed on a cargo ship that had taken it out to an unused oil-drilling platform in the Gulf of Mexico. Another ship had met them at the platform, an Aegis class cruiser, which performed the function of generating the required electricity for the tests. The Aegis cruiser is a marvel of modern naval warfare. It is designed to detect and shoot down anti-ship missiles and aircraft, and is an essential part of any modern naval battle group. The instruments and weapons that fight the battles demand an inordinate amount of electricity. With all of the non-essential systems turned off, it was barely able to generate the amount of electricity required to power the time-warp device.

The test had been performed during nighttime hours. A remote controlled drone aircraft had been purchased from the Israelis, the experts in the field of pilot-less aircraft. Instead of carrying a weapon, a rather recent adaptation of the aircraft from its original reconnaissance-only role, it had been fitted with a payload that allowed it to track the position of as many as 100 stars. The idea was that, as the airplane went back in time, it could verify its position by locating enough stars to calculate not only its position in three dimensional space, but in time as well.

The test had been a success. The time-warp device had been set to open up a channel in time back 150 years. The channel had opened

125

long enough for the drone to be piloted through, then the channel closed, and the drone had been on its own. Four hours later, the channel was re-opened. The drone's 'pilot' (who was actually working from the top of the oil platform) was able to acquire a signal from the drone within 30 seconds, and had piloted the drone back into the present time. The data that the drone had recorded verified that it had indeed been flying above the Gulf of Mexico 150 years in the past for a period of four hours.

The next step was construction of the second-generation time warp drive that could be placed inside an aircraft. That device had been built and shipped to New Mexico for installation into *TimeFlyer*. Testing of the space-warp device, however, would be put off until *TimeFlyer* was housed at Minion Lake in Nevada.

The two aircrews had spent two months on and off in New Mexico, test flying *TimeFlyer*. The aircraft was powered by a series of steam turbines with shafts that transferred the power to the enormous, eight-bladed composite propellers. Each steam turbine was rated to produce the equivalent of 34,000 peak and 27,000 continuous horsepowers. The surge in peak horsepower was seen as essential to get the heavy aircraft to take off from the water.

Flight tests had been relatively uneventful. The aircraft had performed nearly as expected, with one problem that Steve and Tex encountered on their first water takeoff. A flying wing is a relatively inefficient platform for a flying boat, because in order to operate, a wing needs air flowing both over and under it. However, when taking off from the water, most of the lower surface of the wing is submerged. In order to get air moving under the wing, a set of high-volume air pumps were installed that pushed air through a series of holes in the lower forward surface of the flying wing's body when taking off from the water. It had worked – but barely. Steve and Tex had bounced along the surface of the Gulf for a full three and a half miles before finally becoming airborne.

It was during those three and a half miles that Steve knew he had made the right choice in a co-pilot. As the aircraft bounced and floundered, with the steam turbines being driven at their full rated power longer than specified, Steve had gotten quite concerned with the number of systems that seemed to be surpassing their limits. It was at mile three, when the overheating alarm for the main reactor had gone off, that Tex suddenly let go with a wild cowboy yell loud enough to make the reactor technicians sitting in the compartment directly behind them think that something had gone profoundly wrong in the cockpit. Steve spared a glance at Tex to see someone who was having the time of his life. His exuberant Asian features were illuminated with the glow of red and yellow warning lights gleaming all over the control panels. It made Steve laugh, and he had relaxed enough to let the plane try to achieve liftoff for just a few more seconds, and it had.

Several modifications had been made to allow *TimeFlyer* to get airborne more easily from the surface of the water. These included more and higher capacity air pumps, and additional cooling for the engine systems through the lower surfaces of the aircraft, which were in contact with the water. The water sucked away the excess heat being generated as the steam turbines struggled to lift the great bulk, over one million pounds of aircraft, equipment and people, into the air. After those modifications, water takeoffs were less dramatic, although it still took a good two miles of clear water to achieve liftoff.

TimeFlyer flew acceptably, although Steve would have never compared it to flying the A-10. It was like flying an airliner – you were rated on the smoothness and stability of the flight. It responded to control inputs leisurely, as if it just didn't want to do anything but fly in a straight line. The aircraft had the capacity to carry 30 people. On a normal flight, it carried the pilot and first officer, and a crew of eight technicians to monitor and fuss over the nuclear reactor and steam equipment. It was easy to fly, as long as the pilot didn't want anything to happen quickly. It felt more like herding animals than piloting an aircraft – you worked slowly and carefully to get the aircraft heading in the direction you wanted to go, and slowly, it responded to the crew members' input.

Once flight-testing was completed, the aircraft was flown to Minion Lake for installation of the second-generation space-warp drive. That job, which had taken slightly less than one month, was nearly complete. Today, finally, the actual flight schedule was going to be announced.

When Steve saw Tex wander in, he stood up and waved to his partner. Tex ambled over and made his way toward the empty spot on the bleacher next to him. As he got closer, Steve's exclamation of "Doggone!" caused Jill to look up from her book. The entire left side of Tex's face, from his jaw to his hairline, was one huge bruise. It stood out in contrast to the tanned bronze color of the rest of his face. "What did you do, try to wrestle a steer with your ear?"

"I had a choice," responded Tex. "It was the bucking bronco contest. I was in the saddle for seven seconds when I felt myself start to go. I knew I could either go down gracefully without making the eight second mark, or try to stay on another second and get thrown hard. I decided to stay on."

"Didn't it hurt?" asked a sympathetic Jill.

"Not too bad," he paused. "Actually, I ended up with a concussion. It didn't start hurting till yesterday." The right side of his face grinned at them cheerfully. "It was worth it. I won the trophy."

Steve shook his head. "Keep this up and I am going to start calling you two-tone."

"Humph. Keep your names to yourself, Crispy Critter." Tex was referring to Steve's sunburn, which he acquired easily in the desert sun with his characteristically blond hair and fair skin. He gingerly took a seat next to Steve.

"What's the rest of you look like?"

"As good as ever, something I am not going to let you confirm."

Steve chuckled and turned his attention to the microphones set up at one end of the gym. Behind the microphones, a large projection screen had been set up. There was beginning to be some activity. Steve saw Brian Masulis moving around with Dr. Stark, Dr. Choi, and several others he didn't recognize. He looked at Dr. Choi. The man seemed to grow thinner every month, and his hair had started to gray, something that was somewhat unusual for a Korean. He leaned his head closer to Jill. "Dr. Choi doesn't look very good."

"I know. Some of us have been wondering if we should try to do something to try to help him. This project really seems to have stressed him out. He is always tense, and never seems happy anymore. He is a lot different from when I started working with him."

The dignitaries had taken their seats, and Brian Masulis approached the microphone. "Good Morning, Ladies and Gentlemen." He waited until the low buzz of conversation quieted. "I know we're anxious to hear about the schedule. But before we get into that, I want to introduce to you one of our most ardent supporters.

"Major General Greg Collins has had a distinguished career, first enrolling in the Army in 1968. He did two tours of duty in Vietnam, during which he earned the Purple Heart. He was consulted extensively during the Falkland Island crisis, and was a key player in developing strategy for both Gulf Wars. When Dr. Stark first approached the government with his theory, it was General Collins who recognized the potential of the theory and promoted it within the executive branch, ultimately helping to prepare for a presentation to the President. The President also saw the potential, and appointed General Collins as sponsor and chief government liaison for the project. He works tirelessly to support our project back in Washington. Please give a warm welcome to Major General Gregory Collins."

Everyone clapped enthusiastically as General Collins approached the lectern. "Thank you. My remarks will be very brief. First, I want to express my thanks for your efforts here at Minion Lake. Your development and testing of the space-warp drive exceeded our expectations, which were lofty indeed. Second, I want to applaud your drive. I know how hard many of you have been working, and I thank you. Finally, just to make sure you understand the importance of this project, I have arranged for a special guest to join us for a few moments to say a few words." He nodded at someone at the rear of the gym. Behind him, a large silver screen lit up with a projected image. "Our guest will be joining us via a secure video link from back in Washington." The image of the President appeared. "Mr. President, can you hear me?"

"I can hear you very well, General."

The General turned back to the audience. "Ladies and Gentlemen, it is my great pleasure to introduce the President of the United States."

The applause was thunderous. When it died down, the President spoke. "Ladies and Gentlemen of Project Opera, I thank you for that warm welcome. But let me assure you, it is I who applaud you for your efforts and your successes. General Collins has kept me informed of your progress. He and I are amazed and grateful for the pace of development. I would like to personally thank each and every one of you for your contributions to this effort. It is people like you, with your amazing skills, and your willingness to apply them in a coordinated fashion, who make our country so great.

"I understand that you will be announcing the flight schedule today. You and I realize that there will continue to be challenges ahead. Not all of the problems have been solved – in fact, not all of the problems have yet been encountered. But I have faith in you. I have the faith that you will continue to work together, as you have already been doing, to overcome the problems, the obstacles, and the challenges, to deliver to our country a tool that will be the envy of the world for decades to come.

"John F. Kennedy was able to publicly challenge the country to get America started on her journey to the moon. I have chosen to keep Project Opera out of public view for now. But make no mistake, what you are doing right now out in the Nevada desert will make the space race pale into insignificance. You are building a tool that will make the world a safer place, a better place, and a more enjoyable place. A place where we can assure peace and safety for our allies, and ourselves and prove a remarkable deterrent to those who would be our enemies. It is my hope that, with the technology you are developing, the entire human family will be able to live in peace, harmony, and prosperity for hundreds of years to come.

"Again, I applaud your skill, your creativity, your dedication, and your successes. Thank you. God bless you all, and God bless America."

Again, there was thunderous applause, and this time with a standing ovation. The President nodded and smiled, gave two thumbs up, and then started applauding the audience, which he could apparently see in a video screen on his side of the link. Eventually the picture faded, and the audience began to quiet down and take their seats again.

Brian Masulis returned to the lectern. "General Collins, thank you for those words. Please convey our thanks to the President for taking time out of his busy schedule to address us as well." The General, who had taken his seat, nodded and smiled at Brian.

"OK, let's get to the flight schedule. I know you have all been anxious to know how we are going to actually implement our time travel. At this time, we have scheduled four flights into the past. Can we have the visual, please?" The screen lit up with a computer presentation. "As you can see, our first flight will be to travel back into the past roughly 500 years. The first flight will be a four-hour flight. *TimeFlyer* will remain airborne the entire four hours. We will have an array of sensors and video equipment onboard to confirm our position in time and space. In addition, we will be taking extensive photographs of pristine North America. We will be flying over the Sierra Nevada Mountains into California, and then up and down the Pacific coast. Our goal for this first flight is to verify the working of the time travel device. Additionally, through pictures and video, we hope to learn more about the native peoples who once populated the area. Of course, we will try to avoid detection by them. We will maintain a minimum height of 30,000 feet during our flight.

"If that mission is successful, we will be flying a second mission 1000 years into the past. The second mission will last 48 hours. We will be flying to an undisclosed location and landing *TimeFlyer* to obtain biological samples. Of particular interest will be species that have become extinct.

"The third mission will be 4,000 years in the past. We will be exploring some of the islands of the Caribbean. This trip will last for 72 hours. Again, we will be interested in learning more about the culture and biology of the native inhabitants. It is not our intention to interact with any native people on the islands.

"The fourth mission will be traveling 8,000 years into the past. We will be traveling for a full five days. We will be going all the way to the Marshall Islands in the Pacific. In particular, we want to explore Bikini Atoll as it was in its pristine state, before America did its nuclear testing there in the '50's and '60's.

Our final mission will take us back 15,000 years. We will be focusing on a possible land bridge between Alaska and Siberia, the Bering Strait. Hopefully, it will allow us to learn more about how the North American continent was populated. The current theory is that indigenous peoples entered North America via this land bridge and then moved on to populate North, Central, and South America. The length of this mission and specific focus has not been finalized at this time.

"I am sure you all have plenty of questions, as well as other ideas. It would be impossible to try to address all of them in a forum such as this. What we have decided to do is to have you visit our intranet site to post questions and ideas. We have details for each of the trips posted, and discussion forums set up where you can post messages on different topics for each trip. For example, there is forum for culture, another for environment, and so on. Our trip planning team will be viewing those forums extensively, and using your feedback to refine the mission profiles. I know you will have a tremendous amount of input and feedback, and I look forward to working with you as we move forward. Thank you for attending today. There are handouts in the back that list the URLs for the relevant intranet sites. This concludes our meeting."

Jill turned to Steve. "Wow. That schedule sounds very aggressive." Her brow was knitted in concern. "Only five trips, and they are trying to go back 15,000 years."

"Don't you remember our first briefing? Oh, I forgot, you weren't part of the project then. You were apartment shopping while I sat through the introductory briefing, remember? Anyway, Brian told us then that they wanted to travel back as many as one million years. I guess if you want to go that far back, you need an aggressive schedule."

"Hmm." responded Jill, but said nothing more.

* * * *

The next day Jill returned to the lab. It had come as no surprise to Steve that she had become a bit of a star. She turned out to be particularly good at transforming mathematical equations into either words or visual metaphors that allowed her fellow team members to gain a better understanding of Dr. Stark's theory. She had become so useful that she often worked directly with Dr. Stark on theory or Dr. Choi on implementation, then putting together a presentation to help teach others about the subject of interest.

She was sitting in one of their shared meeting rooms, along with Dr. Stark, Dr. Choi and several others, discussing yesterday's presentation and the announced travel schedule. She was trying to lead the others into a discussion relating to the aggressiveness of the schedule. "Do you plan to continue to jump back in time by ever-increasing periods of time?"

"That's the plan," responded Dr. Stark. "There are so many things in natural history about which we only have ideas. Good ideas, well thought out ideas, but ideas. No proof. Examining the Bering Strait, for instance. It probably existed. Evidence supports population of large parts of North America by people who migrated over the Strait. But there is no way to know for sure until we can examine it in real time. Just think of it," he enthused. "Fabulous time to be alive. All kinds of history will be revealed. The lost history of the middle and Far East regained. Documented. Recorded. Real-time video of Napoleon's campaigns, of Alexander the Great's conquests. We could learn why Rome really burned under Nero. Why, the possibilities are absolutely endless. Fabulous. Breathtaking. I'm running out of adjectives."

132

"If everything goes well," put in Dr. Choi.

"God forbid that anything bad happens." agreed Dr. Stark.

Jill found that statement interesting. "Are you a believer, Andy?"

"Huh? A believer? A believer in what?" asked Dr. Stark, pulling himself back into the present.

"In God. You just said 'God forbid that anything bad happens.'"

"Oh. No, definitely not. Heh, just a phrase." He focused his attention on her. "Why? Are you?"

"Oh, yes. I believe in Jesus Christ."

Dr. Stark stared at her. "I can't believe that anyone with your intellect would believe in that superstitious nonsense."

"What do you mean?" she asked.

"I mean, how can you believe in something that is so obviously a fabrication?"

"I don't believe it is a fabrication at all. In fact, there are fields of science that place a tremendous amount of emphasis on the Bible. Archeology, in particular. The Bible has proven to be the most reliable document by far in describing the ancient Middle East."

"Pish-posh. Not real science. Physics is real science. Archeology is just a fancy name for historians who get their hands dirty once in awhile. Now, let me ask you a few questions. How do you relate your beliefs to a book that obviously describes the earth as flat?"

"What do you mean?"

"I mean, if you read the Bible, it often talks about the ends of the earth. In case you hadn't noticed," he continued somewhat sarcastically, "the earth has no ends. It is a globe."'

"That's just a matter of speaking. I don't believe it literally means the earth is flat."

"I can see where this is heading. I think I'll take my leave. Good day, all." said one of the other researchers. Almost all of them stood up and left. Within a matter of seconds, everyone else except Dr. Choi had left.

Dr. Stark was obviously trying to figure out where to begin. "Do you believe that God created the earth in seven days?"

"Actually, it was six days. And yes, I believe that."

"What about the rest of the universe?"

"What about it?"

"Was that created in six days as well?"

"Yes, I believe so."

Dr. Stark shook his head in disgust. "How can you possibly believe that? It has taken the light from some of those stars out there millions of years to get here where we can observe it."

"Yes, that is probably the most difficult thing for someone who believes as I do to explain." admitted Jill. "On the other hand, where did it all come from? You believe that nothing exploded and turned into everything? That sounds equally unlikely."

"So you fall back to groundless superstition. At least I am trying to rely on science and provable theories."

"Alright, let's stick to science, as you say," declared Jill. In a way, she was surprised that she felt so free to talk like this to Dr. Stark. But at the same time, she felt a certain challenge in his probing questions that made her want to push back. "You claim it has taken light millions of years to get here. You are making several assumptions, of course. The most obvious is that the speed of light is constant."

"That's because it is."

"On the contrary. The speed of light varies depending on the material through which it is traveling. In our calculations, we use the speed of light in space, but it is different in water, glass, you know, other things."

"Well, we are talking about light traveling through space, since it is generally accepted that those stars are indeed located in space." Dr. Stark was starting to be openly sarcastic.

"My point is that, if light can slow down, is it not possible that light could also speed up?"

"Doubtful, since the makeup of all the matter in the universe is based on the speed of light. However, let's entertain your idea. Let's say that somehow the speed of light doubled. Now, instead of taking 10 million years for light to reach here, it takes only five million years. That still leaves that religious foolishness quite a problem."

"Unless," Jill countered, "the light took some shortcuts getting here."

"How can you get shorter than a straight line between two points?"

"By bending space," she replied.

Dr. Stark stopped. "Well, it is difficult for me to argue with that, since that is what we are learning how to do here. However, I find it unlikely that space bent into the specific shape to allow the light from hundreds of thousands of stars to find its way here in the pattern we observe."

"But theoretically it is possible."

"Theoretically yes, but statistically an impossibility."

"More likely than the statistical probability of evolution."

Dr. Stark stopped talking for a moment. His face was beginning to turn red. "But we can observe evolution in action all around the world."

"Dr. Stark, I read an article about the statistical likelihood of evolution creating all the life we observe on earth. Do you realize that it is more likely that a tornado tearing through a junkyard would leave behind a fully assembled and functional jetliner than for evolution to have created life as we know it?"

"Well, everybody knows that theory has problems. But let's get back to the universe. If you don't believe in the big bang, offer me a scientific explanation for the existence of matter."

"That seems rather obvious. God just did $E = mc^2$. He took a tremendous amount of energy and turned it into matter."

Dr. Stark looked at her incredulously. "Do you have any idea how much energy it would take to create the universe? It is absolutely incomprehensible."

"Yes. Isn't God awesome?" enthused Jill.

"Awesome?" Dr. Stark blew his top. "What is awesome is your acceptance of intellectual absurdity. I can't believe someone who can explain gravity waves like you can believes all that nonsense." Dr. Stark was shouting now. "Absolutely stultifying. It's intellectual irresponsibility at the most fundamental level. Do you realize that it is people like you who held back the advancement of science for nearly 1000 years during the Dark Ages?"

"That is not true." Jill was getting slightly cowed by Dr. Stark's anger.

"It is absolutely true. Bunches of religious idiots suppressing logical reasoning and provable conclusions, imprisoning, torturing, and killing men of science. Why, if the Black Plague hadn't come along and killed off half of Europe, we would still be ruled by religious fanatics. You realize, of course, that the Renaissance didn't happen until enough people were killed off that the religious establishment lost their control of civilization?"

"It also led to the Reformation, when people got back to the true word of God." replied Jill quietly.

"Arrgh, I give up." Dr. Stark turned and stomped out of the room. Then he popped his head back in. "In the future, you may address me as Dr. Stark. I only allow those who are intellectually honest to call me Andy." And then he was gone.

"Wow. He got really mad," said Jill, trying to regain her composure.

Dr. Choi was silent for a moment. He had been watching the debate rage, and found it a rather interesting dialogue. He had heard some of the ideas that Jill had espoused, but had never taken the time to examine them in depth. "May I ask you something?" he asked.

"Of course."

"All of this is academically interesting. But there is something I don't understand about Christianity. Um, that is what you believe, right?"

"Yes." Jill nodded.

"Well, if God exists, why does he permit such evil in the world?" He was silent for a moment, as if trying to decide what to say next. "I have escaped out of North Korea. When I lived there, I saw terrible things. Why would God permit such things to happen?"

"Dr. Choi, God gives everyone a choice about what they believe. He does not force his will on anyone. If people decide to turn their back on Him, He allows them to make that choice and suffer the consequences."

"But why would God do that? Wouldn't it be better to prevent all the bad things that happen in the world?"

"The Bible doesn't answer that question directly. But I can tell you what I think. Are you aware that there has already been a revolt in Heaven?"

"Um, no."

"In the book of the prophet Isaiah, there is a conflict recorded between God and an angel called Lucifer. Lucifer tried to make himself equal to God. God kicked him out of Heaven. When he left, 1/3 of all of the other angels voluntarily left with Lucifer. This Lucifer is who we know of today as Satan, or the Devil. We believe that those angels have become evil spirits, and that they inhabit this world."

"I still do not understand why God would permit that."

"I believe that God never wants to have another revolt in his home, Heaven. So, he allows all men to make a choice between good and evil. For those who choose good, he will reward with an eternal existence in Heaven with him. For those who choose evil, God will dispose of them in the eternal burning trash heap known as Hell."

Dr. Choi was silent for a several minutes. "That seems a bit farfetched."

"Dr. Choi, what do you know of Jesus?"

"He is supposed to be a great prophet of God who died a cruel death."

"That is true. But there's more. You see, even if we wanted to, you and I could never hope to approach God. No person has lived a perfect life. We have all sinned. We have all made mistakes, done things we should not have done. Here, let me illustrate." She stood and walked over to a printer at the side of the room to pull out a blank piece of paper. Then she came back and sat down by Dr. Choi. "Let's say the left hand side of this paper is God, also known as perfect goodness, with absolutely no fault, sin, or mistake of any kind. On the right hand side is the Devil, also known as perfect evil, with all cruelty, hatred, and spite. Now, here's the pen. Where would you place yourself on this paper?"

Dr. Choi looked at her for a moment, then made a mark toward the middle, but closer to the "God" side of the paper.

"OK, so what you are saying is that you have some good, but also some bad in you. In other words, you are not perfectly good. But you are also not perfectly evil. Am I right?"

"Yes, of course. That is the way of all people."

"I agree. I just think we are probably more evil than good. Anyway, the point is that we can't get to God. We're not perfect."

"But a perfect God could just overlook that."

"If he simply ignored the evil part of us, and allowed us to come into his presence, then he wouldn't be perfectly good anymore, would he?"

"Why not?"

"Because if he allowed any evil, even a small amount, to dwell with him, we couldn't say he was perfect, with no hint of evil near him, could we?"

"I suppose not. And yet, you claim that people can go to live with God. So there must be a way to get rid of this evil."

"You're exactly right. Jesus is the way we can get rid of the evil. You see, God demands that there must be a punishment for sin. That is how we can get rid of our sin. That punishment is death. God has proclaimed that any sin, all sin, must be put to death."

"That sounds rather harsh."

"Yes, but God is perfect. Would you expect any less of God than to have high expectations?"

"I suppose not. So, if we die, then we can lose our sin?"

"No. God didn't mean a physical death, the death of our body. He demands the death of our sinful nature, our very soul."

"But if our body is dead, and our soul is dead, what is left to go to Heaven?"

"Nothing. So there is still a problem, right? We still haven't figured out a way for our souls to live forever with God."

"That's right."

"It's a real problem, all right. Without some help, there is no way that any of us could pay a sufficient price to be forgiven for our sin. That's why we appreciate the sacrifice of Jesus Christ. He saw the predicament of the human race, and asked God if he could pay the price of our sin for us."

"How did he do that?"

"First, he lived among us in human form. His mother was a woman, but his father was God. No man was his father. So he was actually man physically and God spiritually. That allowed him to do the second thing, live a perfect life without any sin at all. He did that, and of course he taught people about God. He also performed many miracles, through the power of God, that are recorded in the Bible,. Finally, he voluntarily took our place to pay for our sin. He was killed, and died a horribly tortured death. He stepped into our position and took our punishment. He was killed physically and spiritually. His death met God's high expectations, and we can lose our sins because of the terrible price he paid. So, you might say that Jesus is our 'Get Out of Hell Free' card."

Dr. Choi sat thinking this through. Finally, he said, "This is a very difficult concept."

"Yes, it is."

"Let me ask you this, then. You claim that Jesus performed miracles. Do you think that miracles can still happen for people today?"

"Absolutely. But a believer has to ask in the right way. They have to meet God's criteria for approaching and asking for salvation first. That means repentance, being truly sorry for sin. After that, baptism as

138

a public testimony of conversion. Then they have to ask for the miracle in the name of Jesus. After that, maybe, God will grant their request. But there is no guarantee."

Jill studied Dr. Choi, who was looking into the surface of the table, obviously thinking deeply. "Dr. Choi, may I ask you something?"

"Of course, you have answered my questions. I should be willing to answer yours."

"I have noticed that you appear to be very, um, not very well. You seemed very stressed and unhappy. Is everything all right? Is the reason you are asking about miracles is because you have a problem?"

Dr. Choi sighed. "There are things that I cannot discuss. I am sorry. But about my health, there is no concern. The project is quite stressful, and there are times that I do not sleep very well."

"May I pray for you?"

"That would be a nice thing for you to do."

So, Jill bowed her head and asked God to bless Dr. Choi. She prayed in faith, and in the name of Jesus. And in her innocence, she had no idea of the enormity of the effort that would be needed to bring peace and comfort to Dr. Choi's soul.

Chapter 8

"There. I think I see it. 10:00 o'clock, say five miles away." Tex was peering intently out the front window of the turboprop. He and Steve were currently assigned the duty of trying to detect *TimeFlyer* when it jumped back to the current time. They were acting as a chase plane for *TimeFlyer*'s first mission. Steve was relieved. Night was approaching. Already the Pacific Ocean below them was dark, and there were only 20 minutes of sunlight left at the altitude they were flying.

"Right on time," replied Steve. "Got to hand it to those folks with the timing. So far, they have been amazingly accurate jumping between times."

"*TimeFlyer* to Chase 1, do you read me?" came the familiar sound of Scoot's voice over the radio.

"Chase 1, we read you loud and clear. Welcome to the modern age, over."

"*TimeFlyer*, thanks. Smooth sailing, just a little bump during each jump. Nothing to it. You going to come alongside and do a visual?"

"Yeah, looks like you are going to be passing to my left. What's your altitude?"

"I'm reading 282." radioed Scoot, meaning he was at 28,200 feet in altitude.

"OK, I'm at 260. I'll stay here and approach underneath and behind."

TimeFlyer had been growing in size in their windscreen. It was slowly transiting right to left across their field of vision. Steve turned the commuter into a gentle left turn, preparing to close the gap between the two aircraft.

They completed the turn, and the commuter plane approached the flying behemoth from underneath. "Tell me when you want to change perspectives." Steve told Tex. Since Steve was flying, Tex was responsible for doing the visual inspection.

"OK. Let's just not get too close. We don't want to pull a *Valkyrie*," warned Tex. He was referring to a terrible accident that had occurred in 1966 when the Air Force was flight-testing a prototype high-speed bomber. *Valkyrie* had just successfully finished being certified for Mach 3 flight, and was flying in formation at subsonic speeds with some other airplanes for publicity photos. The closest aircraft to *Valkyrie* in the formation was an F-104. The photographers, flying around the periphery of the formation in a small business jet, requested the formation close up several times. The pilots complied with each request. Just as the photographers were finishing their work, the F-104 got caught in the vortex of air that trailed from the wing of the huge bomber. The F-104 had flipped upside down and rotated 180 degrees, then been pulled right across *Valkyrie's* back, breaking off both of the aircraft's vertical stabilizers and part of its left wing. The pilot of the F-104 had been killed immediately. The copilot of *Valkyrie* had been unable to eject, and was killed when the aircraft impacted the ground just a little over a minute later. The only other occupant, the pilot, was able to eject just before impact.

Steve eased the commuter airplane in behind *TimeFlyer*, as Tex examined its lower surface. "Everything looks fine. Let's go look up top."

Steve thumbed the microphone. "Chase 1 to *TimeFlyer*. Your underside looks fine. We're going to fall behind, then approach above you from your right." He backed off, then pulled right, climbed to flight level 295, and approached *TimeFlyer* from the right.

Tex examined the upper surface carefully. "Looks OK up here, too. Let's get these birds home."

Steve thumbed the switch. "Everything looks good. I'll get clearance to transit California's airspace. You go first, and I'll follow." After being acknowledged, he flipped the radio to a different frequency and requested the appropriate clearance from California air traffic controllers. The process took just a couple of minutes, and they were able to turn and head inland. It took another 65 minutes before

141

the lights of Minion Lake appeared below them. Steve circled the field twice as *TimeFlyer* touched down and gradually slowed, using up about 6,000 feet of runway before finally pulling off onto the taxiway to head back to her hanger. Steve lined up with the runway, landed, and arrived at his hanger just as *TimeFlyer* was cutting her engines. Steve pulled the turboprop into the hanger and parked it. He and Tex ran through their post-flight inspection quickly, then exited the aircraft and headed for *TimeFlyer*.

The hatch hadn't opened by the time they got to *TimeFlyer*. Shutting down a nuclear powered airplane was not quite the same as parking a commuter aircraft in a hanger. Eventually, a lower hatch popped open on the underside of *TimeFlyer* and a ladder was extended. The flight engineers were the first ones out. It took Scoot and Jake another 10 minutes to complete their post-flight routine and paperwork before they clambered out of the big airplane.

Steve and Tex met them at the bottom of the ladder. "Nothin' to it, man. You just point the nose at the space-warp hole and pop out in another age. Fabulous. What an incredible invention." Scoot was clearly enamored with the big bird and its capabilities.

"Easy as pie." Jake confirmed.

"Alright. Let's get to debriefing." And they all turned toward the meeting room on the side of the hanger.

* * * *

Five days later, anyone who was qualified to be in *TimeFlyer* when she flew had assembled in one of the small auditoriums. They were being briefed on the plans for the next flight. Steve and Tex were the designated pilots for this mission, but Scoot and Jake and their aircrew were in attendance as well. Steve thought he knew everyone who was flight qualified, but there were several people in the room he didn't recognize.

Brian Masulis was giving the briefing. "You already know we plan on going back 1,000 years on this flight," he was saying. "Not only is our jump back in time longer, but the flight is going to last 48 hours. Up to this point, the location has not been disclosed. Here's the reason why. If things go well, we hope to have you land and do a little exploring. In addition, we want you to bring back some biological specimens. A Dodo. Two of them, in fact."

"Steve was already planning on coming back." Scoot's voice interrupted the presentation. "Who else did you have in mind?" Brian couldn't answer immediately because of the burst of laughter from the group. Scoot had made his voice sound so naive and innocent that Steve had to laugh right along with them.

"Alright, quiet down. Quiet down folks." Brian was trying to restore order. "Hey, it wasn't that funny!" The laughter finally subsided enough for him to continue. "Alright, let me try that again. We want you to bring back two birds, Dodo birds to be exact. From the island of Mauritius. It's an island off the east coast of Africa, in the Indian Ocean. Dodo birds were discovered on that island in 1598 and they became extinct less than 100 years later. If you go back 1000 years, the island should not be inhabited by people. We want you to bring back these birds so that we have living proof that we are actually transiting time. Bringing living examples of an extinct species should be convincing enough."

"That is a long flight," observed Steve.

"Yes, that's why the mission will last 48 hours. It will take a good 12 hours to fly there, another 12 hours to fly back. We'll have some places we will want you to fly over on the way there and back. There are some glaciers in the Rocky Mountains that we want you to get a good long look at. That data will be of interest to our climatologists. Then, as you approach Mauritius, you will fly over the island of Madagascar. We'll have you try to spot some human settlements and take pictures of them as well. Unobserved, of course.

"In order to capture the, uh, birds, we're sending along a team of animal handlers. Let me introduce to you Dr. Michael Zalander and Dr. Patricia Shulz." A sprinkling of polite applause welcomed the two people who stood up. "They will be heading up a team of six people total who will be joining you on this expedition.

"*TimeFlyer* is being outfitted so that you all can get some rest on the airplane. We are adding some cots, and some cooking gear, things like that. In essence, you will be traveling in the world's most expensive and spartan recreational vehicle. The animal team will be resting during the flight, the rest of you will be resting while they are out trying to capture the animals."

Listening to the rest of the briefing, Steve wondered how a couple of birds were going to enjoy sitting in *TimeFlyer* for 12 hours. Specifically, how much he would enjoy sitting in *TimeFlyer* for 12 hours along with the birds. He hoped they weren't too noisy. Or stinky.

* * * *

The outbound flight ended up so uneventful Tex started complaining of boredom halfway across the Atlantic. The transition 1000 years back had turned out to feel like nothing more than a couple of air bumps. Their navigation computers had locked on to their reference stars and confirmed a successful transition back in time. They had found and photographed the glaciers without incident. Steve had turned over the controls to Tex and let him fly the rest of the way to their destination. They had indeed found human settlements on Madagascar, and spent almost an hour circling and taking pictures and video of the happenings in a small village on the eastern side of the Island.

They continued on from Madagascar and began their descent toward Mauritius. There were several challenges involved in landing *TimeFlyer*. First, they had to determine where there might be coral reefs, which would rip the bottom out of their aircraft and end any chance of takeoff. They had to determine possible landing and takeoff approaches from eight points of the compass: after all, the wind might shift between landing and takeoff, and they might not be able to takeoff in the same direction as they landed. Second, they had to try to determine at what point they were in the tidal cycle. It would be no good to beach their aircraft at high tide and they try to depart during low tide- they would be firmly grounded until the tide came back in. Last, but certainly not least, they had to watch the weather. A powerful storm would certainly be cause for aborting the mission.

They reached the island and circled it six times, looking for signs of human habitation. There were none, although the birds could be easily seen. After getting a good feel for the geography, including possible coral reefs, Tex turned *TimeFlyer* into the wind and made an uneventful landing on the ocean's surface. They turned the airplane toward the island, intending to get as close as they could to a strip of beach on the island's south side. One of the advantages of *TimeFlyer's* shape was that she had a draft of only five feet, despite her weight. They slowly approached the shore, Tex changing the power settings of the six propellers in order to keep heading toward the beach, and finally bumped gently against the sand. There were two anchors in the front of *TimeFlyer* and two in the stern. Steve deployed all four, and then they began shutdown procedures.

It was only a short time later that they saw the animal capture people piloting their bright yellow inflatable boat toward the shore. Steve had to chuckle as he saw the ungainly flightless Dodos waddling around near the edge of the trees. The animal team was able to walk within a couple feet of the birds before they began to shy away. Steve could see how they had earned the name Dodo. The presence of humans didn't seem to bother them at all. They had lived for hundreds of years on the island with no natural predators, and they were more curious of this invading biped than frightened.

Flight duties finished, they made their way up through the top hatch and into the tropical sunshine. "Now, this is more like it," announced Tex. "A guy could get used to this. I think I'm going to test the water." He stripped off his shirt, shoes, socks, and pants, revealing a red and blue swimsuit underneath. He walked to the back of *TimeFlyer*, where the trailing part of the wing was just slightly above the water, took a deep breath and dove over the side.

Steve walked back and looked down. Tex was frolicking in the waves as if he had never seen an ocean before. "Oh, man, this is great. The water is perfect. Are you going to come in?"

"No, I'd better go get the rifle and stand watch," replied Steve. They had been warned about the possibility of sharks, and Steve didn't feel like losing a limb to a carnivorous fish. He stood and watched as Tex swam and dove. He was soon joined by several of the flight engineers. After about 20 minutes, he saw a smooth torpedo-shaped figure swim a little to the left of where he was standing and glide underneath *TimeFlyer*'s shadow. "Hey, folks, you've got company," he announced.

"OK." Tex reluctantly swam over to *TimeFlyer* and reached up to Steve. "Here, give me a hand."

"Better me than the shark," commented Steve and he helped pull Tex over the edge of the wing. "Help me get these others aboard. Then we better try to get some sleep."

* * * *

General Collins had set up a meeting with Nola and Dan. They were meeting in Nola's office, in the Department of the Interior building. Nola was explaining how a lot of questions were being asked of them about the missing money in the budget. This was the second year when several million dollars of federal money seemed to be missing in the department's budget. Nola and Dan were being pressured on several fronts. The press had picked up the story, and Randy Patchinsky had written an editorial condemning black projects in general, and voicing concern that the practice seemed to be spreading out beyond the military.

After the editorial had run, most of the pressure on Nola and Dan had come, ironically enough, from their own staff. The directors in charge of the individual areas of responsibility hadn't initially picked up on the missing money. Once the editorial ran, however, the directors seemed to attack en masse. Dan couldn't blame them. They were the ones who had to deal with budgets that weren't nearly large enough to allow them to accomplish all of their objectives. The directors had demanded an accounting of the missing money, each of them hoping to gain a bit for use in their own projects. Nola and Dan had repeated the statement about not being able to discuss the money, but they were getting worn down by the sheer number of inquiries. Nola had expressed a concern to Dan that the topic was impacting the morale of the department.

General Collins listened to Nola and Dan as they expressed their concern about the inadequacy of the answers that the General had provided for them. "The biggest concern, of course, is morale." Nola was speaking. "General, I have a very good staff. I am proud of the work that they do, and the way they generally manage to accomplish their tasks with limited resources. However, they have expressed the fact that they feel they are being cheated out of the full measure of their funding. I am afraid that some of them might become frustrated enough to look for other jobs, and I really don't want to face a large turnover in staff because of this."

"Well, I have some good news. You are authorized to reveal a bit more about the project. This is going to go to your function directors only, for now." The General knew full well that as soon as this bit of information was given to Nola's staff, someone would slip it to the press. That was part of the plan. He went on to elaborate. "You are authorized to say that the money is part of a secret project. This secret project is being conducted in cooperation with the military. You are authorized to tell your staff that this is a high-risk project, but also a high reward project. You have decided that the risk is worth taking because the potential results are so positive."

"That's all?" asked Nola.

"That's all for now."

"Have there been any significant developments in the last couple of months that you can tell us about?" pressed Dan. "We want to know that progress is being made."

"I am going to tell you a bit more, but please don't reveal the following information to your staff. This is for your ears alone. Are you comfortable keeping a bit more information from your staff?"

"Absolutely." replied Nola.

"Very well. I can tell you that DNA has been synthesized from fossils. The lab is at the point where the DNA is being injected into living cells. The lab has had some success getting these cells to begin to grow and transcribe the DNA. However, they haven't gotten the cells to grow to a point where they can survive on their own."

"So progress is being made?" This question came from Nola. The General could see that she needed to be reassured that all the attacks she was withstanding were worth the effort.

"Excellent progress is being made. If we continue at this pace, we will be able to provide living examples of extinct species well before the initial projection of five years from the beginning of the project."

"It can't be too soon."

"Nola, think about what it will be like to hold a press conference to reveal a living species that had been driven to extinction," encouraged the General. "Do you think anyone is going to be criticizing you at that point for spending a few million dollars of federal money for helping to sponsor this risky project? Believe me, your staff members, and the press too, will be falling all over themselves wanting to get involved in the project."

Dan grinned at Nola. "We're still going to have people banging on our doors, but for an entirely different reason."

"I can hardly wait," said Nola dryly. But she seemed more content.

"It will be a press conference to remember, believe me," Collins replied. And despite the deception, or maybe because of it, he too was looking forward to the event.

* * * *

Back at the base, Dr. Stark was having a rather intense conversation with Brian Masulis. General Collins was conferenced in via speakerphone. "I tell you, she has absolutely no credibility left. I don't want her on the project."

"Her performance has been excellent. Just because she believes in the Bible isn't grounds to dismiss her," countered Brian.

"Maybe not. But with her belief, she brings an enormous number of prejudices, which can and will affect her work. Religious zealots cannot be objective. It's impossible. They believe in things that cannot be seen or proven. That's not science. Doesn't the fact that she affirms things that cannot even be tested concern you?"

"It's something to be aware of," came the General's voice over the speakerphone. "But she is a fairly talented woman. And she has been very helpful in explaining your theory to your colleagues on base."

"It's not her ability to explain my theory that concerns me. It's her ability to understand, implement, and extend the theory that is at risk. You have to be objective. Losing objectivity could send us off on a tangent that will take years to correct."

"The law is very clear about freedom of religion," responded the General. "Our country has managed to survive over 200 years inhabited by any number of religious people, and our science and technology is the best of any country in the world. It seems to me that we haven't suffered too much from religious zealotry."

"But most of those people are, you know, farmers, plumbers, people who work with their hands and not their heads."

"I disagree," responded the General. "I have met a number of scientists over the years that were quite religious, as well as being quite well respected in their disciplines. In my experience, the two are not mutually exclusive."

Dr. Stark sighed. "But they weren't working in gravity wave theory either."

"That's true," admitted the General. There was silence for a moment. "Andy, I can understand your concern. But there is another angle here that you may not have considered. If we dismiss her, and she finds out the real reason she was fired, she will have the right to file a lawsuit against the government. After that, it will be impossible to keep this thing a secret. We have had amazingly good fortune up to this point keeping *TimeFlyer* under wraps. Are you willing to take the risk of exposing all of this work to the world just so you can get one Christian fired?"

Dr. Stark's face flushed. "I didn't think of that," he muttered.

"Well, I think it is a big risk. Too big to risk firing Jill. She probably isn't the suing type, but all it takes is one slick-talking lawyer to get her to agree to file. And she will have a case."

Dr. Stark swore loudly.

"Look, Dr. Stark," said Brian, "I know you are concerned about her. But I don't think we have enough grounds to dismiss her. I think what you need to do is make sure all of her work is reviewed by yourself or some of your other staff. If you find a mistake, then we will have grounds for dismissal. But until then, I think you are going to have to accommodate her."

"So now I have extra work to review all of the work of our little superstitious angel."

"Don't you review all of her work now?" asked Brian.

"Humph, I don't like this one bit," responded Stark, avoiding the question.

"I agree with Brian," came the General's voice. "If you find a problem with her work, then I don't have a problem dismissing her. But at this point, I don't want to risk a lawsuit."

Without a word, Dr. Stark jumped up and stomped out of the room.

"He walked out." Brian spoke toward the conference phone.

"He'll probably get over it. But keep an eye on him, and let me know if does anything dumb. He's obviously pretty worked up about this," came the General's voice.

"More worked up than I have ever seen him before. I'll watch him, Sir." Brian added.

"OK, talk to you later." And with that, the call ended.

* * * *

Steve was dreaming. He was a boy, fishing at a pond in Kansas with his dad. Night was falling, and the frogs were starting their croaking. He had just hooked a nice size fish when a big frog, the biggest he had ever seen, hopped out of the pond and started croaking at him...

Steve opened his eyes, but the noise didn't stop. It wasn't a croaking, exactly, more like a Hawk with a baritone voice suffering from a head cold. He got up and walked to the door of the room where he had been sleeping. Down the hall, he saw the animal folks moving a cage into the storage area. The horrible noise was coming from inside the cage.

Steve walked down the hall and stepped in. There was already one cage in place, and this second one was being maneuvered and strapped to the wall next to the first. Sure enough, the occupants were two of the strangest birds Steve had ever seen. Their bodies were shaped roughly like a chicken, only much larger. Their heads came up to slightly above his waist. But their beaks were the most unusual. They were big, and there was no obvious transition between their beaks and the rest of their heads. The front of their beaks extended slightly over the edge of the lower beak, and ended in a rather sharp-looking point. The birds were a mix of cream and brown – most of their bodies were brown, but their chest and neck were of a creamy color. The color wasn't unattractive, Steve had to admit. But that beak!

"Easiest animal capture I have ever done." Dr. Zalander was standing next to Steve. "All we did was grab some fruit from one of the Calvaria trees, up higher than the Dodos could reach. Threw it in the cage, and in went the birds. Amazing. Almost no fear of humans at all. I've never seen such docile animals. No wonder they became extinct."

"Will become extinct," corrected Steve.

"Yes, yes, I suppose I am not used to living before my time."

Steve checked his watch. "Looks like we have about 16 hours before we have to leave. Any chance I can get a ride ashore and take a look around?"

"Sure. We'll probably be making another trip in about an hour or so."

"Great. I'll clean up and catch up with you."

The remainder of their time at the island consisted of some hiking and picking up a good supply of fruit from the Calvaria trees. These trees had stopped reproducing when the Dodos became extinct. For some reason, the seeds of the tree needed to be passed through the birds before they would germinate. Dr. Zalandar was not sure what other food would be suitable for the birds, and he wanted to bring along plenty of what he knew they could eat. His counterpart, Dr. Shulz, was spending the entire time on the island, observing the birds and their behavior.

Steve spent eight hours on the island, and then returned to *TimeFlyer* for some more sleep. When he woke up, there were two hours left until departure. He went topside to get some air and check the weather. The wind had picked up, and the ocean looked rougher than it had earlier. It was still sunny and clear, however, and the tide was coming in.

The time for departure arrived, and they got everything stowed. The flight engineers had already fired up the 'tea kettle,' as Tex referred to their nuclear reactor, and Steve raised the anchors. He reversed the propellers. There was a slight grating noise as *TimeFlyer* slipped off her sandy perch, and then they were backing away from the island. When they had backed away a few hundred feet, Steve pitched the propellers forward and turned the aircraft away from the wind. The wind was from the Northwest; probably steady at about 15 miles per hour, he estimated. They could feel *TimeFlyer* begin to pitch and roll as they came out of the shelter of the island and the waves began to work on her. There were whitecaps out there. Steve didn't mind the wind, though. It should help them get airborne.

When they were southeast of the island, Steve increased power and went around the east side of it, traveling south to north. After a few minutes, there was a clear stretch of water toward their northwest. "Ready for takeoff?"

"Air injection system activated. We're ready." reported Tex.

Steve moved all six thrust levers all the way forward. He could feel the surge as *TimeFlyer* started moving forward. The ride was rougher than before as *TimeFlyer* fought through the chop. Steve noticed it was taking a long time to reach flying speed. The wind, which he thought would help them lift off, was raising waves high enough that their steady impact slowed *TimeFlyer* down. They continued to bounce through the chop, *TimeFlyer* straining to break free from the pesky waves that held her back. They struggled along for two miles, then three, then four. The occasional croak of the Dodos was beginning to get more constant. Steve was beginning to worry. Temperatures were OK; the additional cooling along the bottom of the aircraft was working as designed. What worried him was the sickening realization that they might not be able to get airborne.

"Call back to the flight engineers and see if they can get us any more power." Steve ordered. Tex made the call and listened to the reply as Steve maneuvered to clear an island approaching from the horizon.

"They say they're giving you all they've got." Tex reported.

Steve pursed his lips, and continued to try to coax the plane airborne. The five-mile mark passed, then six. "This isn't going to work," he said.

"Too many waves." Tex agreed.

Steve saw another small island on the horizon. With a sudden inspiration, he steered right toward it. They continued to bounce as the island began to grow in their windscreen. It grew bigger, but Steve began to feel the change that he had been hoping for. He gritted his teeth and said a short prayer. If this didn't work, they were going to hit the beach going nearly 100 miles per hour. The bumpy ride suddenly smoothed, *TimeFlyer's* speed jumped 20 miles per hour. The island was now filling their windscreen. Steve pulled back on the yoke, and *TimeFlyer* climbed into the air, barely clearing the trees on the edge of the island.

"Whew, that was a close one," he breathed.

"Good job," responded Tex. "That was one gutsy move."

"I knew the only way we were going to get airborne was to get out of the waves. I figured the leeward side of the island should be a lot calmer, where the island blocks part of the wind. It was, but the effect stayed a lot closer to the island than I thought."

"I figured that is what you were doing. I was just hoping we weren't going to hit a coral reef."

Steve just shook his head. He had been so focused on getting out of the waves that he hadn't even thought of the possibility. He made a mental note to give thanks for a successful takeoff later. One more item in a long list of things to which he owed a debt of gratitude to his Heavenly Father.

* * * *

Four days after *TimeFlyer* returned from its flight to Mauritius, Nola received a call from General Collins. "Good news, Nola. We've got two animals from the project. Remember that news conference I promised? Let's get it scheduled."

Chapter 9

Randy found Melanie at her desk. As he had suspected, she had turned out to be inquisitive enough to be offered a full time job as a reporter at the *Times-Herald*. She had accepted the position as soon as it was offered, which had been in the fall of her Senior year in college. Randy liked to think that at least part of the reason she had accepted the position was because of his mentoring during the previous couple of summers.

"Thought you might like to see this press briefing invitation." He handed her an envelope.

Melanie took the envelope and extracted the letter. It was from the Department of the Interior, inviting the press to a briefing that promised to reveal '...an extraordinary development for science, humanity, and the environment.' But it wasn't that paragraph that was the most enticing. The next to last paragraph requested the press' cooperation for a completely silent environment for a brief part of the conference. It requested that motorized auto-advance mechanisms be removed from cameras, and stated unequivocally that no flash photography would be allowed. 'The stage will be lighted sufficiently to allow photographs to be taken with daylight-rated film.'

"This is different. Have you ever had a press briefing where these conditions were requested?" she asked.

"Nope. Never. And I've been a journalist for almost 22 years. Strangest invitation I've ever received."

"Are you going to attend?"

"Yes. Want to come along?"

"Sure. But why me?"

"Remember Bohemia? I think this must be related."

"Ah, the manure project." Bohemia had long ago been dropped from their lexicon, replaced by the laughable euphemism.

"That's it. Remember when you finally got some information? They said it was a high-risk, high-value project. They must have developed something."

"I think I still have the notes." Melanie put down the letter and swung around to open a file cabinet. She pulled out a folder. "Here it is." She flipped through the few pages it contained, "We got that answer from one of the superintendents. We never did get anything official from anyone over there. When's the briefing?"

"Two weeks from this coming Friday. It will be at the Department of the Interior building."

With the folder still in her lap, Melanie swung around to pull up her calendar on the computer. "What time?"

"10:00 AM sharp."

"It's on the calendar." She was adding the entry as he spoke. "When do we meet?"

"Let's head out of here at 9:00, that should give us plenty of time."

"Are you bringing along a camera crew?"

"I haven't talked to them yet, but I thought I would bring one still camera and one video camera operator."

"Sounds good. Thanks for the invite. It'll be interesting to see what they've really been up to."

* * * *

Gail picked up the phone that was clamoring for her attention. "Hello, Labinsky residence." She listened for a moment, and then covered the receiver. "Dan, go to the bedroom and get on the extension. It's Jill."

Dan put down the paper, rose from his recliner, and went back to their bedroom. He picked up the receiver in time to hear Jill saying "...he is being a real stinker."

"Hi, Jill. Who's being a stinker?" he asked.

"Oh, the lead supervisor on this project. We were getting along great until I told him I was a Christian and believed in the Bible. He just about came unglued. He's been petty and mean ever since. He tries to embarrass me in front of the other researchers, and makes fun of anything he can find. I am getting really tired of it."

"How long ago did you tell him you were a Christian?" asked Gail.

"Almost a month ago. I was hoping that he would just get over it, but he really has it out for Christians. Well, not just Christians, exactly. He seems to have a problem with just about any religion. He says that it gets in the way of objectivity, and that it's a bunch of superstition."

"Sounds like God is using you there," commented Dan.

"Well, maybe. It isn't very much fun, though."

"I'm sorry to hear that. How are things going besides the stinker?" he asked.

"Well, the rest of the project is going well. We're getting really good results from the experiments. Everybody seems very satisfied with our progress. I wish I could tell you more, but you know how it is."

"I understand. How is Steve?"

"Doing just great. He was challenged to a tennis match earlier today, so he's out right now. You know him, he can't back down from a challenge. You know, if someone told him that he couldn't scale Everest barefoot, he would be on the next airplane to Nepal without any shoes. Hey, did I ever tell you about his copilot?" She described Tex and his escapades at the rodeo. "Anyway, he is really a cool customer. Nothing phases him. Steve says he is really bummed if his life isn't in danger at least once a week."

"Heh, sounds like an interesting guy. Hope I get to meet him sometime."

"Just look for the Korean with an English accent in an oversize cowboy hat and boots. He's hard to miss."

"So, when are you going to come home for a visit?" queried Gail. She was always glad to have Jill visit, but she had an ulterior motive. She had worried for years whether Jill was ever going to find a man interested enough in her unique talents to marry her. With that issue settled, her mind was now turning to the possibility of a grandchild or two. Or three. She wanted to see Jill to try to figure out whether or not she was pregnant. She knew she wasn't excited at the thought of having a baby quite yet. But that didn't stop her from hoping for a blessed accident to occur.

"Well, I was wondering if we could come out the weekend after next. I'd like to get back and see you and all the people we left behind by coming to Nevada. How's your calendar look?"

"Hold on a minute, let me check," Gail replied.

"Don't I have that news conference on Friday?" asked Dan.

"Yes. Your father is going to be attending a big news conference. He won't be speaking; he'll just be on the platform. The President will be speaking, along with Dan's boss, Lola Nielson. Then, Sunday evening, we have potluck dinner at church. There's nothing else on the calendar."

"What's the news conference going to be about?" queried Jill.

"Ah, ah, ah... You're not the only one in this family with secrets," answered Dan jovially.

"Well, is it open to the public? If we came out Thursday, could we come and watch?"

"That's a thought," responded Dan. "It's not open to the public, no, but Lola had some tickets yesterday. She said she would give me five if I could use them. I told her no, your mother didn't seem very interested in attending. I can check and see if she still has them. Maybe you could convince your mother to attend."

"If Jill wants to go, I'll go." Gail volunteered.

"Great. Dad, why don't you see if you can get those tickets? Steve and I will fly out on Thursday and spend the weekend with you. We'll probably fly back Sunday afternoon. It will be a nice change of pace."

"OK. I'll send you an e-mail and let you know if those tickets are still available."

* * * *

The morning of the news conference turned out to be cool and overcast. It was scheduled to begin at 10:00 AM, but Dan urged them to get there early. Because of the President's attendance, everyone knew security would be tight, and laggards would be turned away. They left the house at 7:30 and caught the train into the city with the rest of the commuters. They all got off the subway and headed toward the Interior Building.

Once inside, Dan directed them toward the auditorium where the news conference was going to be held, then he went upstairs to his office. Even at this early hour, news crews were in full swing setting up and checking equipment. Since they had over an hour to spare, they toured the museum that was housed in the building. When they returned to the auditorium, they were surprised at the number of news media people in attendance – there were at least twice as many people present as there had been previously. Gail made them stop for a few minutes as she downed a second cup of coffee. Then the family made their way toward the door and went through the security check. Their seats were in row 12, a little to the left of center, and they managed to find them by 9:40. They found that the 20 minutes passed quickly because there was so much activity, as everyone scurried around preparing for the start of the conference. At 9:55, most of the dignitaries were seated on the stage, including Dan, who spotted them and waved briefly. Shortly afterward, powerful lights came up to illuminate the stage. Promptly at 10:00 AM, Nola Nielson stepped forward, introduced herself, and then introduced the President, who stepped from behind the curtain at the side of the stage to take his place at the lectern.

"Thank you, Nola. Ladies and Gentlemen, I take great pleasure in being able to be with you today. I am pleased to announce a tremendous leap forward in technology, which will bring benefits to all of us. Over the last three years, the Department of the Interior has been funding a research effort aimed at gathering biological information for extinct species of plants and animals. Thanks to the tireless efforts of our research teams, they have been able to reconstruct the genetic sequences from a few species. The genetic sequences are beneficial, of course, but it would be more beneficial if we could actually use those sequences to resurrect the plants and animals from extinction. Well, our researches have been able to resurrect one of these animals, which you will see in a few minutes. As you can imagine, this is a tremendous breakthrough for the biological sciences. With this technology, we have the potential to resurrect species that have been dead for hundreds or thousands of years. The challenge for resurrecting species appears to be in getting a suitable quantity of intact genetic material. In one case we have been able to successfully do just that, and we have resurrected it from extinction."

Steve shot a questioning glance at Jill, who returned her own. "Sounds like we're not the only ones messing with extinct species," he whispered. She nodded, and they turned their attention back to the stage.

"I am going to turn the meeting back over to Director Nielsen, who is going to be showing you the results of our research. Nola?"

"Thank you, Mr. President. Ladies and Gentlemen, I am going to have to ask for your cooperation at this time. The animals that I am about to show you seem to be very docile. However, for their safety and yours, I am going to ask you to be very quiet while they are with us up here. We do not want to startle them. I am also going to ask that you refrain from any flash photography while they are on stage, as we requested in the invitation to this press conference. I acknowledge that this is very unusual. If nothing else, I will go down in history as the only person in government who got the press to be silent during a press conference." A swell of laughter stopped her for a second, and she looked up and smiled good-naturedly at her audience. "Now, Ladies and Gentlemen, if I could ask for your complete silence, we will be joined by our miracle animals."

Except for the noise of the cameras clicking, the room became silent. The audience followed Nola's gaze as she turned expectantly toward stage right. A tall, thin man stepped into view, walking backwards, and holding something in his hand. He was obviously trying to lure something out onto the stage. Steve didn't recognize the man at first, because he had his back to them. And then, to Steve's shocked amazement, the two Dodo Birds strutted into view. Steve stared at them, and then at the man leading them on stage.

It was Dr. Michael Zalander.

He led the birds across the stage. The audience was absolutely still. The birds strutted like oversized chickens, and occasionally he rewarded their progress with a piece of some sort of food. Their beaks were just as outrageous as Steve remembered. Occasionally, the birds stopped and looked around curiously. They slowly made their way across the stage, around the lectern, and then disappeared off to stage left.

The stillness lasted for another 20 seconds or so. Then Nola appeared to get some kind of signal from off stage. She turned back to the audience. "Thank you for your cooperation," she said, and that was the end of her control of the conference. Every reporter jumped up, waving their hands wildly in the air shouting questions in her direction. The noise was so intense it started to give Steve a headache. After trying several times to try to regain control of the news conference, Nola finally appeared to give up, and the dignitaries on

158

stage stood up and started making their way offstage. Some went back behind the curtain, but Nola, Dan, and other officials in the Department of the Interior were obviously trying to make themselves available to answer some of the questions from the reporters on a more personal basis. It was utter pandemonium.

"I think we should leave now," shouted Gail at Steve and Jill. They nodded, and the three stood up and made their way to the nearest exit.

The hallway outside was equally as chaotic. Reporters were standing in front of cameras, reporting back to their headquarters the dramatic news of the resurrected Dodo Birds. Gail, Steve and Jill wound their way around three camera/reporter combinations before finally making their way to a quieter section of the hallway.

"My goodness. Are all press conferences like that?" wondered an obviously flustered Gail.

Steve and Jill didn't respond. Jill was looking at Steve with a questioning look in her eyes. He responded to her unanswered question. "Yes, those were the birds." he said.

He glanced back down the hallway toward the press mob and spotted another familiar figure. "Look who else is here," he said. Gail and Jill turned to look. Steve raised his hand and waved to get the man's attention. It was Paul Schneider.

To Steve, it didn't appear that Paul was entirely happy to see them, although he made his way over and shook their hands. "Hello, all. I'm surprised to see you two here." He nodded toward Steve and Jill. "I thought you were working out West."

"We are. We just came home for a long weekend. Dad invited us to the press conference," Jill replied. "We didn't know it was going to turn into a mob."

"It usually isn't like this. We didn't expect the news people to respond this, shall we say, enthusiastically." As soon as Paul had seen Steve and Jill, he started putting the pieces together, and was mentally kicking himself for not seeing the obvious connection between Dan Labinsky, working at the Department of the Interior, and Steve and Jill working at Project Opera. It was a security person's worse nightmare. He was well aware of the amount of work it had taken to lead the press in a direction away from Project Opera. The idea had been to credit the appearance of the birds to a biological breakthrough. There was no doubt the press would be starting to dig around, trying to find out more about this spectacular project. Having them chase the biological angle would keep them busy, and hopefully well away, from making any connection with Project Opera. But now, standing right in front of him, were two people who knew the truth, and could blow the whole cover story wide open. He groaned internally as he tried to think of something else to say. "So, you're just staying for the weekend, you say?"

"Yeah, we're heading back Sunday after church. Will you be there?" asked Steve.

"Plan to. Karen and the kids will be glad to see you. You know how much the boys look up to you," said Paul. Steve smiled and nodded. Ever since they had seen him in uniform, it was obvious they were in awe.

"I won't wear my uniform tomorrow. Maybe I can get them to talk to me," he said.

"They would like that," responded Paul. Then, trying to be casual, he said "Can I talk to you alone for a second?"

"Sure." Steve was still smiling, but his eyes were questioning.

"We'll wander down the hall to look at the displays," said Gail, and she and Jill turned and began walking down the hall.

Paul looked at Steve. "Does Dan know anything?"

"About what?"

"You know."

"I'm not sure what I can say."

Paul sighed and glanced around. No one was within earshot. "OK, I'm going to level with you. I'm head of internal security for Project Opera. I know all about what you guys are doing." He smiled ruefully. "What did you think of our press conference here?"

Steve's mind was racing as well. He was trying to figure out what he could say and what he couldn't. This very well could be a counter-espionage attempt, and he didn't want to say anything that could be construed as violating security. "Well, I guess I would say that it a bit inaccurate," he said slowly.

Paul nodded. "We're doing that on purpose. We want to steer any nosy investigators in the wrong direction. Steve, I'm going to ask you again. Does Dan know anything, especially about your work on Project Opera?"

Steve shook his head. "No, not a thing."

"So the fact that you and Jill are here is a complete coincidence?" pressed Paul.

"Yes." Paul obviously was skeptical. "Look, Jill called her folks a couple of weeks ago and arranged a visit home over the weekend. Dan invited us to the press conference. Since Dan was going to be sitting on stage, and the President was going to attend, it sounded like something important was going to be announced. Dan told us he could get seats, so we agreed to come. We had no idea what was going to be announced today. Dan didn't tell us anything, and we haven't told Dan anything. Believe me, I about fell out of my chair when I saw those birds." Steve stopped talking, suddenly worried that he had said too much.

"Well, I have to say, seeing you two here is a nightmare for me. No offense," Paul added hastily. "But if you, Jill and Dan put your heads together, you could blow this whole thing sky high. Please, Steve, I know you're a good guy, please don't tell Dan anything. And make sure Jill doesn't tell him anything either. The less he knows, the better for everybody."

"Yeah, sure. Hey, we're on your side," said Steve. "I can appreciate what you're trying to do here." He was quiet for a second. "So, are you the one that is sicking all these counter-espionage people on us?"

Paul nodded, "I guess I owe you that. Yeah, that's part of my responsibilities."

"Let's make a deal," said Steve with a smile, knowing full well that Paul had the authority to get him tossed into jail somewhere and throw away the key. "I promise not to say anything to anybody if you pull your spooks off me and Jill." It worked. He could see Paul relax a little bit.

"I'll take that deal. Hey, it really is good to see you. No offense?"

"Absolutely not. Bit of a surprise for everyone today. I do hope to see your family Sunday."

"That you shall," promised Paul. "I'd better get back to the mob." He shook Steve's hand, and then turned away. "See you Sunday."

Steve turned and trotted after Gail and Jill.

* * * *

Jill had been quite obviously curious about Paul talking to Steve alone. Steve hadn't said anything about it until they were on the subway, heading back toward Virginia and the Labinsky home. He managed to get Jill in a seat behind Gail, and ended up talking quietly

161

to her for most of the ride. Gail didn't seem to mind being ignored. Apparently, she was content to enjoy the lulling sounds of the train, after the noise and chaos of the news conference. By the time they got off the train, Jill understood the situation as well as Steve and Paul. He made her promise not to say anything to her parents.

Jill found herself being so careful about what she said for the rest of the weekend that, by the time Sunday morning arrived, she was ready to head back to Nevada. She wasn't used to keeping secrets from her parents. But she still wanted to attend church with them.

Church turned out to be a welcome distraction from the stress of keeping secrets. She enjoyed seeing the people in the congregation where her family had attended for so many years. When Paul, Karen, and their children arrived, the Labinsky family was standing in the hallway. The boys weren't nearly as shy as before. When they spotted Steve, they ran right up to him and tackled his legs. Paul and Karen pulled them off and shooed them away to Sunday School. As they usually did, the adults all sat together during the service.

Afterward, Pastor Howie made a special point of coming up to Steve and Jill to find out how things were going. Jill explained her situation with Dr. Stark. The pastor was sympathetic. "Don't get discouraged. You are obviously right where God wants you to be, and you are standing up for Jesus. There is nothing that pleases God more. There will probably be more challenges ahead. Don't back down. God is obviously trying to get through to Dr. Stark, and he's using you to do it. Maybe some others, too. Keep it up," he encouraged. "And if you need someone to talk to, call me. Day or night. This Dr. Stark would be a powerful ally for Christ if we could get him working on our side."

"I don't see that happening," said Jill with a sad shake of her head.

"Never say never. Remember, the apostle Paul was persecuting Christians too, before he was converted. Sometimes the ones that fight the hardest are the ones who turn out to be the greatest allies."

"Thanks, Pastor. I'll try to remember that," said Jill.

"And how are things going for you, Steve?" he asked next.

"Oh, things are fine." Steve said. "The work isn't really that challenging. I'm mostly flying a commuter plane back and forth across the base, shuttling people and equipment around. I miss my fighter," he acknowledged, "but I think I'm where God wants me to be. He's obviously using Jill right now. I feel like I am just kind of coasting along in life, though."

"Well, be thankful for a bit of a spiritual break. Things won't always be this easy. It's obvious that Jill needs you to stand firm and support her. Use the time to dig deeper into the Bible. You'll never regret doing it."

"Thanks, Pastor. I'll do that," replied Steve.

"It's good to see the two of you. God bless you both," said Pastor Howie, and he turned toward several other members of his flock.

Chapter 10

In preparation for the next flight, *TimeFlyer* was being altered. It was becoming increasingly apparent that the series of air pumps that were supposed to funnel air underneath the aircraft weren't working well. When Steve and Tex showed the video of their takeoff from Mauritius, including nearly hitting the island, Dr. Choi nearly had an apoplectic fit. No one ever remembered the diminutive physicist throwing a temper tantrum before, but he let Steve and Tex have it.

"What do you think you were trying to do?" he yelled at them.

Steve was taken aback, but Tex kept his cool. "Uh, is this a trick question?" he asked. Dr. Choi glared angrily at him. "We were trying to take off."

"What you did was reckless. You could have lost the aircraft."

"We should have stayed there," Tex shot back, "which was the alternative anyway."

"Dr. Choi, we didn't have a choice. We weren't able to get airborne without getting out of the waves." Steve was trying to assuage Dr. Choi's anger and frustration. "In my judgment, it was the best thing to do under the circumstances. We could have stayed until the wind died down and the seas calmed, but we had no idea how long that might have been, and it would have delayed our return to the present. I thought we could achieve liftoff with smoother water and I was right."

"What if you were wrong?"

"Well, like Tex said, we wouldn't be having this conversation, would we?"

"You took a foolish chance."

"I had to take a chance because the air injection system doesn't work well. You know that, Tex and I were the ones who uncovered that problem during flight trials. Can't we focus on fixing the problem?"

"We have tried to find higher capacity air pumps," replied Choi, apparently calming in the face of Steve's reasonable tone. "There doesn't appear to be any."

"Can't you just mount some booster rockets on the back or something?" asked Tex.

"Actually, that's not a bad idea." Scoot and Jake had been silently listening to the exchange, and it was Jake who offered this bit of advice. "On the C-130, there are four locations on each side of the aircraft where booster rockets can be placed to get the aircraft flying on short runways. They only burn for something like 20 seconds, but they sure get the airplane moving. Something like that could probably be used for *TimeFlyer*."

"Not only that, you could probably use something like that to put air into the injection system." added Steve. "After all, a solid rocket motor just gives off a lot of gas, doesn't it? Seems like you could use something like that to generate a large amounts of gas instead of relying on mechanical air pumps."

"It would be better than what we have now." put in Tex.

Dr. Choi still appeared somewhat upset, but he seemed to be calming rapidly. "Well. Perhaps you are right. I don't want to see another video like that again," he said, nodding toward the screen.

"Neither do we," agreed Steve.

* * * *

After the new solid rocket boosters had been installed, *TimeFlyer*'s water takeoff capabilities were tested several times. Four big solid rocket boosters were integrated into the rear of the aircraft, and were designed to be fired in pairs. That would allow two takeoffs from water during a mission. Another two, smaller, solid rocket boosters were used to generate the high pressure and volume of gas that would lift *TimeFlyer* off the surface of the water during the takeoff run. Both aircrews had the opportunity to test the system.

The rocket propulsion made all the difference in the world. When

165

it was Steve and Tex's turn to fly, they flew out over the Pacific Ocean in the pre-dawn darkness and landed on the surface of the ocean shortly after the sun came up. It was a sunny, but somewhat windy, day, with gusts of wind hitting 20 miles per hour. The whitecaps rose up to four feet above the surface. After landing, Steve brought *TimeFlyer* to a full stop, riding in the swells. Then, they throttled up to begin their takeoff run.

He brought *TimeFlyer* up to 50 knots, then called "Boost!" Tex pushed the button that first fired the rockets on the tail, then the booster to supply the air injection system. They felt the surge as the rockets in the rear began to lend their assistance to their effort, but when the air injection system kicked in, they became airborne so rapidly it was like the hand of God had reached down and plucked them out of the water. As soon as air replaced the water underneath the aircraft, the speed jumped, and Steve was able to pull the nose up to reach a climb rate of 2000 feet per minute until the booster rockets burned out.

"Wow. That's a lot better," said Steve.

"It'll do," said the unflappable Tex.

* * * *

The meeting started at noon. The full compliment of both aircrews was in attendance, although the focus would be on Scoot and his crew. In addition, every single technical support group was present, from anthropology to zoology.

Steve and Tex had flown out over the Gulf of Mexico to meet *TimeFlyer*'s return the previous evening. *TimeFlyer* had returned just as expected, but Scoot had reported over the radio that things were weird. Everything with *TimeFlyer* and her crew was fine, but the things they had encountered over 4,000 years ago were puzzling, to say the least. Scoot hadn't gone into detail over the radio, and had insisted on debriefing with only his crew in attendance. Steve and Tex and their crew had waited for two hours to be invited into the debriefing, but at 1:00 AM they had been told to report the following day for a noon meeting.

As Steve was crawling blearily into bed at 1:35 AM, the phone had rung. It was for Jill, who had just sunk into a sound sleep after hearing him come home a couple of minutes before. She was being called in for

166

some urgent analysis of data from the latest *TimeFlyer* mission. As she got dressed, Steve relayed what he knew about the mission, which wasn't much. He had walked with her over to the research building, and then returned to the apartment and fallen asleep immediately.

He had slept until 9:00 AM the next morning, quite unusual for him. He had done his devotions, exercised, and eaten three hours later than usual. On the way to the meeting, he grabbed some carry-out food. He suspected that Jill probably hadn't had much to eat during the night.

The meeting had been moved to the small auditorium. Steve arrived about 10 minutes early to find Jill, exhausted, slumped in one of the seats on the side of the room. It was obvious that there were quite a few in attendance who had stayed up all night. Steve sat down beside her and offered her some of the food.

"Oh, thank you, Honey. You are the best." The food earned him a compliment and a kiss. "I haven't had a bite since I got called in."

"That's what I figured. I grabbed a foot-long sandwich, yogurt and a couple cans of soda. Help yourself." Jill gratefully reached for the yogurt.

"Alright, let's get started." Brian called the meeting to order. "The purpose of this meeting is to try to get answers about the unexpected findings of *TimeFlyer* from the mission that ended yesterday. I'll briefly fill you in on the details, because I know some of you haven't been in the loop yet.

"Yesterday when *TimeFlyer* returned from her mission, Scoot reported some problems with the navigation system." He looked up from his notes. "I guess I should add that there was no significant problem with *TimeFlyer*, and no problem with the health of any of the crew." He turned back to his notes. "During the mission, *TimeFlyer* was able to fly to the Caribbean, we believe, and do some remote observations of the native people, as well as land and spend some time on an island that was not inhabited. However, the crew was never exactly sure they were navigating properly, because their navigation computer was reporting irregular results. When they finally got what they considered reasonable readings, the earth's geography didn't match their maps." Steve looked at Jill in surprise. Jill just nodded tiredly.

"Data from the mission has been analyzed through the night by our technical staff. We are going to be asking for preliminary results from the various teams regarding their analysis of the data. We will allow each team 20 minutes to present their findings, then we will take a short break, and return and open the floor to questions. Three teams will be presenting. First will be Navigation, second Geography, and third Theory. I would respectfully ask that you hold your questions until after the break. I would recommend taking notes. Arnie, why don't you come on up and get us started."

There was a flurry of activity in the audience as notebooks and pens were pulled out, and people who hadn't thought to bring paper or pen borrowed some from their neighbors.

Dr. Arnold Olgierdson stood up and walked up to the lectern. He was holding a manila folder, and there were a few papers hanging out of it. He had the reputation of being quite meticulous. His team must have been working right up until deadline to have something to report, Steve realized.

"Uh, I am not sure exactly where to start," began the astronomer. "I guess I'll just start by going over what we did during the night and what we have concluded so far. When we first reviewed the data early this morning, it didn't seem to make a lot of sense. We reviewed some of the data from the navigation computer. We didn't have time to analyze all of it, you understand, because it has generated several million lines of log files, not to mention the size of the database it generated on the flight.

"The first thing we suspected was some kind of equipment malfunction. We asked our computer wizards to run some checks for us. They reported that the computer seemed to be working as expected. They even went so far as to roll *TimeFlyer* out of her hanger and have the computer plot its position based on the region of the sky it could see early this morning. It reported correctly that it was sitting stationary on the ground at Minion Lake at the correct point in time. We still haven't ruled out an equipment malfunction, of course. But we moved forward based on the assumption that the recorded data was accurate.

"The first thing we noticed was that the computer was having trouble locking on to the proper stars to get a position check. Normally, the computer can locate up to 100 reference stars in under 60 seconds. A little over three stars located every two seconds. However, in this case, it took over three minutes to locate 27 reference stars. Based on those stars, it reported *TimeFlyer*'s position somewhere beyond Jupiter's orbit. Obviously inaccurate. Over the next 30 minutes, it located 13 additional stars, but also went back and removed the original location of four of the original 27 stars. At this point, it was reporting a position over the Gulf of Mexico, 4000 years ago. This was the first reasonable response from the computer.

"We tried to determine why the computer was having trouble locking on to its reference points. The data indicates that there were more stars in the sky 4000 years ago than there are now. In addition, the stars we use for reference points reportedly varied in the intensity of light they were expected to produce. More than half were within expected limits. However, of the stars that varied in intensity, most were brighter, but some were dimmer, and three were so dim they couldn't be detected at all.

"At this point, we suspect a combination of things. First, it is not unreasonable to expect that some of the stars varied in intensity more than anticipated. If we stick to this conclusion, we will be able to reprogram the navigation computer to account for the variations in intensity. More troubling, however, is the computer reporting more stars in the sky, perhaps by as much as 25% more than it reports in our present age. We intend to pursue two possible explanations in the coming days. First would be a problem with the software. Second, as the aircraft goes through the space-warp, it is possible that the sensors being used to plot the positions of the stars is being effected in some manner that we don't fully understand.

"I guess that wraps up our preliminary conclusions. Obviously, we are pleased that the computer was operating well enough that it was able to get our aircrew safely back to the present time and space. But we are going to be doing a lot of work before the next mission to resolve the problems we've observed on this mission." He gathered his papers, shoved them into the folder, and walked back to his seat in the auditorium.

Brian returned to the podium. "Thank you, Arnie. Next up is Geography. Who's going to be speaking from that group? Carol? Great, come on up."

A woman that Steve recognized only by sight walked up to the podium. "Good morning. Well, it's been an interesting night." She had circles under her eyes, and she didn't look nearly as comfortable on stage as Dr. Olgierdson.

Steve felt something press against his shoulder, and turned to see

169

Jill's head resting on it. "Here, let's trade seats," he said in a low voice. "You can rest your head on my left shoulder, and that way I can still take notes with my right hand." Jill nodded, and they swapped seats. Jill's head immediately lolled against his left shoulder.

"...going to explain what was observed from *TimeFlyer*, and then I'll provide a possible alternative explanation." Carol was saying. "When *TimeFlyer* entered space and time 4,000 years ago, it was flying over water. The crew eventually determined they were flying over the Gulf of Mexico. They then flew southeast for a couple hundred miles, skirting the western side of Cuba, recording both still and video footage of the native people. Next, they turned south until they found some islands that seemed uninhabited. These would have been some of the small islands that lie between Cuba and Jamaica.

"Interestingly, because of the observed disparity between what the navigation computer was recording and what they were observing, they departed early and decided to fly back over North America and see if they could visually verify their location. They were unable to do so. If they really were where the navigation computer reported, the following things would have had to be true.

"First, they encountered the North American land mass much earlier than expected. That means that the water level of the ocean would have had to be between 100 and 200 feet lower than it is today. Second, they decided to locate the Grand Canyon. They were unable to do so. What they found instead was a large inland body of water. Third, there was much more vegetation than normally covers Arizona. They were not flying over a desert ecology. In fact, the photographs indicate a decidedly Taiga ecology, which is characterized by dominant coniferous forestation.

"After reviewing, the data, we decided the combination of factors, which I have just related to be quite unlikely, especially as recently as 4,000 years ago, which is almost nothing in overall geological time. So, we decided to see if we could locate a position where *TimeFlyer* might have started, instead of the Gulf of Mexico as they reported, which matched the recorded data. I had Desmond Wallace throw together a few computer slides to help us view the course of *TimeFlyer*. What we did is overlay *TimeFlyer*'s course on several different maps. Can you bring up the first slide?" she nodded to Desmond, who was sitting next to a projector. He turned the unit on, and a map with a red line appeared on the screen. "Here is where *TimeFlyer* reported it was flying. As you can see, they would have flown directly over the Grand Canyon, but they report that there was no Grand Canyon at the expected location. Additionally, this red dot..." she indicated with a laser pointer "...shows the point at which they encountered land." The dot was some distance away from the Texas shoreline, lying in the Gulf of Mexico. "We overlaid this same path on some other maps. Here is a map of *TimeFlyer*'s position overlying the eastern portion of the United States and extending out into the Atlantic Ocean. As you can see, the red dot aligns much more closely to the east coast of the United States.

"This is our current hypothesis. *TimeFlyer* actually emerged from the space-warp event over the Atlantic Ocean, east of North Carolina. The landmass they skirted, which they thought was Cuba, was actually Bermuda. When they turned back to search for the Grand Canyon, the ecology they observed roughly fits some of the ecology found in parts of the eastern United States. When they reached what they believed to be the site of the Grand Canyon, and found a large body of water, we believe they were observing one of the great lakes. It was probably Lake Ontario, although it could have been Lake Erie to the east or even Lake Michigan to the west. We did try to match observations with other locations, but we didn't get any good fits until we were well away from the North American continent, which we believe is unlikely. I could detail some of them here, but my time is just about up, so I won't go into those now." And she too gathered up her notes and returned to her seat in the audience.

Brian returned to the podium. "I suspect that we are going to have a lively debate after our break. OK, finally let's hear from our Theory team. Dr. Stark, are you going to speak? OK, come on up."

Dr. Stark got up and made his way to the podium. While he did so, Steve turned to Jill. "How are you doing?"

"Better. The food helped a lot."

"What do you think of all this?"

"I haven't made up my mind yet. Carol had an interesting hypothesis. I think we're going to be working on this for several weeks, at least." They turned their attention back to the podium.

"Our team decided to go back through the mathematics and re-verify the algorithms," began Dr. Stark with his characteristic abruptness. "We didn't get all the way through last night, but what we did go through seems accurate. We re-ran all of our test cases through

171

the computer, and they came out OK. We also entered the starting position of *TimeFlyer*, and from what we can see, they should have emerged over the Gulf of Mexico." He glanced at Carol. "What Carol proposed is interesting. One of the things we might try to do is try to plot the positions of the stars as recorded on the flight to see if we can get a combination that would show *TimeFlyer* over the Atlantic. When we broke to report here this morning, we were a little over 2/3 of the way through re-proving the theory. While we were doing that, I had Dr. Choi gather a few folks and check the space-warp drive and its control system. I'll turn it over to Dr. Choi to let him share his results."

Dr. Choi came up to the podium as Dr. Stark backed a few steps away. "As Dr. Stark said, I was asked to verify the integrity of the space-warp system. We have gone through the system and it seems to be working properly. We also have quite a number of test cases to use to test the software that does the calculations for the actual space-warp event. Those have all been run, and the tests were all negative. That is to say, the computer operated as expected in all cases. There were no anomalies or unexpected results. We run through this same test suite several times before each mission, so we would have been quite unhappy to have our test results turn out otherwise." Then he backed away from the podium.

When Dr. Stark indicated that he had nothing further to say, Brian again approached the microphone. "Well, we are finishing this first segment a few minutes early. Let's take a 17-minute break instead of 10 minutes. We'll start again at 1:00 sharp."

The audience collectively stood up and began to move, buzzing with conversation. Jill turned her head closer to Steve. "I'm so tired I don't want to move, but I have to go use the bathroom."

"Don't let me get in your way," said Steve. Actually, his left shoulder was aching from the weight of her head, and he was relieved she had offered an excuse for getting it off of his shoulder.

When she returned a few minutes later, she had another request. "Steve, I'm so tired, I don't want to stay for the rest of the meeting. I can read the meeting notes later. Please walk with me back to the apartment."

Steve could see she was absolutely exhausted. She had focused intensely all night long, and now it was afternoon of the following day. "Let me go check to make sure they are taking meeting minutes. If so, I'll go with you." He bounded toward the front of the auditorium, and returned less than 30 seconds later. "Let's go."

They didn't say much on the way back to the apartment. Jill kept one hand on his elbow. He could tell she was tired – she stumbled a couple times and seemed to be walking with her eyes closed part of the time. When they got to the apartment, she walked straight to the bedroom and collapsed on the bed. Steve sat on the edge on the opposite side. "I'm probably going to go over to the hanger. I want to see some of the video from *TimeFlyer*," he told Jill. She didn't answer. She was already asleep.

* * * *

When the meeting was over, Choi slumped in his chair. He, too, was tired from the all-night investigation. A pair of shoes entered his field of vision. He looked up. It was Dr. Stark. "When is the last time you've been off this base, Choi?"

"Seems like a long time." he said, too tired to try to calculate the dates.

"If you were going to take a weekend off, where would you go?"

"San Francisco. Chinatown." Choi said it almost without thinking. He had started to entertain thoughts of going there. It wasn't exactly authentic Korean, but it was about as close as you could get while still living in the United States. Thoughts of his father, mother, and siblings locked up in North Korean camps had raised in him long-suppressed thoughts of Korea, and made him begin to yearn to again experience his childhood culture. Chinatown wasn't exactly Korea, but it was as close as he was going to get in the United States.

"You're going there this weekend. I'll get it arranged. Go get some sleep. You've been working too hard, and I don't want to lose you."

"Thank you," responded Choi with characteristic politeness. He was too tired to argue, too tired to object. They could send him to Australia for all he cared. As long as it had a bed.

* * * *

Steve was watching the video footage from *TimeFlyer* as it flew between either the Gulf of Mexico and Arizona or the Atlantic and one of the Great Lakes. It showed coniferous forest, all right. It also showed a more rugged terrain than he had ever experienced in the east. The hills were higher and sharper. The forest went for mile after mile. There were very few deciduous trees.

Tex wandered in. "Meeting over?" queried Steve.

"Yeah. Everybody agreed that they don't know for sure what happened to the flight. But I think everyone liked Carol's idea that *TimeFlyer* was over the Atlantic. You watching the tape?"

"Uh-huh. It doesn't look like the East Coast, though. It looks more like Texas and Arizona, except with a lot more trees. Mostly evergreens. It's strange. Could the East Coast have once been populated almost entirely by conifers?" he wondered aloud. "If so, when did all the deciduous trees come in?"

"Hey, don't look at me. I don't know much about that stuff. I can tell the difference between a pine tree and an oak, but that's about it. Now, if you could find a horse or a cow in the video, I might be able to give you an informed opinion," said Tex jestingly.

"Actually, that's a great idea. I did see a herd of some kind a few minutes ago. I was focusing so much on terrain I didn't think much about it. Here, let me go back and see if I can find it." He quickly started playing the video backwards. "What kind of animals would there be back then? Probably not horses. How about cattle? Longhorns?"

Tex looked at Steve thoughtfully. "Horses are out. They were brought over by the Spaniards a lot later than 4,000 years ago. Cattle were imported too. The Longhorn is considered native, but it is really just a mix of different European breeds that ran wild for a few hundred years. That means, 4,000 years ago, no cattle either."

"Well, what about bison?"

"You mean buffalo?"

"Yeah. Hey, here it is." He stopped rewinding the video and zoomed in on a section that seemed to be a black mass. "It doesn't look like much here. This is the low resolution recording. They weren't running the high resolution cameras at this point in the flight."

"Can you play the video forward slowly?" requested Tex.

"Sure." Steve did, "Sure looks like bison, doesn't it? There used to be millions of them. I mean, single herds numbered in the millions. They definitely would have existed 4,000 years ago. And, you know what else," Steve was beginning to get excited, "maybe bison were only in the West and not in the East."

"Look on the Internet," suggested Tex. "I bet you could find out."

Steve jumped over to a nearby computer. "OK, let's do a quick search." He pulled up a search engine, typed in 'bison buffalo history', and hit enter. He was presented with thousands of hits.

"Man, think about riding a bison. Now that would be cool," murmured Tex to himself.

Steve was clicking on the links from the search results. The first page confirmed that bison were native, but didn't describe their range very well. But the second page had some maps, with the bison's range highlighted. At their peak, their range covered most of the country from the East Coast to the Rocky Mountains. "Well, nice try. They were on the East Coast too. So that won't help."

"Well, if you come to any conclusions, let me know, Mr. Sherlock Holmes." Tex said.

"I will," Steve replied as he returned to the video from *TimeFlyer*.

* * * *

"It's imperative that we travel back to at least the Mesozoic Era," Dr. Stark was saying. "We've only gone back 4,000 years. In geological time, that's nothing. If we redo a mission every time we have a little trouble, we will never make it back to the time of the dinosaurs."

"I would be more comfortable if we could explain without a doubt what happened on that last flight." came the voice of General Collins over the speakerphone. Dr. Choi was in the room, as was Brian, who was recording the meeting minutes. "I think we should change the next flight to try to duplicate the previous flight and gather more data. Now that we know what to expect, we will be able to set up *TimeFlyer* to record a lot more data that will help understand the situation."

"It would probably be helpful," agreed Dr. Stark. "But if we can reasonably explain what *TimeFlyer* encountered on its last flight, I think we need to continue with the current flight schedule. *TimeFlyer* did just fine on the last flight and I think the risk of continuing to go back in time is low."

"How can you say that, when you're not even sure where *TimeFlyer* was?" said General Collins. "Another mistake could send *TimeFlyer* out into space, and that would be a disaster."

"If we could come up with an explanation, would that be acceptable?"

"I guess that depends on the explanation. What's your plan?"

175

"We are going to take the astronomical data from *TimeFlyer*. We are building a computer program to plot *TimeFlyer*'s position with all possible combinations of star sightings it made on its last mission. We think we will come up with a combination that shows *TimeFlyer* over the Atlantic."

"Sounds like a big job. How soon do you expect to get results?" queried the General.

"Depends on what kind of supercomputer time we get. We don't have access to a supercomputer here. We need your help to get us some computing time. If we can get the program written, do you think you can dig some up for us?"

"Consider it done. The Air Force has one, but I'll have to check availability. If it isn't available, I can always lean on some of our subcontractors. Some of them have machines that would probably work. How much time do you think you're going to need?"

"On a fast machine, probably just a little over two hours."

"How soon will your program be ready?"

"It should be done by tomorrow," responded Dr. Choi.

"Dr. Choi, are you writing the program?" asked the General.

"No, I have several members of my staff writing the program. They are taking the existing programming on *TimeFlyer* and adapting it to calculate results based on millions of combinations of different stars."

"Well, let's get the computer time and see what kind of results we get. I haven't said anything to the President yet, so we have options."

Chapter 11

A week later, Steve and Jill were eating supper in their apartment. Jill was explaining to Steve how Dr. Stark and a couple others had found a possible solution to the puzzle of *TimeFlyer*'s location.

"They ran through the equation that the computer uses to shape the space-warp. They didn't find anything unexpected. Then they started looking at the stars the astronomers used to set their location. The surprising thing is, there were more stars. Very strange. Nobody can explain why. Anyway, they decided to write a program to calculate their possible position using all possible combinations of stars, to see if they could find a pattern that would place them over the Atlantic."

"Must have been some program."

"It was. They actually requested and got some run time on a supercomputer somewhere. It took the program over five hours to run, but they got three sets of results that would have placed them over the Atlantic."

"Did they check the number of results that would have put them over the Gulf?"

"I don't think so."

"What do you think? Where do you think *TimeFlyer* was?"

Jill hesitated. Then she said, "I wouldn't want to say for sure. But I've gone over the space-warp calculations, and I've looked at some of the logs from the navigation computer. I think it was more likely that they were over the Gulf, and then flew on to Arizona."

"But the Grand Canyon wasn't there."

"I know. But the math was right."

Steve sighed. "Well, how could something like the Grand Canyon just suddenly jump out of, uh, I guess that would be dive into, the ground less than 4,000 years ago? That sounds pretty unlikely."

"You know, I've never been to the Grand Canyon," said Jill. "Dad took us to a lot of the National Parks, but never that one. I've always wanted to go there."

"Well, this would be a good time to go. How about we go there this weekend? Maybe we could figure something out. If not, it is an interesting place. I went there when I was about 14 or so with my family. We camped all the way. We hiked down to the bottom, camped overnight, and then hiked back up. It was a really fun trip, but it was hard work. My little brothers just about didn't make it back to the top. I remember there were some college kids there who helped us the last half-mile or so. They overtook us on the trail, and saw how tired my brothers were. They volunteered to carry their packs the rest of the way."

"Well, I'm not sure I'm in good enough shape to hike the canyon. But I would like to go."

"Deal. We'll go this weekend."

* * * *

Steve and Jill decided to start in the guest center. There was a film on the formation of the Grand Canyon, which explained how the canyon formed over millions of years by the ebb and flow of the Colorado River. It went into detail on the colors of the walls of the canyon, how they related to the different layers of rock, and the various ages of the layers. After the movie, they wandered through the visitor center, looking at samples of various fossils found in the area, evidence of Native Americans who lived around the canyon, and the decision to make the Grand Canyon into a National Park. Then they caught the shuttle, which would take them to Trailview Overlook.

Saturday morning dawned bright and clear in Northwest Arizona. It would have been perfect except for the wind, which was steady from the northwest and just a little on the cold side. The view from the overlook was spectacular though. They stood for a while, Jill snuggling up to Steve to keep from getting too cold. The rock strata, with its shades of color, shone in the bright sun. The plateaus that were in the middle of the canyon, and which hadn't been eroded away, stood like sentinels, as if guarding the ancient river that flowed around their feet. They were able to observe hikers on the various trails in the canyon, and marveled at the enormity of what they were observing.

"Let's look at some of the signboards," suggested Steve.

"OK."

They wandered from sign to sign, reading the information about rock strata, sedimentation, native plant and animal species, comments from explorers who had first discovered the canyon, etc. After about an hour, Jill suggested they head back to the visitor center. "I'm getting really cold," she said.

"Me too. Let's see if we can catch the next shuttle."

The waiting area for the shuttle was inside a building, so they were able to sit down and start to warm up. There were several other people waiting for the shuttle as well.

"Colder than it looks out there, isn't it?" queried a neighboring man politely to Steve, observing the fact that Jill was more chilled than she was willing to admit.

"Yeah. We only brought light jackets. Didn't expect it to be this cold." replied Steve.

"The weather around here can fool you," said the man.

"You come here often?"

"I try to make it once a year. It fascinates me. I'm a creationist, you see."

"What's a creationist?" asked Steve. He was rubbing Jill's hands to try to make them warmer.

"It's a person who believes in the literal biblical story of creation, that the earth is only 6,000 to 10,000 years old." he replied.

Steve looked at him, intrigued. The man seemed to be in his 60's. He wore a cap advertising seed corn. He could have been any number of farmers that Steve remembered from his childhood in Kansas. "How do you explain the canyon? Everything we've seen says it is millions of years old."

The stranger smiled at the challenge. "It's not. It was formed between 3,000 and 4,000 years ago. It is the result of a dam breach. The resulting rush of water carved out the canyon very rapidly, in probably less than a week."

Steve stared at him in amazement. Then he stuck out his hand.

"My name's Steve Harrison. This is my wife Jill. Listen, you traveling with anyone? I'd love to hear more. Can we treat you to lunch?"

"My name's Herb Lolling. No, I'm not traveling with anyone. My wife died last year," he said. "I'd be glad to have lunch with you. I get lonely without her. And I'd be glad to tell you what I've learned about the canyon."

The shuttle arrived, so they all stood up and made their way in. "I'm sorry to hear about your wife," said the tender-hearted Jill.

"Well, the Good Lord gives, and the Good Lord takes away. We had 40 good years together, raised five kids. I can't complain. I do miss her, though," sighed Herb.

"Where are you from?"

"I'm from Indiana. Lived and farmed there my whole life, except when I went to school. I have a degree in Geology. My dad told me to get it, thought it might be useful for a farmer to have that knowledge. He was right. Helped me understand what was going on out in the field more than some of my neighbors. I ended up starting a soil sampling business to keep us going during the off-season. I'm retired now, two of my boys have the farm and the business. How about you folks?"

"We're working in Nevada right now. I'm a pilot in the Air Force. My wife is a physicist. I grew up in Kansas, she grew up in the Washington, D.C. suburbs. We've been married for a little over two years now.

Is it OK if we just go to the cafeteria here?" Steve asked as they arrived back at the visitor center..

"That would be fine." Herb said, "I appreciate the invitation to eat with you." They headed into the cafeteria, grabbed trays, and started choosing food.

"He seems like a really nice man." Jill said to Steve, out of Herb's earshot.

"Yeah, I think so too. Maybe he can explain what *TimeFlyer* recorded."

"Well, just be careful what you say. Don't spill any beans." warned Jill.

"Kick me under the table if you think I am starting to say too much." Steve told her and she nodded in agreement.

They needn't have worried. Herb turned out to be a good talker. Once they got him started, he kept himself going. Which was fine with

180

Steve and Jill. The information they were getting from him was fascinating.

"Well, I tell you what, folks. Just appreciate each other. Life can change awful quick. Just be thankful for each day you have together." Herb said as they sat down.

"Are you a believer?" queried Jill, remembering how that simple question had ended up creating such a problem with Dr. Stark.

"I sure am, Young Lady."

"Would you have a quick prayer with us?" asked Steve.

"I would be glad to." They joined hands, and Herb asked God's blessing on their meal and their fellowship.

"So, tell me about this canyon forming 4,000 years ago," Steve prompted.

"Well, let's see. Probably the best place to start is in the flood of Noah's time. You know, we are still learning about the effects of moving water. Unbelievably destructive. There have been spectacular natural accidents showing how much damage moving water can cause. Hurricane Katrina wiping out New Orleans in 2005. Big Thompson canyon, happened in 1975 or '76 if I remember right. Cajon Pass in California in the late 1800's. That one buried a freight train so deep in mud they almost couldn't find it. But the most convincing was Mt. St. Helens. Over the next several years after the volcano blew its top, scientists were able to observe the results. Including the rapid formation of canyons, which look very similar to the Grand Canyon.

"Here's what us kooky Creation Scientists think," continued Herb, winking at Steve and Jill. "At one point, there was no Grand Canyon. If you assume that the area of the Grand Canyon was solid ground, similar to the ground on both sides, you would find that it could hold back a lake that would cover parts of Arizona, New Mexico, Utah, and maybe even parts of Western Colorado. That lake could hold as much water as Lake Michigan three times over. The thought is that the lake overflowed for some reason. Could have been a lot of rain, melting snow and ice from winter, who knows? Probably a combination of all those things. Anyway, once the water found a way out of the lake, it ate a bigger and bigger pathway, and more and more water came pouring through the breach. That much moving water would have caused a tremendous amount of erosion in a very short period of time and that breach ended up being the Grand Canyon." He stopped talking to take a bite of his sandwich.

Steve's mind was whirling. "If there was a lake that huge, wouldn't the climate of the western United States been different than it is now?"

"Absolutely. Temperatures would be a lot more stable, for one thing. More moisture all around, more rainfall. Different plants and animals. More of both, of course. Lots of things would have been different," replied Herb.

"Wouldn't that much water affect the ocean levels too? I assume all that draining water eventually made its way to the ocean." Steve speculated.

"Sure did, right into the Gulf of California. And yes, it would have raised the level of the ocean. Don't know how much though."

"Could it have raised it 150 feet?"

"Well, that sounds like a little too much. It's possible, I guess. Interesting thing about that, though. Let's say the earth was the size of a 12 inch ball. How much water do you think it would take to fill all the oceans of the earth if it was that size?"

"A quart." guessed Jill.

"A pint." was Steve's guess.

They had to wait while Herb took another bite of sandwich. "Actually, only one teaspoon."

"One teaspoon of water would fill all of the world's oceans?" repeated Steve incredulously.

"Yes, if the world were a 12 inch globe."

"But oceans cover three quarters of the surface of the planet."

"That's right, but relatively speaking, they're not very deep. The deepest part of the ocean seems to be about seven miles. Mariana Trench, I believe it's called. Average depth is a lot less than that. Compare that to the width of, say, the Pacific. Thousands of miles wide. Only a few miles deep. It would take a lot less water to fill than most people think."

Steve and Jill looked at each other. The data from *TimeFlyer* was starting to make a lot more sense.

"If a lake that size drained away, it would create a huge environmental catastrophe," said Jill. "I mean, I assume there would be people living around the lake. Their source of life would be gone. And think of all the plants and animals that would be affected." She turned to Herb. "Would God really do something like that?"

"Well, he caused the Red Sea to drown the entire Egyptian Army that was pursing the Israelites as they fled from Egypt." Herb pointed out. "I would call that pretty catastrophic too. One thing you have to understand about Creation Science is that it is based on catastrophes. Huge geological events that caused large scale change in short amounts of time. Oh, I never got back to Mt. St. Helens, did I?" Steve and Jill shook their heads. "Well, two years after Mt. St. Helens blew, scientists saw a canyon form. What happened was this. The volcano continued to spit and burble occasionally over the next several years. Actually, I think it's still active. Anyway, the original explosion in 1980 filled in the bed of the Toutle River, raised the level of the riverbed. In 1982, another small eruption melted a bunch of snow on the mountain, creating a mudslide. The slide cut through the material that was deposited in the Toutle River bed. In a single day, it cut a canyon through the deposited material. The canyon is over 100 feet deep. It is narrow and winding, just like the Grand Canyon. And the walls of the canyon show stratification, just like the Grand Canyon. If you went and looked at it today, it would look like it had been there for hundreds of thousands of years. Except we know it hasn't. Scientists have been able to document the depositing of the material in 1980, and its breach two years later. That's the kind of catastrophism that Creation Scientists believe formed the earth as we see it today."

"That's incredible," breathed Steve. "I've never heard of a, what did you call it, Creation Scientist, before. Are there many of them around?"

"Oh, hard to say. Problem is, mainstream scientists are so determined to hold on to the theory of evolution, and an earth that is billions of years old, that they won't listen to any alternatives. Any scientist who proclaims he believes in a young earth, and not in slow evolutionary change, has to believe in a Creator. That's where the trouble comes. Hard to prove the existence of God to someone who is determined not to listen. I think there are a lot more scientists who believe in God than you and I will ever know. Problem is, they get so persecuted by other scientists, most of them just decide to blend in and go with the flow. Jill, would you have been granted your PhD in physics if your professors knew you believed what I am telling you today?"

"Probably not."

"Well, there you go."

"You're right." she said thoughtfully. "I told one of my colleagues where I work right now that I believe the Bible. He has been making my life miserable ever since. Of course, for a long time I tried to match the creation story with the evolutionary theory."

Herb smiled sympathetically, "Didn't fit together very well, did it?"

"No. I finally just came to the conclusion that evolution didn't happen. But I have some other questions, not about the Grand Canyon. Mind if I ask them?"

Herb chuckled. "Go right ahead. But I'll be stepping a little out of my element."

"Would there have been more stars thousands of years ago?"

"Probably. Here's an interesting thing. Scientists have documented thousands of stars going dark. Guess how many stars they have seen form, or begin to shine."

"A lot less than thousands." answered Steve pragmatically.

"The answer is none. Not one."

"I know what an astronomer would say to you. That is just because we haven't found and cataloged all the existing stars. Besides, it takes millions of years to form a star."

"That's one possibility," acknowledged Herb.

"That colleague that is giving me a hard time, he challenged me about the amount of time it would take for light to travel through space to reach our planet. There are a lot of objects that are millions of light-years away," challenged Jill.

"Einstein's theory was called the theory of...what?" asked Herb.

"Relativity. Even I know that," said Steve.

"What's relative about it?" asked Herb.

"Space and time." said Jill.

"Right. So, is it not possible that, while 24 hours worth of time passed on earth, thousands or millions of years were passing in other parts of the universe? If God created the universe, wouldn't space be expanding shortly after the creation? And if space were expanding, might that not have a significant affect on the passage of time?"

Steve and Jill were quiet for a moment. "That's a pretty wild thought," said Steve finally. He looked at Jill, and recognized her look. She was 'in the zone.' He turned back to Herb. "Is that really possible? Having that much of a difference in the rate of time?"

"Seems to be. Let's start with known facts. We know clocks at different relative heights on earth record times at different rates. The higher the clock is away from the center of the planet, the faster the clock operates. In fact, the difference is large enough that computers have to be programmed to take the different rates of time passage into account. For example, the satellites that are used in the Global Positioning System. Since the satellites are flying around in space, and the GPS receivers are being used on earth's surface, GPS software has to take the different rates of time passage between the satellite clocks and the clocks on the earth's surface into account."

"Amazing. And you're saying that the difference in the passage of time between the satellites and the receivers is explained by Einstein's General Relativity Theory?"

"That's right," said Herb.

"But I assume you're talking fractions of seconds. That's a long way from billions of years difference," said Steve.

"Right again. But before I get too far out of my element, I'd better refer you to someone who understands Relativity a whole lot better than I do. I heard a man talk about this once at a Creation Science conference. His name was Dr. Emil Phelson, he is a professor at some University, I don't remember which one right now. He'd be the one who could answer your questions."

* * * *

The ride back to their hotel was quiet. Steve was glad. He could see Jill's mind was working overtime. Her eyes were open, but she didn't seem to be seeing anything. She was just thinking as hard as she could.

When they finally got back to the hotel, Steve parked and got out of the car. He walked around to the front of the car, waiting for her to join him. She remained sitting in the car. It tickled his sense of humor. He walked over to her door and opened it, "Hey, Brainy Lady, time to get out."

"Oh. Yeah," replied Jill absently. She swung her legs out and tried to stand up. The attempt was unsuccessful, because she still had her seat belt on. Steve couldn't help laughing again. Jill frowned in annoyance at the seatbelt, got it unbuckled, and made a second effort to join him on the side of the car. This one turned out to be more successful.

"I better get you to our room before you wander out onto a street somewhere."

"Um-hmm," said Jill absently. This time, Steve didn't find it quite as funny. He had never seen her quite like this before. He guided her up to the hotel door, into the aisle, and finally into their room. "Where's the computer?" she asked.

"I'll get it out." Steve pulled out Jill's three-year-old laptop and set it on the small desk. He turned it on and watched it boot up. It immediately recognized a wireless connection to the Internet. "There you go."

"Thanks," said Jill. She was utterly absorbed. Steve watched as she typed in a query for Emil Phelson. It didn't take long to find the university where he taught. She picked up the phone.

"Are you going to call him right now?"

"Why not?"

"Well, um, it's Saturday afternoon. I guess it's worth a try."

Jill dialed the number for the university. She reached an operator, who gave her the number for Dr. Phelson, then forwarded her call. The phone rang twice, and then was picked up.

"Hello?"

"Is this Dr. Phelson?" asked Jill.

"Yes it is. With whom am I speaking?"

"My name is Jill Harrison. I was referred to you by someone I met while visiting the Grand Canyon. He said you could explain how the universe was millions of years old, while the earth was only a few thousand years old."

"Ah. That I can do," replied Dr. Phelson.

"Do you have time to explain it now?" she asked.

"Actually, you caught me at a good time. I have about 20 minutes before I can shut down an experiment in progress and go home. Before I start, I need to know how much you know about science. What kind of science background do you have?"

"I have a PhD in physics. My husband is here too, he is an electrical engineer. Can I put you on speakerphone so he can hear the conversation as well?"

"Sure. What's his name?"

Jill hit the button to turn on the speakerphone function. "His name is Steve."

"Alright then, let's get started." He sounded like this was a presentation he had made many times, thought Steve. "Ever heard of a

White Hole?"

"No. I've heard of a Black Hole," said Steve.

"I have. It's the reverse of a Black Hole," said Jill.

"Think you can explain how to reverse a Black Hole?" asked Steve. "Do you just fold it inside out?"

"Actually, that's not a bad explanation." came the voice of Dr. Phelson. "Let's start by having you tell me what you know about a Black Hole."

"Well, it is something in space that contains a bunch of mass, and has a huge amount of gravity. The gravity is so strong that even light cannot escape, which is why it is black." said Steve.

"Right. Now, let's say we have a photon of light that is approaching the Black Hole. Up to a certain point, it can still veer away and escape the strength of the gravitational field. But as it approaches the Black Hole, at a certain point it is going to be sucked in. Escape is impossible. That point is what we call the Event Horizon. With me so far?"

"I think so."

"So as the Black Hole continues to suck in matter, what happens to the diameter of the Event Horizon?" asked Dr. Phelson.

"It gets bigger. I mean, the point at which light can escape from the effects of gravity from the Black Hole gets further away from the center of the Black Hole as the Black Hole sucks in more and more matter."

"Right. OK, now let's talk about a White Hole. A White Hole is a hole in which the effect is reversed. There is a ring of mass around a central point of relatively empty space, which tends to pull light away from the central empty space. The Event Horizon is defined as the closest point to which light can approach the center of that ring of mass before being pulled back toward the outer ring of matter. Light from outside the Event Horizon cannot enter inside, but light and matter from inside the Event Horizon can escape outward. So, if you are standing on the surface of a planet inside the Event Horizon of a White Hole, you can see things going on around you inside the White Hole, but nothing going on outside the Event Horizon, because no light is coming past it."

"So, if you were on the surface of the planet, and you looked toward the Event Horizon, everything would look black," said Steve.

"Right. Good. Now, as that ring of mass that makes up the White

Hole continues to expand outward, what happens to the Event Horizon?"

"I'm not sure." Steve admitted. "I guess the Event Horizon would do the opposite thing from a Black Hole. The Event Horizon from a Black Hole gets larger. So I guess the Event Horizon in an expanding White Hole would get smaller."

"Right. Excellent logic, that is exactly how it works. Now, imagine you were on the surface of Earth as the Event Horizon passed. What would you see?" asked Dr. Phelson.

"I guess everything that was black would suddenly be, uh, not light exactly, but not black anymore either." said Steve awkwardly.

"Oh, I get it." said Jill. "You would be able to see things that you haven't seen before, things that are generating light that were previously outside the event horizon. So, the black sky would suddenly be filled with stars, because their light could reach Earth."

"You two are doing very well. This combination of events would allow the stars to appear on Earth on the fourth day of Creation, as explained in the Creation account in the Bible."

Steve sat quietly, trying to get comfortable with these new ideas. "So you're saying that, when the Earth was created, it was inside the Event Horizon of a White Hole until day four of creation. Then, as the Event Horizon of the expanding White Hole shrank, it passed earth and the stars appeared in the sky."

"Good. I think you've got it," said Dr. Phelson enthusiastically.

"OK, so we maybe have figured out how the stars appeared on day four of creation. But the original question was about the billions of years of time difference."

"That's where the Event Horizon is also important." Dr. Phelson picked up his narrative. "At the Event Horizon, time is also doing strange things. For all practical purposes, it actually is stopped. The nearer you are to the Event Horizon, the slower time goes. That is true of both Black Holes and White Holes. So, as the Event Horizon swept past Earth, time would be going much more slowly on Earth compared to the rest of the Universe. Of course, whatever was on the Earth at that point wouldn't notice the slow time, it would seem normal to them. However, anyone looking down on earth from outside would see time on earth progressing very slowly."

"OK, I think I am beginning to understand." Steve's voice became more intense as he began to grasp the implications. "If I was on Earth as the Event Horizon passed, I would go from seeing nothing in the sky to everything. But since time is going so slowly for me, when I looked up at the universe, it would look like everything far away from me was going very fast. Time would seem normal to me, but time would be going by very quickly for the rest of the universe."

"Exactly. And that explains how the universe can be millions of years old, and yet earth is still only 6,000 years old." concluded Dr. Phelson.

"But it's all relative. The Bible says without doubt that creation happened in six days. That would have to mean six Earth days, while time in other parts of the universe wasn't passing at the same rate," said Steve thoughtfully.

"The creation story is centered on the Earth," explained Dr. Phelson. " In fact, the Bible says the Earth was created before the Sun by several days. All of creation is described relative to Earth. Now that we understand relativity, we see it is quite possible that parts of the universe can be much older than other parts. In fact, the Theory of Relativity requires such things to happen."

"I never put all the pieces together before," commented Jill. "It makes a lot of sense."

"The encouraging thing is that we are finding more and more evidence that our Solar System is quite young." Dr. Phelson continued his lesson. "Astronomers that believe in Creationism have made some remarkably accurate predictions. Here's an example. There was a space probe that did a flyby of Jupiter. It discovered lots of surprising things. One of the surprises was the strength of Jupiter's magnetic field. Very strong, stronger than that of the Sun, in fact. Now, if the universe were actually billions of years old, Jupiter would have a much weaker magnetic field. It would have decayed significantly over time, you see. But it is very strong, which was predicted by Creation Science astronomers before it was discovered. It took the Evolutionary astronomers completely by surprise."

"That's cool," said Steve. "How do regular scientists explain it?"

"Oh, they have theories about self-regenerating magnetic fields and who knows what else. But if a scientist is determined to believe a certain way, they are going to try to get the evidence to fit their own theories. Trouble is, humans are getting knowledgeable enough about the universe that the scientists that believe in a universe billions of years old are running into more and more problems. In fact, I believe that the next few major breakthroughs in astronomy will be from Creation scientists. The traditional scientists are going to be spending so much time trying to fit the data to their billions-of-years theory that they won't be making the breakthroughs."

"Like maybe there really is no dark matter," said Jill thoughtfully.

"That's right," said Dr. Phelson.

"Oh, brother. What is dark matter?" asked Steve.

"Well, scientists are trying to figure out why the universe hasn't collapsed by now." explained Dr. Phelson. "We know that all the galaxies are moving away from each other. There is not enough known mass in the universe to be able to sustain the movement that we observe over billions of years. So, the traditional scientists are trying to find matter that exists, and has mass, to make up the difference. Matter that is dark, that is very difficult to detect. So far, they haven't succeeded."

"But if the universe is young, an expanding universe is easy to explain. There wouldn't need to be any dark matter, right?" queried Steve.

"That's right. I think you two have got it. Does the explanation make sense?" asked Dr. Phelson.

"It makes sense to me." said Jill.

"I think so." said Steve.

"Very good. Well, it's Saturday and I would like to get home. Can I answer any other questions for you?" he asked.

"No, Sir. Thank you for your time. You've been very generous," said Steve.

"Quite welcome. God Bless." And the phone went silent.

"What do you think?" asked Jill, replacing the phone's receiver.

"I think I have a headache from thinking too hard."

"Maybe you're just hungry."

"I can always eat," replied Steve cheerfully.

* * * *

Their supper at a nearby restaurant started off silently, each preoccupied with their own thoughts. After a few minutes of silence, however, Steve raised his head from his French Onion soup and looked at Jill. "So, we've got a theory that explains a young Earth. We have another theory that explains the Grand Canyon formation.

Question is, do we believe them? Would this explain what *TimeFlyer* observed 4,000 years ago?"

"Things make a lot more sense to me." said Jill. "It's just so much information so fast." She sighed. "I would like to know for sure. But there is one thing. These theories do seem to match the Biblical account more closely than anything else I have ever heard."

"Yeah, but do we take the Bible literally? You know, in the Middle Ages, the priests tried to take the Bible literally and ended up convinced that the Sun revolved around the Earth. Are we making the same kind of mistake?"

"I don't think so," said Jill. "The data from *TimeFlyer* can be made to look like *TimeFlyer* was over the Atlantic. But it also can be argued that *TimeFlyer* was over the Gulf of Mexico, where it was supposed to go. To me, it looks more likely that *TimeFlyer* was over the Gulf. In order to make *TimeFlyer* appear over the Atlantic, you have to ignore most of the star locations and focus only on a relative few."

"I wish we had more evidence to support this young Earth idea. Theories are fine, but they are supposed to be testable. How can we test these ideas?"

"I'm not sure," said Jill and their supper became quiet again.

* * * *

On the flight back to Nevada, Steve said, "I think I want to look at the video taken from *TimeFlyer* again. I wonder if there is some way we can compare it to pictures taken more recently."

"How about satellite photos?"

"Hey, that's a great idea. I wonder if that lady from Geography could get us access to some."

"Carol?"

"Yeah. I don't know her. Do you?" asked Steve.

"I've seen her a few times, but never had a conversation with her," Jill answered.

"Well, maybe it's time we made her acquaintance," he replied.

* * * *

Choi felt good. He had enjoyed Chinatown as much as anyone possibly could. He had even found several Koreans, and been able to

191

converse with them in his native language. They were from South Korea, so each side had to work around their accent. But it was nice to talk to people who understood where you were coming from.

He had eaten lunch and supper at different Chinese restaurants, going to a gymnastics show in between, and also wandered through the street market. The merchandise was not quite like Korea, but the crowds of people, the smells, and the noise all reminded him very much of home.

Home. Why was he thinking of it as home, he wondered. This was his home. America. The United States. A place where people from every language, culture and background was welcome, particularly if they had anything to contribute. A place where he could be himself. Where he could both appreciate his Korean heritage and enjoy the blessings of prosperity.

Unlike his family.

Stop that, he told himself firmly. Your father told you to go and never look back. This is the life he wanted you to have. You are doing what he directed you to do. He knew he would probably suffer if you escaped, he reasoned. He was willing to make that sacrifice.

But was his mother, and his brothers, or his sister?

He stopped at a bakery and purchased a pastry. It was as much of a dessert as he ever ate, and he rarely allowed himself to indulge. He had the first-generation inclination against getting fat. But this was special. This was his time to relax and enjoy life.

He was getting tired. Time to go back to the hotel and get some sleep. He decided to save the pastry for later. Perhaps he could find something interesting to watch on television before he turned in. He waved down a taxi, hopped in, and directed the driver back to his hotel.

When he reached his room, the message light on the telephone was blinking. That was a little disappointing. He had hoped to be able to forget about work for the weekend. He retrieved the message. It was from the front desk, telling him that something had been delivered for him and was waiting to be picked up at the front desk.

He considered walking down the stairs for the exercise, but decided against it. He was on the eleventh floor, after all, and he had already gotten plenty of exercise for one day. He rode the elevator down, stepped into the lobby and presented himself at the desk.

"Ah, yes. This is for you." The girl behind the counter was Asian,

192

and pretty. Probably Japanese. She handed him a large envelope. "Is there anything else I can do for you, Dr. Choi?"

"No, thank you."

"Very well. Enjoy your stay."

He went back to his room, wondering why the project manager would send him anything in an envelope at an off site address, when he'd be back in a couple days anyway. Back in his room, he tore it open and reached inside. There was a single sheet of paper, along with a business card. The business card had the address of a dry cleaning shop in Chicago. His hand started shaking.

He picked up the letter and read it.

Dear Dr. Choi,

    We regret to inform you that your father passed away last week. Unfortunately, your mother is in very poor health.

    We hope that you will reconsider your refusal to speak to us. We look forward to speaking with you soon.

    Sun and Moon

Chapter 12

Monday morning, Steve and Jill walked together to the Muriel building. But instead of going to the lab where she usually worked with the other theorists, she stopped at the directory to look up the Geography department. It was in a series of offices on the second floor.

When they walked in to the indicated area, they found a row of desks in an open area. The walls were covered with maps, along with a few whiteboards. A few people were already at their desks. When they entered, a black man sitting at a desk nearest to the door looked up at them, "Good morning," he said, "I don't recognize you two. Can I help you?"

"We were looking for Carol." Steve offered, "I'm Steve Harrison, one of the pilots for *TimeFlyer*. This is my wife Jill."

"Carol's not here right now. I'm Desmond Wallace, I work for her. I recognize you now, you fly with that Texas dude, right? Maybe I can help you."

"We're still kicking around ideas about *TimeFlyer*'s last mission. We wondered if you folks had access to some satellite photos that we could compare to videos taken from *TimeFlyer*."

"I think I can help you with that. Sounds like a smart approach. It's one we haven't taken."

"Do you have the video from *TimeFlyer* here?" asked Jill.

"All of it," nodded Desmond. "It's on the network, we can view any of it right here from our computers."

"I'd like to compare satellite photos of the Grand Canyon to pictures of the same location taken by *TimeFlyer*." said Steve.

"I can probably do that." said Desmond. "Let's see what I can find for satellite images. Why don't you two pull up some chairs." He nodded toward a couple of desks that didn't look used. Steve pushed some chairs over behind Desmond, so that he and Jill could both see his computer screen. "How much of the Canyon do you want to see?"

"I would like to see the Northern point, with a decent amount of land on each side of the Canyon."

"OK." Desmond worked the mouse, and an image appeared. He selected a rectangular section of the picture, and that section expanded to fill the screen. "That's a recent satellite photo. Let's see, two years old. Is that good enough?"

"That's great. Now can we get the same view from the *TimeFlyer* video?" Jill was silent, intently watching the screen as the two men worked on the images.

"Let's see. If I remember right, the Grand Canyon failed to show up about three and a half hours into the video." He made the video jump forward several times until he came to the appropriate section. "This ought to be just about right. Those numbers on the top right of the video are latitude and longitude. At least, what *TimeFlyer* thought was latitude and longitude." He jumped back to the satellite picture. "Hmm, looks like we need to zoom in a little on this one to get to the same apparent height." The screen jumped again. "That's about right."

"Can you draw lines on the pictures?" asked Steve.

"Sure can. What do you want me to draw?"

"On the video, can you draw a line along the shoreline of the lake?" Desmond obligingly traced a rough line around the apparent shoreline of the mysterious lake. "Now, can you trace the same line pattern on the satellite picture?"

"Hmm," Desmond studied the marked up video carefully, then flipped to the satellite photo and drew a rough approximation of the same line. The line stretched from the north side to the south side, and directly across the Canyon's entrance. "Isn't that interesting," he muttered.

Steve looked at Jill. "What do you think?"

"Looks like Herb's explanation fits pretty well."

"Can we get a printout of these two pictures?" Steve asked Desmond.

"Of course. How big do you want them?"

"About the size of a newspaper, if you can do that."

"That's about as big as I can print with a normal printer." He was moving and clicking the mouse rapidly. "Done. They should come out on that printer over there..." he pointed "...in about five minutes." He flipped back and forth between the two images again several times, allowing all three of them to get a good look at each image.

"Let me try something else." said Desmond suddenly. "I want to erase everything in each picture that either belongs to the lake or the canyon." He moved and clicked the mouse, and the lake started to disappear from the video image. When he was done there, he jumped back to the satellite image and started erasing the details of the canyon. When he was done, there was little doubt in any of their minds. "If you factor out the water and the canyon, the rest of the terrain looks very similar."

Steve told him briefly what Herb had related on their visit to the Grand Canyon. When he finished, Desmond looked at him silently for a moment. Then he said, "I know the name of the lake."

"Really? What is it?" asked Steve.

"Lake Bonneville."

"Where is Lake Bonneville?"

"It's gone now. Just a huge dry lakebed where it used to be. It's called the Bonneville Salt Flats now. You've probably heard of it. It's not too far from here. They race cars there now, try to set new land speed records. It's a huge expanse of perfectly flat salt." Desmond explained.

"Can you print these pictures too, please?" asked Steve.

"Sure. I'm going to print some copies for myself, as well." More moves and clicks of the mouse.

"Desmond, are you a Christian?"

"Yes. Southern Baptist. That is, if you consider Southern Baptists Christians," he added with a chuckle. "Why do you ask?"

"Because I think this proves that the Grand Canyon is not millions of years old."

"I'm beginning to think you're right."

"What do you think of Carol's theory?" asked Steve.

"I'm not sure. Actually, I was the one who proposed it. When the data came back from *TimeFlyer*, we were sitting around throwing out ideas. I happened to be looking at a map of the whole US, and I threw out the idea that maybe *TimeFlyer* was over the Atlantic Ocean instead of the Gulf. I didn't really believe it myself, at the time, but Carol jumped all over the idea, and she has me partially convinced it's possible. Have you heard about the results from the supercomputer run?"

"We've heard it." Jill entered the conversation for the first time. "I think it's possible but unlikely. According to the data, it is a lot more likely that *TimeFlyer* was over the Gulf than over the Atlantic. In order to make the Atlantic idea work, you have to ignore the positions of quite a few more stars than you do if you were over the Gulf."

"Seems to me that each side is a possibility," said Desmond reflectively. "I think I'm going to talk this over with Carol."

"Thanks for your help, Desmond." Steve and Jill stood up. "Mind if we check back in a day or two to see how your conversation with Carol goes?"

"Not at all. Stop by anytime. I'll let you know how it goes."

* * * *

After they had gathered up their printouts, they walked out of the Geography department. "Now what?" asked Steve.

"Let's go sit at an empty table in the cafeteria. There probably won't be anyone there right now. We can look at these pictures some more," Jill suggested.

"Good idea." They walked down one level and over to the cafeteria. Sure enough, it was largely deserted and they had their pick of tables.

They sat staring down at the pictures. After about a minute, Jill asked, "How far back are you supposed to go on your next flight?"

"Eight thousand years."

She was silent for a moment as she studied the printouts. When she looked up, Steve was startled to see tears in her eyes. "You can't go."

"Um, you're not getting upset, are you?" he asked carefully.

She shook her head. "No. But you can't go on that flight."

"Why not?"

"Because I don't want to be a widow."

He looked at her in amazement. "Why would you be a widow? Don't you think I can fly *TimeFlyer*?"

"Oh, Steve. It's not about you. It's about time. Don't you see? You'll

197

be flying into nothing. You'll enter a period before time was. Before creation. Before anything existed. *TimeFlyer* can't possibly survive. You'll be killed." A tear was trickling down one cheek.

Steve didn't know what to say. He thought about the past several days, about what Herb and Dr. Phelson had told them. About White Holes and Event Horizons, and the conclusion that time could vary so enormously across the Universe. "So, what you are telling me is that you think the earth is only 6,000 years old? Exactly like the Bible says?"

Jill nodded emphatically. "Yes. It's true, Steve. It's all true. When you go back 8,000 years, you'll be trying to jump back relative to time for the objects that are around us. The Sun, Moon and Earth itself. That means you'll jump back 8,000 Earth years. If you were in some other galaxy, it would probably be OK. But you're not. You're here. It can't possibly work."

"But it's my job. What am I supposed to do, tell them I believe the mission will fail since the ship is going to jump back before the dawn of time? I'll be disobeying orders if I don't fly that mission."

"I don't care if you have to disobey orders. I want to spend the rest of my life with you. I don't want to lose you."

"Oh, man." Steve groaned as he began to realize the implications of Jill's logic. "How did I get myself into this mess?"

Jill giggled unexpectedly through her tears. "We prayed about it, remember?"

"Yeah, and God answers prayer. Oh, man. We went from the frying pan into the fire."

Jill wiped her eyes. "I had to stand up for my beliefs to Dr. Stark. Now it's your turn."

Steve didn't answer. She was right, he concluded. As usual. He knew he couldn't agree to the flight. It would probably result in the loss of the aircraft and crew. The risk was unacceptable. But in order to make his argument, he would have to stand, at least in part, on his belief in the literal interpretation of the Bible, a book that seemed to indicate an Earth roughly 6,000 to 6,500 years old. A book that modern scientists dismissed as irrelevant. A book that Dr. Stark, the brilliant theorist, openly disdained.

The rest of the day looked to be considerably less enjoyable than the past hour.

* * * *

"Come In," called Brian Masulis' from inside his office. Steve opened the door and walked in. "Hi, Steve. How are things?"

"Things are OK. Got a minute?"

"For you? Anytime. What's up?"

"I have decided not to fly the next mission."

Brian sat straight up in his chair. "What?"

"I have decided not to fly the next mission." Steve repeated.

"Why not?"

"Because I believe that the earth was created less than 10,000 years ago, probably about 6,000 years ago and I believe that the lives of all the crew are at risk on this mission."

Brian studied him with a questioning eye. "Let me guess. Biblical literalism."

"Yes, that's part of it."

"What else is part of it?"

"I believe that *TimeFlyer* was actually over the Gulf of Mexico on this last trip, and did fly up to Arizona to check on the existence of the Grand Canyon. I also believe the Grand Canyon had not formed yet."

"But that was 4,000 years ago. The Grand Canyon is hundreds of thousands of years old."

"I believe otherwise."

"Why don't you sit down and tell me about it," requested Brian.

Steve told of their visit to the Grand Canyon over the weekend. He related what they had learned about the rapid formation of the Grand Canyon by a dam breach. He discussed the evidence of rapid canyon formation at Mount St. Helens. "So, that explains the missing Grand Canyon."

"OK, let's say you're right, that the Grand Canyon did form less than 4,000 years ago." Brian said reflectively. "That still leaves a lot of unanswered questions. For example, it is obvious to me that the Universe is millions of years old. There's no question it would take starlight a long time to reach earth from where it started in space."

"That's another thing that was explained to us this weekend," replied Steve, and he went on to explain rapid universe aging and the difference in the passage of time in different parts of the universe.

"So let me see if I have this straight," said Brian. "You think that the earth was formed 6,000 years ago. You also think the rest of the universe is millions, perhaps billions, of years old, even though God created everything at the same instant. The discrepancy in time is possible because of rapid aging due to expansion of the universe in the first few days after creation. Did I get that right?"

"You got it right."

Brian sighed. "This is going to make waves. You know that, right?"

"I know it. I am not looking forward to it. However, I believe that the mission cannot succeed. And, since I am responsible for the welfare of my aircrew, I will not fly."

"Is there anything I can do to change your mind?"

"If the mission were to go back 5,700 years or less, I would fly it."

"Alright. Mind if I write that down? I want to make sure I convey this correctly."

"Not at all."

Brian started jotting notes on a notepad. "OK, let me see. Universe expansion. Rapid aging. And you said, how many years?"

"Five thousand seven hundred. Or less."

"Alright. Well, I need to make some calls about this. Let me do that and I'll get back to you. Where will you be today?"

"I'll probably be in the office in *TimeFlyer*'s hanger."

"OK. Thanks for letting me know." They shook hands, and Steve turned and walked out. Brian reached for the phone.

* * * *

Two hours later, Dr. Stark and Brian were on the phone with General Collins. "I told you that woman was going to be trouble." Dr. Stark was fuming. "You didn't do anything, and now the trouble is spreading. She's got him talked into her religious nonsense. How much more of this are we going to have to put up with?"

There was silence on the speakerphone for so long Brian was afraid the connection was broken. "Hello, are you still there General?" he finally asked.

"Yes, I'm still here. I'm just thinking. What if we were to make an example of these two?"

"How?" demanded Stark.

"I will order Steve to go on the mission. He will refuse. That's a court-martial offense. I'll be there when *TimeFlyer* returns from the mission. As soon as *TimeFlyer* touches down, I will present him with a court-martial. We'll fire Jill at the same time."

"Well, now, that's more like it," Stark declared. "Are you going to tell him ahead of time?"

"Yes, absolutely. He will know exactly what he is risking by refusing to fly. Also, that means Scoot's aircrew will replace Steve's. I also think we should make Steve explain to both aircrews why he is refusing to fly. You know, make sure everybody understands that Steve and Jill are standing on religious arguments. Then, when *TimeFlyer* returns, everybody will see the consequences."

"Yes, yes. That ought to end the nonsense." agreed Dr. Stark happily.

"Brian?"

"Sounds reasonable to me." agreed Brian.

"Alright, that's what we'll do. Just one other thing, Dr. Stark. Is there any chance at all that Steve and Jill are right?"

Dr. Stark turned red. "Poppycock. Pure and utter nonsense. The earth is millions of years old. Now, look, General. I don't want this thing spreading. Sounds like you have doubts too. I don't want everyone getting crazy if they hear Steve explain his idea. This might cause more trouble than it's worth. Maybe we should just get rid of them quietly."

"Don't get yourself all riled up, Andy. I just wanted to make sure you were quite confident." replied the General.

"Confident? I'm so confident I would like to fly on that next mission."

"Not a chance. We agreed to that at the start of the project. OK, Brian, do you think you can get Steve on the phone?"

"Yes, I think I know where he is."

"Alright, conference him in. Andy, I don't want you to be a part of this conversation. It will just be myself, Brian and Steve."

"Alright," Stark agreed and walked out of the office.

The phone began ringing. After a moment, it was picked up. "Hanger. Scoot here."

"Hello Scoot, Brian Masulis. Is Steve there?"

"Yeah, just a second." They could hear muffled conversation in the background.

"Hello, this is Steve."

"Steve, this is General Collins. Brian Masulis is also on the line. He just informed me of your decision. Are you holding to your decision?"

They heard Steve sigh. "Yes, Sir. I am sticking with my decision."

"Steve, I am going to order you to fly that mission. Should you still refuse to fly, you will be directly disobeying orders. I will be present when *TimeFlyer* returns. Upon its return from the mission, you will be presented with a court-martial for failing to follow orders. Does that change your mind?"

"No, Sir, it doesn't. I'm very sorry, Sir, but in this case I believe I have sufficient cause to disobey orders. If it were just me, I would fly. But I am responsible for the rest of my aircrew. Their safety is my concern. I will not knowingly put them in jeopardy."

"That means that Scoot's crew will be put at risk," said Brian.

"I understand that. I wish I could do something about it, but I cannot. His crew is his responsibility, my crew is mine."

"Steve, I am going to have Brian schedule a full meeting with both aircrews. You will explain to them your reasons for not allowing your aircrew to fly the mission, and tell them that Scoot's crew will be flying the mission."

"Yes, Sir."

"Brian, set it up. Steve, do you have any objection to flying a chase plane?"

"No, Sir, none at all."

"Very well, that will be your responsibility for this mission. That's all I have for you."

"Yes, Sir." and Steve hung up the phone.

The General sighed. "Brian, anything else?"

"That's all I have. I thought that would be enough."

"You thought correctly, it is quite enough."

* * * *

Jill spent the day searching the Internet for any and all information she could find on Relativity, Black and White Holes, and Event Horizons. She found some equations that she was able to follow, that validated everything that she had learned so far. She discovered that, in order to avoid a White Hole cosmology, scientists believed that there actually might be a fourth dimension (besides time), which hadn't yet been discovered. She decided that is was more logical to believe in a White Hole than in an undiscovered dimension.

It was glum in the apartment that night. Jill told Steve about her findings. Steve, in turn, related to Jill the reactions from Brian, and then the call from General Collins. JIll's heart was aching for her husband. She knew how difficult it must be for him to have to disobey orders like this. She tried to encourage him, but didn't think she had succeeded. They had prayed together, which seemed to help a little.

The meeting with the aircrews was scheduled for 9:00 AM Thursday morning. Jill had willingly agreed to accompany him. It was now 10:30 PM. In the dark bedroom, he was lying sleepless, staring up at the ceiling.

"You know, Dr. Stark seemed a lot happier today." Jill said, she wasn't sleeping either.

"Well, that's not too surprising. They've found a way to get rid of us both. The troublemakers."

"I suppose you're right."

It was quiet for several minutes.

"I never knew being a Christian could be so hard," Steve said quietly.

"I guess this is persecution." Jill was reflective.

"I hope we're doing what God wants."

"Remember what Jesus said. 'Rejoice when you are persecuted, for great is your reward in Heaven. For so persecuted they the prophets which were before you.' " Jill tried to sound encouraging.

"Well, then, we ought to be getting a nice little account built up in Heaven."

"Yeah. Too bad we can't check the balance once in a while," she said wistfully.

* * * *

By 9:00 AM Thursday, both aircrews had assembled in the auditorium. Brian started the meeting. "The purpose of this meeting is to report a development regarding *TimeFlyer*'s next mission. I have asked Steve Harrison to give the details. Steve?"

Jill gave his arm a squeeze. He stood up and walked to the podium.

"Well, I guess I'll just tell you my decision, and then explain why I made it. I have decided to refuse to fly the next mission on *TimeFlyer*." There was an audible gasp from the assembled group. "That means the rest of my aircrew will also be pulled. Scoot's crew will be flying the next mission, assuming he agrees to do so." The eyes of almost 50 people stared at him incredulously.

"As you probably all know, the next mission is scheduled to go back in time 8,000 years. The reason I am refusing to fly this mission is because I believe our planet was created roughly 6,000 years ago. If I am right, that means traveling back 8,000 years would mean entering a time when nothing existed. Not Earth. Not our solar system. Not even space itself. I don't believe that *TimeFlyer* will survive the trip. Because I am responsible for the safety of my aircrew, I am pulling them off the mission."

The silence in the room was deafening.

"There are three reasons why I believe the earth is only 6,000 years old." Steve went on to explain his findings of the Grand Canyon, his conclusions about its rapid formation, and his explanation of what *TimeFlyer* recorded on its last trip. "I believe that *TimeFlyer* was over the Gulf of Mexico, and did indeed fly to Arizona. I don't believe it was over the Atlantic."

"Second, my wife and I have stumbled across an alternate explanation for the existence of starlight that is millions of years old." He explained the idea of slow earth time and more rapid universe time. "Some preliminary work shows that this is scientifically possible."

"Finally, my wife and I are Christians. The Bible says that all things were created by God, and that the creation happened in six literal days. I believe that is true. I also believe that the timeline presented in the Bible is accurate." He looked up to see Scoot staring down at the floor and shaking his head in disbelief.

"Now, let me tell you what I am risking because of my decision." Steve explained about the expected court-martial. "I am willing to accept a court-martial if I am wrong."

"I expect you will have questions. Brian and I will try to answer them." Steve backed away from the podium, allowing Brian access.

One of Steve's flight engineers raised his hand. "If we disagree with Steve, can we fly anyway?"

"Only if Scoot needs you to fill in on his aircrew," was Brian's reply.

"What if someone on Scoot's aircrew agrees with Steve and Jill and doesn't want to fly?"

"They will face similar consequences. Upon successful conclusion

204

of the mission, if the person is a civilian, they will be fired. If they are military, they will be court-martialed."

Another of Steve's flight engineers raised his hand. "What did you say about the Grand Canyon on that last mission? And what about the lake that Scoot found?"

"The lake was a remnant of the flood of Noah's time," repeated Steve. "If you assume that the Grand Canyon didn't exist, in other words, that the area where the canyon is now was still all solid rock comparable to its surroundings, then it would have been able to hold back a lake that would have covered parts of Utah, Arizona, New Mexico, and Colorado. It would have been huge. Somehow, water from that lake started leaking across the area where the Grand Canyon is now. That caused erosion, which opened up a bigger pathway, which caused more erosion, and all of its geologic repercussions. After a few days, the lake would be drained and you would have the Grand Canyon."

"But it would have had to wear through solid rock," argued the engineer.

"I believe it did. Rapidly," replied Steve. "Moving water can do amazing things."

"So when do you think the Canyon actually formed?" pressed the engineer.

"Sometime after the last flight," replied Steve. There were a few chuckles in the audience, which seemed to discourage the inquisitor from continuing his questioning.

Brian and Steve waited, but there were no other questions. Brian dismissed the meeting.

Scoot was the first one to reach Steve. "Steve, man, what are you doing? You're throwing away your career. Think about what you're doing."

"I have thought about it. A lot."

Tex and Jake were close behind. Jake spoke up. "Hey, Steve, I respect you a lot. And, you know, I'm a Christian too. But, you know, you have to take things with a grain of salt. I mean, I think you are taking this Christian thing way too far. Those stories in the Bible can't all be true. They're just like fairy tales or something."

"I respect your right to disagree with me. But I believe they are all true. And I have heard enough other ideas in the last few days to convince me that things happened just the way the Bible says they did."

"Steve, I have a question." Tex's eyes bored into him. "Are you doing this because you're afraid to fly?"

"No. Like I told Brian, Tex, I am responsible for your safety and the rest of my flight crew. If it were just me, I would probably fly, even knowing that I probably wouldn't survive. But I can't knowingly put all of you at risk. I know you probably don't agree with me, but in my judgment, this is the right decision for you and the rest of the crew."

"I don't want to be associated with a coward," said Tex, half accusingly.

"If I were a coward, I would be flying. Do you have any idea how difficult it is to stand up here and explain that I am not flying partially on religious grounds? That was a whole lot harder than just agreeing to fly the mission and chance the consequences."

Tex stared at him for another moment, then he nodded, apparently satisfied. "Yeah, that speech you made took guts. OK. That's good enough for me."

"You're going along with it?" Scoot stared at Tex in disbelief.

"Not my decision, it's his. I'm just following orders. Are you telling me you have an opening for a co-pilot?" shot back Tex.

"No. I'm his co-pilot, and I'm flying." put in Jake quickly.

Scoot turned back to Steve. "Steve, I get you on this project, man. You're making me look bad."

"I know, Scoot. I'm sorry. But I still believe my decision is correct." he said.

"You know that the theory group figured out how the space-warp formula might have put us over the Atlantic during the last mission, right?"

"Yeah, I heard," said Steve. "They found a set of stars that would place *TimeFlyer* over the Atlantic. The problem is, when you jump back 8,000 years, how are you going to know where you are? Are you going to have to search for a star pattern that will place you over the location you believe yourself to be? How will you ever be sure? How do you know you will be able to get back to the present?"

Scoot shrugged. "It'll work. Just reverse the formula for going backward, and you should go forward, right?"

"I hope that's how it works," replied Steve, "unless there is nothing there."

The four men stood standing around looking at each other. Finally,

206

Steve spoke to Scoot and Jake. "Look, guys, I know this is difficult to absorb. But I'm afraid that if you fly that mission, you are not going to survive. Have you ever considered the possibility that I might be right?"

Scoot snorted. "No way, man. There is no credible scientist alive who agrees with your ideas."

"The idea that the earth was round was pretty radical too, when it was first introduced," said Steve. "There weren't many credible scientists who believed that theory either. But it turned out to be true."

"Well, they were a bunch of dumb bunnies back then."

"OK, let me ask you this. Do you believe in God?"

Scoot sighed. "Man, now you're going to drag me into a religious argument."

"I won't argue with you. I am just going to ask you some questions. Anytime you ask me to, I'll stop."

Scoot nodded resignedly.

"OK, let's get back to my question. Do you believe in God?"

"Yes."

"Do you believe God made everything?"

"Yes."

"If God made everything, he must be pretty smart, right?"

"Yeah, that sounds logical."

"So don't you think, if he made space, since we know space and time are created, that he made time too?"

"Well, I guess we know they are related," admitted Scoot reluctantly.

"So if he created space and time, he can probably manipulate them pretty easily, right? I mean, if you invented something, can't you usually control its behavior to some extent?"

"Well, sometimes. Not always."

"What I am trying to tell you is that I believe that God is able to create the earth in six days, that he did it 6,000 years ago, and he can manipulate time and space to make the universe age more rapidly than earth."

"But we're talking billions of years here." countered Scoot.

"Yeah, I know."

"That is just too much of a stretch for me to believe."

"I'll admit it sounds pretty fantastic. So, have a lot of new ideas. Just think it over."

Scoot shook his head reluctantly. "OK, man. But I still think you're throwing away your career." He and Jake turned and walked toward an exit.

"You got a lot of guts," said Tex quietly to Steve.

Steve recognized it as the compliment that Tex intended. "Thanks, Tex. I appreciate your support."

Tex grinned. "I am not sure I would call it support. After all, I am just following orders. But I have to admire a guy who is willing to stand up for what he believes." And then he too, turned, and walked away.

Jill came up and slid an arm around his waist. "Honey, I am so proud of you. You did great."

"I hope we're right. I'm not looking forward to spending time in prison."

"Oh, we're right. You'll see."

* * * *

For the next several weeks, discussions between the two aircrews raged about Steve's decision and the theory of rapid universe aging. Most dismissed it as pure folly, religious fanaticism taken to the extreme. Most of Steve's aircrew members were quite upset with him. But there were a number of Christians on each team who were struggling to come to terms with Steve's conclusions, and to re-evaluate their own views about the accuracy of history as recorded in the Bible. The arguments grew so intense that, in the end, Dr. Stark had been forced to do a presentation defending prevailing scientific wisdom that the universe, including the earth, was millions of years old. He hadn't been very happy about it, but he had managed to hold his temper in check during the presentation, and most who attended seemed convinced by his explanation.

Dr. Stark's presentation had been open to "...anyone ready to examine the evidence with an unbiased view." Meaning, Steve and Jill figured, that they were not welcome. They did not try to attend.

There were, however, four people who had come to Steve and asked him to explain himself again. Two of them had been from Steve's crew, and two from Scoot's. Steve and Jill had invited them over to their apartment, and the group ended up talking until late into the night. Jill had been invaluable in explaining the mathematical foundation for the theory, which the highly educated nuclear technicians found helpful. At the end of the night, one of the people from Scoot's crew had decided to refuse to fly. The other seemed convinced, but told the group his conviction was to follow orders and fly with his crew, even if it meant risking his life. He did tell them, however, he was taking out extra life insurance on himself to provide for his family in the event he didn't survive the flight.

When Scoot's crewman told Scoot he didn't want to fly, Scoot had taken it well. He had gotten a technician from Steve's crew to agree to replace his missing crew member without informing the people higher up. "Been enough trouble around here," he explained to Steve. "I don't want to stir up the hornet's nest again. No sense getting more people all riled up if we don't have to." Steve was grateful for Scoot's cooperation.

Two weeks before *TimeFlyer's* next flight, Steve and Jill had been astounded when Scoot approached them with his lead flight technician, a stolid and unassuming genius of a man named Delvan Abscomb. They told Steve that they had decided to install an emergency override switch into the cockpit of *TimeFlyer*, which could be reached by either Scoot or Jake. When depressed, the switch would immediately cut power to the space-warp drive and thereby terminate the space-warp event. "Doesn't mean I am falling for your religious hocus-pocus." he told Steve and Jill. "But it never hurts to have more options, right?"

Jake had been somewhat disgusted with Scoot when he learned about the abort button, but in the ensuing 'discussion', had agreed that it probably wouldn't do any harm.

The abort button was installed without consulting any of the other aircrew members. Everyone wanted to keep a low profile. It hadn't taken Delvan long to figure out how to wire the switch into the space-warp drive circuitry. Steve, not too far removed from school with a major in Electrical Engineering, helped review the circuit diagrams for him. The switch itself was placed underneath the lower edge of the instrument panel, out of sight but easily reached by pilot or copilot in the event of an emergency.

The night before the flight, Steve prayed fervently that it wouldn't be necessary.

Chapter 13

In preparation for the 8,000 year mission, all of *TimeFlyer*'s available space had been crammed with supplies. This trip was the five day trip to the Marshall Islands and the Bikini Atoll, where the United States had conducted Nuclear Bomb tests in the 1950's. Scoot's aircrew members were obviously excited about the trip, since there would be time for most of them to lie on the beach and swim. They had even managed to find room for a volleyball and net. There was plenty of work to do as well, of course. As usual, native peoples would be photographed from a distance. In addition, many soil and rock samples were to be taken, specifically to check for radioactivity levels in the age before nuclear testing contaminated some of the islands. Also, there had been requests for some of the crew to take along underwater cameras and try to get some pictures of the wildlife around the abundant coral reefs. Even with the threat of sharks, interest in this part of the mission was high, and there were no shortage of volunteers.

But despite all the eagerness and anticipation, there was a tense undercurrent as well. The closer the day came for the mission, the less anyone seemed willing to discuss the possibility that there might be any kind of risk. People were shorter with each other, and tempers flared more easily. Even Jill, who didn't spend nearly as much time with the aircrews as Steve, noticed the difference.

"I think people have finally just decided to make up their minds and be done with it." she said to Steve the day before the mission.

"They don't want to talk about it anymore. They have decided what they believe, and don't want to consider the fact that they might be wrong."

"It's almost a kind of willful ignorance," he observed.

"I don't know of anyone who likes to be told they are wrong," said Jill. "Everyone has taken a position. The people on the mission have decided we are wrong."

"I would be willing to be wrong for their sake," said Steve.

* * * *

The day of *TimeFlyer's* 8,000 year mission there was a cloud cover, which drastically reduced visibility, so the mission was delayed for two days. When the second day rolled around, conditions turned out to be just about perfect. The atmosphere was clear, with patches of widely scattered clouds and almost unlimited visibility.

The flight was scheduled to take off at 4:00 AM, under the cover of darkness. It would be light at altitude when they reached the Pacific at approximately 5:30 AM. Since the mission had been delayed by two days, there wasn't as much of the usual last-minute bustle surrounding the departure. All those seemingly endless last minute details had already been taken care of before the previous scheduled departure.

Steve arrived at *TimeFlyer's* hanger at 3:30 AM. Jill had decided to accompany him. Despite her continued assurance that the court martial would never materialize, he noticed that she had stayed a lot closer during the last several days. Not that he minded, of course. She was simultaneously a source of encouragement and comfort.

As had become tradition during the previous missions, Brian Masulis volunteered for coffee duty, keeping a ready supply of the hot, black liquid. The detail oriented multi-role library science major had thoughtfully assembled a cadre of coffee makers before the first flight, and had plainly started a tradition that everyone appreciated during these early morning departures. He smiled as Steve and Jill made their way over to the coffee bar. "Morning, folks. Looks like you need some of the good stuff." He handed them each a steaming cup.

"Thanks, Brian. Doing your usual great job," said Steve. Jill just nodded appreciatively.

"Ah, well, we don't want anyone falling asleep in our marvelous contraption. How would that look in the history books?" Brian winked and grinned at them. "Cream and sugar are over there," he nodded toward a table on his right. The normalcy of this little gesture struck Steve as somewhat odd, but he realized that Brian was doing his part to make things seem as normal as possible. Steve appreciated the gesture. He knew he had created quite a bit of stress for Brian and the leadership team.

Steve and Jill got their cream and sugar, then looked around at that assembled crowd. There were more people here than the last flight, even though fewer would be flying on *TimeFlyer*. He got some grins and nods, but also noticed several people trying to avoid his gaze, mostly his own aircrew members. He couldn't blame them. If he hadn't felt so strongly about his decision, he would have been disappointed to miss the flight as well. In fact, he was disappointed, he admitted to himself. It would have been so easy to just dismiss all of his thoughts as religious fantasy and decide to fly the mission anyway.

It was a moment he would always remember as being his most vulnerable. First, he had decided to try and honor God by deciding not to continue to fly the A-10, doing a job that he loved and had dedicated his whole life to pursuing. He was trying, really trying, to honor God, and he had ended up flying a great overgrown whale of an airplane, which was really no more technically challenging than driving his car to the grocery store. Then, when the missions had started to become interesting, he felt like he and Jill had to stand up to defend the Bible. And the reward? If he was wrong, several years sitting in a military prison mourning everything he had given up and wondering how to recover.

Stop it, he told himself firmly. *You heard the arguments, you made your decision, and you're going to stand behind that decision.* As he and Jill moved toward Tex and the other fliers, he silently gave himself a dressing down that would have made his drill sergeant proud.

"Ouch. What are you doing?" Jill pulled her hand out of his. Steve suddenly realized that, in the emotion of the moment, he had started squeezing her hand fiercely.

"Sorry."

Jill looked at him searchingly. She realized that something was going on in his mind. She shook her hand a little to get the blood flowing again. "Are you OK?" she asked quietly.

"Yeah. Sorry about that," he said. Then they were in among the group.

"Morning," said Tex.

"Good morning," responded Steve.

Tex shook his head. His eyes seemed more Asian than usual. "I didn't say good morning. Just morning."

Jake laughed. "I take it you're not a morning person," he teased Tex.

"Not unless he's climbing onto a horse," responded Steve. "You ready to go?"

"Just about. Scoot's up top, doing the visual on the props and upper surface. He'll be back down in a minute or two."

Scoot chose that moment, to pop down the ladder extending from the underside of *TimeFlyer* just a few feet above the ground. "Hey, Guys and Gal," he called as he swaggered toward them, acknowledging Jill's presence. "Everything up top looks fine. We're ready to roll. You?" he looked at Steve.

Tex answered. "We're ready. I've already pre-flighted our plane."

"Usual routine, right? I lead, you follow." Steve said to Scoot.

"I think so. Have you checked with Darren?" Scoot asked, referring to the pilot who was to fly the second chase plane. In a change from the usual procedures, there would be a second chase plane flying today. Dr. Stark had decided that he wanted to view the flight departure, and Steve was glad the physicist had decided to view the proceedings from this second aircraft.

"Actually, I haven't. Anybody seen him?" asked Steve.

Among the general shaking of heads, Tex said "I think I saw him in the hanger office. I'll go check." He trotted off in that direction.

"Well, I guess it is as good a time as any to wish you a good flight," said Steve.

Scoot looked at him. "Thanks, Steve. You've been a good friend. I still say I don't agree with you, but I know you really mean what you say, and I know you totally believe your theory." He stopped talking for a second, then continued. "I hate to say I hope you're wrong, but I hope you're wrong." He tried to grin at him, but the attempt at humor fell short. He stuck out his hand. "See you in five days, Pal."

Steve took Scoot's hand. "Thanks for everything, Scoot. I appreciate you working with the crew." The lump in his throat prevented him from saying anything further. Scoot slapped him on the arm with his left hand. He too seemed to be having difficulty speaking.

Steve released his grip and turned to Jake. "Try to keep this guy in line, OK?" he said, indicating Scoot with a nod of his head.

Jake laughed. "Of everything you've said the last two months, what you just said is the most impossible." Then he sobered. "Take care of yourself, Steve. I'm glad I had a chance to get to know you. You're a great pilot."

Steve nodded as they shook hands. Jill had given Scoot a quick embrace, and did the same to Jake. "You guys are the best," she said. It didn't surprise Steve to note that her eyes were moist.

"Here's Darren," said Scoot, breaking the awkwardness of the moment by getting back to business. "Usually, the chase plane goes first till we reach the jump-off point of the mission. Since you're second chase, you want to follow the two of us?"

"Sure, I'll follow." replied Darren.

"Alright then. One. Two. Three." said Scoot, pointing first to Steve, then himself, then Darren. "Let's get this operation rolling."

The others turned toward their aircraft. Steve paused for a moment, then embraced his wife. "Be back in a few hours." he said.

"I'll be here." she replied. There was nothing more to say.

Steve followed Tex toward the silently waiting turboprop.

* * * *

Steve and Tex were going through the preflight checklist in the turboprop. "Engine 1 start," Steve told Tex.

"Starting Engine 1," replied Tex. The whine of a hydraulic motor resonated through the fuselage as the big four-bladed propeller started to turn, then was drowned out as the turbine fired and the propeller rapidly rose to its rated speed. The sound was impressive. There was the hiss of air being drawn into the turbine, the roar of the turbine's exhaust, and the ferocious buzzing of the big propeller being driven through the air so fast that the tips approached the speed of sound. The plane began to rock gently from the forces being controlled. It was as if the plane were coming alive. "Engine 1 running fine, all pressures normal."

"Engine 2 start." Soon Engine 2, on the right side of the aircraft, was hissing and roaring like its twin on the right.

"Engine 2 running fine, all pressures normal," Tex reported.

Steve called the tower and got permission to taxi to the end of the runway. When they arrived, they held short of the runway and waited for *TimeFlyer* to approach behind them. It was more than 10 minutes later when they saw *TimeFlyer* start to move from its resting spot in front of its hanger trundle toward the taxiway. It took another five minutes before it was approaching them from behind. As it pulled up behind them, Steve requested and received permission to depart.

As they turned onto the runway, they saw *TimeFlyer* moving forward and turning toward the runway's end where they had sat waiting only moments before. The sight never failed to impress Steve. The huge aircraft was moving slowly, its six huge propellers spinning at the top of the six vertical stabilizers. It was an incredible machine.

Steve advanced the pitch levers. The pitch of the blades on their two propellers changed, and they started grabbing big fistfuls of air. The commuter plane started down the runway and quickly reached rotation speed. Steve pulled back on the yoke, and they were airborne once again. They were ordered to circle out to one side of the airstrip. Steve and Tex had a good view of *TimeFlyer* lining up on the end of the runway, sitting for a moment as its crew checked and rechecked everything, and then started moving away from the end of the runway. From their height of 5,000 feet, it looked like *TimeFlyer* was hardly moving. But after consuming a little more than a mile of runway, it lifted off and began its climb to meet them.

After *TimeFlyer* was in the air, the second commuter aircraft lifted off. When all three were at altitude, Steve radioed ahead and got clearance to fly west, over the Sierra Nevada mountain range, over California, and on to the Pacific Ocean. The jump back in time would happen over the Pacific. After that, *TimeFlyer* had a rather boring 16-hour flight past Hawaii and on to the Marshall Islands. There was some buffeting over the mountains, nothing out of the ordinary. Another 40 minutes and they were over the Pacific.

Scoot's voice came over the radio. "OK, let's get into position." Steve acknowledged, and then climbed to 26,000 feet, allowing *TimeFlyer* to pass him underneath. He was above and to the right of *TimeFlyer*; the other chase plane was below and to the left.

Once in position, Steve ordered Tex to turn on the video cameras. Then Steve radioed Scoot and reported they were ready. A moment later, the second chase plane reported in. Then they sat and waited.

* * * *

215

Aboard *TimeFlyer*, Scoot and Jake were finishing their pre-space-warp checklist. There wasn't much to it. Their flight technicians, led by Delvan, had already run the computers through all the self-diagnostic programs, which had reported that everything was functional. The next thing was to make sure the reactor was producing enough steam to generate the electrical power necessary to operate the space-warp device. Once that was done, all Scoot had to do was give the order. It came within a few moments. "Ready to proceed with space-warp," Delvan reported over the intercom.

"Alright, let's do it," Scoot ordered into his headset. "Initiate space-warp."

"Initiating." Delvan replied from the trailing compartment. Scoot both heard and felt the hum indicating that the power was being generated and fed into the space-warp drive. He and Jake peered ahead, looking for the characteristic shimmering glow that accompanied the space-warp event.

The hum continued. Scoot's eyes fell back to the instruments. "See it?" he asked Jake.

"Not yet."

Scoot's eyes stayed on his instruments. Over the 100+ years of flight, the responsibilities of each seat in the cockpit had been pretty well defined. They were generally interchangeable. For this part of the flight, Scoot had volunteered to watch the instruments, while Jake aimed *TimeFlyer* into the middle of the space-warp. Last flight it had been Jake's turn to watch the instruments. Trading duty between the two seats was almost as old as flight itself.

Besides monitoring the flight instruments, there were a couple of other gauges that Scoot was watching. One was the amount of total electrical power being generated and fed into the space-warp device. Another indicated the temperature of the nuclear pile. The reactor could reach max power for only a few minutes each flight. The limiting factor was the ability to shed excess heat, preventing the nuclear pile from melting down. Even though the temperature outside at this altitude was well below freezing, it was still difficult to dump heat into the atmosphere in quantity. Air just didn't pull heat from the skin of the aircraft nearly as well as water did.

"Generating a lot of power. Getting hot, too. See anything?"

"No. Wait, yes! There it is."

****

"Look at that!" exclaimed Tex. Steve just stared. Instead of the usual shimmering glow, a black maw was opening in front of *TimeFlyer*.

Steve reached down and toggled his transmit button. "Scoot! Abort! Something's wrong."

****

Jake had already decided to abort before Steve had finished his radio call. He reached forward and under the instrument panel and pressed the abort button. Scoot's hand hit the back of his a moment later as Scoot reacted to the radio call and reached for the abort button as well.

Jake yanked his hand back to the control yoke, and twisted it savagely to the right. *TimeFlyer* began a leisurely bank. Jake looked forward at the black void opening in front of their aircraft, waiting for that awful blackness to disappear as rapidly as it had materialized.

****

Delvan had wired up the abort button to simultaneously turn off the space-warp drive and turn on a red light on his console. When the red light came on, he jumped into action. The reactor was putting out full power, generating steam as fast as it could. A little more than one third of the total amount of steam being produced in the nuclear reactor was being used to power the generator for the space-warp drive. When that load was suddenly removed, there was just as suddenly a surplus of steam that needed somewhere to go.

Delvan had anticipated this situation, and spent several hours in the days before the mission thinking through the sequence of steps that he would need to take in order to keep the reactor from being damaged when one third of its rated load was suddenly removed. His hands started moving across the control board in front of him. First, he reduced the power output of the reactor. While that immediately slowed down the nuclear reaction, there was a large quantity of heat, already generated, that needed to go somewhere.

Even as he felt *TimeFlyer* began to bank to the right, Delvan was watching the pressure gauge for the steam. It rose rapidly, as he expected. He decided he had better vent some steam, which would simultaneously lower the pressure and release some of the excess heat. He pressed another button on his console and steam exploded out of an emergency release valve at the rear of the aircraft.

* * * *

Steve and Tex watched anxiously to see if *TimeFlyer* would respond to Steve's radioed warning. It did. They saw *TimeFlyer* start to bank to the right. Steve let out a sigh of relief. Another second later, and he realized with horror that *TimeFlyer* wasn't changing direction. It continued to bank, but was getting closer and closer to the blackness.

"They're getting sucked in," said Tex in alarm. With a sickening feeling, Steve realized it was true. *TimeFlyer* had opened a hole into nothingness. Their world was pouring through the opening as fast as it could go, trying to fill the void. The rush of air into the blackness was carrying *TimeFlyer* like a dry leaf in a stiff fall breeze.

TimeFlyer had banked almost 45 degrees. Now it was no longer pointed in its direction of travel, and its nose had started to rise. "Come on, shut that thing down," whispered Steve.

* * * *

At almost the same instant, Jake also realized what was happening. The opening from his world into the void had taken a tremendous amount of energy to generate, but once generated, resisted closing back down. Time and space were being sucked into the nothingness through the void. A struggle commenced between the warped space, which wanted to un-warp, and the flow of matter and time from the current age into nothingness, trying to fill an emptiness that could never be satisfied.

Jake pulled back on the yoke to try to point *TimeFlyer* above the void. He saw the top of the black space appear at the top of his windshield, so he realized that *TimeFlyer* was starting to climb. But still the blackness seemed to be approaching. Jake realized that *TimeFlyer* was being pulled toward the void. There was nothing else to be done. If that blackness didn't disappear, and fast, they were going to be sucked in.

Steve and Tex watched in disbelief as *TimeFlyer* came to the space-warp. The black void was now smaller, but still large enough to accommodate the huge airplane.

* * * *

As soon as the steam being vented by Delvan hit the outside air, it started to condense into water vapor, forming a billowing cloud. Even though it cooled rapidly in the sub-zero air, it still contained enough heat energy to rise. And rise it did, just enough to obscure a clear line of sight between *TimeFlyer* and the chase planes following above and behind on each side.

* * * *

Steve saw the white cloud form behind *TimeFlyer*. "They're venting steam," he reported to Tex. Through the vapor, Steve dimly saw *TimeFlyer* pass into the blackness. There seemed to be a flash, and then the blackness was gone.

And *TimeFlyer* was gone.

Another moment, and their plane started bouncing through the still steaming air currents. Steve held the controls loosely, afraid to over correct. The plane jolted hard once, twice, then reverted to bouncing through what felt like normal turbulence. Then, suddenly, they were cruising along smoothly again.

Steve banked the plane into a hard right turn, circling to try to get back behind where the void had materialized. As they swung around, they heard a radio call coming from Darren in the second chase plane. "Chase 2 to *TimeFlyer*. Please acknowledge, *TimeFlyer*."

Because of the bank, the view for Tex out his right window was down and toward the Pacific more then three miles below. As he scanned the sky for any sign of *TimeFlyer*, as well as trying to spot Chase 2, a flash of something caught his attention. There was something spinning and tumbling through the air on its way down to the surface of the ocean. "Something's falling through the air below us. Let's get down there and figure out what it is," he said to Steve.

Without hesitation, Steve pushed the yoke forward and simultaneously pulled back on the pitch control. Their airplane pitched down so suddenly that Steve and Tex were pushed up against their restraints. Steve held the yoke forward as the nose continued to pitch down until he, too, could see the object tumbling, alternatively dark and reflective, tumbling through the air below. As they got closer, Steve could make out some detail. "Get the camera on that thing," he ordered Tex.

Tex reached for the camera controls. The camera was actually mounted in a clear acrylic pod just behind them on the bottom of the fuselage. He pointed it to the appropriate region of space and started to zoom in. They both recognized it about the same time.

"It's a propeller. And part of one of their vertical stabilizers," said Tex.

Steve reduced the speed of their dive, and started circling the wind-milling propeller. It was turning and twisting, now pointed at them, now down as it did its crazy dance toward the surface of the ocean. The large flat section that had once been the proud tail of that enormous aircraft was whipping around crazily as it fought with the still attached propeller for aerodynamic stability. They followed it down, Steve being careful not to get too close.

It took almost four minutes before the piece impacted the surface of the Pacific. Every 30 seconds, they could hear Chase 2 calling *TimeFlyer* on the radio, trying vainly to get a response. Steve leveled the aircraft to avoid becoming part of the aquatic environment themselves. The piece hit the ocean's surface, raising a spout of water. For another few seconds, the piece seemed to rest on the swells. One of the propeller blades seemed to reach in agony toward the blue sky above. Then, slowly, the piece slipped beneath the surface of the waves and was gone.

"Man, oh man." said Tex. Steve felt sick. He couldn't say anything. He rolled the pitch control forward and felt their own propellers bite into the air. Then he pulled back on the yoke and pointed the nose of his aircraft back up toward the beckoning blue.

"Going to call the other plane?" asked Tex.

"You do it." Steve's voice was choked with emotion.

Tex thumbed the transmit button. "Chase 1 to Chase 2."

"Go ahead, Chase 1," came Darren's voice over the radio.

"What's your altitude?"

"We're at 221 feet," came the response, meaning they were at 22,100 feet. "We are at your 7 o'clock."

"Roger. We'll climb back to 221 feet as well. You can pull alongside."

It seemed to take a long time to climb back to altitude. All the time, Tex was scanning the sky, looking for anything else that might give them a clue as to *TimeFlyer*. When they reached altitude 221, the second chase plane came along their right side, about a quarter of a mile away.

"We've been calling them over the radio, but there's no response," reported Darren.

Steve's emotions turned to anger as he thumbed the microphone to respond. "They're not going to respond. We followed one of their propellers all the way down to the Pacific." He released the transmit button. "Idiot!"

"They're just being prudent," said Tex quietly.

"You go ahead and return to base." Darren's voice sounded nonplussed. "We'll stay out here for another half hour or so to see if we can get them to respond."

"They don't have enough fuel for that, do they?" Tex asked Steve.

"Probably wouldn't hurt to ask," said a still irritable Steve. He thumbed the microphone switch. "Chase 2, do you have enough fuel to stay on station for another 30 minutes?"

It was several moments before Darren responded. "We won't have enough fuel to get all the way back to Minion Lake, but we can reach Edwards and refuel there."

"Roger, Chase 1 is heading for the barn," Steve responded.

The ride home was quiet, neither of the men trusting themselves to speak their thoughts. Passage over California and back to Nevada was thankfully non-eventful. Steve got immediate clearance to land, and pulled up to the plane's hanger less than one minute after touchdown. They completed post-flight quickly. When they got off the plane, Jill was there waiting. So were most of his aircrew, along with Dr. Choi. They had heard the radio conversations between the aircraft, and knew something was seriously wrong. As Steve opened the exit door of the chase plane, it was plain something was not right by the pained expression on his normally upbeat face. They watched as he lowered the boarding ladder and descended from the aircraft, followed by Tex. They waited for him to speak. Finally, one of his aircrew asked, "So, what happened?"

"Their space-warp drive opened a hole into nothing. They couldn't shut it down in time, and they got sucked in." Steve stopped for a second, and then plunged ahead. "Some debris popped back out through the space-warp right before it collapsed. We followed it down to the Pacific."

Jill came up and slid an arm around his waist. That gentle gesture overwhelmed him. He pulled her close, buried his head in her thick black hair, and started sobbing. He wept for Scoot and Jake. He wept for Delvan and the rest of the lost aircrew. He wept for the loss of the magnificent *TimeFlyer*. And, as so many men of God have done through the ages, he wept for the decision makers who had ignored the warnings and allowed such an unnecessary tragedy.

Chapter 14

Five days later, Steve and Jake were again ordered to take up chase plane duty, to fly out over the Pacific, and meet *TimeFlyer* if it should return from wherever it had disappeared. After viewing the video recorded by their cameras, almost everyone agreed that the reappearance of *TimeFlyer* was more than a little unlikely. However, orders were orders, and even Steve had to admit that it would be irresponsible not to try to meet the huge aircraft if it should reappear.

Steve had asked the mechanics to install some extra-capacity fuel tanks to allow them to loiter above the Pacific for more than six hours. Every 15 minutes, they sent out radio calls for *TimeFlyer*. At the end of six hours of loitering time, they returned to a subdued airbase.

When Steve and Tex descended the steps of their turboprop, General Collins was there with Brian Masulis, along with a few others. Steve walked up to General Collins and saluted smartly. "Permission to speak, Sir."

"Granted," responded Collins.

"Am I going to receive a court-martial?"

"Not at this time," the General admitted with a frown.

"I request permission to visit with Carla, Scoot's wife. How should I report the status of *TimeFlyer*'s aircrew?"

"They are missing in action."

"Any presumption about their status?" pressed Steve.

The General hesitated for a long moment. As much as he wanted to deny the obvious, there wasn't really any hope for the re-appearance of *TimeFlyer*. If the machine had been able to transit back through time, the crew had strict orders to reappear in the current time five days after their mission departure date, no matter how long their mission lasted. Since *TimeFlyer* had not materialized, it was only logical to conclude that its reappearance was highly unlikely.

"You can report that the aircraft is overdue and presumed lost," he finally said, with obvious reluctance. But then his voice hardened. "Make sure you reveal nothing of the nature of the mission or our operations here. All information continues to remain above Top Secret at a Need to Know Level. Family members of missing crew members do not qualify."

Steve understood how hard it must have been for the General to make the admission of the failure of the mission. "Yes, Sir. Thank you, Sir." he responded quietly.

* * * *

Steve and Jill spent the afternoon gathering and packing Scoot's personal belongings. Then they called Carla, where she and Scoot had taken up residence in a Denver suburb. They reached an answering machine, so Steve left his cell phone number and asked her to call. She called back about an hour later.

"Hello, Carla. Have you been told about the status of Scoot's mission?"

"Yes. An Air Force officer came here about noon. Can you tell me anything?"

"Jill and I would like to come visit you in person. May we come?"

"Oh yes, please do. When can you get here?"

Jill had already been checking into available flights. "I think we can be there by about 10:00 in the morning tomorrow," responded Steve.

"Come as soon as you can."

The next morning, their journey started at 5:00 AM with a hop from Minion Lake to Las Vegas International, and from there to Denver with a 7:20 AM departure. They landed in Denver at 9:08, picked up a rental car, and drove out to Scoot and Carla's house.

Scoot and Carla lived in a two-story house in Aurora, a suburb east of Denver. It took 35 minutes to make their way to the house. During the drive, Steve and Jill discussed what they thought they could and couldn't say.

"Do you think I should tell Carla about my refusal to fly the mission and Scoot taking my place?" Steve asked Jill.

"No, I don't think so. It will just make her grief more pronounced, and she might blame you."

"Well, that doesn't leave me able to say much," said Steve as he merged onto I-70 West.

Jill sighed. "I know. I guess all we can really do is be there for her."

* * * *

When they arrived in front of the attractive bi-level house, they noted that there were already several vehicles parked on the street. They parked their rental car in an empty spot a couple of doors down and walked back to ring the doorbell. It was answered by Carla's father, whom they had met at the wedding that now seemed so long ago.

"Steve and Jill. Come in." Welcoming them graciously with a firm handshake, he closed the door behind them and nodded toward the half-length stairway that led up. "Carla's in the living room."

Jill seemed reluctant, so Steve led the way up the stairs. They found Carla sitting on the couch. There were several other people in the room. She stood up when she saw them and embraced them both in turn. "Thank you so much for coming," she said softly.

Carla's father introduced them to the others in the room. "You probably remember my wife, Cecilia? This is our pastor, Jeremiah Johnson. And you probably remember Karisa Adams who was maid of honor." Steve and Jill circled the room, shaking hands and renewing the acquaintances. When they got back to Carla, her father nodded to the others. "We'll go downstairs for a few minutes so you can visit in private," he said.

"Thank you," said Jill. The others made their way single file down the stairs into the partially finished family room located on the lower of the house's three levels.

Carla turned to Steve. "I guess you were right after all," she told him with a sad smile.

The comment took Steve off balance. "I'm sorry?" he responded.

Carla looked at him searchingly. "Didn't Scoot take over this mission from you? That's what he told me."

225

Steve and Jill glanced at each other in surprise. Steve turned back to Carla. "I wasn't sure what Scoot told you. Yes, he did fly the mission for me."

"How much can you tell me?"

"Why don't you tell me what you know, and I'll see what details I can fill in," Steve responded.

Carla told Steve that she knew Scoot was flying some kind of experimental aircraft, and that the mission was considered somewhat dangerous but not necessarily high risk. "He never even told me what kind of airplane he was flying, said it was top secret. I initially thought it was a small airplane like a fighter, but when he mentioned other people flying with him, I guessed it was something larger."

"It was larger than a fighter. Fourteen people were lost in the accident," said Steve.

"Why didn't Scoot recognize the danger like you did?" Carla asked, her dark eyes pleading with Steve for answers that she suspected he couldn't give.

"I guess Scoot was more of a risk taker. Actually, he did recognize that there was some risk, and he made some changes to the airplane that he thought might help prevent the accident I feared. Unfortunately, it seems that those changes didn't work."

"And they can't even recover his body?"

Steve shook his head no. "I'm sorry. There is nothing left to recover."

"Did he... did he suffer?" asked Carla. Steve could tell she was struggling to hold her composure.

"Not at all. I can tell you that the accident happened so quickly, I am sure he felt nothing. It happened out over the Pacific, which is one of the reasons there is so little to recover."

"So everything fell into the ocean? And the military can't recover anything?"

"The water is too deep to make recovery of anything possible," Steve said, hoping he wouldn't have to lie further.

They sat in silence for a few moments.

"We did bring Scoot's personal belongings with us. They are out in the car. Should we go get them?" asked Steve when the silence got awkward.

"Yes, thank you," said Carla graciously.

"I'll get his things," Steve told Jill. She nodded and he rose to go

226

out to the car.

When he returned, he brought Scoot's suitcase back into the living room, set it on the floor, and opened it. Inside were most of the clothes that Scoot had kept on base. Carla's eyes filled with tears when she saw the familiar items.

Jill had wrapped some of the pictures on his desk in the clothing to protect them. She extracted the first of the pictures from the clothing. It was a picture of Scoot and Carla on their wedding day. She handed it to Carla, who looked at it through her tears. She raised her head to look at them. "He probably hadn't told you that I'm pregnant, had he?" And she clutched the picture to her bosom and wept.

* * * *

Steve and Jill ended up staying most of the day. Before they left, Carla had decided on a date for a funeral service eight days later. Steve and Jill decided to return to Minion Lake, to stay in contact with the arrangements for other members of Scoot and Jake's aircrew. Steve wasn't looking forward to the next month. There was going to be a tremendous amount of grieving.

Because of the flight schedules, they didn't get back to Minion Lake until the following evening. When they got off the commuter plane at their airbase, several members of Steve's aircrew met them. They had become quite a bit more respectful of him after the loss of their beloved time machine. "There's an all-hands meeting tomorrow morning," they reported.

"What about?"

"Rumor has it that Dr. Stark is going to explain what happened to *TimeFlyer*."

"I know what happened to *TimeFlyer*," said Steve with a frown.

Jill grimaced, "I bet he doesn't agree."

* * * *

The staff had gathered in the auditorium. Most people chose to sit in the same seats where they had sat in previous meetings, exhibiting a human characteristic familiar to meeting goers around the world. As a result, most of the seats that Scoot and his crew would have occupied were empty. Seeing the empty seats caused a fresh wave of grief to

227

stab at Steve's wounded soul.

As usual, Brian Masulis got up and called the meeting to order. Then he detailed the purpose of the meeting. "Dr. Stark is going to explain to you what they believe happened to *TimeFlyer*. Then, General Collins will give us his thoughts about the status of the project. Dr. Stark?"

Dr. Stark made his way to the podium. "Ladies and Gentlemen, as Brian has said, my purpose today is to explain what we believe happened to *TimeFlyer*. First, let me make it clear that I believe *TimeFlyer* is lost, along with the aircrew. This is a terrible tragedy, and I admit that the fault is partially mine."

Steve and Jill looked at each other in surprise. After Dr. Stark's behavior toward them over the past several months, they were not expecting him to capitulate to any of their beliefs or theories. They were certainly surprised at his admission of failure.

"First, let me review the sequence of events that led up to the loss of *TimeFlyer*," continued the physicist. "The first mission was a 500 year jump back in time, which went quite well. The second jump, 1,000 years back, also went well. However, on the third mission, which jumped back 4,000 years, some anomalies that we did not fully understand, and perhaps still don't, were recorded. When *TimeFlyer* jumped back 4,000 years in time, several things happened that caused some difficulty in locating its position in space and time. First, the navigation system seemed to have difficulty locating the necessary reference stars. Second, the terrain they observed didn't match what they were expecting.

"Because of these anomalies, several areas of our technical staff reviewed the data and determined, with over a 97% degree of probability, that *TimeFlyer* had actually emerged from this third space-warp event over the Atlantic, instead of over the Gulf of Mexico as it was supposed to. Based on those results, my team spent quite a few hours pouring over the data, the machinery, and the theory, trying to explain the unexpected results. We determined that some adjustments to the instrumentation were necessary. We implemented those changes on *TimeFlyer* before the next mission.

"This is what we believed happened. When the computers in *TimeFlyer* made the calculations to jump back in time, something was still not quite right. Instead of opening a space-warp back to the exact same location over the earth's surface as it was departing from, it

228

actually opened a space-warp ending somewhere in space, beyond Earth's atmosphere. Probably somewhere along the path of Earth's orbit, but at a position where the Earth was not located in its orbit at that particular time. The space-warp ended in a vacuum. The atmosphere on our side rushed through the space-warp in a vain effort to fill the vacuum, which of course it could not do. As it did so, *TimeFlyer* was caught in the airflow and was pulled into the vacuum of deep space."

Steve could feel Jill tensing at this explanation as Stark continued, "We believe that *TimeFlyer* tried to halt the space-warp, but was unable to close it in time to prevent catastrophe. Now, I know this is a very sensitive topic, so I want to be very careful in what I say. I know that some of you might have been persuaded that this flight failed because it was going back in time to an age before the universe existed. I want to make sure that you understand none of us in a leadership position on this project agree with that explanation. *TimeFlyer* opened a space-warp that ended in deep space."

"That miserable dog," Steve heard Jill mutter angrily.

"What that means is that we need to do more work on the theory. Perhaps we made an error somewhere in our calculations. Obviously, one of the things we will be checking is the change we made to the space-warp equation. Another possibility, of course, is that *TimeFlyer* was in another position that we haven't yet determined on its third trip back into time, which would have caused us to modify the space-warp equation the wrong way. Another possibility, which I think less likely but still within the realm of possibility is that the orbit of the Earth has shifted over the centuries. This might have been caused by a meteor of sufficient size impacting the earth, or perhaps even the fact that the earth had not captured the moon as a satellite 8,000 years ago. If the Earth didn't yet have its moon, its orbital path around the sun would be different enough that it might result in what we saw with *TimeFlyer*. There are a number of possibilities and we will be exploring each of them very carefully.

"At any rate, I know that we all mourn the tragic loss of our aircrew. I, as well, am deeply grieved by this loss and I extend my sincerest sympathies and condolences to you all. That concludes my remarks. General?"

Dr. Stark and General Collins traded places. While they were doing so, Jill leaned over to Steve. "I can't believe that he just won't acknowledge the truth," she said fiercely. "I mean, he won't even consider the possibility." Steve nodded grimly.

The General had to reach up and pull the microphone down lower so he could talk comfortably. "I appreciate what Dr. Stark has just expressed. I, too, want to express my sympathies to all of you. This is a tragic loss for science, as well as being a tragic personal loss for all of you.

"My purpose here today is to explain what is going to happen to Project Opera. I know this will affect many of you. Before I begin, please understand that we don't have all of the details worked out yet. Because of that, I will not be taking questions today. Over the next couple of weeks, more information will be forthcoming about how we will be proceeding.

"As most of you know, this is the second phase of Project Opera. The first phase was the theoretical phase, in which Dr. Stark's theory was tested and validated by a number of his peers. Once that work was complete, we began this second stage of the project, which was to actually implement his theory into a working model. The result, obviously, was *TimeFlyer*.

"What we are going to do now, as we move forward, is to pare down the project and return it to Stage 1. We will be going back through the theory. We will have a considerable advantage, of course, of the data from the three successful missions. We believe this will give us the advantage to prevent a tragedy, such as we have experienced, to occur in the future. Of course, many of you were hired for the express purpose of helping with Stage 2 of Project Opera. For those of you who are civilians, we will be terminating your contracts. For military personnel, we will be contacting the appropriate offices in the military to get you reassigned. None of this is going to happen for at least another four weeks. That will give all of you time to search and apply for other work that fits your considerable talents. I trust you will all be able to find work that is challenging, rewarding, and profitable.

"Before we dismiss, I also want to say one other thing. Despite the tragedy, the work that you have done here is revolutionary. You have performed, as a team, extraordinarily well. You have accomplished great things in a short period of time. It has been extremely rewarding to see you come together and make such significant progress. Remember, even Orville and Wilber Wright's first airplane crashed on its fourth flight and had to be rebuilt. Just because we have our setbacks, doesn't mean our quest and our purpose is ending. Indeed, we have hardly begun. To all of you, again, I say thank you.. General."

General Collins went to the podium. "Before we dismiss, I regret having to warn you again. This project never happened. You know nothing about any theory related to the warping of space-time. Your loved ones will never know why you spent time in the Nevada desert. If you discuss this project, and authorities find out, you will be thrown into a dungeon and the key will be lost. The technology we have developed here continues to be one of America's most closely held secrets, and will be for a long time to come. Please be aware that, just because we are scaling back the project, does not mean the technology is any less valuable.

"That concludes our meeting for today."

* * * *

After the meeting, General Collins walked with Dr. Stark and Dr. Choi back to Dr. Stark's office. "We need to talk about how to decommission the staff," said the General. "I suppose the aircraft support people will be the first to go, seeing as we don't have an aircraft. Our commuter aircraft can be supported out of the main base here at Nellis."

"I have a concern," responded Dr. Stark.

"Go ahead."

"I'm not sure we are ever going to be able to revive the program."

The two others looked at him in surprise. "What do you mean?" asked the General.

"Look, we know people talk. This technology is not going to stay secret. It's amazing it has stayed secret up till now, actually."

"Well, we have to plan for that possibility."

"What I mean is, we now have a bunch of people who have heard about this young earth foolishness from the Harrisons. That has the potential of stopping further research in its tracks."

"I'm afraid I'm not following you," said the General with a frown.

"What I mean is this, we had this unfortunate situation where we lost *TimeFlyer*. We obviously did something wrong with the space-warp calculations and lost the aircraft. But it happened to occur at the same time that the Harrisons were poisoning people's minds with this 'Earth created 6,000 years ago' nonsense. The fact that we lost

TimeFlyer when we were trying to discredit Steve and Jill Harrison is a coincidence. But I suspect it may cause a lot of people to take their explanation seriously."

"So instead of getting rid of the problem, we made it bigger," said the General.

"Yes. Much bigger. Not only that, these people are going to be a big deterrent for getting more space-warp trials set up in the future. I am afraid this could set our experimentation back for a generation. If the President gets wind of this, he will never authorize more work in this area." Dr. Stark sighed in frustration. "You know, the American people are quite superstitious. Quite a lot of them claim to believe that the Bible is literal fact. The only way to convince folks like them is to show them, beyond a shadow of a doubt, that what they believe is nonsense. Do you know how many years it took for the average person to accept the fact that the Earth is not flat? Over 400 years! And professional scientists are still fighting some of those same superstitious fallacies. It hasn't affected physics research too much, but the chemistry and biology people are fighting this nonsense all the time. There are people out there claiming to be scientists that go around to churches and preach this Creationism stuff. And the public eats it up. Do you know how much credibility those factions will gain if word of our situation gets out?"

"I hardly think it is as bad as you make it out to be."

"No? Where is America rated in its University level math and science graduates?"

"Lower than a whole lot of other nations," admitted the General.

"Twenty-seventh! There are twenty-six nations that demonstrate more math and science knowledge than our University graduates who are supposedly at the same level. The actual number of students getting advanced math and science degrees continues to fall as well. America is already starting to fall noticeably behind."

"This is true," agreed Choi.

"Come now. We are the most advanced country on earth, by far."

"The only reason is that other countries are having a difficult time converting their research into practical applications. The reason is money and America has it. We can take advantage of our research. Did you know, for example, who came up with the stealth technology for aircraft?"

"America."

"No. A Russian researcher, but America is the only country that has been able to afford to develop and implement the technology."

"Let's assume your argument is correct," said the General, "what you are telling me is that the best inventors and researchers in the world will continue to emigrate to America to take advantage of their ingenuity."

"But that is happening less and less. The Israelis are leading in drone technology. Japan is way ahead of us in robotics. Singapore is ahead of us in artificial intelligence. Nowadays, most of the advances in computers comes from Hong Kong and other places in East Asia. America is definitely falling behind."

"But they have a long way to go to catch up with us."

Stark sighed. "I am not getting my point across," forcing himself to speak more calmly than he felt. "Let me try to explain it a different way. Are you aware that major technological jumps have generally occurred at similar times in various locations?" The General shook his head. "When Orville and Wilbur Wright first flew, there were two other groups of people who were working on building their own flying machines. The Wright brothers beat the others by a matter of weeks. Same story with the invention of the telephone. Same story with the discovery of the effects of radioactivity. Same story with the invention of radio. In every case, there were multiple independent groups across the globe that developed these inventions almost simultaneously."

"Go on," said the General. He was beginning to see where this was leading.

"I predict that within 10 years, a researcher in some other country will independently discover what I have already discovered. If something gets in the way of our ability to continue to develop and refine this technology, we will fall behind. And if that country is sufficiently motivated, they could figure out how to use the technology for tyranny."

"So what you're saying is that we are already in a race with this space-warp technology," said the General.

"Exactly."

"And you think that the people we had here, who listened to the Harrisons, will ultimately get in the way of developing this technology?"

"That's right."

"And America will fall behind, like we were at the beginning of the space race in the 60's."

"Exactly. But the stakes will be much higher." agreed Stark.

General Collins pondered that for a bit. "We cannot afford to let that happen."

"Now you're getting the picture," he said enthusiastically.

"What to you propose we do about it?"

Dr. Stark spoke for several more minutes. They argued for a bit, but finally the General seemed to acquiesce to his point of view. "I'll need to go to the President for this," he said.

"The President will never agree."

"But he might be willing to look the other way when it happens," said the General.

"Well then, go talk to the President."

* * * *

Dr. Choi walked back to his office and thought about what he had heard. He was dismayed that Dr. Stark should go to such desperate measures to keep his theory viable. But he had to agree with the assessment that someone else would probably make the same discovery soon enough, and that it might very well be someone outside of America.

As Director of Implementation, he knew his job was gone. There would be nothing more to implement, at least for several years while the theory was refined again. If there were nothing to implement, he would not be living on base. And if he were not living on base, and continued to refuse to cooperate with the North Koreans and their demands to return to North Korea, he had no doubt he would find himself on the losing side of a gun. Once the project was over, and the North Koreans decided he was not going to tell them what he had been working on, they would get rid of him. In fact, he decided, a gun would be a blessing. He had no doubt they would be willing to kidnap and torture him into telling them what he knew. He understood the North Korean pride and arrogance as few others could. They simply would not stop until they got what they wanted. After all, it was well known that they had kidnapped Japanese citizens and transported them to North Korea. They had been trying to learn more about Japan and its culture, to make it easier to infiltrate their agents into Japanese society. They were ruthless. But what could he do about it?

He didn't want to allow himself to be returned to North Korea. He knew the kind of life that awaited him there. It might be worth it to get his family out of prison. But there was no guarantee that they would actually release them. They were the worst kind of liars. It was very possible that they would bring him back to North Korea and make him a prisoner as well. So that was a poor option.

On the other hand, doing nothing was a poor option too. That meant certain death, and possibly torture as well.

He could go to the American authorities. Choi figured there was about a 25% chance they would believe him, but whether or not they cared enough to try to protect him was another matter. If they didn't come through, he was back to essentially doing nothing.

He thought of going in to hiding on his own, and he immediately dismissed that possibility as well. Their pictures of him in his apartment in Canada made him realize how thoroughly they had watched him. If he did manage to evade them, it would be only a matter of time until they found him.

Choi sighed. The only possible way out of this mess was if Jill's God would provide a miracle. As much as he respected Jill, Steve, and their beliefs, he didn't think their God would perform a miracle for him. He had a lot of respect for them, he admitted. The idea they had promoted about a rapidly aging universe and a slowly aging earth was quite intriguing. And, he admitted, they had accurately predicted the loss of *TimeFlyer*, even if Dr. Stark didn't agree on the reason for its loss.

Steve and Jill. A pretty good pilot married to a female physics genius. A very strange couple, he decided, but quite talented and apparently devoted to each other. And now their life was in danger, too. He respected their willingness to take risks and stand up for what they believed. There ought to be more people like them, he decided. Even if their beliefs ended up to be nothing but religious superstition, as Dr. Stark claimed, they had a lot going for them. He didn't like the fact that Dr. Stark and General Collins had decided to murder them and make their deaths look like an accident.

Wait a minute, he thought. Steve and Jill. Pilot and female physics genius. Both had extensive knowledge of *TimeFlyer* and the space-warp theory. One flew the machine. One could explain how it worked. He wondered if North Korea would rather have two experts with specialized knowledge of their project rather than just himself. Maybe he could work out a deal. Trade Steve and Jill for his family emigration from North Korea, and freedom from their tyranny for the rest of his life.

Wait a minute, Choi, argued with himself. What if North Korea gained the space-warp knowledge? Wouldn't they ultimately become a threat to America? Then, instead of threatening just him, they would be able to threaten America herself. That wasn't a pleasant thought.

Then he remembered his tunnel-detecting machine from so many years ago. He remembered how they had searched for an appropriate machine on which to implement his technology. How they had finally managed to scrape up that ridiculous excuse for a tractor. That project had been given national priority! He chuckled to himself. What could North Korea possibly do with the knowledge gained from Dr. Stark's space-warp theory? They could barely manage to scrape up a tractor to stop people from tunneling to freedom. They would never be able to build a machine to take advantage of the theory. It would take millions of dollars to build such a machine. At least eight figures, he calculated, probably nine. It would never happen.

And what about Steve and Jill? Well, he thought to himself, better that they were alive in North Korea than dead in America, ignoring the fact that he had preferred the opposite when it was his life in question.

He left his office and walked back to his apartment. Inside, he went to his bedroom and opened the third drawer. He pulled out the business card from a certain Chinese dry cleaning shop in Chicago. Then he turned and headed for the phone.

Chapter 15

The red phone was actually more computer than telephone. It contained a computer chip with a special set of circuits for handling cryptography. The installers told him it was the most secure device America had ever built. Anyone trying to listen in on the call would hear nothing but electronic static. If run through a modem connected to a computer, the electronic static would be translated into sets of incomprehensible digits and symbols. When a call was made between two red phones, the phones would agree on an encryption/decryption scheme before allowing any communication. The encryption scheme was based on a randomly-generated encryption/decryption key. Each phone generated its own key and exchanged it with the phone on the other side of the connection.

The technology was limited almost exclusively to military applications. Paul had learned about the technology almost by accident. He had been attending a coordination meeting between the Department of Homeland Security and the Defense Department. The meeting had been held at the Pentagon. During the visit, one of the military attendees had been summoned by a call on the 'red phone.' Paul's detail-oriented nature had jumped on that little piece of information. After his military hosts had reluctantly revealed the phone's capabilities, he had inquired about getting one for himself. The military had successfully resisted until Project Opera. There was no question that such a project was the type of project for which the red phone had been designed.

It had turned out to be both a blessing and a curse. A blessing because Paul could be fairly sure he could communicate securely using the device. A curse because, when the red phone rang, you had to answer. Even his secretary wasn't allowed access. He had to drop whatever he was doing when it rang. After all, it might be the President.

It was ringing now. He turned and picked up the receiver, waiting for the phone to indicate that the encryption had been established between itself and the caller. After a few seconds, a light on the front of the phone glowed green and a tone sounded in his ear.

"Hello, Paul Schneider."

"Good morning, Paul. This is John Brier."

"Hello, John. How are things?"

"Well, I'm not sure. Any reason why a weapons expert would need to be involved in the project?"

"Not that I know of," Paul replied. "Why?"

"I was reviewing the list of people being granted access to come on site, like I always do, but the background check on one person didn't add up. He was listed as an aircraft technician, but his records don't say anything about aircraft maintenance. His military records indicate he is a weapons and demolition expert."

"Where is this person supposed to be working?"

"It says here he is going to be doing some maintenance on the commuter airplanes. You know, those turboprop airplanes they use for hauling people around the base. I guess that's why they have him listed as an aircraft technician."

"Any chance of a mix-up?"

"No, and that is strange too. General Collins apparently approved it. I got off the phone with him just a few minutes ago to verify this request. He told me I was to allow this person access to the base as an aircraft technician. Then he warned me again about the secrecy of the project. Well, it was more like a threat, actually."

"So you are telling me that General Collins told you to approve a weapons expert coming on base disguised as an aircraft technician, and this person is supposed to be working on one of the turboprop airplanes?"

"You got it," John confirmed.

"When is this person supposed to be coming on base?" queried Paul.

"In three weeks, and he is supposed to stay for a month. Of course, he probably won't stay that long. Usually, for people with short term engagements, the requester puts in more time than they think they will need, in case they do have to stay longer than originally anticipated."

"And you talked to Collins personally about this?"

"Yep, just got off the phone with him," repeated John.

"That's very strange."

"That's what I thought too. Anyway, I thought you ought to know."

"OK, thanks for the tip. Can you give me this person's name and service number?" Paul copied down the information, then thanked John and promised to get back to him.

Paul sat in his chair, still holding the phone. This was going to take some hard thinking. What possible use could the General have in assigning a weapons expert to an airplane? And why wasn't he being told about it? He didn't like any of the answers that came to mind.

Paul slowly replaced the phone, but his brain was running in high gear. He knew that *TimeFlyer* had been lost in an accident during its last flight. The project was going back to Stage 1 status, which meant a lot of people were being released from the project. The official story was that they had gotten some of the math wrong and *TimeFlyer* had been severely damaged by the space-warp attempt. This had to be related to the loss of *TimeFlyer*, thought Paul. Obviously, losing *TimeFlyer* was a huge setback.

Could the General want someone out of the way? Maybe more than one person? Why? What would he possibly gain from getting rid of any of the people on the project?

He needed to get more information. He needed information from someone who was involved in the day-to-day operation of the project, someone who could give him more details. He thought about calling Brian Masulis, but he rejected that idea almost immediately. Brian had worked quite closely with General Collins. Paul didn't want the General to know he was sniffing around. He wondered who else he might talk to. Could he go to visit Minion Lake at this point without arousing suspicion? Risky, he decided, but he might have to try.

Then he remembered the press conference, and the shock of seeing Steve and Jill. They could probably tell him what was going on. He wondered about the possibility of covertly getting them back to Washington, D.C. He probably wouldn't be able to arrange it himself.

But he and Dan Labinsky, Jill's father, had been close for several years now. Maybe he could leverage their friendship to find out what was going on at Minion Lake.

Maybe it was time for Dan to get a little closer to the action. Paul was beginning to think he was going to need all the information he could get. On the one hand, getting Dan involved was a gross violation of security. On the other, assigning a weapons expert to the project disguised as an aircraft technician was a gross violation of protocol. Was he willing to take the risk of a security breach with Dan Labinsky in order to figure out what was going on in Nevada without letting anyone involved in the project know what he was doing?

The answer was obvious. He picked up his regular phone and called Dan.

* * * *

Dr. Choi had never been to Chicago before. It reminded him of several cities, and none of them, all at the same time. It had some buildings as big as those in New York, but there were not nearly as many. It was closer to the size of San Francisco, but it was flat. He was impressed with the lakefront. Chicago was one of the few cities with the foresight to annex the property along their waterfront and dedicate it to recreation and tourism. Too many cities had just turned their waterfronts into docks and wharves. Convenient for commerce, but ugly.

He had arrived yesterday. He had little motivation to go out, but his hotel room overlooked the lakeshore, so he had gone down and done some walking. He was supposed to meet Sun and Moon at a Chinese Restaurant at noon. During his walk, he rehearsed his offer. Rehearsing the offer made him nervous, but the sunshine and pleasant weather calmed him, somewhat.

At 11:45, he flagged down a taxi, providing the address of the restaurant in Chicago's Chinatown. It didn't amount to much, he thought, especially compared with the one in San Francisco. He entered the specified restaurant and, as directed, told the young man who came to seat him that he enjoyed a view of the sun and moon. The young man had taken him to a booth set apart in the back, in the corner of the restaurant. Sun and Moon joined him a moment later with a third person, who was introduced as Wind.

240

"So, Comrade Choi, you have requested to meet with us," said Sun. "How may we be of service today?"

"I want my family freed. I am prepared to make an arrangement," began Choi. "Sun, you are right when you say that I was working on a top secret military project. That project is coming to a close, and I will leave it within three weeks. I can guarantee that what the Americans have developed is revolutionary. However, I cannot explain it all." He saw Sun's eyes narrow. He raised a hand. "Just wait. Allow me to finish. I am merely an assistant. I have been tasked to help solve implementation problems. Primarily, that dealt with the problem of bleeding off excess heat from a very unique device. The exact details of that device were not revealed to me." He lied as convincingly as he could.

"However, there are two people on the project that I think would be able to provide much more detail than I ever could. These two people are a married couple. The husband has been trained to operate the device. The woman, however, is the real prize. She has a PhD in applied physics, which she earned at the age of 21. She worked closely with the researcher on whose theories this work was based. She can explain every detail of every part of the device, as well as the theory behind it."

"A woman can explain this theory?" Gender equity was not a North Korean strong suit.

"Far better than I, in fact. I will not tell you any more about the project at this time, for two reasons. First, if I told you, you would not believe me. The idea is so advanced that it sounds too fantastic to be true. Second, if I did give you information, you would want details, which I cannot adequately provide. I will tell you the following things, however. The device requires so much power that a nuclear reactor was built to power it. The device also needed to be airborne, so a custom airplane was built that was actually powered by that same nuclear reactor. Third, the one thing I will tell you is that what the Americans have discovered is more significant than the development of nuclear physics during World War II."

"More significant than the development of the atomic bomb?" queried Sun skeptically.

"Yes, and with greater implications for national security than the atomic bomb."

"I see. So, if you do not agree to return to North Korea, what are you proposing?"

"I propose that I hand these two people, the man and his wife, to you. In return, you will deliver to me here all my relatives you have imprisoned, along with their children. And you will leave all of us alone for the rest of our lives."

"We believe that you would probably have enough knowledge that you would be useful to North Korea, even if you did not know all the details." Sun replied.

"Well, here is a reason why you might consider my proposal. If I came to North Korea and just told you about the implementation of this device, and could not explain the theory behind it, many of your brightest scientists would have to figure out the theory. That might take years. It certainly will take a single year. Why not get someone who can detail the entire theory and be that much further ahead? After all, the Americans already have it in operation. North Korea is already behind. You will need to catch up quickly."

Sun, Moon, and Wind looked at each other. Then Wind stood, "I need to make a telephone call," he announced, and walked into the kitchen.

"You realize, of course, that if anything you have presented is not completely factual, it will not be good for you," Sun threatened.

"Oh, I quite realize that. But you will not be disappointed, I guarantee. These two people can explain everything, and get you into design and development very quickly."

"Let us assume we accept your offer. Have you thought about how we might get these two?" Sun asked.

"Yes, as a matter of fact I have. The man is a pilot. He flies back and forth from Las Vegas and the base all the time. I will arrange to fly with them. When he comes in to land in Las Vegas, instead of going to the usual terminal, I will get him to go to an alternate location where you can get him and his wife. There are facilities for small aircraft at the Las Vegas airport. When we get to the alternate location, these two people and I will get out of the aircraft and go with you. You will provide aliases for me and my family so we can hide. Also, I will want my features surgically altered so that I am not easily recognized."

"We can easily arrange for those things," agreed Sun.

"Also, I will want to see my family in this country before I provide this couple. If I see that you have made the effort to get my family into this country, then I will have much more confidence that you will do

242

what you say."

"What if we do not agree to your demands?" asked Sun.

"Then you will have to either kill me or torture me to try and get information. And when you force the information out of me, it will be incomplete and fragmented. And it will sound so fantastic that you will be tempted not to believe me. Much better to get this couple into North Korea and have time to get all the information you need."

Wind returned to the table. "We are interested in your proposal. However, we do not believe your claim that this development is more significant than the atomic bomb. Can you give us any more information to back up this claim?"

"I will tell you this. Do you remember the story of the Dodo birds? How the government discovered a way to resurrect extinct species?" Sun and Rain nodded. "The project I am working on made that happen. But this project is not a biology project, it is a physics project. The government presented it as a biology project to lead inquisitive minds in the wrong direction. Those birds were produced with the help of the device on the aircraft that I have described."

"How could this be?" demanded Sun.

"I will say no more. I have told you that what they have developed is almost too fantastic to believe. I have told you it is more important than the atomic bomb. You may choose to believe me or not. I know my life is on the line, that is a reason you may believe me. If you choose not to believe me, you will come to regret that decision. Of course, I will suffer. But when you get the information out of me, and you verify it, and learn that you could have had so much more, your own superiors will not deal kindly with you." He saw the three of them look at each other, and he knew he had them.

"We will have to discuss this," said Wind.

"The time for discussion is past. Within a month, this opportunity will be gone. The project is shutting down, and the people are leaving. I would encourage you to act immediately."

"Please excuse us for a minute." Sun and Wind both got up and walked away. Moon stayed with Choi. Neither of them said anything. Less than three minutes later, the two returned.

"We agree to your proposal. Shall we discuss the details?" Sun asked.

The meeting lasted well into the evening.

* * * *

Paul was sitting in Dan Labinsky's office. They made the usual small talk. Each man respected the other. Dan was one of Paul's spiritual mentors, and the two of them had spent significant amounts of time together. They had lunched together once a month for the past several years. Their families knew each other from church. Paul appreciated Dan's spiritual wisdom, as well as his ability to communicate his knowledge. Dan enjoyed Paul's willingness to be open and apply the Biblical principles that Dan had revealed.

"You've got something on your mind." prompted Dan.

"Dan, you know I am working in the Department of Homeland Security. What you don't know is that I am head of internal security for a very secret project being conducted by the military." Dan's eyebrows rose in surprise. "Yes, I know that is unusual. The President himself wanted our department to be involved with the security. The military wasn't very happy about it, but the President didn't back down. Eventually, they had to agree to move forward."

"Sound's like you've been placed in a very important position. That could only mean good things for your career."

"Thanks. I think so, too. Or I did until I received a very unusual phone call this morning. It leads me to believe there are some things going on that I don't understand and I need more information. I need someone who is actually on site, doing the work, and involved in the politics of the thing."

"Well, it never hurts to get more information. Security can be a very tricky thing. Sounds like good judgment to me."

"I need more than just your opinion on this one," Paul admitted.

"How can I help?" Dan asked.

"This is the project that Steve and Jill are working on in Nevada."

"I see. Do you want to talk to them?"

"Yes, but I want to get them to come out here without raising suspicion. Would you contact Steve and Jill and get them to come out this weekend?" It was Thursday.

"Hmm. You want me to get them to come out right away without raising suspicion. That might be tricky," Dan said with a frown.

"That's why I need your help. I thought maybe you could think up a crisis in the family that would get them to drop everything and come out right away. Will you help?"

244

"Well, I don't know. Are you sure it is really that urgent?" asked Dan skeptically.

"I believe that it is a matter of life or death. I just don't know who is being targeted. Steve or Jill may be able to shed some light on some things I have heard, help me put the pieces together. I really need their input. I don't know who else I can trust."

"Well, if you really think that Steve and Jill could help, I can try to get them out here. Do you have any ideas about what might motivate them to get on the next plane?"

"How about if the doctor had discovered a tumor somewhere in your body? You have been feeling pain, but thought it was just age or something. They don't know if it is cancer or not, but will be doing more tests this weekend, and you want them to come to be with you and Gail," suggested Paul.

"I suppose that would do it. That means Gail will have to be in on the plot."

"I know. I would like to avoid having her involved, but I haven't come up with a better idea," admitted Paul.

"Well, I think we can trust Gail. She's a good woman. Might be a little hard on her, though."

"Can she keep a secret? This is going to be pretty unusual for her. She will probably start worrying about what's going on. You know her a lot better than I do."

"She can keep a secret. I trust her completely and I think I can make her understand that you need to ask them about their work."

"OK, let's start making the phone calls. you probably want to call Gail first, then Jill."

Dan picked up the phone, then hesitated and looked back at Paul. "You're sure you think they can be helpful? I hate to raise a false alarm unless you really think it is absolutely necessary."

"I could go there and try to talk to them, but I know I will be watched. I can't think of an alternative. To my knowledge, no one on the project knows about our relationship. If you can get Steve and Jill out here, I can talk to them in a completely confidential manner. I have reason to believe that Steve and Jill may be able to shed some light on the things that I have heard. Especially Jill. She is pretty high up in the project, working with the top dogs. Please, Dan, I know I am asking a lot, but I really do believe that this may be a matter of life or death for someone, maybe more than one person and I think they will be quite helpful."

"OK." Dan relented, and picked up the phone to call his wife.

* * * *

Less than an hour later, Steve walked in to their apartment. Jill nearly leaped into his arms. "Dad just called. They found a tumor in his abdomen. He needs to go in for more tests this weekend. They want us to come home as soon as possible."

Steve shook his head. "Oh no. Did they say what organ?"

"They said kidney or liver, couldn't tell which." Steve could tell Jill was shaken by the news. He tried to comfort her as best he could. "They don't even know if it is cancer. There is a chance it is just a benign tumor. But Dad said the doctor said the odds of it being benign were pretty small because of its location." Jill unsuccessfully tried to hold back her tears. "Oh, Steve. What else is going to go wrong?"

Steve didn't say much. He just held her. After a few minutes, she grew calmer. "I'm OK. Thanks for coming right away."

"You're welcome. They want both of us to come out?"

"Yes. Dad said he would really like me to be able to stay into Monday or Tuesday, but they would at the least like both of us to come out for the weekend."

"Tickets will be expensive at the last minute," warned Steve.

"I don't care, we can afford them."

"Let me call the travel people and see what we can get. Have you checked your schedule with, uh, whoever? I don't even know who you would need to talk to."

"I talked with Brian Masulis. He said to take whatever time I need," she said.

"I'll have to talk to Brian too, I suppose. We'll probably have to get a pilot from Nellis to cover me. I am supposed to be doing shuttle duty this weekend. And we'll have to miss the memorial service for Delvan, too." Steve went to the phone and started making the necessary calls.

* * * *

They arrived at Reagan National Friday afternoon. Gail met them at the airport and drove them home. She seemed tense. When Jill asked about more details, she just said to wait and ask her father. She was still so shocked, she said, that she hadn't really absorbed any of the details.

When they arrived home, they were surprised to find Paul Schneider there. Paul explained, as gently as he could, that Dan's illness was fake and he had been the cause of all the concern. He apologized profusely as Jill shed tears of relief.

Steve was somewhat offended that Paul would be willing to manipulate him and Jill so callously. But then he remembered meeting Paul at the press briefing, and how concerned Paul had been that they not reveal anything about project Opera to Dan. Something really unusual was going on, and it took only a few seconds to decide the unusual thing probably had to do with the project.

Once Jill had calmed down, Paul turned to Gail. "If you don't mind, I would like to speak to the rest of your family. There is really no benefit that you could gain from our discussion."

"That's fine with me. I think I'll go shopping." Gail responded.

"Oh, now you owe me." Dan teased Paul. "Gail goes shopping to relax. You owe me whatever she spends tonight."

"Start at the dollar store." Paul called to Gail's departing back.

"Actually, I think I need a new car," she called back in reply and the humor helped everyone relax.

"Before we go too far, I think we need to fill Dan in on the project," said Paul.

"That's easy," Steve volunteered. " I helped capture those Dodo birds that were at your press conference."

"What!?"

Steve explained *TimeFlyer*, and how they had flown back in time and space to capture the birds. When he was done, Dan shook his head. "Now I know why our department got pulled into this thing. We were the distraction."

"Exactly," emphasized Paul, "and it worked beautifully. The press is still poking their nose into every biology lab they can find that has ever done any work for the government." He chuckled. "Some of the lab folks are getting kind of tired of their probes. The newsies can be pretty persistent."

"But an actual time machine. That's incredible!" Dan exclaimed,

"OK, now I need to explain why I needed to talk to the two of you." Paul inclined his head toward Steve and Jill. "I got a call this past week from someone on the project. General Collins seems to be

247

interested in having a demolition expert work on one of those commuter planes that you folks use out there."

"A demolition expert? You mean, someone who blows up things?" asked Steve.

"Yes, and he is supposed to be coming on base with the credentials of an aircraft technician. Any idea why he might be doing something like that?"

Steve and Jill looked at each other. "Us." said Steve.

"You? Both of you? Why?" asked the shocked security chief.

Steve told the whole story about the way they stood up to most of the rest of the project because of their belief in a young earth. He told how they had predicted the loss of *TimeFlyer*, and how it had actually happened. He told them about Dr. Stark's subsequent denial of their idea, and his allegation that the equation had instead caused *TimeFlyer* to jump into space somewhere along Earth's orbital path.

"But that's Dr. Stark. Why would General Collins be doing the dirty work?" queried a perplexed Paul.

"How bad does General Collins want this technology?" responded Steve.

"Pretty bad, I guess," Paul replied.

"Right. See, if our story gets out, it upsets all kind of established science. The entire scientific community will be forced to examine their assumptions, about almost everything. Evolution couldn't possibly happen. Biology would have to be viewed as the work of a divine creator. Physics? The same. Think about all the astronomers and their presupposition that the universe and the earth are all billions of years old. They would have to go back to square one to understand the universe. If that happens, do you think there will be much interest in pursuing this space-warp thing? It will be overshadowed by all the other things that will be happening in the scientific community."

"Wouldn't have to be that way. Theories could be modified at the same time that this space-warp stuff is happening," objected Paul.

"Not according to Dr. Stark," put in Jill. "He's been ranting at me for over two months now, ever since I told him I believed in the Bible. He thinks our scientific progress is being constrained by our religious beliefs. He won't even consider a young Earth perspective because he says it is just religious superstition. It really triggers his hot button."

"I'll verify that. Jill has mentioned her trouble with this Dr. Stark several times over the past couple of months," put in Dan. "She didn't

248

reveal anything," he put in hastily to Paul, seeing his alarmed look. "She just said that she told another researcher that she believed in the Bible, and he started giving her a really hard time."

"So you think they're in cahoots?" asked Paul.

"Absolutely," put in Steve firmly. "There's another reason, too. They probably don't want anyone to tell an inquiry board that they were warned about the possible loss of *TimeFlyer*. If they can attribute it to bad math, it is seen as a tragic mistake, nothing more. If we get up and tell our side of the story, it makes them negligent. There has got to be laws that would incriminate them."

"Whew. That's sufficient motive, all right." agreed Paul.

"So, what do we do about it?" asked Steve.

There were no good answers to that question.

* * * *

It seemed to Choi that Stark had grown more reluctant to discuss the 'accident' that was planned to take the life of Steve and Jill. But Choi knew he needed the information, in order to be able to get Steve and Jill in a position to be kidnapped and taken to North Korea before they were killed. After pressing for additional information, Stark told him that an auto accident was being planned after Steve and Jill had been dismissed from the project.

"You are sure an auto accident will do it?" asked Choi. It didn't seem like a very good plan to him.

"I'm sure," assured Stark. "General Collins has many trained men in the military that make it their business to know how to kill people."

"It seems like such a waste of talent," volunteered Choi, wondering what kind of response he would get.

"Tragic, yes, but absolutely necessary for the advancement of science. We cannot risk having this technology discovered and implemented by a foreign power." And with that response, Choi reluctantly admitted to himself that Stark really was going to carry out his plan.

Chapter 16

The communication pathway had been Jill's idea. The idea was that there needed to be an easy way to communicate securely between Steve and Jill in Nevada, and Paul Schneider in Washington. Jill's father agreed to be the intermediate contact. All messages between Steve and Jill in Nevada, and Paul Schneider, were to be relayed by Dan.

No one doubted that the phone lines and e-mail were being monitored. In the course of her research activities, however, Jill had encountered more than a few convenient tools for secure communications. She decided on embedding encrypted messages in photographs, and sending them back and forth over e-mail. The technique, known as steganography, hides messages in picture files, such as those that are recorded with a digital camera.

Saturday morning, Jill sat down at Dan's computer at home and generated public and private keys for her father's use, as well as for Steve and herself. A trip to the nearest shopping center yielded two cheap digital cameras and several USB memory sticks on which to store their keys.

Paul returned to the Krantz home Saturday afternoon. Jill walked Steve, Paul, and her father through the encryption/stenography steps several times to make sure they were comfortable with the procedures. She also showed them how to avoid storing the images on the hard drives. Once the images were deleted from memory, there would be no record of the message. By the end of the day on Saturday, they were embedding messages into pictures and sending them back and forth like old pros.

When Paul returned home that afternoon, he put in a call to John Brier on the red phone, which had been installed in his home as well as his office. Paul thanked John for the warning, and asked him to report any activity related to the demolition expert. Without revealing anything else, Paul let John know that the information he had provided had been quite valuable.

* * * *

That same weekend, Dr. Choi had flown to Phoenix, Arizona, then rented a car and driven on to Tucson. He stayed overnight at a hotel that served a continental breakfast. He was breakfasting at 8:15, just as arranged, when he was joined by Sun and Moon.

"We have a two hour trip ahead of us. You will meet your family at the end of the journey. However, you will have to accept one of our requests before we leave."

"What is that?" asked Choi.

"You must remain blindfolded for the entire trip."

"Don't you trust me?" he demanded.

"Not completely. This is just a precaution on our part. We will try to make sure you are comfortable."

Choi wondered if he were placing his life in his hands. "How do I know this is not a trick?" He tried to sound in control.

"Inside that utility van is one of your brothers. We are telling you so that you do not cry out or draw attention to us when you see him."

They went outside, Choi hardly daring to hope. There was a utility van parked outside, with a ladder rack on top, complete with a ladder. Sun opened the side door, and Choi peered in.

"Hello, Daesang," said a voice quietly in Korean. Choi jumped into the van and embraced the man whose body he did not recognize, but whose voice brought back memories from more than fifteen years before.

* * * *

Steve and Jill spent the rest of the weekend with Dan and Gaii, and then returned to Minion Lake on Monday. Steve had already begun flying shuttle missions every day, moving the large project group off of the base. Every day he checked for any unusual activity around the commuter planes. His pre-flight inspections took so long that Tex began to wonder what was going on. After several flights, Steve had leveled with him. Since they always flew together, Steve figured Tex had a right to know someone might be trying to plant a bomb on their airplane.

Tex started helping Steve with the pre-flight inspections.

Jill and her father mailed at least one picture back and forth every day. The messages embedded in the pictures always came through the e-mail scanners without a problem. Unfortunately, there was no news to report. Paul checked with John Brier every week, but John had heard nothing more.

Most of the folks leaving Minion Lake the first week were the technicians who had helped maintain *TimeFlyer*. Some were specialized in aircraft, and some in the operation of nuclear reactors. The next wave were the support staff – cooks, housekeeping, and the retired military folks who had run the stores in the mall. Finally, it was the turn for the scientific staff who had been brought on board for the actual project implementation. Three round trips per day had Steve and Tex working nearly 10 hours every day, shuttling the workers out. The base was rapidly becoming a ghost town. Only the administration building was kept open, as the theoretical physicists continued their work.

Then, three weeks later on a Tuesday afternoon, John Brier put in a call to Paul Schneider. The aircraft technician was scheduled to arrive on base the following day. There was no reason for John to deny his entry onto the base, as the individual in question had the appropriate clearances allowing access to ultra-top-secret projects. The information was passed through Dan to Jill, who had the information less then three hours later. Jill printed the message, then decided to go meet Steve at the aircraft hanger where the turboprop was parked during the night.

Steve was not particularly surprised at the timing. Jill was supposed to fly out on Thursday. Steve and Tex were going to fly one more day, on Friday, and then their jobs would be completed as well. So, if Jill and Steve really were being targeted, it almost had to be the Thursday flight. And as the sun sank low in the west, Steve, Jill and Tex held a strategy meeting, standing in the lengthy shadow cast by the aircraft.

"You know anything about munitions?" Steve asked Tex hopefully.

Tex shook his head. "Nothing beyond what we learned in basic training. Not unless they've got four legs," He replied.

"Well, we have to act like everything's normal," said Steve. "Thank goodness I've been coming an hour early every day to pre-flight the aircraft. At least that won't raise any suspicion. We'd better have a toolkit on board."

"Tools I've got," said Tex. He nodded at the plane. "Are these here critters metric or English?"

"Metric, but we better have both. Who knows how this thing is going to be mounted."

"Where are we going to put the tools? Probably ought to have them aboard ahead of time. It would look kind of suspicious if I walked in Thursday morning lugging a toolbox." Tex said.

"If we're careful, we can put them in the electronics compartment behind and below the pilot's seat." said Steve. "But we'll have to strap the toolbox in tight. I don't want the thing coming loose and killing some of our electrical circuits. Otherwise, I don't know another good place to put them where we can get to them easily during a flight. Why don't you ask one of the folks flying out tomorrow to put your toolbox in with their luggage? Then it will be loaded into the luggage compartment along with all the other stuff. We just won't unload it at the end of the flight, we'll hide it in the electrical compartment."

"That works. Alright, I'm going to go visit a few friends who will be flying tomorrow, to see if I can pawn off my toolbox in their luggage." He turned to head back to the living quarters, then turned back to them. "Um, can I ask a personal question?"

"Sure." said Steve.

"You guys are, like, praying to God about this, right?"

"Yeah. Tex, I'm surprised. After your rodeo adventures and nearly hitting an island with *TimeFlyer*, I didn't think anything made you cautious."

"Well," said Tex, "there's a difference between risking your life and knowing that someone's actually out to kill you. Risking your life can be fun. But I don't want to die because some fool planted a bomb in my airplane."

"We're praying," said Jill, "and so are my Dad and Mom, and Paul and Karen Schneider. Don't worry, Tex. God's got us in his hands."

"I hope so," he said.

As Steve and Jill walked toward their own apartment, Steve said "There's something else I want you to get for me."

"Sure, what's that?" asked Jill.

"Mercury."

"You mean, the liquid metal mercury?"

"Yes. We may not need it at all. But if we need it, it'll come in really useful. I don't care how you get it. Break open some thermometers or a barometer. Just make sure you get it to me before Thursday morning. Oh, and one more thing. An extra toothbrush."

"Whatever for?"

Steve told her. Jill nodded and promised she would bring the materials.

On the way back to their apartment, they met Dr. Choi. "Hello, Doc. Out for a stroll?" queried Steve pleasantly.

"Yes. Work is almost done. Still flying out tomorrow?" inquired the physicist.

"I am." said Jill. "But Steve has to fly one more day. He'll be done Friday."

"I see. What flight will you be flying tomorrow?" Dr. Choi asked Jill.

"First flight in the morning."

"Ah, me too. So, we will fly out together." Choi seemed pleased.

"Dr. Choi, have you thought any more about Jesus since we talked awhile back?" asked Jill. It seemed as good a time as any to broach the subject, and she had reminded herself to follow up with him on more than one occasion.

"Yes, I have thought about it. But I still do not see how such a good God could allow so much evil in the world. And besides, North Korea was once considered a mainly Christian nation. Why would a God allow his people to be ruled and killed by such tyrants as those who run the country now?"

"I don't know the answers to all your questions. But the Bible says that God will set all things right in the end. We have to believe that God is able to do that," Jill explained.

He shook his head. "It is difficult to believe."

"Dr. Choi, what did you mean that North Korea was once considered a Christian nation?" asked Steve.

"Before the communists, there were many Christians in North Korea. Catholics. Baptists. Presbyterians. Many others, all over the country. South Korea still has many Christians. In fact, South Korea sends missionaries to America." Dr. Choi appeared to get a kick out of that.

"Did the communists outlaw Christianity?" asked Steve.

"All religions, except the worship of the leader of the country. No other religion is allowed. Many Christians were killed when the communists took over. Some were starved to death. You see, the leaders of North Korea are evil. That is what I cannot understand. If your God is so powerful, why does he allow these things?"

"It is a hard question," agreed Steve, "but God has allowed it. And the Bible tells us that those who die because of their faith will have a special place in Heaven. There have been terrible things done to Christians ever since Jesus was killed. God has warned us in the Bible that we will be persecuted because of our faith. Sometimes that is part of being a Christian."

"Well, thank you for your concern. However, I do not wish to become a Christian," Dr. Choi replied. "But we are friends, are we not? I do hope to fly with you on Saturday."

"Good," said Jill, "we'll see you then."

* * * *

Thursday dawned clear and cool. Steve would have been surprised if it had been any other way. One thing you could count on was consistency in this dry desert climate. He found himself heading toward the hanger 15 minutes early, and he had to check himself. Nothing unusual, he told himself firmly. He decided to spend the extra 15 minutes praying. If there was a day where he might need God's intervention, this was it.

He arrived at the hanger five minutes before Tex. When Tex walked in, Steve saw that his pants seemed to be hanging off him heavily. "Let me guess," Steve said with a grin. "You wouldn't make it through an airport metal detector."

Tex grinned cheerfully. "Kept back some of the tools I thought might be most useful. Decided to bring them in this morning separately. If there's been any monkey business, I wouldn't be surprised if my toolbox is gone." He climbed aboard, followed by

Steve. They walked into the cockpit. Tex raised the lid to the electronics compartment. "Sure enough. It's not there."

Steve felt his adrenaline begin to flow. "This must be the day. What tools did you bring along?" Tex revealed a couple of adjustable wrenches, two metal files, a wire cutter, and a regular and needlenose pliers. "Good choices. Those will come in handy. Let's do our pre-flight like normal. We'll start outside."

Tex deposited the tools in the map pocked on his side of the cockpit. Then they walked outside and began their pre-flight. Everything looked normal. After that, they climbed up the ladder and into the aircraft. "I'm going to check under the luggage compartment," said Tex. He walked forward into the luggage compartment, dropped to his knees, and opened the small hatch that led into the area below. Normally it contained nothing but the hydraulic and electrical lines. Today there was obviously something else. Tex motioned Steve to join him. Steve peered inside. It was a black box, about one foot long, three feet wide, and six inches high. It appeared to be made out of metal.

"Thank the Good Lord we were warned," said Steve. "We would never have found it if we hadn't. Why don't you get started getting that thing out of there? I'll finish the pre-flight."

"OK." Tex went to the cockpit and retrieved his tools, then returned and reached into the hole.

The rest of the pre-flight check turned up nothing unusual. Steve returned to the luggage compartment. "How's it going?"

"Man, they really have this thing tied in. It's bolted to the airframe with four bolts. I got one of them out, working on another one. But there's two that I don't think I am going to be able to reach. The good news is there are no wires or anything attached to it. Must have a battery inside it."

"I've been thinking about that. What do you think triggers it?"

"I would guess one of three things. Either a timer, set for a certain time after we depart," grunted Tex, bending over into the compartment. "Least reliable. What if we got delayed for some reason? Then this thing would go off while we're still on the ground. Second possibility, an altitude sensor. But I would bet on a GPS system. Once we get a certain number of miles away from our departure point, boom. Military is in love with GPS."

"Well, ten minutes before we head to pick up our first load. Guess I'll be in the cockpit. Holler if you think I can lend a hand."

The next ten minutes were frustrating. Nothing to do but sit and worry. He could hear Tex moving around, and the occasional clank of metal on metal. After ten minutes, he returned to the luggage compartment.

"Time to go. How are you doing?"

"Got two bolts out. But those other two look a lot harder. I don't know if I am going to be able to get them out. I wonder how they got this thing in here."

"Jill got some mercury from the lab. Want to try it?"

Tex pulled himself out of the compartment and grinned up at Steve. "Why didn't I think of that? That's the best news I've heard all year. Let me have it." Steve went to the cockpit and returned with a small vial of the silver liquid metal.

"Here's my toothbrush to apply it," he said.

"Great idea." Tex gingerly held the two items and then bent down into the compartment again. "I'm going to start with the mercury right away." Tex announced. "No sense trying to keep messing with the wrenches. You aren't going to taxi to the terminal yet, are you?"

"Not while that thing's on board. I'll think up an excuse to delay our departure. How much time do you think it's going to take?"

"Fifteen minutes."

Tex bent down into the compartment and placed put several drops of mercury on some of the aluminum pieces to which the black box was attached. When the mercury touched the aluminum, the aluminum began to turn brown and flake off. Tex watched, fascinated. He remembered being told about this phenomenon when he was in flight training. It was one of a thousand little pieces of information that pilots accumulate.

Aluminum is a rather peculiar metal. The metal itself is rather soft, and has very little strength. However, it combines readily with the oxygen in the air, and the surface of the aluminum turns into an air-tight coating of aluminum oxide. It is this tiny layer of aluminum oxide that gives aluminum its characteristic strength. Because the aluminum oxide coating is air-tight, it also prevents additional oxygen from getting into metal. It is very different from iron. When oxygen combines with iron, the resulting rust has almost no strength and will crumble away to nothing.

However, when mercury is placed on aluminum, it disrupts the aluminum oxide coating. The coating starts to flake and peel. It loses its air-tight quality, allowing more oxygen to attack the underlying aluminum. Essentially, it allows the aluminum to turn into an aluminum/mercury oxide rust with no strength. However, because aluminum is much more chemically active than iron, the reaction also happens at a much faster speed.

Tex remembered the story one of his classmates had told, sitting around during a break one day. It was rumored that during WWII, American commandos would parachute close to enemy airfields with nothing more than a spray bottle of mercury. They would try to get to the enemy aircraft and spray some of the mercury inside in wings, where the damage hopefully wouldn't be noticed. Then, at some point in the next couple of days, when the wing was being stressed during flight, the damage would allow the entire wing to fail and tear off the rest of the airplane. Tex wondered if the story were really true. After watching the mercury attack the airframe, he didn't doubt it would work. He reached in with the toothbrush, scrubbed some of the aluminum oxide away, and put another drop of mercury on each side. In less than 10 minutes, he was able to reach in with the pliers and bend the weakened aluminum up and out of the way, extracting the box as he did so.

Tex pulled his head out of the compartment. "It's free. That mercury was a great idea. Now what do I do with it?"

"I've been thinking about that. How about we just leave it on a bench in the hanger? We can leave a note on it to let them know we found it."

"Why would we want them to know we've found it?" said a perplexed Tex.

"Well, I was thinking, if they know we know about their assassination attempt, they might not want to try again the future, right? I mean, they would know we could get them in a lot of trouble."

"A little trouble would suit me just fine," said Tex in an angry tone.

"But we can't win that way. We will be playing right into their hands if they can accuse us of causing trouble. They'll toss us in jail and throw away the key. If, that is, we're lucky. I say we just leave the thing here and let them know we're on to them."

"Maybe you're right," admitted Tex. "I guess it's worth a try. I wouldn't mind going a few rounds in a boxing ring with General Collins, though. Especially if his hands were tied behind his back."

"Just take the thing and put it on a workbench," encouraged Steve. Without another word, Tex picked up the box and walked toward the exit of the aircraft. He was back less than a minute later.

"Alright, done. I hope it works. Let's get out of here," said Tex when he returned. He gathered up the tools, slammed the compartment hatch, and marched forward to join Steve in the cockpit. They got the engines started, and started moving toward the terminal.

With its metal roof and transparent sides, the terminal was nothing more than a glorified bus stop. It was about 20 by 20 feet and inside there were about 30 people. Some of their luggage was inside, some outside. Steve and Tex got the job of loading the luggage. *Ah, the benefits of being a military pilot,* thought Steve. They parked the airplane, shut down the engines, and Steve clambered out. Tex opened the luggage compartment door from the inside, and Steve started lifting bags up to him. Once that job was complete, Tex pulled the door closed as Steve walked to the back of the aircraft and climbed the ladder into the passenger compartment. He counted the number of passengers as he moved forward. The count matched what he had been told to expect.

Once that chore was completed, he turned around and walked back to where Jill was sitting. She was just a few seats aft of the luggage compartment bulkhead on the left hand side of the airplane. Dr. Choi was sitting across the aisle from her. He sat in the empty seat next to her. "How are you doing?"

"Fine. How are you?" she said searchingly.

"Great. We got rid of the unrequested option package," said Steve quietly. He leaned over to kiss her, then stood up and moved toward the cockpit. After he got seated, he and Tex restarted the engines, then taxied out to the runway. Air traffic was so light now that there were no air traffic controllers. Everything was being done visually. Steve checked for inbound aircraft, then pulled out onto the runway and advanced the pitch control. The turboprop gained speed quickly and rose into the air. After a few minutes of climbing, Steve banked right in preparation to head back to the main part of Nellis.

Tex had been sitting quietly. "Mind if I fly for awhile?"

"You're airplane," said Steve.

Tex placed his hands and feet on the controls. "My airplane," he smiled. Steve pulled his hands and feet away from the controls.

"I wonder what's next," said Steve.

"Nothing, I hope," was the reply.

They reached cruising altitude and leveled off. Less than a minute later, the cockpit door opened, and Dr. Choi entered.

Steve glanced back. "Hi, Dr. Choi. What's up?"

"I am hijacking this airplane. I have a bomb," he announced.

Steve and Tex looked at each other incredulously. "Um, we got rid of one before we took off," said Steve.

"This is no joke," said Choi harshly.

"We're not joking either, you lunatic. We left it on a workbench back in the hanger." said Tex hotly.

Dr. Choi looked at them. He seemed confused. As tense as he was, he suddenly realized that Stark had not told him the truth. *They meant for me to be killed too,* he realized in shock. *They must have decided they couldn't trust me with knowledge of the assassination attempt, and decided to do away with all of us at once.* The realization put to silence any doubts he had about completing the kidnapping attempt. "I am carrying mine. It is strapped to my body," he told Steve and Tex.

Tex started to laugh. He turned to Steve. "Man, I've got to hang with you more often. Do you always party like this?"

Steve tried to ignore Tex. "OK, so you have *another* bomb. What do *you* want?" he said to Dr. Choi.

"When we land at Las Vegas airport, you will drive over to a private hanger," he directed.

"OK. That's easy enough. Which one?" asked Steve.

"Never mind now," said Choi.

"Dr. Choi, I have to tell the air traffic controllers where I am heading before I land. That way they can tell me which way to go when I get ready to pull off the runway."

"How soon before you must tell?"

"Ten to fifteen minutes."

"OK, I will tell you then."

"Why are you doing this?"

"I need to take you and Jill somewhere. Now you will stop asking questions."

Steve decided it would be wise to stop asking questions.

The next few minutes passed slowly. Eventually, Steve turned to Dr. Choi. "I need to call air traffic control. What is the hanger number?"

"Thirty-four."

"Alright." Steve thumbed the transmit switch and contacted air traffic control.

"No tricks." said Choi. He was leaning forward, his head almost between Steve and Tex's.

"No tricks." repeated Steve. He requested permission for the initial approach, and then was handed off to final approach. He told them he was heading to private hanger 34.

"Roger, Nellis 255. You are cleared to land on 32R. Exit on taxiway 5R and contact ground control."

"Nellis 255," acknowledged Steve. Tex turned the airplane to line up with the runway. Approach was smooth, and in a couple more seconds the big 32R painted on the end of the runway was flashing by underneath. Tex let the airplane settle slowly. The right wheel bumped, then the left. Tex let the nose come down, and then he eased the pitch controller back. The propellers fought to push the air forward, slowing the airplane down rapidly. Tex pushed against both pedals with his feet. The aircraft's brakes came on, and they slowed down some more. He saw 5R approaching, put the propeller pitch back into neutral, and continued to brake slowly. The airplane was going about 35 miles per hour as he eased into the turn. Steve thumbed the microphone and requested further instructions from ground control.

"Nellis 255, turn right on 15L and go 6000 feet. Turn in to the private hanger ramp at 7L. Hanger 34 will be ahead of you slightly to your left."

"Nellis 255," acknowledged Steve. Tex turned right again onto 15L and started cruising down the taxiway. He had one hand on the propeller's pitch control, his other on the yoke. Suddenly, without warning, he pushed on both pedals as hard as he could, at the same time pulling the propeller's pitch all the way back.

The action was completely unexpected by everyone but Tex. The plane slowed as if it had run into a wall. Dr. Choi, who wasn't belted in, was thrown forward. His head cracked against the top of the instrument panel. Then he dropped down across the engine and propeller controls between the two seats. Tex grabbed him and pushed him back. Then he undid his seatbelt and leaped over the control area to land astride Choi. He needn't have worried. The physicist was out cold. Blood started to drip off a deep cut on the top of his head.

"Smooth move," said Steve.

Tex unfolded the small jump seat from the wall, picked up Dr. Choi and roughly threw him into it. His head rolled, and he nearly fell out of the seat. Tex grabbed the front of his shirt and pushed him up against the wall. As he did so, he felt something under Choi's shirt. "It feels like he has something strapped to his body," he reported.

Steve was on the microphone, apologizing to the passengers for the quick stop. The airplane was sitting still on the taxiway. He released the brake and let the airplane start moving again.

Tex ripped open the shirt. Around Choi's stomach, there appeared to be some kind of thick belt with a pouch that bulged every few inches. There was a buckle on the front of it, and a button on each side of the buckle. Tex looked at it closely, then loosened the buckle and pulled it off.

"Can you work with him in the luggage compartment?" asked Steve.

"Sure." Tex supported Dr. Choi with one hand while he opened the door between the cockpit and the luggage compartment, then grabbed Dr. Choi under each arm. He awkwardly dragged Dr. Choi around the door. Steve glanced back as Dr. Choi's legs, than feet disappeared through the door.

Steve was thinking rapidly up in the cockpit. He got on the intercom again and requested Jill join him in the cockpit. Thirty seconds later, Jill poked her head in. "What's going on up here? It looks like Dr. Choi got hurt. Is that why we stopped?"

"Where's your cell phone?" Steve asked her urgently.

"In my purse, back in my seat."

"Go get it. Hurry."

"Why?"

"Jill, it's an emergency. Don't ask questions, just go get your phone."

Jill disappeared around the cockpit door into the luggage compartment. "Steve asked me to go get my cell phone," she told Tex.

He nodded and tried to pull Dr. Choi further to one side of the compartment. "Try not to let anyone see in here." he told her.

She opened the door into the passenger compartment, slipped through, and closed the door behind her. She walked back to her seat, opened the overhead bin, grabbed her purse, and headed for the cockpit. Again, she slipped through the luggage compartment door, stepped over Tex and Dr. Choi, and into the cockpit. She showed Steve the phone.

"Excellent. Call Paul Schneider. Hurry."

"I don't have his number."

"Then call your Dad."

She pushed the appropriate speed dial button. When she heard it ringing, she gave it to Steve.

"Dad? This is Steve. Listen, we've just been hijacked. We overpowered the hijacker." He saw Jill's eyes grow wide as she listened to his side of the conversation. "Please get Paul Schneider on the phone right now." Steve waited impatiently. Then, "Paul, this is Steve Harrison. Listen, lots of things just happened. We were just hijacked, but managed to overpower the hijacker. We are at Las Vegas airport, heading for private hanger number 34. We need some help, now." Steve paused to listen. "No, we're still in the airplane, just turning in toward the hanger now from the taxiway."

Jill leaned forward. "Shouldn't we be heading someplace else?" she whispered to Steve. He didn't answer. He was braking the airplane, getting ready to turn off the taxiway. He turned the airplane, and found himself facing a row of hangers on the other side of a pad where airplanes were parked out in the open. He allowed the airplane to approach the hanger slowly. Looking around, he found an area that looked big enough to sit without blocking any of the other aircraft. He turned in, stopped the airplane, and set the parking brake.

"Paul, we just parked the airplane. We are going to have to be going now. I am going to leave the phone on. Track the signal. We won't be talking on it anymore." He lowered the phone and sighed.

"Why did we come here?" Jill asked in confusion.

"We're going with Dr. Choi," said Steve.

"To a hospital?"

"He was trying to hijack us. He wants us to go with him somewhere. I have the feeling we need to take him wherever he needs to go."

"What? Are you nuts?" Jill demanded.

"I don't think so. Look, Jill. Remember what Jesus said? If your enemy hungers, feed him, if he is thirsty, give him a drink? If he asks you to go a mile with him, go with him two miles?"

"Yes, but that didn't apply to hijacking."

"It applies to everything. We're going to go wherever Dr. Choi wants us to go. God will protect us."

"I'm not going," said Jill resolutely.

"Jill, listen to me," said Steve. "I listened to you when you told me about your conviction about taking the lives of people. That's what got us into this mess, remember?" She nodded resignedly. "Well, now I'm telling you what the Bible says, and I want you to accommodate my convictions."

"But we don't know where we're going," She protested.

"Though I make my bed in Hell, or dwell in the uttermost parts of the sea, even there will thy hand lead me, and thy right hand shall guide me," Steve quoted to her.

"I will only go if we pray," she said.

Steve climbed out of his seat and grabbed her hands. "Father, we are giving ourselves into the hands of our enemy. We don't know what he wants. We don't know where we are going. Please protect us and make us strong. In Jesus' name, Amen." He opened his eyes. "Come on, let's go." He opened the door and slid around it into the luggage compartment.

Dr. Choi was sitting dazedly on a pile of suitcases. He was pressing a strip of cloth against his head. Steve saw that Tex had ripped Choi's shirt and was using it to soak up some of the blood.

"Dr. Choi, can you hear me?" Steve asked. He nodded silently. "Was it me and Jill that you wanted?" He nodded again. "Are we supposed to get out of the airplane here?" Another nod. "Is someone going to meet us?" Another nod. "Do you eat baseballs for breakfast?" A pause, and a slight shake of his head. "Well, I guess we know he's thinking logically." Steve turned to Tex, "Jill and I are getting off here with Dr. Choi. It's your airplane now."

"You are? That's what he wanted you to do. You don't have to do it now." said Tex in confusion.

"I know. We are doing it anyway." He turned to Dr. Choi. "Can you walk?" He reached down and pulled him to his feet. The diminutive physicist swayed drunkenly. Steve grabbed his left arm and slung it over his shoulder, then put his right arm around his waist. "Come on, let's go. Jill, do you have your phone?"

"Yes."

"Is it still on?"

"Yes."

"Go open the door." he said to Tex.

Tex shook his head. "I thought I was the crazy one," he said as he opened the door between the cargo compartment and the passenger area. "Let me go first, I can open the door and let down the ladder." He walked into the passenger compartment. People looked at him confusingly. "We'll be underway in a moment, Ladies and Gentlemen. We are having a bit of a medical problem with Dr. Choi. Please clear the aisle and the door." A few of the passengers in the rear had already stood up and were waiting by the door. "Sorry, folks, you aren't getting off here. Please get back in your seats." They moved reluctantly back into their seats. Tex reached the passenger door, opened it, and lowered the folding aluminum ladder. Steve arrived a moment later, half-guiding and half-supporting Dr. Choi. Tex looked at Steve. "I'm confused. Are you part of this conspiracy too?"

"No, but I am following Jesus. Help me get him down this ladder."

"Here. I'll hold him. You go down first, and then I'll lower him down."

Steve climbed down, then turned. Tex got Dr. Choi to the top step. As Steve guided his feet, Dr. Choi managed to make his way down the ladder, partially falling from the last step into Steve's waiting arms. Jill followed a moment later. Steve slung Dr. Choi's arm over his shoulder again. "Alright, where's the welcoming party?" He peered down the aisle between hanger 34 and the next hanger on his left. At the end of the aisle, a couple of people waved at them. "There they are. Let's go."

Dr. Choi mumbled something. "What?" asked Steve.

"Don't go. Bad people," said Dr. Choi.

"Who are they?"

"From North Korea. They want you and Jill. Take back to North Korea," Dr Choi slurred drunkenly.

"Well, I hope that's not where we end up," said Steve. "Let's go," he repeated again to Jill and they set off.

It seemed like a long walk. On each side of them was a metal building, each with a series of large folding doors that could accommodate a small aircraft. He could see the men up ahead talking back and forth and staring at them. It seemed they didn't know whether to wait or to come and help. Steve soldiered on, Jill beside him. The men waited and chattered. When Steve finally got close, he said, "Hey, how about some help for your pal here?"

There was a gate in the fence with an electronic lock on it. One of the men pushed a code and opened it, then held it open so Steve and Dr. Choi could get through. On the other side of the fence was a panel van with a ladder rack. One of the men opened the door. Steve led Dr. Choi over to it, and then sat him down on the edge of the door.

"What happened to him?" asked the taller of the two men. They were staring at Steve, Jill and Dr. Choi like they were seeing ghosts. They had good reason to stare. Dr. Choi was on his feet, but there was blood on his face and only the remains of his shirt flapped loosely around his torso in the slight breeze. They were obviously trying to figure out why their hijacker was a bloody wreck, and why he was being transported by his captives.

"He hit his head."

"Did he ask you to come here?"

Steve nodded. "You might say that."

The man looked at Dr. Choi's bare torso. "Where is his belt?"

"You mean the bomb? We took it off in the airplane."

More obvious confusion. "Why are you here?"

"Because Dr. Choi wanted us to come here." Steve didn't mind letting them be confused. The more time they spent here, the greater their chances of safety. He was praying that Paul was getting some police agency somewhere to track Jill's phone signal.

The two men chattered back and forth in a language Steve didn't recognize. Finally, one of the men said to Steve, "Are you the police?"

"No, I'm a pilot. I flew that airplane back there." He nodded toward the turboprop.

More chatter. Finally, the tall man turned back to Steve. "Will you all get in the van, please?" he asked politely.

Steve climbed into the van, then turned to pull in Dr. Choi. Jill helped push him in, then she climbed in. The smaller of the two men climbed in behind her and pulled the door shut. The other man walked around and climbed in the driver's seat. The van backed out of the parking spot and pulled away.

"So, how do you like Nevada?" asked Steve, trying to keep the men off balance as long as possible. The man frowned at Steve, shook his head, and put his finger to his lips. Steve turned back to Dr. Choi. "How are you doing?"

"My head hurts."

"I bet it does. You need stitches." Blood was still dripping from his head in a steady rhythm. Steve ripped another piece of shirt off what remained and pressed it on the wound. It was saturated almost immediately. He turned to the short man. "Dr. Choi needs to go to a

266

hospital."

"That is not possible," said the tall man from the driver's seat. Steve hadn't figured it would be, but it didn't hurt to ask.

Dr. Choi was looking at Steve. "Why did you come?" he said weakly.

"Because Jesus said that if someone asks you to go with him one mile, you go with him two. If he asks for your coat, give him your coat and your shirt, too," he answered.

"You are a good man," said Dr. Choi.

"No, Dr. Choi. Jesus is a good man. We follow Jesus. You just don't understand what that means."

"You are right. I do not understand," replied Dr. Choi. Then he closed his eyes and leaned his head back against the side of the van.

They traveled for about 15 minutes. Traffic was heavy. They turned a couple of times, and then seemed to bump up some sort of driveway. The van pulled into the shadow of a building and stopped.

The tall man walked around, opened a door in the side of the building, and opened the van door. "All out," he ordered. The glare of the Nevada sunshine leaped in at them, stinging their eyes after the relative darkness of the van's interior. The small man got out first, followed by Jill.

Steve helped Dr. Choi sit up. "Ooh. Everything is spinning," he said.

"You probably have a concussion. Just sit still a minute. When you feel better, we'll get out."

The tall man stuck his head in the door. "Out!" he repeated impatiently.

"Just a minute. Dr. Choi is about to pass out," said Steve. Dr. Choi nodded at Steve, and then started scooting himself toward the door. Steve followed. Choi climbed unsteadily out the door and stood up. Steve followed, grabbing him again. The tall stranger made no attempt to help them. Steve helped Dr. Choi into the building. They were led down a short hallway, and then pointed toward a door. Steve guided Dr. Choi in and the door was closed behind them.

Steve looked around the room. It had a concrete floor and ceiling and was lit by a single light bulb hanging from the middle of the ceiling. The walls were concrete block, and in the distant past had been painted a whitish-color. There were several people sitting against the wall around the perimeter of the room.

After the door was closed, the others in the room stood up. But they seemed afraid to approach the newcomers. Steve looked at them more closely. They were all Asian. There were two men and four women. One of the women seemed very old, the others appeared to be in their mid-30's, he judged, the men perhaps were just a little older. There were four children clinging to the legs of two of the women.

"Hi. I'm Steve. Who are you?" inquired Steve politely. No one answered. "Dr. Choi, do you know who these people are?"

Instead of answering, Dr. Choi pulled himself loose from Steve's grasp and walked unsteadily toward them. A moment later they were a mass of arms and legs wrapping around each other, with Dr. Choi in the middle. They all seemed to be talking at once. Dr. Choi turned his head toward Steve. "This is my family from North Korea. I have not seen them since I left North Korea over 15 years ago."

Steve and Jill both stared in amazement. Tears and cries mingled with a steady stream of a lilting foreign tongue. Now it was Steve and Jill's turn to be confused.

But Steve realized he didn't have time to enjoy the reunion. He turned to Jill. "Still got the phone?" he asked. Jill nodded, dug into the pocket of her sweater, and pulled it out. Steve put it up to his ear. "Hello, anyone there?"

"This is Paul Schneider. Who am I speaking to?" came the familiar voice.

"Paul, this is Steve."

"Steve! Are you alright? Where are you?"

"We are alright. I'm not sure where we are. Are you tracking the phone's signal?"

"Yes, we're working with the Las Vegas police. Can you give us any information that would help us find you?"

"Yes. We were driven here in a white panel van. It has a ladder rack, and there is at least one ladder on it. The van is parked in the shadow of a building, next to a door in the side of the building. The building is a concrete block construction. I think it is about two stories tall."

"OK, that's excellent. Hold on." Steve heard the information being relayed in the background. Then, "Is Jill with you?"

"Yes, she's here. So is Dr. Choi. Also we have two additional men, four additional women, and three children. Dr. Choi told us they were his family." The family members had by now recognized that Dr. Choi

268

was wounded, because they were apparently telling him to sit down against the wall. "They are acting like family, that's for sure."

"OK, the police are looking for you. What can you tell me about your immediate surroundings?"

"We're in an inner room with no windows. I would say 10 feet by 20 feet with a single lightbulb." Steve heard footsteps approaching. He pulled the phone down and managed to put it in the pocket of Jill's sweater before the door was opened. The tall man walked in and looked at the group. Steve was surprised to see Dr. Choi's family freeze in fear.

The man motioned to Steve. "You. Come with me."

Steve looked at him, trying to decide whether to comply or not. Judging by the reaction of Dr. Choi's family, this individual was someone with whom they would not choose to spend quality time. Well, a little too late for second thoughts, he told himself firmly.

He felt Jill grab his arm with both hands. "Don't go!" she whispered desperately.

"It's OK, Babe. Just pray," Steve responded. He kissed her, then tore himself loose from her grasp, and followed the tall man out the door. It was pulled shut as soon as he walked through.

Chapter 17

Jill watched in shock as Steve walked out the door. She was so frightened, she thought she would collapse where she stood. She had counted on him being there for her through all of this. But she suddenly realized that there was no guarantee they would be kept together. It was this, more than anything that made her aware of the danger they were in.

But what had Steve told her before he left? "Pray." So she did. Right there, in that small room, a prisoner, in the company of ten people, only one other who spoke English, she bowed her head and silently asked God to protect them and get them out of this, if it was his will. And when she finished, she felt the calming presence of the Holy Spirit fill her with a peace that was as unexpected as it was unrealistic.

She turned and walked over to Dr. Choi. His family moved aside, making a place for her as she came. She sat down next to him. "How do you feel?" she asked him.

"Better," he said, "I am not feeling so dizzy now."

"Good. Has the bleeding stopped?"

"I think maybe yes."

Jill breathed a sigh of relief. Even though Dr. Choi had apparently turned on them, she didn't want to see him hurt.

"Why did you come?" he asked.

"Steve said we should come. He reminded me that in the Bible, Jesus said that if someone asks us to go with him a mile, we should walk two miles. If someone asks for our coat, we should give not only our coat, but our shirt as well."

"You put yourself in danger."

"The Bible says that the hairs of our head are numbered, and that God sees everything that happens to us. I believe God knows where we are. We are not in danger if we are doing what God wants us to do."

"But I was going to..." he stopped.

"What?"

"I was going to trade you to North Korea so I could get my family." And Dr. Choi broke down and wept.

"Oh." Realization dawned on Jill. She looked at Dr. Choi's family that was standing around them. "Well, now you have your family."

"But we are all prisoners," said Dr. Choi through his tears.

"Only as long as God allows."

"God would never forgive me after what I have done," said Dr. Choi through his tears.

"Dr. Choi, remember when we talked about how Jesus paid the price for our sins?" He nodded. "Well, God watched his son die a terrible death. The price for sin has been paid. All sin. My sin. And your sin. Dr. Choi, God wants you to be able to escape from your sin. He wants everyone to take advantage of the free gift of salvation. The more people take advantage of that free gift, the more God likes it. Freedom is here, Dr. Choi."

"God could never accept me."

Jill thought about that for a moment. "I see that you are twice a prisoner," she said finally.

"What? What did you say?" he asked.

"I said that you are twice a prisoner. You are a prisoner here. I am too, apparently. But I have freedom from my sins in Jesus. You don't. Dr. Choi, if you don't take advantage of the gift of salvation right now, for the rest of your life, you will be afraid to die. Because you know there is no other way to get rid of your sin and guilt. If you repent and ask Jesus to come into your life, that sin and guilt can be washed away. You will never have to be overwhelmed with guilt again."

The tears had stopped and Dr. Choi sat still. Then he asked, "Does this mean that God will grant me a miracle so that my family can still be free?"

"No, not necessarily. God's in control of our lives. We might be rescued. If we are, then you will probably have to go to court. God

271

saves us from our sins, but he doesn't necessarily take away the consequences of our sins. Salvation means you will not fear to face God after you die, because you will know that Jesus paid the price for what you have done. It means you will not have to live for eternity in Hell, being endlessly punished for your sins because you didn't allow Jesus to take them away."

Dr. Choi nodded understandingly. "Your God likes to forgive sin?"

"Oh, very much. The price has been paid. The more people come to Jesus, the happier God is."

"Then I want to make your God happy. I want to come to Jesus. I do not want to always feel guilty for what I have done."

"Dr. Choi, are you sorry for your sins?"

Dr. Choi hung his head. "I am very sorry," he whispered.

"Then you are repenting, and that's what God asks us to do. All you have to do is ask Jesus to come and clean out your heart."

"I am not sure what to say."

"Just talk to Him. Tell God that you want the blood of Jesus to take away your sin."

And so he did. Dr. Choi bowed his head, closed his eyes, and asked God to forgive his treachery. When he was done, he looked up at Jill. "My sins are gone?"

Jill felt tears of happiness welling up in her eyes. "Yes, Dr. Choi. They are gone. And you have made God happy. Very happy."

"I will tell my family." He turned and started talking to them in his native language. Jill smiled as she realized that, in his own way, Dr. Choi was speaking in tongues.

* * * *

Steve was led down a hall to a larger open area. He realized that they were in the service area of an empty service station. There were concrete block walls on three sides of him, but the fourth wall featured three tall garage doors. The doors had narrow windows about half way up. On the floor, there were marks in each of the three bays where hydraulic lifts had once lifted vehicles off the floor to be serviced.

Two folding chairs had been placed facing each other. "Sit," indicated the man. Steve sat and waited.

"Why did you come?" demanded the tall man.

272

"Dr. Choi wanted us to come."

"What happened to him? How did he get hurt?"

"Well, he was in the cockpit, and the other pilot put on the brakes hard. He didn't have a seatbelt on, and he hit his head on the control panel."

"You did this, yes?"

"No. The other pilot was the one that put on the brakes."

"So he was hurt in the airplane?"

"Yes, he was hurt while he was in the airplane."

"What happened to his belt?"

"We took it off."

"Where is it?"

"Still on the airplane."

"So why did you come?" The tall man was obviously getting frustrated by the simple answers that contained not a trace of logic.

"Because I am a Christian. Jesus said to help your enemy."

The man sneered. "Jesus told you to come to us?"

"Yes."

"There is no Jesus. There is no Christian."

"You are wrong."

The man stood staring at him. Then he said, "You are lying." Steve said nothing. There didn't seem to be anything to say. "Why are you lying to me?"

"I am not lying to you."

"You are lying," screamed the man at him. Again, Steve didn't say anything. This seemed to work the man into more of a frenzy. "Why did you come?"

"I told you. Jesus said to help your enemy."

"You are the police."

"I am a pilot. I flew the airplane here."

"But you are police."

"I am a member of the United States Air Force. But I am not a police officer."

"Why are you lying?" demanded the man.

"Look, why do you think I am lying? You saw that Dr. Choi was hurt when we arrived, right? You saw me help him off the plane and bring him to you. You know his bomb belt is gone. He got hurt on the airplane. But he told us he wanted me and my wife to come to you. So, after he got hurt, I thought about what Jesus would do, and I decided

273

to come anyway."

The man clearly couldn't grasp what Steve was trying to say. "Who made you come?" he demanded.

"No one made me come. I came voluntarily."

"I do not believe that. Now you will tell me the truth." He turned and nodded at the other man. The other man walked over to Steve and slapped him across the face. Steve's cheek stung, and his left eye began to water from the force of the blow. "Now, tell me why you have come."

"I told you. I came because that is what I thought Jesus would do." Steve was beginning to dislike this man in a rather fundamental way. On the other hand, he realized for the first time in his life, that he was thankful for the SERE training he received while a cadet at the Academy. The Survive-Evade-Resist-Escape training was appropriately brutal, but it taught survival skills in a way no textbook was able to do. The cadets has been dropped into the brush, made to survive several days with just their wits, then they were 'captured' and pulled into a makeshift POW camp to learn the fine art of denying information to their 'enemies.' It was no picnic. It was just something to be endured. At least, that's what he had thought until now.

"There is no Jesus. You will learn Juche."

"What is Juche?"

"Juche is self-reliance. Juche is our great leader, Kim Sung Il."

"Who is Kim Sung Eel?"

The man glared at Steve. "He is the great leader of the Democratic People's Republic of Korea."

"The country that starves its people?"

This time his other cheek was slapped. "No one starves in Democratic People's Republic of Korea. That is a lie."

As Steve head was turned toward the garage doors by the force of the blow, he thought he saw a bit of movement at one of the windows. Hoping that help was rallying outside, he decided to get these people really mad and keep them distracted. "That is the truth. Your people are starving while the great president steals their food."

"You lie!" shrieked the man. Steve put his arms up around his head as the two men began to beat him with their fists. He bent over to protect himself as much as he could. As the blows rained down on him, he began to wonder if he had done the wrong thing. Suddenly the blows stopped. Steve peered up. The two men were panting, staring

274

down at him.

"If I'm lying, why are you getting so angry?" he asked.

"I ask the questions here," said the man.

"Why? Afraid of the truth?"

They started in on him again. Steve had just bent double when there was a flash and a tremendous BOOM. The flash was so bright that for a moment he couldn't see. As his sight came back, he thought he saw black figures moving through the smoke in the room. One of them seemed to be coming up to him. "On the floor," barked the black suited figure. Steve lowered himself to the floor. He felt himself being frisked. "OK, you can get up. Are you Steve Harrison?"

"Yeah. Who are you?"

"Las Vegas SWAT. Where's your wife?"

"Down the hall on the right, through the door."

"Anyone in there with her?"

"Dr. Choi from the project and the members of his family. No bad guys, I don't think."

The man nodded, and then seemed to be speaking to someone else through some kind of a radio system. "I've got Steve Harrison here. He says his wife and other friendlies are in the inner room, probably no bad guys. No guarantee."

Steve nodded wearily. His head was ringing from the explosion and the slaps. He was suddenly more tired than he believed possible. Another minute passed, and then Jill stepped around the corner. She gave a little cry and rushed up to him. He stood up to meet her and she flung herself into his arms. "Oh, Steve. Are you alright?"

"I'm OK. Are you?"

"I'm OK too. Oh, thank the Good Lord you're alright."

Steve held her. "They slapped me around a little. But I think they are going to end up regretting that." He looked over at the two men. They were laying face down on the floor. Their ankles had been cuffed, and their wrists cuffed behind them. An obviously physically fit man, dressed entirely in black, was standing behind them, pointing a rather impressive looking gun at their backs.

"They sure are." said the first man in black that had approached Steve. "OK, I just got the all clear signal." He pulled off the black face mask to reveal a black face. "These two have broken more laws than I ever knew existed. Not to mention they seem to be sponsored by a foreign power. They'll probably be classified as foreign terrorists." he shook his head. "Stupidity knows no limits, I guess." The other black clad figures in the room were pulling off their masks as well.

"Steve, Dr. Choi just became a Christian." Jill smiled up at him. "Isn't that wonderful?"

"That's great. Do you think he meant it?"

"No doubt. He told his family what he was doing, and why he was doing it. He told me they want to find out more."

"Hallelujah. That sounds even better." He sighed, feeling the tension begin to run off of him. Next he turned back to the SWAT team member. "Now what?"

"Well, I guess we'll want to be talking to you folks for awhile. Not here. Probably take you back downtown, someplace more comfortable than this." He looked distastefully around the old auto shop. "I was afraid to throw that stun grenade in here. Thought it might light up some old gas fumes of something. What a hole."

"Yeah. I wonder how they found this place."

"That's just one of many things we'll be asking them."

Steve released Jill. "You know my name. What's yours?"

The man grinned. "I'm Andre. Put 'er there." They shook hands. "We saw what they were doing to you. That took guts."

"I was hoping you were outside when I started egging them on."

"Great play. Kept them distracted, all right. Need a job? We're always looking for good folks on the SWAT team."

Steve smiled tiredly and shook his head. "No, thanks." He turned to Jill. "Still have your phone?"

Jill pulled it out and held it up to her ear. "Hello?" no response. She looked at the display. "Battery died."

"We better get your Dad on the phone. He's probably had a heart attack by now."

"We have a phone outside in the truck." Andre turned and led the way.

* * * *

They took Steve and Jill to the Las Vegas police station. Andre, who seemed to be the commander of the SWAT team, showed them to a small conference room. "I'll be back in a few minutes. You folks need anything to drink?"

"Any chance for some food?" asked Steve, before Jill could ask for water.

Andre laughed. "I guess it is lunchtime already. Yeah. How's a submarine sandwich from the vending machine?"

"That would be great, thanks."

"Some water too, please," called Jill as Andre turned and headed out the door. "Did you hear what he said? Lunchtime already. It feels like a week since we got on that airplane."

"Yeah, I know what you mean. Hard to believe we only got on the airplane a couple hours ago."

"Steve, what do you think they are going to do to Dr. Choi?"

"I have no idea, Love." He stopped to think about that. "If they try to pursue the hijacking charges, I assume that Project Opera will be blown wide open. Of course, once we explain to the police about the other bomb and Dr. Stark, I doubt they will be able to keep anything quiet."

"Do you think it's safe to tell the police what happened?"

"It's the best thing to do. Look," he said, straightening suddenly and looking at her more intensely. "Paul Schneider said that bomb was planted with the permission of General Collins. That makes it a military operation. We need to get the police on our side. They are civilian, not military. If we tell them about the plot, they can start to investigate, and it will be in their best interest to keep us safe."

"But what about the space-warp technology?"

"We don't have to tell them about all that, we just have to tell them we were working on a secret military project at Nellis, and that we can't explain everything. But we need to tell them about both the bomb plot and the hijacking."

"What a mess." Jill sighed.

"Yeah. Have you thought that this might bring down the President? Project Opera was kind of his baby. Remember when he addressed us at that meeting? If this gets all the way up to General Collins' level, it's going to be political chaos."

They were silent for a few moments. Then Steve said, "Remember when we decided that God was calling me away from being a fighter pilot because I might have to kill people?"

"Of course." replied Jill.

"Well, I never imagined how many people would end up trying to kill me because of that decision." They looked at each other, and then started laughing. The laughter felt good. Steve felt the stress of the last few hours start to drain away.

The door opened and Andre walked back in balancing several submarine sandwiches, soft drinks and bottled water. Behind him strode Tex. "Nothing like an armed escort to make a guy feel secure," he said as he walked in and spied Steve and Jill. "Safest I've felt in two weeks."

Steve was still smiling, and his smile deepened when he saw his copilot. "Hey, Tex, good to see you. What happened after we got off the airplane?"

Tex walked over to a chair and sat down. "Well, there were lots of questions from the passengers, you can imagine. I just went back to the cockpit, called the tower, and reported a hijacking. What a mistake that was. I was trying to explain that the wounded hijacker was already gone, carried away by the pilot and his wife." He shook his head. "I am still not sure they believe me. Anyway, all of a sudden these squad cars start pulling up around the airplane. Cops are jumping out with their guns drawn. I can hear the passengers starting to come unglued. So I get on the intercom and try to tell them the danger is past, but the police don't understand that yet." He shook his head again. "What a zoo. Anyway, it took about 20 minutes before the cops finally were willing to come aboard and verify the story. After that, they took me to some sort of security office at the airport. After a bit of an argument, they let me call the service people to tell them about the mercury eating away the airplane. That was another 20 minutes of confusion." He sighed and flopped his head against the back of the chair with his eyes closed. "Anyway, I was just getting off the phone with the service people when some more cops come in and tell me they are bringing me down here. And here I am." He opened his eyes and looked at Steve and Jill. "What's your story?"

Steve told him briefly what had happened. Andre was still in the room, listening to the entire conversation while he set the food and drinks on the table in front of them. He shook his head several times as he heard Steve's story.

"Do you think they really are from North Korea?" asked Tex.

"They were sure acting like it. They were starting to preach Juche to me, told me Jesus was a lie. I guess Juche is some kind of a state religion over there. They told me they worshiped Kim Sung Eel, their great president. I asked if that was the president who let all the people starve. They didn't like that very much."

"I imagine not." interjected Andre dryly.

Tex looked at Steve, dumbfounded. He opened his mouth, then snapped it shut again. Finally, he managed to say, "You are either the stupidest or the bravest guy I have ever met. I haven't decided which yet."

Steve grinned. "Tex, you should know by now. I am a Christian. When Jesus is on your side, your life is different."

"I'll say. Before I met you, I thought rodeo was exciting."

"Well, most Christians probably don't have experiences exactly like ours every day."

"So what kind of experiences do most Christians have?" asked Tex.

Steve knew an opportunity when he heard it, so he began to explain the plan of salvation through the blood of Jesus.

As Steve talked, Jill listened quietly. At the same time, she thought about the bombs and the hijacking. She thought about the terror of that moment when Steve had left her in the room with Dr. Choi and his family. She thought about the political ramifications of everything that had happened. It was almost overwhelming. She decided to stop thinking about it and listen to Steve explaining God's plan of salvation to Tex.

And as she sat and listened to her husband explaining that marvelous story of Jesus' love and self-sacrifice, she was struck again by the lengths to which Jesus had gone to pay for the sins of the whole world. And she realized that God had kept them safe from their enemies. Despite all the danger they had faced, the doubt she had felt, and the fear, and the uncertain future, she suddenly realized that she had been safe in God's hand, that He had guided them through the fires of persecution, hate, and hypocrisy. The fact that they were still alive was nothing short of a miracle.

She thought about God's divine protection, and His love. About Jesus, who gave himself into his enemies' hands when he knew he would be brutally tortured and killed, in order to save mankind from their sins. And as she sat next to Steve, with his arm around her shoulders, listening to him explain the plan of salvation to Tex, she decided that there was no other place in the world where she would rather be.